The Maid-At-Arms

Robert W. Chambers

Contents

THE MAID-AT-ARMS

BY

Robert W. Chambers

TO
MISS KATHARINE HUSTED

PREFACE

After a hundred years the history of a great war waged by a successful nation is commonly reviewed by that nation with retrospective complacency.

Distance dims the panorama; haze obscures the ragged gaps in the pageant until the long lines of victorious armies move smoothly across the horizon, with never an abyss to check their triumph.

Yet there is one people who cannot view the past through a mirage. The marks of the birth-pangs remain on the land; its struggle for breath was too terrible, its scars too deep to hide or cover.

For us, the pages of the past turn all undimmed; battles, brutally etched, stand clear as our own hills against the sky--for in this land we have no haze to soften truth.

Treading the austere corridor of our Pantheon, we, too, come at last to victory--but what a victory! Not the familiar, gracious goddess, wide-winged, crowned, bearing wreaths, but a naked, desperate creature, gaunt, dauntless, turning her iron face to the west.

The trampling centuries can raise for us no golden dust to cloak the flanks of the starved ranks that press across our horizon.

Our ragged armies muster in a pitiless glare of light, every man distinct, every battle in detail.

Pangs that they suffered we suffer.

The faint-hearted who failed are judged by us as though they failed before the nation yesterday; the brave are re-enshrined as we read; the traitor, to us, is no grotesque Guy Fawkes, but a living Judas of to-day.

We remember that Ethan Allen thundered on the portal of all earthly kings at

Ticonderoga; but we also remember that his hatred for the great state of New York brought him and his men of Vermont perilously close to the mire which defiled Charles Lee and Conway, and which engulfed poor Benedict Arnold.

We follow Gates's army with painful sympathy to Saratoga, and there we applaud a victory, but we turn from the commander in contempt, his brutal, selfish, shallow nature all revealed. We know him. We know them all--Ledyard, who died stainless, with his own sword murdered; Herkimer, who died because he was not brave enough to do his duty and be called a coward for doing it; Woolsey, the craven Major at the Middle Fort, stammering filthy speeches in his terror when Sir John Johnson's rangers closed in; Poor, who threw his life away for vanity when that life belonged to the land! Yes, we know them all--great, greater, and less great--our grandfather Franklin, who trotted through a perfectly cold and selfishly contemptuous French court, aged, alert, cheerful to the end; Schuyler, calm and imperturbable, watching the North, which was his trust, and utterly unmindful of self or of the pack yelping at his heels; Stark, Morgan, Murphy, and Elerson, the brave riflemen; Spencer, the interpreter; Visscher, Helmer, and the Stoners.

Into our horizon, too, move terrible shapes--not shadowy or lurid, but living, breathing figures, who turn their eyes on us and hold out their butcher hands: Walter Butler, with his awful smile; Sir John Johnson, heavy and pallid--pallid, perhaps, with the memory of his broken parole; Barry St. Leger, the drunken dealer in scalps; Guy Johnson, organizer of wholesale murder; Brant, called Thayendanegea, brave, terrible, faithful, but--a Mohawk; and that frightful she-devil, Catrine Montour, in whose hot veins seethed savage blood and the blood of a governor of Canada, who smote us, hip and thigh, until the brawling brooks of Tryon ran blood!

No, there is no illusion for us; no splendid armies, banner--laden, passing through unbroken triumphs across the sunset's glory; no winged victory, with smooth brow laurelled to teach us to forget the holocaust. Neither can we veil our history, nor soften our legends. Romance alone can justify a theme inspired by truth; for Romance is more vital than history, which, after all, is but the fleshless skeleton of Romance.

R.W.C.
BROADALBIN,
May 26, 1902.

I

THE ROAD TO VARICKS'

We drew bridle at the cross-roads; he stretched his legs in his stirrups, raised his arms, yawned, and dropped his huge hands upon either thigh with a resounding slap.

"Well, good-bye," he said, gravely, but made no movement to leave me.

"Do we part here?" I asked, sorry to quit my chance acquaintance of the Johnstown highway.

He nodded, yawned again, and removed his round cap of silver-fox fur to scratch his curly head.

"We certainly do part at these cross-roads, if you are bound for Varicks'," he said.

I waited a moment, then thanked him for the pleasant entertainment his company had afforded me, and wished him a safe journey.

"A safe journey?" he repeated, carelessly. "Oh yes, of course; safe journeys are rare enough in these parts. I'm obliged to you for the thought. You are very civil, sir. Good-bye."

Yet neither he nor I gathered bridle to wheel our horses, but sat there in mid-road, looking at each other.

"My name is Mount," he said at length; "let me guess yours. No, sir! don't tell me. Give me three sportsman's guesses; my hunting-knife against the wheat straw you are chewing!"

"With pleasure," I said, amused, "but you could scarcely guess it."

"Your name is Varick?"

I shook my head.

"Butler?"

"No. Look sharp to your knife, friend."

"Oh, then I have guessed it," he said, coolly; "your name is Ormond--and I'm glad of it."

"Why are you glad of it?" I asked, curiously, wondering, too, at his knowledge of me, a stranger.

"You will answer that question for yourself when you meet your kin, the Varicks and Butlers," he said; and the reply had an insolent ring that did not please me, yet I was loath to quarrel with this boyish giant whose amiable company I had found agreeable on my long journey through a land so new to me.

"My friend," I said, "you are blunt."

"Only in speech, sir," he replied, lazily swinging one huge leg over the pommel of his saddle. Sitting at ease in the sunshine, he opened his fringed hunting-shirt to the breeze blowing.

"So you go to the Varicks?" he mused aloud, eyes slowly closing in the sunshine like the brilliant eyes of a basking lynx.

"Do you know the lord of the manor?" I asked.

"Who? The patroon?"

"I mean Sir Lupus Varick."

"Yes; I know him--I know Sir Lupus. We call him the patroon, though he's not of the same litter as the Livingstons, the Cosbys, the Phillipses, Van Rensselaers, and those feudal gentlemen who juggle with the high justice, the middle, and the low--and who will juggle no more."

"Am I mistaken," said I, "in taking you for a Boston man?"

"In one sense you are," he said, opening his eyes. "I was born in Vermont."

"Then you are a rebel?"

"Lord!" he said, laughing, "how you twist our English tongue! 'Tis his Majesty across the waters who rebels at our home-made Congress."

"Is it not dangerous to confess such things to a stranger?" I asked, smiling.

His bright eyes reassured me. "Not to all strangers," he drawled, swinging his free foot over his horse's neck and settling his bulk on the saddle. One big hand fell, as by accident, over the pan of his long rifle. Watching, without seeming to, I saw his forefinger touch the priming, stealthily, and find it dry.

"You are no King's man," he said, calmly.

"Oh, do you take me for a rebel, too?" I demanded.

"No, sir; you are neither the one nor the other--like a tadpole with legs, neither frog nor pollywog. But you will be."

"Which?" I asked, laughing.

"My wisdom cannot draw that veil for you, sir," he said. "You may take your chameleon color from your friends the Varicks and remain gray, or from the Butlers and turn red, or from the Schuylers and turn blue and buff."

"You credit me with little strength of character," I said.

"I credit you with some twenty-odd years and no experience."

"With nothing more?"

"Yes, sir; with sincerity and a Spanish rifle--which you may have need of ere this month of May has melted into June."

I glanced at the beautiful Spanish weapon resting across my pommel.

"What do you know of the Varicks?" I asked, smiling.

"More than do you," he said, "for all that they are your kin. Look at me, sir! Like myself, you wear deer-skin from throat to ankle, and your nose is ever sniffing to windward. But this is a strange wind to you. You see, you smell, but your eyes ask, 'What is it?' You are a woodsman, but a stranger among your own kin. You have never seen a living Varick; you have never even seen a partridge."

"Your wisdom is at fault there," I said, maliciously.

"Have you seen a Varick?"

"No; but the partridge--"

"Pooh! a little creature, like a gray meadow-lark remoulded! You call it partridge, I call it quail. But I speak of the crested thunder--drumming cock that struts all ruffed like a Spanish grandee of ancient times. Wait, sir!" and he pointed to a string of birds' footprints in the dust just ahead. "Tell me what manner of creature left its mark there?"

I leaned from my saddle, scanning the sign carefully, but the bird that made it was a strange bird to me. Still bending from my saddle, I heard his mocking laugh, but did not look up.

"You wear a lynx-skin for a saddle-cloth," he said, "yet that lynx never squalled within a thousand miles of these hills."

"Do you mean to say there are no lynxes here?" I asked.

"Plenty, sir, but their ears bear no black-and-white marks. Pardon, I do not mean to vex you; I read as I run, sir; it is my habit."

"So you have traced me on a back trail for a thousand miles--from habit," I said, not exactly pleased.

"A thousand miles--by your leave."

"Or without it."

"Or without it--a thousand miles, sir, on a back trail, through forests that blossom like gigantic gardens in May with flowers sweeter than our white water-lilies abloom on trees that bear glossy leaves the year round; through thickets that spread great, green, many-fingered hands at you, all adrip with golden jasmine; where pine wood is fat as bacon; where the two oaks shed their leaves, yet are ever in foliage; where the thick, blunt snakes lie in the mud and give no warning when they deal death. So far, sir, I trail you, back to the soil where your baby fingers first dug-- soil as white as the snow which you are yet to see for the first time in your life of twenty-three years. A land where there are no hills; a land where the vultures sail all day without flapping their tip-curled wings; where slimy dragon things watch from the water's edge; where Greek slaves sweat at indigo-vats that draw vultures like carrion; where black men, toiling, sing all day on the sea-islands, plucking cotton-blossoms; where monstrous horrors, hornless and legless, wallow out to the sedge and graze like cattle--"

"Man! You picture a hell!" I said, angrily, "while I come from paradise!"

"The outer edges of paradise border on hell," he said. "Wait! Sniff that odor floating."

"It is jasmine!" I muttered, and my throat tightened with a homesick spasm.

"It is the last of the arbutus," he said, dropping his voice to a gentle monotone. "This is New York province, county of Tryon, sir, and yonder bird trilling is not that gray minstrel of the Spanish orange-tree, mocking the jays and the crimson fire-birds which sing 'Peet! peet!' among the china-berries. Do you know the wild partridge-pea of the pine barrens, that scatters its seeds with a faint report when the pods are touched? There is in this land a red bud which has burst thundering into crimson bloom, scattering seeds o' death to the eight winds. And every seed breeds a battle, and every root drinks blood!"

He straightened in his stirrups, blue eyes ablaze, face burning under its heavy mask of tan and dust.

"If I know a man when I see him, I know you," he said. "God save our country, friend, upon this sweet May day."

"Amen, sir," I replied, tingling. "And God save the King the whole year round!"

"Yes," he repeated, with a disagreeable laugh, "God save the King; he is past all human aid now, and headed straight to hell. Friend, let us part ere we quarrel. You will be with me or against me this day week. I knew it was a man I addressed, and no tavern-post."

"Yet this brawl with Boston is no affair of mine," I said, troubled. "Who touches the ancient liberties of Englishmen touches my country, that is all I know."

"Which country, sir?"

"Greater Britain."

"And when Greater Britain divides?"

"It must not!"

"It has."

I unbound the scarlet handkerchief which I wore for a cap, and held it between my fingers to dry its sweat in the breeze. Watching it flutter, I said:

"Friend, in my country we never cross the branch till we come to it, nor leave the hammock till the river-sands are beneath our feet. No hunting-shirt is sewed till the bullet has done its errand, nor do men fish for gray mullet with a hook and line. There is always time to pray for wisdom."

"Friend," replied Mount, "I wear red quills on my moccasins, you wear bits of sea-shell. That is all the difference between us. Good-bye. Varick Manor is the first house four miles ahead."

He wheeled his horse, then, as at a second thought, checked him and looked back at me.

"You will see queer folk yonder at the patroon's," he said. "You are accustomed to the manners of your peers; you were bred in that land where hospitality, courtesy, and deference are shown to equals; where dignity and graciousness are expected from the elders; where duty and humility are inbred in the young. So is it with us--except where you are going. The great patroon families, with their vast estates, their patents, their feudal systems, have stood supreme here for years. Theirs is the power of life and death over their retainers; they reign absolute in their manors, they account only to God for their trusts. And they are great folk, sir, even yet--these Livingstons, these Van Rensselaers, these Phillipses, lords of their manors still; Dutch of descent, polished, courtly, proud, bearing the title of patroon as a noble bears his coronet."

He raised his hand, smiling. "It is not so with the Varicks. They are patroons, too, yet kin to the Johnsons, of Johnson Hall and Guy Park, and kin to the Ormond-Butlers. But they are different from either Johnson or Butler--vastly different from the Schuylers or the Livingstons--"

He shrugged his broad shoulders and dropped his hand: "The Varicks are all mad, sir. Good-bye."

He struck his horse with his soft leather heels; the animal bounded out into the western road, and his rider swung around once more towards me with a gesture partly friendly, partly, perhaps, in menace. "Tell Sir Lupus to go to the devil!" he cried, gayly, and cantered away through the golden dust.

I sat my horse to watch him; presently, far away on the hill's crest, the sun caught his rifle and sparkled for a space, then the point of white fire went out, and there was nothing on the hill-top save the dust drifting.

Lonelier than I had yet been since that day, three months gone, when I had set out from our plantation on the shallow Halifax, which the hammock scarcely separates from the ocean, I gathered bridle with listless fingers and spoke to my mare. "Isene, we must be moving eastward--always moving, sweetheart. Come, lass, there's grain somewhere in this Northern land where you have carried me." And to myself, muttering aloud as I rode: "A fine name he has given to my cousins the Varicks, this giant forest-runner, with his boy's face and limbs of iron! And he was none too cordial concerning the Butlers, either--cousins, too, but in what degree they must tell me, for I don't know--"

The road entering the forest, I ceased my prattle by instinct, and again for the thousandth time I sniffed at odors new to me, and scanned leafy depths for those familiar trees which stand warden in our Southern forests. There were pines, but they were not our pines, these feathery, dark-stemmed trees; there were oaks, but neither our golden water oaks nor our great, green-and-silver live-oaks. Little, pale flowers bloomed everywhere, shadows only of our bright blossoms of the South; and the rare birds I saw were gray and small, and chary of song, as though the stillness that slept in this Northern forest was a danger not to be awakened. Loneliness fell on me; my shoulders bent and my head hung heavily. Isene, my mare, paced the soft forest-road without a sound, so quietly that the squatting rabbit leaped from between her forelegs, and the slim, striped, squirrel-like creatures crouched paralyzed as we passed ere they burst into their shrill chatter of fright or anger, I know not which.

Had I a night to spend in this wilderness I should not know where to find a palmetto-fan for a torch, where to seek light-wood for splinter. It was all new to me; signs read riddles; tracks were sealed books; the east winds brought rain, where at home they bring heaven's own balm to us of the Spanish grants on the seaboard; the northwest winds that we dread turn these Northern skies to sapphire, and set bees a-humming on every bud.

There was no salt in the air, no citrus scent in the breeze, no heavy incense of the great magnolia bloom perfuming the wilderness like a cathedral aisle where a young bride passes, clouded in lace.

But in the heat a heavy, sweetish odor hung; balsam it is called, and mingled, too, with a faint scent like our bay, which comes from a woody bush called sweet-fern. That, and the strong smell of the bluish, short-needled pine, was ever clogging my nostrils and confusing me. Once I thought to scent a 'possum, but the musky taint came from a rotting log; and a stale fox might have crossed to windward and I not noticed, so blunted had grown my nose in this unfamiliar Northern world.

Musing, restless, dimly confused, and doubly watchful, I rode through the timber-belt, and out at last into a dusty, sunny road. And straightway I sighted a house. The house was of stone, and large and square and gray, with only a pillared porch instead of the long double galleries we build; and it had a row of windows in the roof, called dormers, and was surrounded by a stockade of enormous timbers, in the four corners of which were set little forts pierced for rifle fire.

Noble trees stood within the fortified lines; outside, green meadows ringed the place; and the grass was thick and soft, and vivid as a green jewel in color--such grass as we never see save for a spot here and there in swampy places where the sun falls in early spring.

The house was yet a hundred rods away to the eastward. I rode on slowly, noticing the neglected fences on either hand, and thought that my cousin Varick might have found an hour to mend them, for his pride's sake.

Isene, my mare, had already scented the distant stables, and was pricking forward her beautiful ears as I unslung my broad hat of plaited palmetto and placed it on my head, the better to salute my hosts when I should ride to their threshold in the Spanish fashion we followed at home.

So, cantering on, I crossed a log bridge which spanned a ravine, below which I saw a grist-mill; and so came to the stockade. The gate was open and unguarded, and I guided my mare through without a challenge from the small corner forts, and rode straight to the porch, where an ancient negro serving-man stood, dressed in a tawdry livery too large for him. As I drew bridle he gave me a dull, almost sullen glance, and it was not until I spoke sharply to him that he shambled forward and descended the two steps to hold my stirrup.

"Is Sir Lupus at home?" I asked, looking curiously at this mute, dull-eyed black, so different from our grinning lads at home.

"Yaas, suh, he done come home, suh."

"Then announce Mr. George Ormond," I said.

He stared, but did not offer to move.

"Did you hear me?" I asked, astonished.

"Yaas, suh, I done hear yoh, suh."

I looked him over in amazement, then walked past him towards the door.

"Is you gwine look foh Mars' Lupus?" he asked, barring my way with one wrinkled, blue-black hand on the brass door-knob. "Kaze ef you is, you don't had better, suh."

I could only stare.

"Kaze Mars' Lupus done say he gwine kill de fustest man what 'sturb him, suh," continued the black man, in a listless monotone. "An' I spec' he gwine do it."

"Is Sir Lupus abed at this hour?" I asked.

"Yaas, suh."

There was no emotion in the old man's voice. Something made me think that he had given the same message to visitors many times.

I was very angry at the discourtesy, for he must have known when to expect me from my servant, who had accompanied me by water with my boxes from St. Augustine to Philadelphia, where I lingered while he went forward, bearing my letter with him. Yet, angry and disgusted as I was, there was nothing for me to do except to swallow the humiliation, walk in, and twiddle my thumbs until the boorish lord of the manor waked to greet his invited guest.

"I suppose I may enter," I said, sarcastically.

"Yaas, suh; Miss Dorry done say: 'Cato,' she say, 'ef de young gem'man come when Mars' Lupus am drunk, jess take care n' him, Cato; put him mos' anywhere 'cep in mah bed, Cato, an' jess call me ef I ain' busy 'bout mah business--'"

Still rambling on, he opened the door, and I entered a wide hallway, dirty and disordered. As I stood hesitating, a terrific crash sounded from the floor above.

"Spec' Miss Dorry busy," observed the old man, raising his solemn, wrinkled face to listen.

"Uncle," I said, "is it true that you are all mad in this house?"

"We sho' is, suh," he replied, without interest.

"Are you too crazy to care for my horse?"

"Oh no, suh."

"Then go and rub her down, and feed her, and let me sit here in the hallway. I want to think."

Another crash shook the ceiling of solid oak; very far away I heard a young girl's laughter, then a stifled chorus of voices from the floor above.

"Das Miss Dorry an' de chilluns," observed the old man.

"Who are the others?"

"Waal, dey is Miss Celia, an' Mars' Harry, an' Mars' Ruyven, an' Mars' Sam'l, an' de babby, li'l Mars' Benny."

"All mad?"

"Yaas, suh."

"I'll be, too, if I remain here," I said. "Is there an inn near by?"

"De Turkle-dove an' Olives."

"Where?"

"'Bout five mile long de pike, suh."

"Feed my horse," I said, sullenly, and sat down on a settle, rifle cradled between my knees, and in my heart wrath immeasurable against my kin the Varicks.

II

IN THE HALLWAY

So this was Northern hospitality! This a Northern gentleman's home, with its cobwebbed ceiling, its little window-panes opaque with stain of rain and dust, its carpetless floors innocent of wax, littered with odds and ends--here a battered riding-cane; there a pair of tarnished spurs; yonder a scarlet hunting-coat a-trail on the banisters, with skirts all mud from feet that mayhap had used it as a mat in rainy weather!

I leaned forward and picked up the riding-crop; its cane end was capped with heavy gold. The spurs I also lifted for inspection; they were beautifully wrought in silver.

Faugh! Here was no poverty, but the shiftlessness of a sot, trampling good things into the mire!

I looked into the fireplace. Ashes of dead embers choked it; the andirons, smoke-smeared and crusted, stood out stark against the sooty maw of the hearth.

Still, for all, the hall was made in good and even noble proportion; simple, as should be the abode of a gentleman; over-massive, perhaps, and even destitute of those gracious and symmetrical galleries which we of the South think no shame to take pride in; for the banisters were brutally heavy, and the rail above like a rampart, and for a newel-post some ass had set a bronze cannon, breech upward; and it was green and beautiful, but offensive to sane consistency.

Standing, the better to observe the hall on all sides, it came to me that some one had stripped a fine English mansion of fine but ancient furniture, to bring it across an ocean and through a forest for the embellishment of this coarse house. For there were pictures in frames showing generals and statesmen of the Ormond-Butlers, one even of the great duke who fled to France; and there were pictures of the Varicks before they mingled with us Irish--apple-cheeked Dutchmen, cadaverous youths bearing match-locks, and one, an admiral, with star and sash across his varnish-cracked corselet of blue steel, looking at me with pale, smoky eyes.

Rusted suits of mail, and groups of weapons made into star shapes and circles, points outward, were ranged between the heavy pictures, each centred with a moth-ravaged stag's head, smothered in dust.

As I slowly paced the panelled wall, nose in air to observe these neglected trophies, I came to another picture, hung all alone near the wall where it passes under the staircase, and at first, for the darkness, I could not see.

Imperceptibly the outlines of the shape grew in the gloom from a deep, rich background, and I made out a figure of a youth all cased in armor save for the helmet, which was borne in one smooth, blue-veined hand.

The face, too, began to assume form; rounded, delicate, crowned with a mass of golden hair; and suddenly I perceived the eyes, and they seemed to open sweetly, like violets in a dim wood.

"What Ormond is this?" I muttered, bewitched, yet sullen to see such feminine roundness in any youth; and, with my sleeve of buckskin, I rubbed the dust from the gilded plate set in the lower frame.

"The Maid-at-Arms," I read aloud.

Then there came to me, at first like the far ring of a voice scarcely heard through southern winds, the faint echo of a legend told me ere my mother died--perhaps told me by her in those drifting hours of a childhood nigh forgotten. Yet I seemed to see white, sun-drenched sands and the long, blue swell of a summer sea, and I heard winds in the palms, and a song--truly it was my mother's; I knew it now--and, of a sudden, the words came borne on a whisper of ancient melody:

> "This for the deed she did at Ashby Farms,
> Helen of Ormond, Royal Maid-at-Arms!"

Memory was stirring at last, and the gray legend grew from the past, how a maid, Helen of Ormond, for love of her cousin, held prisoner in his own house at Ashby-de-la-Zouch, sheared off her hair, clothed her limbs in steel, and rode away to seek him; and how she came to the house at Ashby and rode straight into the gateway, forcing her horse to the great hall where her lover lay, and flung him, all in chains, across her saddle-bow, riding like a demon to freedom through the Desmonds, his enemies. Ah! now my throat was aching with the memory of the song, and of that strange line I never understood--"Wearing the ghost-ring!"--and, of themselves, the words grew and died, formed on my silent lips:

> "This for the deed she did at Ashby Farms,
> Helen of Ormond, Royal Maid-at-Arms!
>
> "Though for all time the lords of Ormond be
> Butlers to Majesty,
> Yet shall new honors fall upon her
> Who, armored, rode for love to Ashby Farms;
> Let this her title be: A Maid-at-Arms!
>
> "Serene mid love's alarms,
> For all time shall the Maids-at-Arms,
> Wearing the ghost-ring, triumph with their constancy.
> And sweetly conquer with a sigh
> And vanquish with a tear
> Captains a trembling world might fear.
>
> "This for the deed she did at Ashby Farms,
> Helen of Ormond, Royal Maid-at-Arms!"

Staring at the picture, lips quivering with the soundless words, such wretched loneliness came over me that a dryness in my throat set me gulping, and I groped my way back to the settle by the fireplace and sat down heavily in homesick solitude.

Then hate came, a quick hatred for these Northern skies, and these strangers of the North who dared claim kin with me, to lure me northward with false offer of council and mockery of hospitality.

I was on my feet again in a flash, hot with anger, ready with insult to meet insult, for I meant to go ere I had greeted my host--an insult, indeed, and a deadly one among us. Furious, I bent to snatch my rifle from the settle where it lay, and, as I flung it to my shoulder, wheeling to go, my eyes fell upon a figure stealing down the stairway from above, a woman in flowered silk, bare of throat and elbow, fingers scarcely touching the banisters as she moved.

She hesitated, one foot poised for the step below; then it fell noiselessly, and she stood before me.

Anger died out under the level beauty of her gaze. I bowed, just as I caught a trace of mockery in the mouth's scarlet curve, and bowed the lower for it, too, straightening slowly to the dignity her mischievous eyes seemed to flout; and her lips, too, defied me, all silently--nay, in every limb and from every finger-tip she seemed to flout me, and the slow, deep courtesy she made me was too slow and far too low, and her recovery a marvel of plastic malice.

"My cousin Ormond?" she lisped;--"I am Dorothy Varick."

We measured each other for a moment in silence.

There was a trace of powder on her bright hair, like a mist of snow on gold; her gown's yoke was torn, for all its richness, and a wisp of lace in rags fell, clouding the delicate half-sleeve of China silk.

Her face, colored like palest ivory with rose, was no doll's face, for all its symmetry and a forgotten patch to balance the dimple in her rounded chin; it was even noble in a sense, and, if too chaste for sensuous beauty, yet touched with a strange and pensive sweetness, like 'witched marble waking into flesh.

Suddenly a voice came from above: "Dorothy, come here!"

My cousin frowned, glanced at me, then laughed.

"Dorothy, I want my watch!" repeated the voice.

Still looking at me, my cousin slowly drew from her bosom a huge, jewelled watch, and displayed it for my inspection.

"We were matching mint-dates with shillings for father's watch; I won it," she observed.

"Dorothy!" insisted the voice.

"Oh, la!" she cried, impatiently, "will you hush?"

"No, I won't!"

"Then our cousin Ormond will come up-stairs and give you what Paddy gave the kettle-drum--won't you?" she added, raising her eyes to me.

"And what was that?" I asked, astonished.

Somebody on the landing above went off into fits of laughter; and, as I reddened, my cousin Dorothy, too, began to laugh, showing an edge of small, white teeth under the red lip's line.

"Are you vexed because we laugh?" she asked.

My tongue stung with a retort, but I stood silent. These Varicks might forget their manners, but I might not forget mine.

She honored me with a smile, sweeping me from head to foot with her bright eyes. My buckskins were dirty from travel, and the thrums in rags; and I knew that she noted all these matters.

"Cousin," she lisped, "I fear you are something of a macaroni."

Instantly a fresh volley of laughter rattled from the landing--such clear, hearty laughter that it infected me, spite my chagrin.

"He's a good fellow, our cousin Ormond!" came a fresh young voice from above.

"He shall be one of us!" cried another; and I thought to catch a glimpse of a flowered petticoat whisked from the gallery's edge.

I looked at my cousin Dorothy Varick; she stood at gaze, laughter in her eyes, but the mouth demure.

"Cousin Dorothy," said I, "I believe I am a good fellow, even though ragged and respectable. If these qualities be not bars to your society, give me your hand in fellowship, for upon my soul I am nigh sick for a welcome from somebody in this unfriendly land."

Still at gaze, she slowly raised her arm and held out to me a fresh, sun-tanned hand; and I had meant to press it, but a sudden shyness scotched me, and, as the soft fingers rested in my palm, I raised them and touched them with my lips in silent respect.

"You have pretty manners," she said, looking at her hand, but not withdrawing it from where it rested. Then, of an impulse, her fingers closed on mine firmly, and she looked me straight in the eye.

"You are a good comrade; welcome to Varicks', cousin Ormond!"

Our hands fell apart, and, glancing up, I perceived a group of youthful barbarians on the stairs, intently watching us. As my eyes fell on them they scattered, then closed in together defiantly. A red-haired lad of seventeen came down the steps, offering his hand awkwardly.

"I'm Ruyven Varick," he said. "These girls are fools to bait men of our age--" He broke off to seize Dorothy by the arm. "Give me that watch, you vixen!"

His sister scornfully freed her arm, and Ruyven stood sullenly clutching a handful of torn lace.

"Why don't you present us to our cousin Ormond?" spoke up a maid of sixteen.

"Who wants to make your acquaintance?" retorted Ruyven, edging again towards his sister.

I protested that I did; and Dorothy, with mock empressement, presented me to Cecile Butler, a slender, olive-skinned girl with pretty, dark eyes, who offered me her hand to kiss in such determined manner that I bowed very low to cover my smile, knowing that she had witnessed my salute to my cousin Dorothy and meant to take nothing less for herself.

"And those boys yonder are Harry Varick and Sam Butler, my cousins," observed Dorothy, nonchalantly relapsing into barbarism to point them out separately with her pink-tipped thumb; "and that lad on the stairs is Benny. Come on, we're to throw hunting-knives for pennies. Can you?--but of course you can."

I looked around at my barbarian kin, who had produced hunters' knives from recesses in their clothing, and now gathered impatiently around Dorothy, who appeared to be the leader in their collective deviltries.

"All the same, that watch is mine," broke out Ruyven, defiantly. "I'll leave it to our cousin Ormond--" but Dorothy cut in: "Cousin, it was done in this manner: father lost his timepiece, and the law is that whoever finds things about the house may keep them. So we all ran to the porch where father had fallen off his horse last night, and I think we all saw it at the same time; and I, being the older and stronger--"

"You're not the stronger!" cried Sam and Harry, in the same breath.

"I," repeated Dorothy, serenely, "being not only older than Ruyven by a year, but also stronger than you all together, kept the watch, spite of your silly clamor--and mean to keep it."

"Then we matched shillings for it!" cried Cecile.

"It was only fair; we all discovered it," explained Dorothy. "But Ruyven matched with a Spanish piece where the date was under the reverse, and he says he won. Did he, cousin?"

"Mint-dates always match!" said Ruyven; "gentlemen of our age understand that, Cousin George, don't we?"

"Have I not won fairly?" asked Dorothy, looking at me. "If I have not, tell me."

With that, Sam Butler and Harry set up a clamor that they and Cecile had been unfairly dealt with, and all appealed to me until, bewildered, I sat down on the stairs and looked wistfully at Dorothy.

"In Heaven's name, cousins, give me something to eat and drink before you bring your lawsuits to me for judgment," I said.

"Oh," cried Dorothy, biting her lip, "I forgot. Come with me, cousin!" She seized a bell-rope and rang it furiously, and a loud gong filled the hall with its brazen din; but nobody came.

"Where the devil are those blacks?" said Dorothy, biting off her words with a crisp snap that startled me more than her profanity. "Cato! Where are you, you lazy--"

"Ahm hyah, Miss Dorry," came a patient voice from the kitchen stairs.

"Then bring something to eat--bring it to the gun-room instantly--something for Captain Ormond--and a bottle of Sir Lupus's own claret--and two glasses--"

"Three glasses!" cried Ruyven.

"Four!" "Five!" shouted Harry and Cecile.

"Six!" added Samuel; and little Benny piped out, "Theven!"

"Then bring two bottles, Cato," called out Dorothy.

"I want some small-beer!" protested Benny.

"Oh, go suck your thumbs," retorted Ruyven, with an elder brother's brutality; but Dorothy ordered the small-beer, and bade the negro hasten.

"We all mean to bear you company, Cousin," said Ruyven, cheerfully, patting my arm for my reassurance; and truly I lacked something of assurance among these kinsmen of mine, who appeared to lack none.

"You spoke of me as Captain Ormond," I said, turning with a smile to Dorothy.

"Oh, it's all one," she said, gayly; "if you're not a captain now, you will be soon, I'll wager--but I'm not to talk of that before the children--"

"You may talk of it before me," said Ruyven. "Harry, take Benny and Sam and Cecile out of earshot--"

"Pooh!" cried Harry, "I know all about Sir John's new regiment--"

"Will you hush your head, you little fool!" cut in Dorothy. "Servants and asses have long ears, and I'll clip yours if you bray again!"

The jingling of glasses on a tray put an end to the matter; Cato, the black, followed by two more blacks, entered the hall bearing silver salvers, and at a nod from Dorothy we all trooped after them.

"Guests first!" hissed Dorothy, in a fierce whisper, as Ruyven crowded past me, and he slunk back, mortified, while Dorothy, in a languid voice and with the air of a duchess, drawled, "Your arm, cousin," and slipped her hand into my arm, tossing her head with a heavy-lidded, insolent glance at poor Ruyven.

And thus we entered the gun-room, I with Dorothy Varick on my arm, and behind me, though I was not at first aware of it, Harry, gravely conducting Cecile in a similar manner, followed by Samuel and Benny, arm-in-arm, while Ruyven trudged sulkily by himself.

III
COUSINS

There was a large, discolored table in the armory, or gun-room, as they called it; and on this, without a cloth, our repast was spread by Cato, while the other servants retired, panting and grinning like over-fat hounds after a pack-run.

And, by Heaven! they lacked nothing for solid silver, my cousins the Varicks, nor yet for fine glass, which I observed without appearance of vulgar curiosity while Cato carved a cold joint of butcher's roast and cracked the bottles of wine--a claret that perfumed the room like a garden in September.

"Cousin Dorothy, I have the honor to raise my glass to you," I said.

"I drink your health, Cousin George," she said, gravely--"Benny, let that wine alone! Is there no small-beer there, that you go coughing and staining your bib over wine forbidden? Take his glass away, Ruyven! Take it quick, I say!"

Benny, deprived of his claret, collapsed moodily into a heap, and sat swinging his legs and clipping the table, at every kick of his shoon, until my wine danced in my glass and soiled the table.

"Stop that, you!" cried Cecile.

Benny subsided, scowling.

Though Dorothy was at some pains to assure me that they had dined but an hour before, that did not appear to blunt their appetites. And the manner in which they drank astonished me, a glass of wine being considered sufficient for young ladies at home, and a half-glass for lads like Harry and Sam. Yet when I emptied my glass Dorothy emptied hers, and the servants refilled hers when they refilled mine, till I grew anxious and watched to see that her face flushed not, but had my anxiety for my pains, as she changed not a pulse-beat for all the red wine she swallowed.

And Lord! how busy were her little white teeth, while her pretty eyes roved about, watchful that order be kept at this gypsy repast. Cecile and Harry fell to struggling for a glass, which snapped and flew to flakes under their clutching fingers, drenching them with claret.

"Silence!" cried Dorothy, rising, eyes ablaze. "Do you wish our cousin Ormond to take us for manner-less savages?"

"Why not?" retorted Harry. "We are!"

"Oh, Lud!" drawled Cecile, languidly fanning her flushed face, "I would I had drunk small-beer--Harry, if you kick me again I'll pinch!"

"It's a shame," observed Ruyven, "that gentlemen of our age may not take a glass of wine together in comfort."

"Your age!" laughed Dorothy. "Cousin Ormond is twenty-three, silly, and I'm eighteen--or close to it."

"And I'm seventeen," retorted Ruyven.

"Yet I throw you at wrestling," observed Dorothy, with a shrug.

"Oh, your big feet! Who can move them?" he rejoined.

"Big feet? Mine?" She bent, tore a satin shoe from her foot, and slapped it down on the table in challenge to all to equal it--a small, silver-buckled thing of Paddington's make, with a smart red heel and a slender body, slim as the crystal slipper of romance.

There was no denying its shapeliness; presently she removed it, and, stooping, slowly drew it on her foot.

"Is that the shoe Sir John drank your health from?" sneered Ruyven.

A rich flush mounted to Dorothy's hair, and she caught at her wine-glass as though to throw it at her brother.

"A married man, too," he laughed--"Sir John Johnson, the fat baronet of the Mohawks--"

"Damn you, will you hold your silly tongue?" she cried, and rose to launch the glass, but I sprang to my feet, horrified and astounded, arm outstretched.

"Ruyven," I said, sharply, "is it you who fling such a taunt to shame your own kin? If there is aught of impropriety in what this man Sir John has done, is it not our affair with him in place of a silly gibe at Dorothy?"

"I ask pardon," stammered Ruyven; "had there been impropriety in what that fool, Sir John, did I should not have spoke, but have acted long since, Cousin Ormond."

"I'm sure of it," I said, warmly. "Forgive me, Ruyven."

"Oh, la!" said Dorothy, her lips twitching to a smile, "Ruyven only said it to plague me. I hate that baronet, and Ruyven knows it, and harps ever on a foolish drinking-bout where all fell to the table, even Walter Butler, and that slow adder Sir John among the first. And they do say," she added, with scorn, "that the baronet did find one of my old shoon and filled it to my health--damn him!--"

"Dorothy!" I broke in, "who in Heaven's name taught you such shameful oaths?"

"Oaths?" Her face burned scarlet. "Is it a shameful oath to say 'Damn him'?"

"It is a common oath men use--not gentlewomen," I said.

"Oh! I supposed it harmless. They all laugh when I say it--father and Guy Johnson and the rest; and they swear other oaths--words I would not say if I could--but I did not know there was harm in a good smart 'damn!'"

She leaned back, one slender hand playing with the stem of her glass; and the flush faded from her face like an afterglow from a serene horizon.

"I fear," she said, "you of the South wear a polish we lack."

"Best mirror your faults in it while you have the chance," said Harry, promptly.

"We lack polish--even Walter Butler and Guy Johnson sneer at us under father's nose," said Ruyven. "What the devil is it in us Varicks that set folk whispering and snickering and nudging one another? Am I parti-colored, like an Oneida at a scalp-dance? Does Harry wear bat's wings for ears? Are Dorothy's legs crooked, that they all stare?"

"It's your red head," observed Cecile. "The good folk think to see the noon-sun setting in the wood--"

"Oh, tally! you always say that," snapped Ruyven.

Dorothy, leaning forward, looked at me with dreamy blue eyes that saw beyond me.

"We are doubtless a little mad, ... as they say," she mused. "Otherwise we seem to be like other folk. We have clothing befitting, when we choose to wear it; we were schooled in Albany; we are people of quality, like the other patroons; we lack nothing for servants or tenants--what ails them all, to nudge and stare and grin when we pass?"

"Mr. Livingston says our deportment shocks all," murmured Cecile.

"The Schuylers will have none of us," added Harry, plaintively--"and I admire them, too."

"Oh, they all conduct shamefully when I go to school in Albany," burst out Sammy; "and I thrashed that puling young patroon, too, for he saw me and refused my salute. But I think he will render me my bow next time."

"Do the quality not visit you here?" I asked Dorothy.

"Visit us? No, cousin. Who is to receive them? Our mother is dead."

Cecile said: "Once they did come, but Uncle Varick had that mistress of Sir John's to sup with them and they took offence."

"Mrs. Van Cortlandt said she was a painted hussy--" began Harry.

"The Van Rensselaers left the house, vowing that Sir Lupus had used them shamefully," added Cecile; "and Sir Lupus said: 'Tush! tush! When the Van Rensselaers are too good for the Putnams of Tribes Hill I'll eat my spurs!' and then he laughed till he cried."

"They never came again; nobody of quality ever came; nobody ever comes," said Ruyven.

"Excepting the Johnsons and the Butlers," corrected Sammy.

"And then everybody geths tight; they were here lath night and Uncle Varick is sthill abed," said little Benny, innocently.

"Will you all hold your tongues?" cried Dorothy, fiercely. "Father said we were not to tell anybody that Sir John and the Ormond-Butlers visited us."

"Why not?" I asked.

Dorothy clasped both hands under her chin, rested her bare elbows on the table, and leaned close to me, whispering confidentially: "Because of the war with the Boston people. The country is overrun with rebels--rebel troops at Albany, rebel gunners at Stanwix, rebels at Edward and Hunter and Johnstown. A scout of ten men came here last week; they were harrying a war-party of Brant's Mohawks, and Stoner was with them, and that great ox in buckskin, Jack Mount. And do you know what he said to father? He said, 'For Heaven's sake, turn red or blue, Sir Lupus, for if you don't we'll hang you to a crab-apple and chance the color.' And father said,

'I'm no partisan King's man'; and Jack Mount said, 'You're the joker of the pack, are you?' And father said, 'I'm not in the shuffle, and you can bear me out, you rogue!' And then Jack Mount wagged his big forefinger at him and said, 'Sir Lupus, if you're but a joker, one or t'other side must discard you!' And they rode away, priming their rifles and laughing, and father swore and shook his cane at them."

In her eagerness her lips almost touched my ear, and her breath warmed my cheek.

"All that I saw and heard," she whispered, "and I know father told Walter Butler, for a scout came yesterday, saying that a scout from the Rangers and the Royal Greens had crossed the hills, and I saw some of Sir John's Scotch loons riding like warlocks on the new road, and that great fool, Francy McCraw, tearing along at their head and crowing like a cock."

"Cousin, cousin," I protested, "all this--all these names--even the causes and the manners of this war, are incomprehensible to me."

"Oh," she said, in surprise, "have you in Florida not heard of our war?"

"Yes, yes--all know that war is with you, but that is all. I know that these Boston men are fighting our King; but why do the Indians take part?"

She looked at me blankly, and made a little gesture of dismay.

"I see I must teach you history, cousin," she said. "Father tells us that history is being made all about us in these days--and, would you believe it? Benny took it that books were being made in the woods all around the house, and stole out to see, spite of the law that father made--"

"Who thaw me?" shouted Benny.

"Hush! Be quiet!" said Dorothy.

Benny lay back in his chair and beat upon the table, howling defiance at his sister through Harry's shouts of laughter.

"Silence!" cried Dorothy, rising, flushed and furious. "Is this a corn-feast, that you all sit yelping in a circle? Ruyven, hold that door, and see that no one follows us--"

"What for?" demanded Ruyven, rising. "If you mean to keep our cousin Ormond to yourself--"

"I wish to discuss secrets with my cousin Ormond," said Dorothy, loftily, and stepped from her chair, nose in the air, and that heavy-lidded, insolent glance which once before had withered Ruyven, and now withered him again.

"We will go to the play-room," she whispered, passing me; "that room has a bolt; they'll all be kicking at the door presently. Follow me."

Ere we had reached the head of the stairs we heard a yell, a rush of feet, and she laughed, crying: "Did I not say so? They are after us now full bark! Come!"

She caught my hand in hers and sped up the few remaining steps, then through the upper hallway, guiding me the while her light feet flew; and I, embarrassed, bewildered, half laughing, half shamed to go a-racing through a strange house in such absurd a fashion.

"Here!" she panted, dragging me into a great, bare chamber and bolting the door, then leaned breathless against the wall to listen as the chase galloped up, clamoring, kicking and beating on panel and wall, baffled.

"They're raging to lose their new cousin," she breathed, smiling across at me with a glint of pride in her eyes. "They all think mightily of you, and now they'll be mad to follow you like hound-pups the whip, all day long." She tossed her head. "They're good lads, and Cecile is a sweet child, too, but they must be made to understand that there are moments when you and I desire to be alone together."

"Of course," I said, gravely.

"You and I have much to consider, much to discuss in these uncertain days," she said, confidently. "And we cannot babble matters of import to these children--"

"I'm seventeen!" howled Ruyven, through the key-hole. "Dorothy's not eighteen till next month, the little fool--"

"Don't mind him," said Dorothy, raising her voice for Ruyven's benefit. "A lad who listens to his elders through a key-hole is not fit for serious--"

A heavy assault on the door drowned Dorothy's voice. She waited calmly until the uproar had subsided.

"Let us sit by the window," she said, "and I will tell you how we Varicks stand betwixt the deep sea and the devil."

"I wish to come in!" shouted Ruyven, in a threatening voice. Dorothy laughed, and pointed to a great arm-chair of leather and oak. "I will sit there; place it by the window, cousin."

I placed the chair for her; she seated herself with unconscious grace, and motioned me to bring another chair for myself.

"Are you going to let me in?" cried Ruyven.

"Oh, go to the--" began Dorothy, then flushed and glanced at me, asking pardon in a low voice.

A nice parent, Sir Lupus, with every child in his family ready to swear like Flanders troopers at the first breath!

Half reclining in her chair, limbs comfortably extended, Dorothy crossed her ankles and clasped her hands behind her head, a picture of indolence in every line and curve, from satin shoon to the dull gold of her hair, which, as I have said, the powder scarcely frosted.

"To comprehend properly this war," she mused, more to herself than to me, "I suppose it is necessary to understand matters which I do not understand; how it chanced that our King lost his city of Boston, and why he has not long since sent his soldiers here into our county of Tryon."

"Too many rebels, cousin," I suggested, flippantly. She disregarded me, continuing quietly;

"But this much, however, I do understand, that our province of New York is the centre of all this trouble; that the men of Tryon hold the last pennyweight, and that the balanced scales will tip only when we patroons cast in our fortunes, ... either with our King or with the rebel Congress which defies him. I think our hearts, not our interests, must guide us in this affair, which touches our honor."

Such pretty eloquence, thoughtful withal, was not what I had looked for in this new cousin of mine--this free-tongued maid, who, like a painted peach-fruit all unripe, wears the gay livery of maturity, tricking the eye with a false ripeness.

"I have thought," she said, "that if the issues of this war depend on us, we patroons should not draw sword too hastily--yet not to sit like house-cats blinking at this world-wide blaze, but, in the full flood of the crisis, draw!--knowing of our own minds on which side lies the right."

"Who taught you this?" I asked, surprised to over-bluntness.

"Who taught me? What? To think?" She laughed. "Solitude is a rare spur to thought. I listen to the gentlemen who talk with father; and I would gladly join and have my say, too, but that they treat me like a fool, and I have my questions for my pains. Yet I swear I am dowered with more sense than Sir John Johnson, with his pale eyes and thick, white flesh, and his tarnished honor to dog him like the shadow of a damned man sold to Satan--"

"Is he dishonored?"

"Is a parole broken a dishonor? The Boston people took him and placed him on his honor to live at Johnson Hall and do no meddling. And now he's fled to Fort Niagara to raise the Mohawks. Is that honorable?"

After a moment I said: "But a moment since you told me that Sir John comes here."

She nodded. "He comes and gees in secret with young Walter Butler--one of your Ormond-Butlers, cousin--and old John Butler, his father, Colonel of the Rangers, who boast they mean to scalp the whole of Tryon County ere this blood-feud is ended. Oh, I have heard them talk and talk, drinking o' nights in the gun-room, and the escort's horses stamping at the porch with a man to each horse, to hold the poor brutes' noses lest they should neigh and wake the woods. Councils of war, they call them, these revels; but they end ever the same, with Sir John borne off to bed too drunk to curse the slaves who shoulder his fat bulk, and Walter Butler, sullen, stunned by wine, a brooding thing of malice carved in stone; and father roaring his same old songs, and beating time with his long pipe till the stem snaps, and he throws the glowing bowl at Cato--"

"Dorothy, Dorothy," I said, "are these the scenes you find already too familiar?"

"Stale as last month's loaf in a ratty cupboard."

"Do they not offend you?"

"Oh, I am no prude--"

"Do you mean to say Sir Lupus sanctions it?"

"What? My presence? Oh, I amuse them; they dress me in Ruyven's clothes and have me to wine--lacking a tenor voice for their songs--and at first, long ago, their wine made me stupid, and they found rare sport in baiting me; but now they tumble, one by one, ere the wine's fire touches my face, and father swears there is no man in County Tryon can keep our company o' nights and show a steady pair of legs like mine to bear him bedwards."

After a moment's silence I said: "Are these your Northern customs?"

"They are ours--and the others of our kind. I hear the plain folk of the country speak ill of us for the free life we lead at home--I mean the Palatines and the canting

Dutch, not our tenants, though what even they may think of the manor house and of us I can only suspect, for they are all rebels at heart, Sir John says, and wear blue noses at the first run o' king's cider."

She gave a reckless laugh and crossed her knees, looking at me under half-veiled lids, smooth and pure as a child's.

"Food for the devil, they dub us in the Palatine church," she added, yawning, till I could see all her small, white teeth set in rose.

A nice nest of kinsmen had I uncovered in this hard, gray Northern forest! The Lord knows, we of the South do little penance for the pleasures a free life brings us under the Southern stars, yet such license as this is not to our taste, and I think a man a fool to teach his children to review with hardened eyes home scenes suited to a tavern.

Yet I was a guest, having accepted shelter and eaten salt; and I might not say my mind, even claiming kinsman's privilege to rebuke what seemed to me to touch the family honor.

Staring through the unwashed window-pane, moodily brooding on what I had learned, I followed impatiently the flight of those small, gray swallows of the North, colorless as shadows, whirling in spirals above the cold chimneys, to tumble in like flakes of gray soot only to drift out again, wind--blown, aimless, irrational, sense-less things. And again that hatred seized me for all this pale Northern world, where the very birds gyrated like moon-smitten sprites, and the white spectre of virtue sat amid orgies where bloodless fools caroused.

"Are you homesick, cousin?" she asked.

"Ay--if you must know the truth!" I broke out, not meaning to say my fill and ease me. "This is not the world; it is a gray inferno, where shades rave without reason, where there is no color, no repose, nothing but blankness and unreason, and an air that stings all living life to spasms of unrest. Your sun is hot, yet has no balm; your winds plague the skin and bones of a man; the forests are unfriendly; the waters all hurry as though bewitched! Brooks are cold and tasteless as the fog; the unsalted, spiceless air clogs the throat and whips the nerves till the very soul in the body strains, fluttering to be free! How can decent folk abide here?"

I hesitated, then broke into a harsh laugh, for my cousin sat staring at me, lips parted, like a fair shape struck into marble by a breath of magic.

"Pardon," I said. "Here am I, kindly invited to the council of a family whose interests lie scattered through estates from the West Indies to the Canadas, and I requite your hospitality by a rudeness I had not believed was in me."

I asked her pardon again for the petty outburst of an untravelled youngster whose first bath in this Northern air-ocean had chilled his senses and his courtesy.

"There is a land," I said, "where lately the gray bastions of St. Augustine reflected the gold and red of Spanish banners, and the blue sea mirrors a bluer sky. We Ormonds came there from the Western Indies, then drifted south, skirting the Matanzas to the sea islands on the Halifax, where I was born, an Englishman on Spanish soil, and have lived there, knowing no land but that of Florida, treading no city streets save those walled lanes of ancient Augustine. All this vast North is new to me, Dorothy; and, like our swamp-haunting Seminoles, my rustic's instinct finds hostility in what is new and strange, and I forget my breeding in this gray maze which half confuses, half alarms me."

"I am not offended," she said, smiling, "only I wonder what you find distasteful here. Is it the solitude?"

"No, for we also have that."

"Is it us?"

"Not you, Dorothy, nor yet Ruyven, nor the others. Forget what I said. As the Spaniards have it, 'Only a fool goes travelling,' and I'm not too notorious for my wisdom, even in Augustine. If it be the custom of the people here to go mad, I'll not sit in a corner croaking, 'Repent and be wise!' If the Varicks and the Butlers set the pace, I promise you to keep the quarry, Mistress Folly, in view--perhaps outfoot you all to Bedlam!... But, cousin, if you, too, run this uncoupled race with the pack, I mean to pace you, neck and neck, like a keen whip, ready to turn and lash the first who interferes with you."

"With me?" she repeated, smiling. "Am I a youngster to be coddled and protected? You have not seen our hunting. I lead, my friend; you follow."

She unclasped her arms, which till now had held her bright head cradled, and sat up, hands on her knees, grave as an Egyptian goddess guarding tombs.

"I'll wager I can outrun you, outshoot you, outride you, throw you at wrestle, cast the knife or hatchet truer than can you, catch more fish than you--and bigger ones at that!"

With an impatient gesture, peculiarly graceful, like the half-salute of a friendly swordsman ere you draw and stand on guard:

"Read the forest with me. I can outread you, sign for sign, track for track, trail in and trail out! The forest is to me Te-ka-on-do-duk [the place with a sign-post]. And when the confederacy speaks with five tongues, and every tongue split into five forked dialects, I make no answer in finger-signs, as needs must you, my cousin of the Se-a-wan-ha-ka [the land of shells]. We speak to the Iroquois with our lips, we People of the Morning. Our hands are for our rifles! Hiro [I have spoken]!"

She laughed, challenging me with eye and lip.

"And if you defy me to a bout with bowl or bottle I will not turn coward, neah-wen-ha [I thank you]! but I will drink with you and let my father judge whose legs best carry him to bed! Koue! Answer me, my cousin, Tahoontowhe [the night hawk]."

We were laughing now, yet I knew she had spoken seriously, and to plague her I said: "You boast like a Seminole chanting the war-song."

"I dare you to cast the hatchet!" she cried, reddening.

"Dare me to a trial less rude," I protested, laughing the louder.

"No, no! Come!" she said, impatient, unbolting the heavy door; and, willy-nilly, I followed, meeting the pack all sulking on the stairs, who rose to seize me as I came upon them.

"Let him alone!" cried Dorothy; "he says he can outcast me with the war-hatchet! Where is my hatchet? Sammy! Ruyven! find hatchets and come to the painted post."

"Sport!" cried Harry, leaping down-stairs before us. "Cecile, get your hatchet--get mine, too! Come on, Cousin Ormond, I'll guide you; it's the painted post by the spring--and hark, Cousin George, if you beat her I'll give you my silvered powder-horn!"

Cecile and Sammy hastened up, bearing in their arms the slim war-hatchets, cased in holsters of bright-beaded hide, and we took our weapons and started, piloted by Harry through the door, and across the shady, unkempt lawn to the stockade gate.

Dorothy and I walked side by side, like two champions in amiable confab before a friendly battle, intimately aloof from the gaping crowd which follows on the flanks of all true greatness.

Out across the deep-green meadow we marched, the others trailing on either side with eager advice to me, or chattering of contests past, when Walter Butler and Brant--he who is now war-chief of the loyal Mohawks--cast hatchets for a silver girdle, which Brant wears still; and the patroon, and Sir John, and all the great folk from Guy Park were here a-betting on the Mohawk, which, they say, so angered Walter Butler that he lost the contest. And that day dated the silent enmity between Brant and Butler, which never healed.

This I gathered amid all their chit-chat while we stood under the willows near the spring, watching Ruyven pace the distance from the post back across the greensward towards us.

Then, making his heel-mark in the grass, he took a green willow wand and set it, all feathered, in the turf.

"Is it fair for Dorothy to cast her own hatchet?" asked Harry.

"Give me Ruyven's," she said, half vexed. Aught that touched her sense of fairness sent a quick flame of anger to her cheeks which I admired.

"Keep your own hatchet, cousin," I said; "you may have need of it."

"Give me Ruyven's hatchet," she repeated, with a stamp of her foot which Ruyven hastened to respect. Then she turned to me, pink with defiance:

"It is always a stranger's honor," she said; so I advanced, drawing my light, keen weapon from its beaded sheath, which I had belted round me; and Ruyven took station by the post, ten paces to the right.

The post was painted scarlet, ringed with white above; below, in outline, the form of a man--an Indian--with folded arms, also drawn in white paint. The play was simple; the hatchet must imbed its blade close to the outlined shape, yet not "wound" or "draw blood."

"Brant at first refused to cast against that figure," said Harry, laughing. "He consented only because the figure, though Indian, was painted white."

I scarce heard him as I stood measuring with my eyes the distance. Then, taking one step forward to the willow wand, I hurled the hatchet, and it landed quivering in the shoulder of the outlined figure on the post.

"A wound!" cried Cecile; and, mortified, I stepped back, biting my lip, while Harry notched one point against me on the willow wand and Dorothy, tightening her girdle, whipped out her bright war-axe and stepped forward. Nor did she even pause to scan the post; her arm shot up, the keen axe-blade glittered and flew, sparkling and whirling, biting into the post, chuck! handle a-quiver. And you could not have laid a June willow-leaf betwixt the Indian's head and the hatchet's blade.

She turned to me, lips parted in a tormenting smile, and I praised the cast and took my hatchet from Ruyven to try once more. Yet again I broke skin on the thigh of the pictured captive; and again the glistening axe left Dorothy's hand, whirring to a safe score, a grass-stem's width from the Indian's head.

I understood that I had met my master, yet for the third time strove; and my axe whistled true, standing point-bedded a finger's breadth from the cheek.

"Can you mend that, Dorothy?" I asked, politely.

She stood smiling, silent, hatchet poised, then nodded, launching the axe. Crack! came the handles of the two hatchets, and rattled together. But the blade of her hatchet divided the space betwixt my blade and the painted face, nor touched the outline by a fair hair's breadth.

Astonishment was in my face, not chagrin, but she misread me, for the triumph died out in her eyes, and, "Oh!" she said; "I did not mean to win--truly I did not," offering her hands in friendly amend.

But at my quick laugh she brightened, still holding my hands, regarding me with curious eyes, brilliant as amethysts.

"I was afraid I had hurt your pride--before these silly children--" she began.

"Children!" shouted Ruyven. "I bet you ten shillings he can outcast you yet!"

"Done!" she flashed, then, all in a breath, smiled adorably and shook her head. "No, I'll not bet. He could win if he chose. We understand each other, my cousin Ormond and I," and gave my hands a little friendly shake with both of hers, then dropped them to still Ruyven's clamor for a wager.

"You little beast!" she said, fiercely; "is it courteous to pit your guests like game-cocks for your pleasure?"

"You did it yourself!" retorted Ruyven, indignantly--"and entered the pit yourself."

"For a jest, silly! There were no bets. Now frown and vapor and wag your finger--do! What do you lack? I will wrestle you if you wait until I don my buckskins. No? A foot-race?--and I'll bet you your ten shillings on myself! Ten to five--to three--to one! No? Then hush your silly head!"

"Because," said Ruyven, sullenly, coming up to me, "she can outrun me with her long legs, she gives herself the devil's own airs and graces. There's no living with her, I tell you. I wish I could go to the war."

"You'll have to go when father declares himself," observed Dorothy, quietly polishing her hatchet on its leather sheath.

"But he won't declare for King or Congress," retorted the boy.

"Wait till they start to plague us," murmured Dorothy. "Some fine July day cows will be missed, or a barn burned, or a shepherd found scalped. Then you'll see which way the coin spins!"

"Which way will it spin?" demanded Ruyven, incredulous yet eager.

"Ask that squirrel yonder," she said, briefly.

"Thanks; I've asked enough of chatterers," he snapped out, and came to the tree where we were sitting in the shadow on the cool, thick carpet of the grass--such grass as I had never seen in that fair Southland which I loved.

The younger children gathered shyly about me, their active tongues suddenly silent, as though, all at once, they had taken a sudden alarm to find me there.

The reaction of fatigue was settling over me--for my journey had been a long one that day--and I leaned my back against the tree and yawned, raising my hand to hide it.

"I wonder," I said, "whether anybody here knows if my boxes and servant have arrived from Philadelphia."

"Your boxes are in the hallway by your bed-chamber," said Dorothy. "Your servant went to Johnstown for news of you--let me see--I think it was Saturday--"

"Friday," said Ruyven, looking up from the willow wand which he was peeling.

"He never came back," observed Dorothy. "Some believe he ran away to Albany, some think the Boston people caught him and impressed him to work on the fort at Stanwix."

I felt my face growing hot.

"I should like to know," said I, "who has dared to interfere with my servant."

"So should I," said Ruyven, stoutly. "I'd knock his head off." The others stared. Dorothy, picking a meadow-flower to pieces, smiled quietly, but did not look up.

"What do you think has happened to my black?" I asked, watching her.

"I think Walter Butler's men caught him and packed him off to Fort Niagara," she said.

"Why do you believe that?" I asked, angrily.

"Because Mr. Butler came here looking for boat-men; and I know he tried to bribe Cato to go. Cato told me." She turned sharply to the others. "But mind you say nothing to Sir Lupus of this until I choose to tell him!"

"Have you proof that Mr. Butler was concerned in the disappearance of my servant?" I asked, with an unpleasant softness in my voice.

"No proof," replied Dorothy, also very softly.

"Then I may not even question him," I said.

"No, you can do nothing--now."

I thought a moment, frowning, then glanced up to find them all intently watching me.

"I should like," said I, "to have a tub of clean water and fresh clothing, and to sleep for an hour ere I dress to dine with Sir Lupus. But, first, I should like to see my mare, that she is well bedded and--"

"I'll see to her," said Dorothy, springing to her feet. "Ruyven, do you tell Cato to wait on Captain Ormond." And to Harry and Cecile: "Bowl on the lawn if you mean to bowl, and not in the hallway, while our cousin is sleeping." And to Benny: "If you tumble or fall into any foolishness, see that you squall no louder than a kitten mewing. Our cousin means to sleep for a whole hour."

As I rose, nodding to them gravely, all their shy deference seemed to return; they were no longer a careless, chattering band, crowding at my elbows to pluck my sleeves with, "Oh, Cousin Ormond" this, and "Listen, cousin," that; but they stood in a covey, close together, a trifle awed at my height, I suppose; and Ruyven and Dorothy conducted me with a new ceremony, each to outvie the other in politeness of language and deportment, calling to my notice details of the scenery in stilted phrases which nigh convulsed me, so that I could scarce control the set gravity of my features.

At the house door they parted company with me, all save Ruyven and Dorothy. The one marched off to summon Cato; the other stood silent, her head a little on one side, contemplating a spot of sunlight on the dusty floor.

"About young Walter Butler," she began, absently; "be not too short and sharp with him, cousin."

"I hope I shall have no reason to be too blunt with my own kin," I said.

"You may have reason--" She hesitated, then, with a pretty confidence in her eyes, "For my sake please to pass provocation unnoticed. None will doubt your courage if you overlook and refuse to be affronted."

"I cannot pass an affront," I said, bluntly. "What do you mean? Who is this quarrelsome Mr. Butler?"

"An Ormond-Butler," she said, earnestly; "but--but he has had trouble--a terrible disappointment in love, they say. He is morose at times--a sullen, suspicious man, one of those who are ever seeking for offence where none is dreamed of; a man quick to give umbrage, quicker to resent a fancied slight--a remorseless eye that fixes you with the passionless menace of a hawk's eye, dreamily marking you for a victim. He is cruel to his servants, cruel to his animals, terrible in his hatred of these Boston people. Nobody knows why they ridiculed him; but they did. That adds to the fuel which feeds the flame in him--that and the brooding on his own grievances--"

She moved nearer to me and laid her hand on my sleeve. "Cousin, the man is mad; I ask you to remember that in a moment of just provocation. It would grieve me if he were your enemy--I should not sleep for thinking."

"Dorothy," I said, smiling, "I use some weapons better than I do the war-axe. Are you afraid for me?"

She looked at me seriously. "In that little world which I know there is much that terrifies men, yet I can say, without boasting, there is not, in my world, one living creature or one witch or spirit that I dread--no, not even Catrine Montour!"

"And who is Catrine Montour?" I asked, amused at her earnestness.

Ere she could reply, Ruyven called from the stairs that Cato had my tub of water all prepared, and she walked away, nodding a brief adieu, pausing at the door to give me one sweet, swift smile of friendly interest.

IV
SIR LUPUS

I had bathed and slept, and waked once more to the deep, resonant notes of a conch-shell blowing; and I still lay abed, blinking at the sunset through the soiled panes of my western window, when Cato scraped at the door to enter, bearing my sea-boxes one by one.

Reaching behind me, I drew the keys from under my pillow and tossed them to the solemn black, lying still once more to watch him unlock my boxes and lay out my clothes and linen to the air.

"Company to sup, suh; gemmen from de No'th an' Guy Pahk, suh," he hinted, rolling his eyes at me and holding up my best wristbands, made of my mother's lace.

"I shall dress soberly, Cato," said I, yawning. "Give me a narrow queue-ribbon, too."

The old man mumbled and muttered, fussing about among the boxes until he found a full suit of silver-gray, silken stockings, and hound's-tongue shoes to match.

"Dishyere clothes sho' is sober," he reflected aloud. "One li'l gole vine a-craw-lin' on de cuffs, nuvver li'l gole vine a-creepin' up de wes'coat, gole buckles on de houn'-tongue--Whar de hat? Hat done loose hisse'f! Here de hat! Gole lace on de hat--Cap'in Ormond sho' is quality gemm'n. Ef he ain't, how come dishyere gole lace on de hat?"

"Come, Cato," I remonstrated, "am I dressing for a ball at Augustine, that you stand there pulling my finery about to choose and pick? I tell you to give me a sober suit!" I snatched a flowered robe from the bed's foot-board, pulled it about me, and stepped to the floor.

Cato brought a chair and bowl, and, when I had washed once more I seated myself while the old man shook out my hair, dusted it to its natural brown, then fell to combing and brushing. My hair, with its obstinate inclination to curl, needed neither iron nor pomade; so, silvering it with my best French powder, he tied the short queue with a black ribbon and dusted my shoulders, critically considering me the while.

"A plain shirt," I said, briefly.

He brought a frilled one.

"I want a plain shirt," I insisted.

"Dishyere sho't am des de plaines' an' de--"

"You villain, don't I know what I want?"

"No, suh!"

And, upon my honor, I could not get that black mule to find me the shirt that I wished to wear. More than that, he utterly refused to permit me to dress in a certain suit of mouse-color without lace, but actually bundled me into the silver-gray, talking volubly all the while; and I, half laughing and wholly vexed, almost minded to go burrowing myself among my boxes and risk peppering silk and velvet with hair-powder.

But he dressed me as it suited him, patting my silk shoes into shape, smoothing coat-skirt and flowered vest-flap, shaking out the lace on stock and wrist with all the delicacy and cunning of a lady's-maid.

"Idiot!" said I, "am I tricked out to please you?"

"You sho' is, Cap'in Ormond, suh," he said, the first faint approach to a grin that I had seen wrinkling his aged face. And with that he hung my small-sword, whisked the powder from my shoulders with a bit of cambric, chose a laced handkerchief for me, and, ere I could remonstrate, passed a tiny jewelled pin into my powdered hair, where it sparkled like a frost crystal.

"I'm no macaroni!" I said, angrily; "take it away!"

"Cap'in Ormond, suh, you sho' is de fines' young gemm'n in de province, suh," he pleaded. "Dess regahd yo'se'f, suh, in dishyere lookum-glass. What I done tell you? Look foh yo'se'f, suh! Cap'in Butler gwine see how de quality gemm'n fixes up! Suh John Johnsing he gwine see! Dat ole Kunnel Butler he gwine see, too! Heah yo' is, suh, dess a-bloomin' lak de pink-an'-silver ghos' flower wif de gole heart."

"Cato," I asked, curiously, "why do you take pride in tricking out a stranger to dazzle your own people?"

The old man stood silent a moment, then looked up with the mild eyes of an aged hound long privileged in honorable retirement.

"Is you sho' a Ormond, suh?"

"Yes, Cato."

"Might you come f'om de Spanish grants, suh, long de Halifax?"

"Yes, yes; but we are English now. How did you know I came from the Halifax?"

"I knowed it, suh; I knowed h'it muss be dat-away!"

"How do you know it, Cato?"

"I spec' you favor yo' pap, suh, de ole Kunnel--"

"My father!"

"Mah ole marster, suh; I was raised 'long Matanzas, suh. Spanish man done cotch me on de Tomoka an' ship me to Quebec. Ole Suh William Johnsing, he done buy me; Suh John, he done sell me; Mars Varick, he buy me; an' hyah ah is, suh-- heart dess daid foh de Halifax san's."

He bent his withered head and laid his face on my hands, but no tear fell.

After a moment he straightened, snuffled, and smiled, opening his lips with a dry click.

"H'it's dat-a-way, suh. Ole Cato dess 'bleged to fix up de young marster. Pride o' fambly, suh. What might you be desirin' now, Mars' Ormond? One li'l drap o' musk on yoh hanker? Lawd save us, but you sho' is gallus dishyere day! Spec' Miss Dorry gwine blink de vi'lets in her eyes. Yaas, suh. Miss Dorry am de only one, suh; de onliest Ormond in dishyere fambly. Seem mos' lak she done throw back to our folk, suh. Miss Dorry ain' no Varick; Miss Dorry all Ormond, suh, dess lak you an' me! Yaas, suh, h'its dat-a-way; h'it sho' is, Mars' Ormond."

I drew a deep, quivering breath. Home seemed so far, and the old slave would never live to see it. I felt as though this steel-cold North held me, too, like a trap-- never to unclose.

"Cato," I said, abruptly, "let us go home."

He understood; a gleam of purest joy flickered in his eyes, then died out, quenched in swelling tears.

He wept awhile, standing there in the centre of the room, smearing the tears away with the flapping sleeves of his tarnished livery, while, like a committed panther, I paced the walls, to and fro, to and fro, heart aching for escape.

The light in the west deepened above the forests; a long, glowing crack opened between two thunderous clouds, like a hint of hidden hell, firing the whole sky. And in the blaze the crows winged, two and two, like witches flying home to the infernal pit, now all ablaze and kindling coal on coal along the dark sky's sombre brink.

Then the red bars faded on my wall to pink, to ashes; a fleck of rosy cloud in mid-zenith glimmered and went out, and the round edges of the world were curtained with the night.

Behind me, Cato struck flint and lighted two tall candles; outside the lawn, near the stockade, a stable-lad set a conch-horn to his lips, blowing a deep, melodious cattle-call, and far away I heard them coming--tin, ton! tin, ton! tinkle!--through the woods, slowly, slowly, till in the freshening dusk I smelled their milk and heard them lowing at the unseen pasture-bars.

I turned sharply; the candle-light dazzled me. As I passed Cato, the old man bowed till his coat-cuffs hung covering his dusky, wrinkled fingers.

"When we go, we go together, Cato," I said, huskily, and so passed on through the brightly lighted hallway and down the stairs.

Candle-light glimmered on the dark pictures, the rusted circles of arms, the stags' heads with their dusty eyes. A servant in yellow livery, lounging by the door, rose from the settle as I appeared and threw open the door on the left, announcing, "Cap'm Ormond!" in a slovenly fashion which merited a rebuke from somebody.

The room into which the yokel ushered me appeared to be a library, low of ceiling, misty with sour pipe smoke, which curled and floated level, wavering as the door closed behind me.

Through the fog, which nigh choked me with its staleness, I perceived a bulky gentleman seated at ease, sucking a long clay pipe, his bulging legs cocked up on a card-table, his little, inflamed eyes twinkling red in the candle-light.

"Captain Ormond?" he cried. "Captain be damned; you're my cousin, George Ormond, or I'm the fattest liar south of Montreal! Who the devil put 'em up to captaining you--eh? Was it that minx Dorothy? Dammy, I took it that the old Colonel had come to plague me from his grave--your father, sir! And a cursed fine fellow, if he was second cousin to a Varick, which he could not help, not he!--though I've heard him damn his luck to my very face, sir! Yes, sir, under my very nose!"

He fell into a fit of fat coughing, and seized a glass of spirits-and-water which stood on the table near his feet. The draught allayed his spasm; he wiped his broad, purple face, chuckled, tossed off the last of the liquor with a smack, and held out a mottled, fat hand, bare of wrist-lace. "Here's my heart with it, George!" he cried. "I'd stand up to greet you, but it takes ten minutes for me to find these feet o' mine, so I'll not keep you waiting. There's a chair; fill it with that pretty body of yours; cock up your feet--here's a pipe--here's snuff--here's the best rum north o' Norfolk, which that ass Dunmore laid in ashes to spite those who kicked him out!"

He squeezed my hand affectionately. "Pretty bird! Dammy, but you'll break a heart or two, you rogue! Oh, you are your father all over again; it's that way with you Ormonds--all alike, and handsome as that young devil Lucifer; too proud to be proud o' your dukes and admirals, and a thousand years of waiting on your King. As lads together your father used to take me by the ear and cuff me, crying, 'Beast! beast! You eat and drink too much! An Ormond's heart lies not in his belly!' And I kicked back, fighting stoutly for the crust he dragged me from. Dammy, why not? There's more Dutch Varick than Irish Ormond in me. Remember that, George, and we shall get on famously together, you and I. Forget it, and we quarrel. Hey! fill that tall Italian glass for a toast. I give you the family, George. May they keep tight hold on what is theirs through all this cursed war-folly. Here's to the patroons, God bless 'em!"

Forced by courtesy to drink ere I had yet tasted meat, I did my part with the best grace I could muster, turning the beautiful glass downward, with a bow to my host.

"The same trick o' grace in neck and wrist," he muttered, thickly, wiping his lips. "All Ormond, all Ormond, George, like that vixen o' mine, Dorothy. Hey! It's not too often that good blood throws back; the mongrel shows oftenest; but that big chit of a lass is no Varick; she's Ormond to the bones of her. Ruyven's a red-head; there's red in the rest o' them, and the slow Dutch blood. But Dorothy's eyes are like those wild iris-blooms that purple all our meadows, and she has the Ormond hair--that thick, dull gold, which that French Ormond, of King Stephen's time, was dowered with by his Saxon mother, Helen. Eh? You see, I read it in that book your father left us. If I'm no Ormond, I like to find out why, and I love to dispute the Ormond claim which Walter Butler makes--he with his dark face and hair, and those dusky, golden eyes of his, which turn so yellow when I plague him--the mad wild-cat that he is."

Another fit of choking closed his throat, and again he soaked it open with his chilled toddy, rattling the stick to stir it well ere he drained it at a single, gobbling gulp.

A faint disgust took hold on me, to sit there smothering in the fumes of pipe and liquor, while my gross kinsman guzzled and gabbled and guzzled again.

"George," he gasped, mopping his crimsoned face, "I'll tell you now that we Varicks and you Ormonds must stand out for neutrality in this war. The Butlers mean mischief; they're mad to go to fighting, and that means our common ruin. They'll be here to-night, damn them."

"Sir Lupus," I ventured, "we are all kinsmen, the Butlers, the Varicks, and the Ormonds. We are to gather here for self-protection during this rebellion. I am sure that in the presence of this common danger there can arise no family dissension."

"Yes, there can!" he fairly yelled. "Here am I risking life and property to persuade these Butlers that their interest lies in strictest neutrality. If Schuyler at Albany knew they visited me, his dragoons would gallop into Varick Manor and hang me to my barn door! Here am I, I say, doing my best to keep 'em quiet, and there's Sir John Johnson and all that bragging crew from Guy Park combating me--nay, would you believe their impudence?--striving to win me to arm my tenantry for this King of England, who has done nothing for me, save to make a knight of me to curry favor with the Dutch patroons in New York province--or state, as they call it now! And now I have you to count on for support, and we'll whistle another jig for them to-night, I'll warrant!"

He seized his unfilled glass, looked into it, and pushed it from him peevishly.

"Dammy," he said, "I'll not budge for them! I have thousands of acres, hundreds of tenants, farms, sugar-bushes, manufactories for pearl-ash, grist-mills, saw-mills, and I'm damned if I draw sword either way! Am I a madman, to risk all this? Am I a common fool, to chance anything now? Do they think me in my dotage? Indeed, sir, if I drew blade, if I as much as raised a finger, both sides would come swarming all over us--rebels a-looting and a-shooting, Indians whooping off my cattle, firing my barns, scalping my tenants--rebels at heart every one, and I'd not care tuppence who scalped 'em but that they pay me rent!"

He clinched his fat fists and beat the air angrily.

"I'm lord of this manor!" he bawled. "I'm Patroon Varick, and I'll do as I please!"

Amazed and mortified at his gross frankness, I sat silent, not knowing what to say. Interest alone swayed him; the right and wrong of this quarrel were nothing to him; he did not even take the trouble to pay a hypocrite's tribute to principle ere he turned his back on it; selfishness alone ruled, and he boasted of it, waving his short, fat arms in anger, or struggling to extend them heavenward, in protest against these people who dared urge him to declare himself and stand or fall with the cause he might embrace.

A faint disgust stirred my pulse. We Ormonds had as much to lose as he, but yelled it not to the skies, nor clamored of gain and loss in such unseemly fashion, ignoring higher motive.

"Sir Lupus," I said, "if we can remain neutral with honor, that surely is wisest. But can we?"

"Remain neutral! Of course we can!" he shouted.

"Honorably?"

"Eh? Where's honor in this mob-rule that breaks out in Boston to spot the whole land with a scurvy irruption! Honor? Where is it in this vile distemper which sets old neighbors here a-itching to cut each other's throats? One says, 'You're a Tory! Take that!' and slips a knife into him. T'other says, 'You're a rebel!' Bang!-- and blows his head off! Honor? Bah!"

He removed his wig to wipe his damp and shiny pate, then set the wig on askew and glared at me out of his small, ruddy eyes.

"I'm for peace," he said, "and I care not who knows it. Then, whether Tory or rebel win the day, here am I, holding to my own with both hands and caring nothing which rag flies overhead, so that it brings peace and plenty to honest folk. And, mark me, then we shall live to see these plumed and gold-laced glory-mongers slinking round to beg their bread at our back doors. Dammy, let 'em bellow now! Let 'em shout for war! I'll keep my mills busy and my agent walking the old rent-beat. If they can fill their bellies with a mess of glory I'll not grudge them what they can snatch; but I'll fill mine with food less spiced, and we'll see which of us thrives best--these sons of Mars or the old patroon who stays at home and dips his nose into nothing worse than old Madeira!"

He gave me a cunning look, pushed his wig partly straight, and lay back, puffing quietly at his pipe.

I hesitated, choosing my words ere I spoke; and at first he listened contentedly, nodding approval, and pushing fresh tobacco into his clay with a fat forefinger.

I pointed out that it was my desire to save my lands from ravage, ruin, and ultimate confiscation by the victors; that for this reason he had summoned me, and I had come to confer with him and with other branches of our family, seeking how best this might be done.

I reminded him that, from his letters to me, I had acquired a fair knowledge of the estates endangered; that I understood that Sir John Johnson owned enormous tracts in Tryon County which his great father, Sir William, had left him when he died; that Colonel Claus, Guy Johnson, the Butlers, father and son, and the Varicks, all held estates of greatest value; and that these estates were menaced, now by Tory, now by rebel, and the lords of these broad manors were alternately solicited and threatened by the warring factions now so bloodily embroiled.

"We Ormonds can comprehend your dismay, your distress, your doubts," I said. "Our indigo grows almost within gunshot of the British outpost at New Smyrna; our oranges, our lemons, our cane, our cotton, must wither at a blast from the cannon of Saint Augustine. The rebels in Georgia threaten us, the Tories at Pensacola warn us, the Seminoles are gathering, the Minorcans are arming, the blacks in the Carolinas watch us, and the British regiments at Augustine are all itching to ravage and plunder and drive us into the sea if we declare not for the King who pays them."

Sir Lupus nodded, winked, and fell to slicing tobacco with a small, gold knife.

"We're all Quakers in these days--eh, George? We can't fight--no, we really can't! It's wrong, George,--oh, very wrong." And he fell a-chuckling, so that his paunch shook like a jelly.

"I think you do not understand me," I said.

He looked up quickly.

"We Ormonds are only waiting to draw sword."

"Draw sword!" he cried. "What d'ye mean?"

"I mean that, once convinced our honor demands it, we cannot choose but draw."

"Don't be an ass!" he shouted. "Have I not told you that there's no honor in this bloody squabble? Lord save the lad, he's mad as Walter Butler!"

"Sir Lupus," I said, angrily, "is a man an ass to defend his own land?"

"He is when it's not necessary! Lie snug; nobody is going to harm you. Lie snug, with both arms around your own land."

"I meant my own native land, not the miserable acres my slaves plant to feed and clothe me."

He glared, twisting his long pipe till the stem broke short.

"Well, which land do you mean to defend, England or these colonies?" he asked, staring.

"That is what I desire to learn, sir," I said, respectfully. "That is why I came North. With us in Florida, all is, so far, faction and jealousy, selfish intrigue and prejudiced dispute. The truth, the vital truth, is obscured; the right is hidden in a petty storm where local tyrants fill the air with dust, striving each to blind the other."

I leaned forward earnestly. "There must be right and wrong in this dispute; Truth stands naked somewhere in the world. It is for us to find her. Why, mark me, Sir Lupus, men cannot sit and blink at villany, nor look with indifference on a struggle to the death. One side is right, t'other wrong. And we must learn how matters stand."

"And what will it advance us to learn how matters stand?" he said, still staring, as though I were some persistent fool vexing him with unleavened babble. "Suppose these rebels are right--and, dammy, but I think they are--and suppose our King's troops are roundly trouncing them--and I think they are, too--do you mean to say you'd draw sword and go a-prowling, seeking for some obliging enemy to knock you in the head or hang you for a rebel to your neighbor's apple-tree?"

"Something of that sort," I said, good-humoredly.

"Oh, Don Quixote once more, eh?" he sneered, too mad to raise his voice to the more convenient bellow which seemed to soothe him as much as it distressed his listener. "Well, you've got a fool's mate in Sir George Covert, the insufferable dandy! And all you two need is a pair o' Panzas and a brace of windmills. Bah!" He grew angrier. "Bah, I say!" He broke out: "Damnation, sir! Go to the devil!"

I said, calmly: "Sir Lupus, I hear your observation with patience; I naturally receive your admonition with respect, but your bearing towards me I resent. Pray, sir, remember that I am under your roof now, but when I quit it I am free to call you to account."

"What! You'd fight me?"

"Scarcely, sir; but I should expect somebody to make your words good."

"Bah! Who? Ruyven? He's a lad! Dorothy is the only one to--" He broke out into a hoarse laugh. "Oh, you Ormonds! I might have saved myself the pains. And now you want to flesh your sword, it matters not in whom--Tory, rebel, neutral folk, they're all one to you, so that you fight! George, don't take offence; I naturally swear at those I differ with. I may love 'em and yet curse 'em like a sailor! Know me better, George! Bear with me; let me swear at you, lad! It's all I can do."

He spread out his fat hands imploringly, recrossing his enormous legs on the card-table. "I can't fight, George; I would gladly, but I'm too fat. Don't grudge me a few kindly oaths now and then. It's all I can do."

I was seized with a fit of laughter, utterly uncontrollable. Sir Lupus observed me peevishly, twiddling his broken pipe, and I saw he longed to launch it at my head, which made me laugh till his large, round, red face grew grayer and foggier through the mirth-mist in my eyes.

"Am I so droll?" he snapped.

"Oh yes, yes, Sir Lupus," I cried, weakly. "Don't grudge me this laugh. It is all I can do."

A grim smile came over his broad face.

"Touched!" he said. "I've a fine pair on my hands now--you and Sir George Covert--to plague me and prick me with your wit, like mosquitoes round a drowsy man. A fine family conference we shall have, with Sir John Johnson and the Butlers shooting one way, you and Sir George Covert firing t'other, and me betwixt you, singing psalms and getting all your arrows in me, fore and aft."

"Who is Sir George Covert?" I asked.

"One o' the Calverts, Lord Baltimore's kin, a sort of cousin of the Ormond-Butlers, a supercilious dandy, a languid macaroni; plagues me, damn his impudence, but I can't hate him--no! Hate him? Faith, I owe him more than any man on earth ... and love him for it--which is strange!"

"Has he an estate in jeopardy?" I inquired.

"Yes. He has a mansion in Albany, too, which he leases. He bought a mile on the great Vlaic and lives there all alone, shooting, fishing, playing the guitar o' moony nights, which they say sets the wild-cats wilder. Mark me, George, a petty mile square and a shooting shanty, and this languid ass says he means to fight for it. Lord help the man! I told him I'd buy him out to save him from embroiling us all, and what d' ye think? He stared at me through his lorgnons as though I had been some queer, new bird, and, says he, 'Lud!' says he,' there's a world o' harmless sport in you yet, Sir Lupus, but you don't spell your title right,' says he. 'Change the a to an o and add an ell for good measure, and there you have it,' says he, a-drawling. With which he minced off, dusting his nose with his lace handkerchief, and I'm damned if I see the joke yet in spelling patroon with an o for the a and an ell for good measure!"

He paused, out of breath, to pour himself some spirits. "Joke?" he muttered. "Where the devil is it? I see no wit in that." And he picked up a fresh pipe from the rack on the table and moistened the clay with his fat tongue.

We sat in silence for a while. That this Sir George Covert should call the patroon a poltroon hurt me, for he was kin to us both; yet it seemed that there might be truth in the insolent fling, for selfishness and poltroonery are too often linked.

I raised my eyes and looked almost furtively at my cousin Varick. He had no neck; the spot where his bullet head joined his body was marked only by a narrow and soiled stock. His eyes alone relieved the monotony of a stolid countenance; all else was fat.

Sunk in my own reflections, lying back in my arm-chair, I watched dreamily the smoke pouring from the patroon's pipe, floating away, to hang wavering across the room, now lifting, now curling downward, as though drawn by a hidden current towards the unwaxed oaken floor.

No, there was no Ormond in him; he was all Varick, all Dutch, all patroon.

I had never seen any man like him save once, when a red-faced Albany merchant came a-waddling to the sea-islands looking for cotton and indigo, and we all despised him for the eagerness with which he trimmed his shillings at the Augustine taverns. Thrift is a word abused, and serves too often as a mask for avarice.

As I sat there fashioning wise saws and proverbs in my busy mind, the hall door opened and the first guest was announced--Sir George Covert.

And in he came, a well-built, lazy gentleman of forty, swinging gracefully on a pair o' legs no man need take shame in; ruffles on cuff and stock, hair perfumed, powdered, and rolled twice in French puffs, and on his hand a brilliant that sparkled purest fire. Under one arm he bore his gold-edged hat, and as he strolled forward, peering coolly about him through his quizzing glass, I thought I had never seen such graceful assurance, nor such insolently handsome eyes, marred by the faint shadows of dissipation.

Sir Lupus nodded a welcome and blew a great cloud of smoke into the air.

"Ah," observed Sir George, languidly, "Vesuvius in irruption?"

"How de do," said Sir Lupus, suspiciously.

"The mountain welcomes Mohammed," commented Sir George. "Mohammed greets the mountain! How de do, Sir Lupus! Ah!" He turned gracefully towards me, bowing. "Pray present me, Sir Lupus."

"My cousin, George Ormond," said Sir Lupus. "George first, George second," he added, with a sneer.

"No relation to George III., I trust, sir?" inquired Sir George, anxiously, offering his cool, well-kept hand.

"No," said I, laughing at his serious countenance and returning his clasp firmly.

"That's well, that's well," murmured Sir George, apparently vastly relieved, and invited me to take snuff with him.

We had scarcely exchanged a civil word or two ere the servant announced Captain Walter Butler, and I turned curiously, to see a dark, graceful young man enter and stand for a moment staring haughtily straight at me. He wore a very elegant black-and-orange uniform, without gorget; a black military cloak hung from his shoulders, caught up in his sword-knot.

With a quick movement he raised his hand and removed his officer's hat, and I saw on his gauntlets of fine doeskin the Ormond arms, heavily embroidered. Instantly the affectation displeased me.

"Come to the mountain, brother prophet," said Sir George, waving his hand towards the seated patroon. He came, lightly as a panther, his dark, well-cut features softening a trifle; and I thought him handsome in his uniform, wearing his own dark hair unpowdered, tied in a short queue; but when he turned full face to greet Sir George Covert, I was astonished to see the cruelty in his almost perfect features, which were smooth as a woman's, and lighted by a pair of clear, dark-golden eyes.

Ah, those wonderful eyes of Walter Butler--ever-changing eyes, now almost black, glimmering with ardent fire, now veiled and amber, now suddenly a shallow yellow, round, staring, blank as the eyes of a caged eagle; and, still again, piercing, glittering, narrowing to a slit. Terrible mad eyes, that I have never forgotten--never, never can forget.

As Sir Lupus named me, Walter Butler dropped Sir George's hand and grasped mine, too eagerly to please me.

"Ormond and Ormond-Butler need no friends to recommend them each to the other," he said. And straightway fell a-talking of the greatness of the Arrans and the Ormonds, and of that duke who, attainted, fled to France to save his neck.

I strove to be civil, yet he embarrassed me before the others, babbling of petty matters interesting only to those whose taste invites them to go burrowing in parish records and ill-smelling volumes written by some toad-eater to his patron.

For me, I am an Ormond, and I know that it would be shameful if I turned rascal and besmirched my name. As to the rest--the dukes, the glory, the greatness--I hold it concerns nobody but the dead, and it is a foolishness to plague folks' ears by boasting of deeds done by those you never knew, like a Seminole chanting ere he strikes the painted post.

Also, this Captain Walter Butler was overlarding his phrases with "Cousin Ormond," so that I was soon cloyed, and nigh ready to damn the relationship to his face.

Sir Lupus, who had managed to rise by this time, waddled off into the drawing-room across the hallway, motioning us to follow; and barely in time, too, for there came, shortly, Sir John Johnson with a company of ladies and gentlemen, very gay in their damasks, brocades, and velvets, which the folds of their foot-mantles, capuchins, and cardinals revealed.

The gentlemen had come a-horseback, and all wore very elegant uniforms under their sober cloaks, which were linked with gold chains at the throat; the ladies, prettily powdered and patched, appeared a trifle over-colored, and their necks and shoulders, innocent of buffonts, gleamed pearl-tinted above their gay breast-knots. And they made a sparkling bevy as they fluttered up the staircase to their cloak-room, while Sir John entered the drawing-room, followed by the other gentlemen, and stood in careless conversation with the patroon, while old Cato disembarrassed him of cloak and hat.

Sir John Johnson, son of the great Sir William, as I first saw him was a man of less than middle age, flabby, cold-eyed, heavy of foot and hand. On his light-colored hair he wore no powder; the rather long queue was tied with a green hair-ribbon; the thick, whitish folds of his double chin rested on a buckled stock.

For the rest, he wore a green-and-gold uniform of very elegant cut--green being the garb of his regiment, the Royal Greens, as I learned afterwards--and his buff-topped boots and his metals were brilliant and plainly new.

When the patroon named me to him he turned his lack-lustre eyes on me and offered me a large, damp hand.

In turn I was made acquainted with the several officers in his suite--Colonel John Butler, father of Captain Walter Butler, broad and squat, a withered prophecy of what the son might one day be; Colonel Daniel Claus, a rather merry and battered Indian fighter; Colonel Guy Johnson, of Guy Park, dark and taciturn; a Captain Campbell, and a Captain McDonald of Perth.

All wore the green uniform save the Butlers; all greeted me with particular civility and conducted like the respectable company they appeared to be, politely engaging me in pleasant conversation, desiring news from Florida, or complimenting me upon my courtesy, which, they vowed, had alone induced me to travel a thousand miles for the sake of permitting my kinsmen the pleasure of welcoming me.

One by one the gentlemen retired to exchange their spurred top-boots for white silk stockings and silken pumps, and to arrange their hair or stick a patch here and there, and rinse their hands in rose-water to cleanse them of the bridle's odor.

They were still thronging the gun-room, and I stood alone in the drawing-room with Sir George Covert, when a lady entered and courtesied low as we bowed together.

And truly she was a beauty, with her skin of rose-ivory, her powdered hair a-gleam with brilliants, her eyes of purest violet, a friendly smile hovering on her fresh, scarlet mouth.

"Well, sir," she said, "do you not know me?" And to Sir George: "I vow, he takes me for a guest in my own house!"

And then I knew my cousin Dorothy Varick.

She suffered us to salute her hand, gazing the while about her indifferently; and, as I released her slender fingers and raised my head, she, rounded arm still extended as though forgotten, snapped her thumb and forefinger together in vexation with a "Plague on it! There's that odious Sir John!"

"Is Sir John Johnson so offensive to your ladyship?" inquired Sir George, lazily.

"Offensive! Have you not heard how the beast drank wine from my slipper! Never mind! I cannot endure him. Sir George, you must sit by me at table--and you, too, Cousin Ormond, or he'll come bothering." She glanced at the open door of the gun-room, a frown on her white brow. "Oh, they're all here, I see. Sparks will fly ere sun-up. There's Campbell, and McDonald, too, wi' the memory of Glencoe still stewing betwixt them; and there's Guy Johnson, with a price on his head--and plenty to sell it for him in County Tryon, gentlemen! And there's young Walter Butler, cursing poor Cato that he touched his spur in drawing off his boots--if he strikes Cato I'll strike him! And where are their fine ladies, Sir George? Still primping at the mirror? Oh, la!" She stepped back, laughing, raising her lovely arms a little. "Look at me. Am I well laced, with nobody to aid me save Cecile, poor child, and Benny to hold the candles--he being young enough for the office?"

"Happy, happy Benny!" murmured Sir George, inspecting her through his quizzing-glass from head to toe.

"If you think it a happy office you may fill it yourself in future, Sir George," she said. "I never knew an ass who failed to bray in ecstasy at mention of a pair o' stays."

Sir George stared, and said, "Aha! clever--very, very clever!" in so patronizing a tone that Dorothy reddened and bit her lip in vexation.

"That is ever your way," she said, "when I parry you to your confusion. Take your eyes from me, Sir George! Cousin Ormond, am I dressed to your taste or not?"

She stood there in her gown of brocade, beautifully flowered in peach color, dainty, confident, challenging me to note one fault. Nor could I, from the gold hair-pegs in her hair to the tip of her slim, pompadour shoes peeping from the lace of her petticoat, which she lifted a trifle to show her silken, flowered hose.

And--"There!" she cried, "I gowned myself, and I wear no paint. I wish you would tell them as much when they laugh at me."

Now came the ladies, rustling down the stairway, and the gentlemen, strolling in from their toilet and stirrup-cups in the gun-room, and I noted that all wore service-swords, and laid their pistols on the table in the drawing-room.

"Do they fear a surprise?" I whispered to Sir George Covert.

"Oh yes; Jack Mount and the Stoners are abroad. But Sir John has a troop of his cut-throat horsemen picketed out around us. You see, Sir John broke his parole, and Walter Butler is attainted, and it might go hard with some of these gentlemen if General Schuyler's dragoons caught them here, plotting nose to nose."

"Who is this Jack Mount?" I asked, curiously, remembering my companion of the Albany road.

"One of Cresap's riflemen," he drawled, "sent back here from Boston to raise the country against the invasion. They say he was a highwayman once, but we Tories"--he laughed shamelessly--"say many things in these days which may not help us at the judgment day. Wait, there's that little rosebud, Claire Putnam, Sir John's flame. Take her in to table; she's a pretty little plaything. Lady Johnson, who was Polly Watts, is in Montreal, you see." He made a languid gesture with outspread hands, smiling.

The girl he indicated, Mistress Claire Putnam, was a fragile, willowy creature, over-thin, perhaps, yet wonderfully attractive and pretty, and there was much of good in her face, and a tinge of pathos, too, for all her bright vivacity.

"If Sir John Johnson put her away when he wedded Miss Watts," said Sir George, coolly, "I think he did it from interest and selfish calculation, not because he ceased to love her in his bloodless, fishy fashion. And now that Lady Johnson has fled to Canada, Sir John makes no pretence of hiding his amours in the society which he haunts; nor does that society take umbrage at the notorious relationship so impudently renewed. We're a shameless lot, Mr. Ormond."

At that moment I heard Sir John Johnson, at my elbow, saying to Sir Lupus:

"Do you know what these damned rebels have had the impudence to do? I can scarce credit it myself, but it is said that their Congress has adopted a flag of thirteen stripes and thirteen stars on a blue field, and I'm cursed if I don't believe they mean to hoist the filthy rag in our very faces!"

V
A NIGHT AT THE PATROON'S

Under a flare of yellow candle-light we entered the dining-hall and seated ourselves before a table loaded with flowers and silver, and the most beautiful Flemish glass that I have ever seen; though they say that Sir William Johnson's was finer.

The square windows of the hall were closed, the dusty curtains closely drawn; the air, though fresh, was heavily saturated with perfume. Between each window, and higher up, small, square loop-holes pierced the solid walls. The wooden flap-hoods of these were open; through them poured the fresh night air, stirring the clustered flowers and the jewelled aigrets in the ladies' hair.

The spectacle was pretty, even beautiful; at every lady's cover lay a gift from the patroon, a crystal bosom-glass, mounted in silver filigree, filled with roses in scented water; and, at the sight, a gust of hand-clapping swept around the table, like the rattle of December winds through dry palmettos.

In a distant corner, slaves, dressed fancifully and turbaned like Barbary blacka-moors, played on fiddles and guitars, and the music was such as I should have en-joyed, loving all melody as I do, yet could scarcely hear it in the flutter and chatter rising around me as the ladies placed the bosom-bottles in their stomachers and opened their Marlborough fans to set them waving all like restless wings.

Yet, under this surface elegance and display, one could scarcely choose but note how everywhere an amazing shiftlessness reigned in the patroon's house. Cobwebs canopied the ceiling-beams with their silvery, ragged banners afloat in the candle's heat; dust, like a velvet mantle, lay over the Dutch plates and teapots, ranged on shelves against the panelled wall midway 'twixt ceiling and unwaxed floor; the gaudy yellow liveries of the black servants were soiled and tarnished and ill fitting, and all wore slovenly rolls, tied to imitate scratch-wigs, the effect of which was amazing. The passion for cleanliness in the Dutch lies not in their men folk; a Dutch mistress of this manor house had died o' shame long since--or died o' scrubbing.

I felt mean and ungracious to sit there spying at my host's table, and strove to forget it, yet was forced to wipe furtively spoon and fork upon the napkin on my knees ere I durst acquaint them with my mouth; and so did others, as I saw; but they did it openly and without pretence of concealment, and nobody took offence.

Sir Lupus cared nothing for precedence at table, and said so when he seated us, which brought a sneer to Sir John Johnson's mouth and a scowl to Walter Butler's brow; but this provincial boorishness appeared to be forgotten ere the decanters had slopped the cloth twice, and fair faces flushed, and voices grew gayer, and the rattle of silver assaulting china and the mellow ring of glasses swelled into a steady, melodious din which stirred the blood to my cheeks.

We Ormonds love gayety--I choose the mildest phrase I know. Yet, take us at our worst, Irish that we are, and if there be a taint of license to our revels, and if we drink the devil's toast to the devil's own undoing, the vital spring of our people remains unpolluted, the nation's strength and purity unsoiled, guarded forever by the chastity of our women.

Savoring my claret, I glanced askance at my neighbors; on my left sat my cousin Dorothy Varick, frankly absorbed in a roasted pigeon, yet wielding knife and fork with much grace and address; on my right Magdalen Brant, step-cousin to Sir John, a lovely, soft-voiced girl, with velvety eyes and the faintest dusky tint, which showed the Indian blood through the carmine in her fresh, curved cheeks.

I started to speak to her, but there came a call from the end of the table, and we raised our glasses to Sir Lupus, for which civility he expressed his thanks and gave us the ladies, which we drank standing, and reversed our glasses with a cheer.

Then Walter Butler gave us "The Ormonds and the Earls of Arran," an amazing vanity, which shamed me so that I sat biting my lip, furious to see Sir John wink at Colonel Claus, and itching to fling my glass at the head of this young fool whose brain seemed cracked with brooding on his pedigree.

Meat was served ere I was called on, but later, a delicious Burgundy being decanted, all called me with a persistent clamor, so that I was obliged to ask permission of Sir Lupus, then rise, still tingling with the memory of the silly toast offered by Walter Butler.

"I give you," I said, "a republic where self-respect balances the coronet, where there is no monarch, no high-priest, but only a clean altar, served by the parliament of a united people. Gentlemen, raise your glasses to the colonies of America and their ancient liberties!"

And, amazed at what I had said, and knowing that I had not meant to say it, I lifted my glass and drained it.

Astonishment altered every face. Walter Butler mechanically raised his glass, then set it down, then raised it once more, gazing blankly at me; and I saw others hesitate, as though striving to recollect the exact terms of my toast. But, after a second's hesitation, all drank sitting. Then each looked inquiringly at me, at neighbors, puzzled, yet already partly reassured.

"Gad!" said Colonel Claus, bluntly, "I thought at first that Burgundy smacked somewhat of Boston tea."

"The Burgundy's sound enough," said Colonel John Butler, grimly.

"So is the toast," bawled Sir Lupus. "It's a pacific toast, a soothing sentiment, neither one thing not t'other. Dammy, it's a toast no Quaker need refuse."

"Sir Lupus, your permission!" broke out Captain Campbell. "Gentlemen, it is strange that not one of his Majesty's officers has proposed the King!" He looked straight at me and said, without turning his head: "All loyal at this table will fill. Ladies, gentlemen, I give you his Majesty the King!"

The toast was finished amid cheers. I drained my glass and turned it down with a bow to Captain Campbell, who bowed to me as though greatly relieved.

The fiddles, bassoons, and guitars were playing and the slaves singing when the noise of the cheering died away; and I heard Dorothy beside me humming the air and tapping the floor with her silken shoe, while she moistened macaroons in a glass of Madeira and nibbled them with serene satisfaction.

"You appear to be happy," I whispered.

"Perfectly. I adore sweets. Will you try a dish of cinnamon cake? Sop it in Burgundy; they harmonize to a most heavenly taste.... Look at Magdalen Brant, is she not sweet? Her cousin is Molly Brant, old Sir William's sweetheart, fled to Canada.... She follows this week with Betty Austin, that black-eyed little mischief-maker on Sir John's right, who owes her diamonds to Guy Johnson. La! What a gossip I grow!

But it's county talk, and all know it, and nobody cares save the Albany blue-noses and the Van Cortlandts, who fall backward with standing too straight--"

"Dorothy," I said, sharply, "a blunted innocence is better than none, but it's a pity you know so much!"

"How can I help it?" she asked, calmly, dipping another macaroon into her glass.

"It's a pity, all the same," I said.

"Dew on a duck's back, my friend," she observed, serenely. "Cousin, if I were fashioned for evil I had been tainted long since."

She sat up straight and swept the table with a heavy-lidded, insolent glance, eyebrows raised. The cold purity of her profile, the undimmed innocence, the childish beauty of the curved cheek, touched me to the quick. Ah! the white flower to nourish here amid unconcealed corruption, with petals stainless, with bloom undimmed, with all its exquisite fragrance still fresh and wholesome in an air heavy with wine and the odor of dying roses.

I looked around me. Guy Johnson, red in the face, was bending too closely beside his neighbor, Betty Austin. Colonel Claus talked loudly across the table to Captain McDonald, and swore fashionable oaths which the gaunt captain echoed obsequiously. Claire Putnam coquetted with her paddle-stick fan, defending her roses from Sir George Covert, while Sir John Johnson stared at them in cold disapproval; and I saw Magdalen Brant, chin propped on her clasped hands, close her eyes and breathe deeply while the wine burned her face, setting torches aflame in either cheek. Later, when I spoke to her, she laughed pitifully, saying that her ears hummed like bee-hives. Then she said that she meant to go, but made no movement; and presently her dark eyes closed again, and I saw the fever pulse beating in her neck.

Some one had overturned a silver basin full of flowers, and a servant, sopping up the water, had brushed Walter Butler so that he flew into a passion and flung a glass at the terrified black, which set Sir Lupus laughing till he choked, but which enraged me that he should so conduct in the presence of his host's daughter.

Yet if Sir Lupus could not only overlook it, but laugh at it, I, certes, had no right to rebuke what to me seemed a gross insult.

Toasts flew fast now, and there was a punch in a silver bowl as large as a bushel-

-and spirits, too, which was strange, seeing that the ladies remained at table.

Then Captain Campbell would have all to drink the Royal Greens, standing on chairs, one foot on the table, which appeared to be his regiment's mess custom, and we did so, the ladies laughing and protesting, but finally planting their dainty shoes on the edge of the table; and Magdalen Brant nigh fell off her chair--for lack of balance, as Sir George Covert protested, one foot alone being too small to sustain her.

"That Cinderella compliment at our expense!" cried Betty Austin, but Sir Lupus cried: "Silence all, and keep one foot on the table!" And a little black slave lad, scarce more than a babe, appeared, dressed in a lynx-skin, bearing a basket of pretty boxes woven out of scented grass and embroidered with silk flowers.

At every corner he laid a box, all exclaiming and wondering what the surprise might be, until the little black, arching his back, fetched a yowl like a lynx and ran out on all fours.

"The gentlemen will open the boxes! Ladies, keep one foot on the table!" bawled Sir Lupus. We bent to open the boxes; Magdalen Brant and Dorothy Varick, each resting a hand on my shoulder to steady them, peeped curiously down to see. And, "Oh!" cried everybody, as the lifted box-lids discovered snow-white pigeons sitting on great gilt eggs.

The white pigeons fluttered out, some to the table, where they craned their necks and ruffled their snowy plumes; others flapped up to the loop-holes, where they sat and watched us.

"Break the eggs!" cried the patroon.

I broke mine; inside was a pair of shoe-roses, each set with a pearl and clasped with a gold pin.

Betty Austin clapped her hands in delight; Dorothy bent double, tore off the silken roses from each shoe in turn, and I pinned on the new jewelled roses amid a gale of laughter.

"A health to the patroon!" cried Sir George Covert, and we gave it with a will, glasses down. Then all settled to our seats once more to hear Sir George sing a song.

A slave passed him a guitar; he touched the strings and sang with good taste a song in questionable taste:

"Jeanneton prend sa faucille."
A delicate melody and neatly done; yet the verse--

> "Le deuxieme plus habile
> L'embrassant sous le menton"--

made me redden, and the envoi nigh burned me alive with blushes, yet was rapturously applauded, and the patroon fell a-choking with his gross laughter.

Then Walter Butler would sing, and, I confess, did it well, though the song was sad and the words too melancholy to please.

"I know a rebel song," cried Colonel Claus. "Here, give me that fiddle and I'll fiddle it, dammy if I don't--ay, and sing it, too!"

In a shower of gibes and laughter the fiddle was fetched, and the Indian fighter seized the bow and drew a most distressful strain, singing in a whining voice:

> "Come hearken to a bloody tale,
>   Of how the soldiery
> Did murder men in Boston,
>   As you full soon shall see.
> It came to pass on March the fifth
>   Of seventeen-seventy,
> A regiment, the twenty-ninth.
>   Provoked a sad affray!"

"Chorus!" shouted Captain Campbell, beating time:

> "Fol-de-rol-de-rol-de-ray--
> Provoked a sad affray!"

"That's not in the song!" protested Colonel Claus, but everybody sang it in whining tones.

"Continue!" cried Captain Campbell, amid a burst of laughter. And Claus gravely drew his fiddle-bow across the strings and sang:

"In King Street, by the Butcher's Hall
  The soldiers on us fell,
Likewise before their barracks
  (It is the truth I tell).
And such a dreadful carnage
  In Boston ne'er was known;
They killed Samuel Maverick--
  He gave a piteous groan."

And, "Fol-de-rol!" roared Captain Campbell, "He gave a piteous groan!"

"John Clark he was wounded,
  On him they did fire;
James Caldwell and Crispus Attucks
  Lay bleeding in the mire;
Their regiment, the twenty-ninth,
  Killed Monk and Sam I Gray,
While Patrick Carr lay cold in death
  And could not flee away--

"Oh, tally!" broke out Sir John; "are we to listen to such stuff all night?"

More laughter; and Sir George Covert said that he feared Sir John Johnson had no sense of humor.

"I have heard that before," said Sir John, turning his cold eyes on Sir George. "But if we've got to sing at wine, in Heaven's name let us sing something sensible."

"No, no!" bawled Claus. "This is the abode of folly to-night!" And he sang a catch from "Pills to Purge Melancholy," as broad a verse as I cared to hear in such company.

"Cheer up, Sir John!" cried Betty Austin; "there are other slippers to drink from--"

Sir John stood up, exasperated, but could not face the storm of laughter, nor could Dorothy, silent and white in her anger; and she rose to go, but seemed to think better of it and resumed her seat, disdainful eyes sweeping the table.

"Face the fools," I whispered. "Your confusion is their victory."

Captain McDonald, stirring the punch, filled all glasses, crying out that we should drink to our sweethearts in bumpers.

"Drink 'em in wine," protested Captain Campbell, thickly. "Who but a feckless McDonald wud drink his leddy in poonch?"

"I said poonch!" retorted McDonald, sternly. "If ye wish wine, drink it; but I'm thinkin' the Argyle Campbells are better judges o' blood than of red wine.

"Stop that clan-feud!" bawled the patroon, angrily.

But the old clan-feud blazed up, kindled from the ever-smouldering embers of Glencoe, which the massacre of a whole clan had not extinguished in all these years.

"And why should an Argyle Campbell judge blood?" cried Captain Campbell, in a menacing voice.

"And why not?" retorted McDonald. "Breadalbane spilled enough to teach ye."

"Teach who?"

"Teach you!--and the whole breed o' black Campbells from Perth to Galway and Fonda's Bush, which ye dub Broadalbin. I had rather be a Monteith and have the betrayal of Wallace cast in my face than be a Campbell of Argyle wi' the memory o' Glencoe to follow me to hell."

"Silence!" roared the patroon, struggling to his feet. Sir George Covert caught at Captain Campbell's sleeve as he rose; Sir John Johnson stood up, livid with anger.

"Let this end now!" he said, sternly. "Do officers of the Royal Greens conduct like yokels at a fair? Answer me, Captain Campbell! And you, Captain McDonald! Take your seat, sir; and if I hear that cursed word 'Glencoe' 'again, the first who utters it faces a court-martial!"

Partly sobered, the Campbell glared mutely at the McDonald; the latter also appeared to have recovered a portion of his senses and resumed his seat in silence, glowering at the empty glasses before him.

"Now be sensible, gentlemen," said Colonel Claus, with a jovial nod to the patroon; "let pass, let pass. This is no time to raise the fiery cross in the hills. Gad, there's a new pibroch to march to these days--

"Pibroch o' Hirokoue!   Pibroch o' Hirokonue!"

he hummed, deliberately, but nobody laughed, and the grave, pale faces of the women turned questioningly one to the other.

Enemies or allies, there was terror in the name of "Iroquois." But Walter Butler looked up from his gloomy meditation and raised his glass with a ghastly laugh.

"I drink to our red allies," he said, slowly drained his glass till but a color remained in it, then dipped his finger in the dregs and drew upon the white table-cloth a blood-red cross.

"There's your clan-sign, you Campbells, you McDonalds," he said, with a terrifying smile which none could misinterpret.

Then Sir George Covert said: "Sir William Johnson knew best. Had he lived, there had been no talk of the Iroquois as allies or as enemies."

I said, looking straight at Walter Butler: "Can there be any serious talk of turning these wild beasts loose against the settlers of Tryon County?"

"Against rebels," observed Sir John Johnson, coldly. "No loyal man need fear our Mohawks."

A dead silence followed. Servants, clearing the round table of silver, flowers, cloth--all, save glasses and decanters--stepped noiselessly, and I knew the terror of the Iroquois name had sharpened their dull ears. Then came old Cato, tricked out in flame-colored plush, bearing the staff of major-domo; and the servants in their tarnished liveries marshalled behind him and filed out, leaving us seated before a bare table, with only our glasses and bottles to break the expanse of polished mahogany and soiled cloth.

Captain McDonald rose, lifted the steaming kettle from the hob, and set it on a great, blue tile, and the gentlemen mixed their spirits thoughtfully, or lighted long, clay pipes.

The patroon, wreathed in smoke, lay back in his great chair and rattled his toddy-stick for attention--an unnecessary noise, for all were watching him, and even Walter Butler's gloomy gaze constantly reverted to that gross, red face, almost buried in thick tobacco-smoke, like the head of some intemperate and grotesquely swollen Jupiter crowned with clouds.

The plea of the patroon for neutrality in the war now sweeping towards the Mohawk Valley I had heard before. So, doubtless, had those present.

He waxed pathetic over the danger to his vast estate; he pointed out the conservative attitude of the great patroons and lords of the manors of Livingston, Cosby, Phillipse, Van Rensselaer, and Van Cortlandt.

"What about Schuyler?" I asked.

"Schuyler's a fool!" he retorted, angrily. "Any landed proprietor here can become a rebel general in exchange for his estate! A fine bargain! A thrifty dicker! Let Philip Schuyler enjoy his brief reign in Albany. What's the market value of the glory he exchanged for his broad acres? Can you appraise it, Sir John?"

Then Sir John Johnson arose, and, for the only moment in his career, he stood upon a principle--a fallacious one, but still a principle; and for that I respected him, and have never quite forgotten it, even through the terrible years when he razed and burned and murdered among a people who can never forget the red atrocities of his devastations.

Glancing slowly around the table, with his pale, cold eyes contracting in the candle's glare, he spoke in a voice absolutely passionless, yet which carried the conviction to all that what he uttered was hopelessly final:

"Sir Lupus complains that he hazards all, should he cast his fortunes with his King. Yet I have done that thing. I am to-day a man with a price set on my head by these rebels of my own country. My lands, if not already confiscated by rebel commissioners, are occupied by rebels; my manor-houses, my forts, my mills, my tenants' farms are held by the rebels and my revenues denied me. I was confined on parole within the limits of Johnson Hall. They say I broke my parole, but they lie. It was only when I had certain news that the Boston rebels were coming to seize my person and violate a sacred convention that I retired to Canada."

He paused. The explanation was not enough to satisfy me, and I expected him to justify the arming of Johnson Hall and his discovered intrigues with the Mohawks which set the rebels on the march to seize his person. He gave none, resuming quietly:

"I have hazarded a vast estate, vaster than yours, Sir Lupus, greater than the estates of all these gentlemen combined. I do it because I owe obedience to the King who has honored me, and for no other reason on earth. Yet I do it in fullest confidence and belief that my lands will be restored to me when this rebellion is stamped on and trodden out to the last miserable spark."

He hesitated, wiped his thin mouth with his laced handkerchief, and turned directly towards the patroon.

"You ask me to remain neutral. You promise me that, even at this late hour, my surrender and oath of neutrality will restore me my estates and guarantee me a peaceful, industrious life betwixt two tempests. It may be so, Sir Lupus. I think it would be so. But, my friend, to fail my King when he has need of me is a villainy I am incapable of. The fortunes of his Majesty are my fortunes; I stand or fall with him. This is my duty as I see it. And, gentlemen, I shall follow it while life endures."

He resumed his seat amid absolute silence. Presently the patroon raised his eyes and looked at Colonel John Butler.

"May we hear from you, sir?" he asked, gravely.

"I trust that all may, one day, hear from Butler's Rangers," he said.

"And I swear they shall," broke in Walter Butler, his dark eyes burning like golden coals.

"I think the Royal Greens may make some little noise in the world," said Captain Campbell, with an oath.

Guy Johnson waved his thin, brown hand towards the patroon: "I hold my King's commission as intendant of Indian affairs for North America. That is enough for me. Though they rob me of Guy Park and every acre, I shall redeem my lands in a manner no man can ever forget!"

"Gentlemen," added Colonel Claus, in his bluff way, "you all make great merit of risking property and life in this wretched teapot tempest; you all take credit for unchaining the Mohawks. But you give them no credit. What have the Iroquois to gain by aiding us? Why do they dig up the hatchet, hazarding the only thing they have--their lives? Because they are led by a man who told the rebel Congress that the covenant chain which the King gave to the Mohawks is still unspotted by dishonor, unrusted by treachery, unbroken, intact, without one link missing! Gentlemen, I give you Joseph Brant, war-chief of the Mohawk nation! Hiro!"

All filled and drank--save three--Sir George Covert, Dorothy Varick, and myself.

I felt Walter Butler's glowing eyes upon me, and they seemed to burn out the last vestige of my patience.

"Don't rise! Don't speak now!" whispered Dorothy, her hand closing on my arm.

"I must speak," I said, aloud, and all heard me and turned on me their fevered eyes.

"Speak out, in God's name!" said Sir George Covert, and I rose, repeating, "In God's name, then!"

"Give no offence to Walter Butler, I beg of you," whispered Dorothy.

I scarcely heard her; through the candle-light I saw the ring of eyes shining, all watching me.

"I applaud the loyal sentiments expressed by Sir John Johnson," I said, slowly. "Devotion to principle is respected by all men of honor. They tell me that our King has taxed a commonwealth against its will. You admit his Majesty's right to do so. That ranges you on one side. Gentlemen," I said, deliberately, "I deny the right of Englishmen to take away the liberties of Englishmen. That ranges me on the other side."

A profound silence ensued. The ring of eyes glowed.

"And now," said I, gravely, "that we stand arrayed, each on his proper side, honestly, loyally differing one from the other, let us, if we can, strive to avert a last resort to arms. And if we cannot, let us draw honorably, and trust to God and a stainless blade!"

I bent my eyes on Walter Butler; he met them with a vacant glare.

"Captain Butler," I said, "if our swords be to-day stainless, he who first dares employ a savage to do his work forfeits the right to bear the arms and title of a soldier."

"Mr. Ormond! Mr. Ormond!" broke in Colonel Claus. "Do you impeach Lord George Germaine?"

"I care not whom I impeach!" I said, hotly. "If Lord George Germaine counsels the employment of Indians against Englishmen, rebels though they be, he is a monstrous villain and a fool!"

"Fool!" shouted Colonel Campbell, choking with rage. "He'd be a fool to let these rebels win over the Iroquois before we did!"

"What rebel has sought to employ the Indians?" I asked. "If any in authority have dreamed of such a horror, they are guilty as though already judged and damned!"

"Mr. Ormond," cut in Guy Johnson, fairly trembling with fury, "you deal very freely in damnation. Do you perhaps assume the divine right which you deny your King?"

"And do you find merit in crass treason, sir?" burst out McDonald, striking the table with clinched fist.

"Treason," cut in Sir John Johnson, "was the undoing of a certain noble duke in Queen Anne's time."

"You are in error," I said, calmly.

"Was James, Duke of Ormond, not impeached by Mr. Stanhope in open Parliament?" shouted Captain McDonald.

"The House of Commons," I replied, calmly, "dishonored itself and its traditions by bringing a bill of attainder against the Duke of Ormond. That could not make him a traitor."

"He was not a traitor," broke out Walter Butler, white to the lips, "but you are!"

"A lie," I said.

With the awful hue of death stamped on his face, Walter Butler rose and faced me; and though they dragged us to our seats, shouting and exclaiming in the uproar made by falling chairs and the rush of feet, he still kept his eyes on me, shallow, yellow, depthless, terrible eyes.

"A nice scene to pass in women's presence!" roared the patroon. "Dammy, Captain Butler, the fault lies first with you! Withdraw that word 'traitor,' which touches us all!"

"He has so named himself," said Walter Butler, "Withdraw it! You foul your own nest, sir!"

A moment passed. "I withdraw it," motioned Butler, with parched lips.

"Then I withdraw the lie," I said, watching him.

"That is well," roared the patroon. "That is as it should be. Shall kinsmen quarrel at such a time? Offer your hand, Captain Butler. Offer yours, George."

"No," I said, and gazed mildly at the patroon.

Sir George Covert rose and sauntered over to my chair. Under cover of the hubbub, not yet subsided, he said: "I fancy you will shortly require a discreet friend."

"Not at all, sir," I replied, aloud. "If the war spares Mr. Butler and myself, then

I shall call on you. I've another quarrel first." All turned to look at me, and I added, "A quarrel touching the liberties of Englishmen." Sir John Johnson sneered, and it was hard to swallow, being the sword-master that I am.

But the patroon broke out furiously. "Mr. Ormond honors himself. If any here so much as looks the word 'coward,' he will answer to me--old and fat as I am! I've no previous engagement; I care not who prevails, King or Congress. I care nothing so they leave me my own! I'm free to resent a word, a look, a breath--ay, the flutter of a lid, Sir John!"

"Thanks, uncle," I said, touched to the quick. "These gentlemen are not fools, and only a fool could dream an Ormond coward."

"Ay, a fool!" cried Walter Butler. "I am an Ormond! There is no cowardice in the blood. He shall have his own time; he is an Ormond!"

Dorothy Varick raised her bare, white arm and pointed straight at Walter Butler. "See that your sword remains unspotted, sir," she said, in a clear voice. "For if you hire the Iroquois to do your work you stand dishonored, and no true man will meet you on the field you forfeit!"

"What's that?" cried Sir John, astonished, and Sir George Covert cried:

"Brava! Bravissima! There speaks the Ormond through the Varick!"

Walter Butler leaned forward, staring at me. "You refuse to meet me if I use our Mohawks?"

And Dorothy, her voice trembling a little, picked up the word from his grinning teeth. "Mohawks understand the word 'honor' better than do you, Captain Butler, if you are found fighting in their ranks!"

She laid her hand on my arm, still facing him.

"My cousin shall not cross blade with a soiled blade! He dare not--if only for my own poor honor's sake!"

Then Colonel Claus rose, thumping violently on the table, and, "Here's a pretty rumpus!" he bawled, "with all right and all wrong, and nobody to snuff out the spreading flame, but every one a-flinging tallow in a fire we all may rue! My God! Are we not all kinsmen here, gathered to decent council how best to save our bacon in this pot a-boiling over? If Mr. Ormond and Captain Butler must tickle sword-points one day, that is no cause for dolorous looks or hot words--no! Rather is it a family trick, a good, old-fashioned game that all boys play, and no harm, either.

Have I not played it, too? Has any gentleman present not pinked or been pinked on that debatable land we call the field of honor? Come, kinsmen, we have all had too much wine--or too little."

"Too little!" protested Captain Campbell, with a forced laugh; and Betty Austin loosed her tongue for the first time to cry out that her mouth was parched wi' swallowing so many words all piping-hot. Whereat one or two laughed, and Colonel John Butler said:

Neither Mr. Ormond nor Sir George Covert are rebels. They differ from us in this matter touching on the Iroquois. If they think we soil our hands with warpaint, let them keep their own wristbands clean, but fight for their King as sturdily as shall we this time next month."

"That is a very pleasant view to take," observed Sir George, with a smile.

"A sensible view," suggested Campbell.

"Amiable," said Sir George, blandly.

"Oh, let us fill to the family!" broke in McDonald, impatiently. "It's dry work cursing your friends! Fill up, Campbell, and I'll forget Glencoe ... while I'm drinking."

"Mr. Ormond," said Walter Butler, in a low voice, "I cannot credit ill of a man of your name. You are young and hot-blooded, and you perhaps lack as yet a capacity for reflection. I shall look for you among us when the time comes. No Ormond can desert his King."

"Let it rest so, Captain Butler," I said, soberly. "I will say this: when I rose I had not meant to say all that I said. But I believe it to be the truth, though I chose the wrong moment to express it. If I change this belief I will say so."

And so the outburst of passion sank to ashes; and if the fire was not wholly extinguished, it at least lay covered, like the heart of a Seminole council-fire after the sachems have risen and departed with covered heads.

Drinking began again. The ladies gathered in a group, whispering and laughing their relief at the turn affairs were taking--all save Dorothy, who sat serenely beside me, picking the kernels from walnut-shells and sipping a glass of port.

Sir John Johnson found a coal in the embers on the hearth, and, leaning half over the table, began to draw on the table-cloth a rude map of Tryon County.

"All know," he said, "that the province of New York is the key to the rebel strength. While they hold West Point and Albany and Stanwix, they hold Tryon County by the throat. Let them occupy Philadelphia. Who cares? We can take it when we choose. Let them hold their dirty Boston; let the rebel Washington sneak around the Jerseys. Who cares? There'll be the finer hunting for us later. Gentlemen, as you know, the invasion of New York is at hand--has already begun. And that's no secret from the rebels, either; they may turn and twist and double here in New York province, but they can't escape the trap, though they saw it long ago."

He raised his head and glanced at me.

"Here is a triangle," he said; "that triangle is New York province. Here is Albany, the objective of our three armies, the gate of Tryon County, the plague-spot we are to cleanse, and the military centre. Now mark! Burgoyne moves through the lakes, south, reducing Ticonderoga and Edward, routing the rats out of Saratoga, and approaches Albany--so. Clinton moves north along the Hudson to meet him--so--forcing the Highlands at Peekskill, taking West Point or leaving it for later punishment. Nothing can stop him; he meets Burgoyne here, at Albany."

Again he looked at me. "You see, sir, that from two angles of the triangle converging armies depart towards a common objective."

"I see," I said.

"Now," he resumed, "the third force, under Colonel Barry St. Leger--to which my regiment and the regiment of Colonel Butler have the honor to be attached--embarks from Canada, sails up the St. Lawrence, disembarks at Oswego, on Lake Erie, marches straight on Stanwix, reduces it, and joins the armies of Clinton and Burgoyne at Albany."

He stood up, casting his bit of wood-coal on the cloth before him.

"That, sir," he said to me, "is the plan of campaign, which the rebels know and cannot prevent. That means the invasion of New York, the scouring out of every plague-spot, the capture and destruction of every rebel between Albany and the Jerseys."

He turned with a cold smile to Colonel Butler. "I think my estates will not remain long in rebel hands," he said.

"Do you not understand, Mr. Ormond?" cried Captain Campbell, twitching me by the sleeve, an impertinence I passed, considering him overflushed with wine. "Do you not comprehend how hopeless is this rebellion now?"

"How hopeless?" drawled Sir George, looking over my shoulder, and, as though by accident, drawing Campbell's presumptuous hand through his own arm.

"How hopeless?" echoed Campbell. "Why, here are three armies of his Majesty's troops concentrating on the heart of Tryon County. What can the rebels do?"

"The patroons are with us, or have withdrawn from the contest," said Sir John; "the great folk, military men, and we of the landed gentry are for the King. What remains to defy his authority?"

"Of what kidney are these Tryon County men?" I asked, quietly. Sir John Johnson misunderstood me.

"Mr. Ormond," said Sir John, "Tryon County is habited by four races. First, the Scotch-Irish, many of them rebels, I admit, but many also loyal. Balance these against my Highlanders, and cross quits. Second, the Palatines--those men whose ancestors came hither to escape the armies of Louis XIV. when they devastated the Palatinate. And again I admit these to be rebels. Third, those of Dutch blood, descended from brave ancestors, like our worthy patroon here. And once more I will admit that many of these also are tainted with rebel heresies. Fourth, the English, three-quarters of whom are Tories. And now I ask you, can these separate handfuls of mixed descent unite? And, if that were possible, can they stand for one day, one hour, against the trained troops of England?"

"God knows," I said.

VI
DAWN

I had stepped from the dining-hall out to the gun-room. Clocks in the house were striking midnight. In the dining-room the company had now taken to drinking in earnest, cheering and singing loyal songs, and through the open door whirled gusts of women's laughter, and I heard the thud of guitar-strings echo the song's gay words.

All was cool and dark in the body of the house as I walked to the front door and opened it to bathe my face in the freshening night. I heard the whippoorwill in the thicket, and the drumming of the dew on the porch roof, and far away a sound like ocean stirring--the winds in the pines.

The Maker of all things has set in me a love for whatsoever He has fashioned in His handiwork, whether it be furry beast or pretty bird, or a spray of April willow, or the tiny insect-creature that pursues its dumb, blind way through this our common world. So come I by my love for the voices of the night, and the eyes of the stars, and the whisper of growing things, and the spice in the air where, unseen, a million tiny blossoms hold up white cups for dew, or for the misty-winged things that woo them for their honey.

Now, in the face of this dark, soothing truce that we call night, which is a buckler interposed between the arrows of two angry suns, I stood thinking of war and the wrong of it. And all around me in the darkness insects sang, and delicate, gauzy creatures chirked and throbbed and strummed in cadence, while the star's light faintly silvered the still trees, and distant monotones of the forest made a sustained and steady rushing sound like the settling ebb of shallow seas. That to my conscience I stood committed, I could not doubt. I must draw sword, and draw it soon, too--not for Tory or rebel, not for King or Congress, not for my estates nor for my kin, but for the ancient liberties of Englishmen, which England menaced to destroy.

That meant time lost in a return to my own home; and yet--why? Here in this county of Tryon one might stand for liberty of thought and action as stanchly as at home. Here was a people with no tie or sympathy to weld them save that common love of liberty--a scattered handful of races, without leaders, without resources, menaced by three armies, menaced, by the five nations of the great confederacy-- the Iroquois.

To return to the sea islands on the Halifax and fight for my own acres was useless if through New York the British armies entered to the heart of the rebellion, splitting the thirteen colonies with a flaming wedge.

At home I had no kin to defend; my elder brother had sailed to England, my superintendent, my overseers, my clerks were all Tory; my slaves would join the Minorcans or the blacks in Georgia, and I, single-handed, could not lift a finger to restrain them.

But here, in the dire need of Tryon County, I might be of use. Here was the very forefront of battle where, beyond the horizon, invasion, uncoiling hydra folds, already raised three horrid, threatening crests.

Ugh!--the butcher's work that promised if the Iroquois were uncaged! It made me shudder, for I knew something of that kind of war, having seen a slight service against the Seminoles in my seventeenth year, and against the Chehaws and Tallassies a few months later. Also in November of 1775 I accompanied Governor Tonyn to Picolata, but when I learned that our mission was the shameful one of securing the Indians as British allies I resigned my captaincy in the Royal Rangers and returned to the Halifax to wait and watch events.

And now, thoughtful, sad, wondering a little how it all would end, I paced to and fro across the porch. The steady patter of the dew was like the long roll beating- -low, incessant, imperious--and my heart leaped responsive to the summons, till I found myself standing rigid, staring into the darkness with fevered eyes.

The smothered, double drumming of a guitar from the distant revel assailed my ears, and a fresh, sweet voice, singing:

"As at my door I chanced to be
     A-spinning,
       Spinning,
A grenadier he winked at me
     A-grinning,
       Grinning!
As at my door I chanced to be
A grenadier he winked at me.
And now my song's begun, you see!

"My grenadier he said to me.
     So jolly,
       Jolly,
'We tax the tea, but love is free,
     Sweet Molly,
       Molly!'
My grenadier he said to me,
'We tax the tea, but love is free!'
And so my song it ends, you see,
     In folly,
       Folly!"

I listened angrily; the voice was Dorothy Varick's, and I wondered that she had the heart to sing such foolishness for men whose grip was already on her people's throats.

In the dining-hall somebody blew the view-halloo on a hunting-horn, and I heard cheers and the dulled roar of a chorus:

"--Rally your men!
Campbell and Cameron,
Fox-hunting gentlemen,
Follow the Jacobite back to his den!
Run with the runaway rogue to his runway,

Stole-away!

Stole-away!

Gallop to Galway,

Back to Broadalbin and double to Perth;

Ride! for the rebel is running to earth!"

And the shrill, fierce Highland cry, "Gralloch him!" echoed the infamous catch, till the night air rang faintly in the starlight.

"Cruachan!" shouted Captain Campbell; "the wild myrtle to clan Campbell, the heather to the McDonalds! An't--Arm, chlanna!"

And a great shout answered him: "The army! Sons of the army!"

Sullen and troubled and restless, I paced the porch, and at length sat down on the steps to cool my hot forehead in my hands.

And as I sat, there came my cousin Dorothy to the porch to look for me, fanning her flushed face with a great, plumy fan, the warm odor of roses still clinging to her silken skirts.

"Have they ended?" I asked, none too graciously.

"They are beginning," she said, with a laugh, then drew a deep breath and waved her fan slowly. "Ah, the sweet May night!" she murmured, eyes fixed on the north star. "Can you believe that men could dream of war in this quiet paradise of silence?"

I made no answer, and she went on, fanning her hot cheeks: "They're off to Oswego by dawn, the whole company, gallant and baggage." She laughed wickedly. "I don't mean their ladies, cousin."

"How could you?" I protested, grimly.

"Their wagons," she said, "started to-day at sundown from Tribes Hill; Sir John, the Butlers, and the Glencoe gentlemen follow at dawn. There are post-chaises for the ladies out yonder, and an escort, too. But nobody would stop them; they're as safe as Catrine Montour."

"Dorothy, who is this Catrine Montour?" I asked.

"A woman, cousin; a terrible hag who runs through the woods, and none dare stop her."

"A real hag? You mean a ghost?"

"No, no; a real hag, with black locks hanging, and long arms that could choke an ox."

"Why does she run through the woods?" I asked, amused.

"Why? Who knows? She is always seen running."

"Where does she run to?"

"I don't know. Once Henry Stoner, the hunter, followed her, and they say no one but Jack Mount can outrun him; but she ran and ran, and he after her, till the day fell down, and he fell gasping like a foundered horse. But she ran on."

"Oh, tally," I said; "do you believe that?"

"Why, I know it is true," she replied, ceasing her fanning to stare at me with calm, wide eyes. "Do you doubt it?"

"How can I?" said I, laughing. "Who is this busy hag, Catrine Montour?"

"They say," said Dorothy, waving her fan thoughtfully, "that her father was that Count Frontenac who long ago governed the Canadas, and that her mother was a Huron woman. Many believe her to be a witch. I don't know. Milk curdles in the pans when she is running through the forest ... they say. Once it rained blood on our front porch."

"Those red drops fall from flocks of butterflies," I said, laughing. "I have seen red showers in Florida."

"I should like to be sure of that," said Dorothy, musing. Then, raising her starry eyes, she caught me laughing.

"Tease me," she smiled. "I don't care. You may even make love to me if you choose."

"Make love to you!" I repeated, reddening.

"Why not? It amuses--and you're only a cousin."

Astonishment was followed by annoyance as she coolly disqualified me with a careless wave of her fan, wafting the word "cousin" into my very teeth.

"Suppose I paid court to you and gained your affections?" I said.

"You have them," she replied, serenely.

"I mean your heart?"

"You have it."

"I mean your--love, Dorothy?"

"Ah," she said, with a faint smile, "I wish you could--I wish somebody could."

I was silent.

"And I never shall love; I know it, I feel it--here!" She pressed her side with a languid sigh that nigh set me into fits o' laughter, yet I swallowed my mirth till it choked me, and looked at the stars.

"Perhaps," said I, "the gentle passion might be awakened with patience ... and practice."

"Ah, no," she said.

"May I touch your hand?"

Indolently fanning, she extended her fingers. I took them in my hands.

"I am about to begin," I said.

"Begin," she said.

So, her hand resting in mine, I told her that she had robbed the skies and set two stars in violets for her eyes; that nature's one miracle was wrought when in her cheeks roses bloomed beneath the snow; that the frosted gold she called her hair had been spun from December sunbeams, and that her voice was but the melodies stolen from breeze and brook and golden-throated birds.

"For all those pretty words," she said, "love still lies sleeping."

"Perhaps my arm around your waist--"

"Perhaps."

"So?"

"Yes."

And, after a silence:

"Has love stirred?"

"Love sleeps the sounder."

"And if I touched your lips?"

"Best not."

"Why?"

"I'm sure that love would yawn."

Chilled, for unconsciously I had begun to find in this child-play an interest unexpected, I dropped her unresisting fingers.

"Upon my word," I said, almost irritably, "I can believe you when you say you never mean to wed."

"But I don't say it," she protested.

"What? You have a mind to wed?"

"Nor did I say that, either," she said, laughing.

"Then what the deuce do you say?"

"Nothing, unless I'm entreated politely."

"I entreat you, cousin, most politely," I said.

"Then I may tell you that, though I trouble my head nothing as to wedlock, I am betrothed."

"Betrothed!" I repeated, angrily disappointed, yet I could not think why.

"Yes--pledged."

"To whom?"

"To a man, silly."

"A man!"

"With two legs, two arms, and a head, cousin."

"You ... love him?"

"No," she said, serenely. "It's only to wed and settle down some day."

"You don't love him?"

"No," she repeated, a trifle impatiently.

"And you mean to wed him?"

"Listen to the boy!" she exclaimed. "I've told him ten times that I am betrothed, which means a wedding. I am not one of those who break paroles."

"Oh ... you are now free on parole."

"Prisoner on parole," she said, lightly. "I'm to name the day o' punishment, and I promise you it will not be soon."

"Dorothy," I said, "suppose in the mean time you fell in love?"

"I'd like to," she said, sincerely.

"But--but what would you do then?"

"Love, silly!"

"And ... marry?"

"Marry him whom I have promised."

"But you would be wretched!"

"Why? I can't fancy wedding one I love. I should be ashamed, I think. I--if I loved I should not want the man I loved to touch me--not with gloves."

"You little fool!" I said. "You don't know what you say."

"Yes, I do!" she cried, hotly. "Once there was a captain from Boston; I adored him. And once he kissed my hand and I hated him!"

"I wish I'd been there," I muttered.

She, waving her fan to and fro, continued: "I often think of splendid men, and, dreaming in the sunshine, sometimes I adore them. But always these day-dream heroes keep their distance; and we talk and talk, and plan to do great good in the world, until I fall a-napping.... Heigho! I'm yawning now." She covered her face with her fan and leaned back against a pillar, crossing her feet. "Tell me about London," she said. But I knew no more than she.

"I'd be a belle there," she observed. "I'd have a train o' beaux and macaronis at my heels, I warrant you! The foppier, the more it would please me. Think, cousin-- ranks of them all a-simper, ogling me through a hundred quizzing-glasses! Heigho! There's doubtless some deviltry in me, as Sir Lupus says."

She yawned again, looked up at the stars, then fell to twisting her fan with idle fingers.

"I suppose," she said, more to herself than to me, "that Sir John is now close to the table's edge, and Colonel Claus is under it.... Hark to their song, all off the key! But who cares?... so that they quarrel not.... Like those twin brawlers of Glencoe, ... brooding on feuds nigh a hundred years old.... I have no patience with a brooder, one who treasures wrongs, ... like Walter Butler." She looked up at me.

"I warned you," she said.

"It is not easy to avoid insulting him," I replied.

"I warned you of that, too. Now you've a quarrel, and a reckoning in prospect."

"The reckoning is far off," I retorted, ill-humoredly.

"Far off--yes. Further away than you know. You will never cross swords with Walter Butler."

"And why not?"

"He means to use the Iroquois."

I was silent.

"For the honor of your women, you cannot fight such a man," she added, quietly.

"I wish I had the right to protect your honor," I said, so suddenly and so bitterly that I surprised myself.

"Have you not?" she asked, gravely. "I am your kinswoman."

"Yes, yes, I know," I muttered, and fell to plucking at the lace on my wrist-bands.

The dawn's chill was in the air, the dawn's silence, too, and I saw the calm morning star on the horizon, watching the dark world--the dark, sad world, lying so still, so patient, under the ancient sky.

That melancholy--which is an omen, too--left me benumbed, adrift in a sort of pained contentment which alternately soothed and troubled, so that at moments I almost drowsed, and at moments I heard my heart stirring, as though in dull expectancy of beatitudes undreamed of.

Dorothy, too, sat listless, pensive, and in her eyes a sombre shadow, such as falls on children's eyes at moments, leaving their elders silent.

Once in the false dawn a cock crowed, and the shrill, far cry left the raw air emptier and the silence more profound. I looked wistfully at the maid beside me, chary of intrusion into the intimacy of her silence. Presently her vague eyes met mine, and, as though I had spoken, she said: "What is it?"

"Only this: I am sorry you are pledged."

"Why, cousin?"

"It is unfair."

"To whom?"

"To you. Bid him undo it and release you."

"What matters it?" she said, dully.

"To wed, one should love," I muttered.

"I cannot," she answered, without moving. "I would I could. This night has witched me to wish for love--to desire it; and I sit here a-thinking, a-thinking.... If love ever came to me I should think it would come now--ere the dawn; here, where all is so dark and quiet and close to God.... Cousin, this night, for the first moment in all my life, I have desired love."

"To be loved?"

"No, ... to love."

I do not know how long our silence lasted; the faintest hint of silver touched the sky above the eastern forest; a bird awoke, sleepily twittering; another piped out fresh and clear, another, another; and, as the pallid tint spread in the east, all the woodlands burst out ringing into song.

In the house a door opened and a hoarse voice muttered thickly. Dorothy paid no heed, but I rose and stepped into the hallway, where servants were guiding the patroon to bed, and a man hung to the bronze-cannon post, swaying and mumbling threats--Colonel Claus, wig awry, stock unbuckled, and one shoe gone. Faugh! the stale, sour air sickened me.

Then a company of gentlemen issued from the dining-hall, and, as I stepped back to the porch to give them room, their gray faces were turned to me with meaningless smiles or blank inquiry.

"Where's my orderly?" hiccoughed Sir John Johnson. "Here, you, call my rascals; get the chaises up! Dammy, I want my post-chaise, d' ye hear?"

Captain Campbell stumbled out to the lawn and fumbled about his lips with a whistle, which he finally succeeded in blowing. This accomplished, he gravely examined the sky.

"There they are," said Dorothy, quietly; and I saw, in the dim morning light, a dozen horsemen stirring in the shadows of the stockade. And presently the horses were brought up, followed by two post-chaises, with sleepy post-boys sitting their saddles and men afoot trailing rifles.

Colonel Butler came out of the door with Magdalen Brant, who was half asleep, and aided her to a chaise. Guy Johnson followed with Betty Austin, his arm around her, and climbed in after her. Then Sir John brought Claire Putnam to the other chaise, entering it himself behind her. And the post-boys wheeled their horses out through the stockade, followed at a gallop by the shadowy horsemen.

And now the Butlers, father and son, set toe to stirrup; and I saw Walter Butler kick the servant who held his stirrup--why, I do not know, unless the poor, tired fellow's hands shook.

Up into their saddles popped the Glencoe captains; then Campbell swore an oath and dismounted to look for Colonel Claus; and presently two blacks carried him out and set him in his saddle, which he clung to, swaying like a ship in distress, his riding-boots slung around his neck, stockinged toes clutching the stirrups.

Away they went, followed at a trot by the armed men on foot; fainter and fainter sounded the clink, clink of their horses' hoofs, then died away.

In the silence, the east reddened to a flame tint. I turned to the open doorway; Dorothy was gone, but old Cato stood there, withered hands clasped, peaceful eyes on me.

"Mawnin', suh," he said, sweetly. "Yaas, suh, de night done gone and de sun mos' up. H'it dat-a-way, Mars' George, suh, h'it jess natch'ly dat-a-way in dishyere world--day, night, mo' day. What de Bible say? Life, def, mo' life, suh. When we's daid we'll sho' find it dat-a-way."

VII
AFTERMATH

Cato at my bedside with basin, towel, and razor, a tub of water on the floor, and the sun shining on my chamber wall. These, and a stale taste on my tongue, greeted me as I awoke.

First to wash teeth and mouth with orris, then to bathe, half asleep still; and yet again to lie a-thinking in my arm-chair, robed in a banyan, cheeks all suds and nose sniffing the scented water in the chin-basin which I held none too steady; and I said, peevishly, "What a fool a man is to play the fool! Do you hear me, Cato?"

He said that he marked my words, and I bade him hold his tongue and tell me the hour.

"Nine, suh."

"Then I'll sleep again," I muttered, but could not, and after the morning draught felt better. Chocolate and bread, new butter and new eggs, put me in a kinder humor. Cato, burrowing in my boxes, drew out a soft, new suit of doeskin with new points, new girdle, and new moccasins.

"Oh," said I, watching him, "am I to go forest-running to-day?"

"Mars' Varick gwine ride de boun's," he announced, cheerfully.

"Ride to hounds?" I repeated, astonished. "In May?"

"No, suh! Ride de boun's, suh."

"Oh, ride the boundaries?"

"Yaas, suh."

"Oh, very well. What time does he start?"

"'Bout noontide, suh."

The old man strove to straighten my short queue, but found it hopeless, so tied it close and dusted on the French powder.

"Curly head, curly head," he muttered to himself. "Dess lak yo' pap's!... an' Miss Dorry's. Law's sakes, dishyere hair wuf mo'n eight dollar."

"You think my hair worth more than eight dollars?" I asked, amused.

"H'it sho'ly am, suh."

"But why eight dollars, Cato?"

"Das what the redcoats say; eight dollars fo' one rebel scalp, suh."

I sat up, horrified. "Who told you that?" I demanded.

"All de gemmen done say so--Mars' Varick, Mars' Johnsing, Cap'in Butler."

"Bah! they said it to plague you, Cato," I muttered; but as I said it I saw the old slave's eyes and knew that he had told the truth.

Sobered, I dressed me in my forest dress, absently lacing the hunting-shirt and tying knee-points, while the old man polished hatchet and knife and slipped them into the beaded scabbards swinging on either hip.

Then I went out, noiselessly descending the stairway, and came all unawares upon the young folk and the children gathered on the sunny porch, busy with their morning tasks.

They neither saw nor heard me; I leaned against the doorway to see the pretty picture at my ease. The children, Sam and Benny, sat all hunched up, scowling over their books.

Close to a fluted pillar, Dorothy Varick reclined in a chair, embroidering her initials on a pair of white silk hose, using the Rosemary stitch. And as her delicate fingers flew, her gold thimble flashed like a fire-fly in the sun.

At her feet, cross-legged, sat Cecile Butler, velvet eyes intent on a silken petticoat which she was embroidering with pale sprays of flowers.

Ruyven and Harry, near by, dipped their brushes into pans of brilliant French colors, the one to paint marvellous birds on a silken fan, the other to decorate a pair of white satin shoes with little pink blossoms nodding on a vine.

Loath to disturb them, I stood smiling, silent; and presently Dorothy, without raising her eyes, called on Samuel to read his morning lesson, and he began, breathing heavily:

"I know that God is wroth at me
  For I was born in sin;
My heart is so exceeding vile
  Damnation dwells therein;
Awake I sin, asleep I sin,
  I sin with every breath,
When Adam fell he went to hell
  And damned us all to death!"

He stopped short, scowling, partly from fright, I think.

"That teaches us to obey God," said Ruyven, severely, dipping his brush into the pink paint-cake.

"What's the good of obeying God if we're all to go to hell?" asked Cecile.

"We're not all going to hell," said Dorothy, calmly. "God saves His elect."

"Who are the elect?" demanded Samuel, faintly hopeful.

"Nobody knows," replied Cecile, grimly; "but I guess--"

"Benny," broke in Dorothy, "read your lesson! Cecile, stop your chatter!" And Benny, cheerful and sceptical, read his lines:

"When by thpectators I behold
  What beauty doth adorn me,
Or in a glath when I behold
  How thweetly God did form me.
Hath God thuch comeliness bethowed
  And on me made to dwell?--
What pity thuch a pretty maid
  Ath I thoud go to hell!"

And Benny giggled.

"Benjamin," said Cecile, in an awful voice, "are you not terrified at what you read?"

"Huh!" said Benny, "I'm not a 'pretty maid'; I'm a boy."

"It's all the same, little dunce!" insisted Cecile.

"Doeth God thay little boyth are born to be damned?" he asked, uneasily.

"No, no," interrupted Dorothy; "God saves His elect, I tell you. Don't you remember what He says?

> "'You sinners are, and such a share
>   As sinners may expect;
> Such you shall have; for I do save
>   None but my own elect.'

"And you see," she added, confidently, "I think we all are elect, and there's nothing to be afraid of. Benny, stop sniffing!"

"Are you sure?" asked Cecile, gloomily.

Dorothy, stitching serenely, answered: "I am sure God is fair."

"Oh, everybody knows that," observed Cecile. "What we want to know is, what does He mean to do with us."

"If we're good," added Samuel, fervently.

"He will damn us, perhaps," said Ruyven, sucking his paint-brush and looking critically at his work.

"Damn us? Why?" inquired Dorothy, raising her eyes.

"Oh, for all that sin we were born in," said Ruyven, absently.

"But that's not fair," said Dorothy.

"Are you smarter than a clergyman?" sneered Ruyven.

Dorothy spread the white silk stocking over one knee. "I don't know," she sighed, "sometimes I think I am."

"Pride," commented Cecile, complacently. "Pride is sin, so there you are, Dorothy."

"There you are, Dorothy!" said I, laughing from the doorway; and, "Oh, Cousin Ormond!" they all chorused, scrambling up to greet me.

"Have a care!" cried Dorothy. "That is my wedding petticoat! Oh, he's slopped water on it! Benny, you dreadful villain!"

"No, he hasn't," said I, coming out to greet her and Cecile, with Samuel and Benny hanging to my belt, and Harry fast hold of one arm. "And what's all this about wedding finery? Is there a bride in this vicinity?"

Dorothy held out a stocking. "A bride's white silken hose," she said, complacently.

"Embroidered on the knee with the bride's initials," added Cecile, proudly.

"Yours, Dorothy?" I demanded.

"Yes, but I shall not wear them for ages and ages. I told you so last night."

"But I thought Dorothy had best make ready," remarked Cecile. "Dorothy is to carry that fan and wear those slippers and this petticoat and the white silk stockings when she weds Sir George."

"Sir George who?" I asked, bluntly.

"Why, Sir George Covert. Didn't you know?"

I looked at Dorothy, incensed without a reason.

"Why didn't you tell me?" I asked, ungraciously.

"Why didn't you ask me?" she replied, a trifle hurt.

I was silent.

Cecile said: "I hope that Dorothy will marry him soon. I want to see how she looks in this petticoat."

"Ho!" sneered Harry, "you just want to wear one like it and be a bridesmaid and primp and give yourself airs. I know you!"

"Sir George Covert is a good fellow," remarked Ruyven, with a patronizing nod at Dorothy; "but I always said he was too old for you. You should see how gray are his temples when he wears no powder."

"He has fine eyes," murmured Cecile.

"He's too old; he's forty," repeated Ruyven.

"His legs are shapely," added Cecile, sentimentally.

Dorothy gave a despairing upward glance at me. "Are these children not silly?" she said, with a little shrug.

"We may be children, and we may be silly," said Ruyven, "but if we were you we'd wed our cousin Ormond."

"All of you together?" inquired Dorothy.

"You know what I mean," he snapped.

"Why don't you?" demanded Harry, vaguely, twitching Dorothy by the apron.

"Do what?"

"Wed our cousin Ormond."

"But he has not asked me," she said, smiling.

Harry turned to me and took my arm affectionately in his.

"You will ask her, won't you?" he murmured. "She's very nice when she chooses."

"She wouldn't have me," I said, laughing.

"Oh yes, she would; and then you need never leave us, which would be pleasant for all, I think. Won't you ask her, cousin?"

"You ask her," I said.

"Dorothy," he broke out, eagerly. "You will wed him, won't you? Our cousin Ormond says he will if you will. And I'll tell Sir George that it's just a family matter, and, besides, he's too old--"

"Yes, tell Sir George that," sneered Ruyven, who had listened in an embarrassment that certainly Dorothy had not betrayed. "You're a great fool, Harry. Don't you know that when people want to wed they ask each other's permission to ask each other's father, and then their fathers ask each other, and then they ask each--"

"Other!" cried Dorothy, laughing deliciously. "Oh, Ruyven, Ruyven, you certainly will be the death of me!"

"All the same," said Harry, sullenly, "our cousin wishes to wed you."

"Do you?" asked Dorothy, raising her amused eyes to me.

"I fear I come too late," I said, forcing a smile I was not inclined to.

"Ah, yes; too late," she sighed, pretending a doleful mien.

"Why?" demanded Harry, blankly.

Dorothy shook her head. "Sir George would never permit me such a liberty. If he would, our cousin Ormond and I could wed at once; you see I have my bride's stockings here; Cecile could do my hair, Sammy carry my prayer-book, Benny my train, Ruyven read the service--"

Harry, flushing at the shout of laughter, gave Dorothy a dark look, turned and eyed me, then scowled again at Dorothy.

"All the same," he said, slowly, "you're a great goose not to wed him.... And you'll be sorry ... when he's dead!"

At this veiled prophecy of my approaching dissolution, all were silent save Dorothy and Ruyven, whose fresh laughter rang out peal on peal.

"Laugh," said Harry, gloomily; "but you won't laugh when he's killed in the war, ... and scalped, too."

Ruyven, suddenly sober, looked up at me. Dorothy bent over her needle-work and examined it attentively.

"Are you going to the war?" asked Cecile, plaintively.

"Of course he's going; so am I," replied Ruyven, striking a careless pose against a pillar.

"On which side, Ruyven?" inquired Dorothy, sorting her silks.

"On my cousin's side, of course," he said, uneasily.

"Which side is that?" asked Cecile.

Confused, flushing painfully, the boy looked at me; and I rescued him, saying, "We'll talk that over when we ride bounds this afternoon. Ruyven and I understand each other, don't we, Ruyven?"

He gave me a grateful glance. "Yes," he said, shyly.

Sir George Covert, a trifle pallid, but bland and urbane, strolled out to the porch, saluting us gracefully. He paused beside Dorothy, who slipped her needle through her work and held out her hand for him to salute.

"Are you also going to the wars?" she asked, with a friendly smile.

"Where are they?" he inquired, pretending a fierce eagerness. "Point out some wars and I'll go to 'em post haste!"

"They're all around us," said Sammy, solemnly.

"Then we'd best get to horse and lose no time, Mr. Ormond," he observed, passing his arm through mine. In a lower voice he added: "Headache?"

"Oh no," I said, hastily.

"Lucky dog. Sir Lupus lies as though struck by lightning. I'm all a-quiver, too. A man of my years is a fool to do such things. But I do, Ormond, I do; ass that I am. Do you ride bounds with Sir Lupus?"

"If he desires it," I said.

"Then I'll see you when you pass my villa on the Vlaie, where you'll find a glass of wine waiting. Do you ride, Miss Dorothy?"

"Yes," she said.

A stable lad brought his horse to the porch. He took leave of Dorothy with a grace that charmed even me; yet, in his bearing towards her I could detect the tender pride he had in her, and that left me cold and thoughtful.

All liked him, though none appeared to regard him exactly as a kinsman, nor accorded him that vague shade of intimacy which is felt in kinship, not in comradeship alone, and which they already accorded me.

Dorothy walked with him to the stockade gate, the stable lad following with his horse; and I saw them stand there in low-voiced conversation, he lounging and switching at the weeds with his riding-crop; she, head bent, turning the gold thimble over and over between her fingers. And I wondered what they were saying.

Presently he mounted and rode away, a graceful, manly figure in the saddle, and not turning like a fop to blow a kiss at his betrothed, nor spurring his horse to show his skill--for which I coldly respected him.

Harry, Cecile, and the children gathered their paints and books and went into the house, demanding that I should follow.

"Dorothy is beckoning us," observed Ruyven, gathering up his paints.

I looked towards her and she raised her hand, motioning us to come.

"About father's watch," she said. "I have just consulted Sir George, and he says that neither I nor Ruyven have won, seeing that Ruyven used the coin he did--"

"Very well," cried Ruyven, triumphantly. "Then let us match dates again. Have you a shilling, Cousin Ormond?"

"I'll throw hunting-knives for it," suggested Dorothy.

"Oh no, you won't," retorted her brother, warily.

"Then I'll race you to the porch."

He shook his head.

She laughed tauntingly.

"I'm not afraid," said Ruyven, reddening and glancing at me.

"Then I'll wrestle you."

Stung by the malice in her smile, Ruyven seized her.

"No, no! Not in these clothes!" she said, twisting to free herself. "Wait till I put on my buckskins. Don't use me so roughly, you tear my laced apron. Oh! you great booby!" And with a quick cry of resentment she bent, caught her brother, and swung him off his feet clean over her left shoulder slap on the grass.

"Silly!" she said, cheeks aflame. "I have no patience to be mauled." Then she laughed uncertainly to see him lying there, too astonished to get up.

"Are you hurt?" she asked.

"Who taught you that hold?" he demanded, indignantly, scrambling to his feet. "I thought I alone knew that."

"Why, Captain Campbell taught you last week and ... I was at the window ... sewing," she said, demurely.

Ruyven looked at me, disgusted, muttering, "If I could learn things the way she does, I'd not waste time at King's College, I can tell you."

"You're not going to King's College, anyhow," said his sister. "York is full o' loyal rebels and Tory patriots, and father says he'll be damned if you can learn logic where all lack it."

She held out her hand, smiling. "No malice, Ruyven, and we'll forgive each other."

Her brother met the clasp; then, hands in his pockets, followed us back through the stockade towards the porch. I was pleased to see that his pride had suffered no more than his body from the fall he got, which augured well for a fair-minded man-hood.

As we approached the house I heard hollow noises within, like groans; and I stopped, listening intently.

"It is Sir Lupus snoring," observed Ruyven. "He will wake soon; I think I had best call Tulip," he added, exchanging a glance with his sister; and entered the house calling, "Cato! Cato! Tulip! Tulip! I say!"

"Who is Tulip?" I asked of Dorothy, who lingered at the threshold folding her embroidery into a bundle.

"Tulip? Oh, Tulip cooks for us--black as a June crow, cousin. She is voodoo."

"Evil-eye and all?" I asked, smiling.

Dorothy looked up shyly. "Don't you believe in the evil-eye?"

I was not perfectly sure whether I did or not, but I said "No."

"To believe is not necessarily to be afraid," she added, quickly.

Now, had I believed in the voodoo craft, or in the power of an evil-eye, I should also have feared. Those who have ever witnessed a sea-island witch-dance can bear me out, and I think a man may dread a hag and be no coward either. But distance and time allay the memories of such uncanny works. I had forgotten whether I was afraid or not. So I said, "There are no witches, Dorothy."

She looked at me, dreamily. "There are none ... that I fear."

"Not even Catrine Montour?" I asked, to plague her.

"No; it turns me cold to think of her running in the forest, but I am not afraid."

She stood pensive in the doorway, rolling and unrolling her embroidery. Harry and Cecile came out, flourishing alder poles from which lines and hooks dangled. Samuel and Benny carried birchen baskets and shallow nets.

"If we're to have Mohawk chubbs," said Cecile, "you had best come with us, Dorothy. Ruyven has a book and has locked himself in the play-room."

But Dorothy shook her head, saying that she meant to ride the boundary with us; and the children, after vainly soliciting my company, trooped off towards that same grist-mill in the ravine below the bridge which I had observed on my first arrival at Varick Manor.

"I am wondering," said Dorothy, "how you mean to pass the morning. You had best steer wide of Sir Lupus until he has breakfasted."

"I've a mind to sleep," I said, guiltily.

"I think it would be pleasant to ride together. Will you?" she asked; then, laughing, she said, frankly, "Since you have come I do nothing but follow you.... It is long since I have had a young companion, ... and, when I think that you are to leave us, it spurs me to lose no moment that I shall regret when you are gone."

No shyness marred the pretty declaration of her friendship, and it touched me the more keenly perhaps. The confidence in her eyes, lifted so sweetly, waked the best in me; and if my response was stumbling, it was eager and warm, and seemed to please her.

"Tulip! Tulip!" she cried, "I want my dinner! Now!" And to me, "We will eat what they give us; I shall dress in my buckskins and we will ride the boundary and register the signs, and Sir Lupus and the others can meet us at Sir George Covert's pleasure-house on the Vlaie. Does it please you, Cousin George?"

I looked into her bright eyes and said that it pleased me more than I dared say, and she laughed and ran up-stairs, calling back to me that I should order our horses and tell Cato to tell Tulip to fetch meat and claret to the gun-room.

I whistled a small, black stable lad and bade him bring our mounts to the porch, then wandered at random down the hallway, following my nose, which scented the kitchen, until I came to a closed door.

Behind that door meats were cooking--I could take my oath o' that--so I opened the door and poked my nose in.

"Tulip," I said, "come here!"

An ample black woman, aproned and turbaned, looked at me through the steam of many kettles, turned and cuffed the lad at the spit, dealt a few buffets among the scullions, and waddled up to me, bobbing and curtsying.

"Aunt Tulip," I said, gravely, "are you voodoo?"

"Folks says ah is, Mars' Ormon'," she said, in her soft Georgia accent.

"Oh, they do, do they? Look at me, Aunt Tulip. What do my eyes tell you of me?"

Her dark eyes, fixed on mine, seemed to change, and I thought little glimmers of pure gold tinted the iris, like those marvellous restless tints in a gorgeous bubble. Certainly her eyes were strange, almost compelling, for I felt a faint rigidity in my cheeks and my eyes returned directly to hers as at an unspoken command.

"Can you read me, aunty?" I asked, trying to speak easily, yet feeling the stiffness growing in my cheeks.

"Ah sho' can," she said, stepping nearer.

"What is my fate, then?"

"Ah 'spec' yo' gwine fine yo'se'f in love," she said, softly; and I strove to smile with ever-stiffening lips.

A little numbness that tingled spread over me; it was pleasant; I did not care to withdraw my eyes. Presently the tightness in my face relaxed, I moved my lips, smiling vaguely.

"In love," I repeated.

"Yaas, Mars' Ormon'."

"When?"

"'Fore yo' know h'it, honey."

"Tell me more."

"'Spec' ah done tole yo' too much, honey." She looked at me steadily. "Pore Mars' Gawge," she murmured, "'spec' ah done tole yo' too much. But it sho' am a-comin', honey, an' h'it gwine come pow'ful sudden, an' h'it gwine mek yo' pow'ful sick."

"Am I to win her?"

"No, honey."

"Is there no hope, Aunt Tulip?"

She hesitated as though at fault; I felt the tenseness in my face once more; then, for one instant, I lost track of time; for presently I found myself standing in the hallway watching Sir Lupus through the open door of the gun-room, and Sir Lupus was very angry.

"Dammy!" he roared, "am I to eat my plate? Cato! I want my porridge!"

Confused, I stood blinking at him, and he at table, bibbed like a babe, mad as a hornet, hammering on the cloth with a great silver spoon and bellowing that they meant to starve him.

"I don't remember how I came here," I began, then flushed furiously at my foolishness.

"Remember!" he shouted. "I don't remember anything! I don't want to remember anything! I want my porridge! I want it now! Damnation!"

Cato, hastening past me with the steaming dish, was received with a yelp. But at last Sir Lupus got his spoon into the mess and a portion of the mess into his mouth, and fell to gobbling and growling, paying me no further attention. So I closed the door of the gun-room on the great patroon and walked to the foot of the stairway.

A figure in soft buckskins was descending--a blue-eyed, graceful youth who hailed me with a gesture.

"Dorothy!" I said, fascinated.

Her fringed hunting-shirt fell to her knees, the short shoulder-cape from throat to breast; gay fringe fluttered from shoulder to wrist, and from thigh to ankle; and her little scarlet-quilled moccasins went pat-patter-pat as she danced down the stairway and stood before me, sweeping her cap from her golden head in exaggerated salute.

She seemed smaller in her boy's dress, fuller, too, and rounder of neck and limb; and the witchery of her beauty left me silent--a tribute she found delightful, for she blushed very prettily and bowed again in dumb acknowledgment of the homage all too evident in my eyes.

Cato came with a dish of meat and a bottle of claret; and we sat down on the stairs, punishing bottle and platter till neither drop nor scrap remained.

"Don't leave these dishes for Sir Lupus to fall over!" she cried to Cato, then sprang to her feet and was out of the door before I could move, whistling for our horses.

As I came out the horses arrived, and I hastened forward to put her into her saddle, but she was up and astride ere I reached the ground, coolly gathering bridle and feeling with her soft leather toes for the stirrups.

Astonished, for I had never seen a girl so mounted, I climbed to my saddle and wheeled my mare, following her out across the lawn, through the stockade and into the road, where I pushed my horse forward and ranged up beside her at a gallop, just as she reached the bridge.

"See!" she cried, with a sweep of her arm, "there are the children down there fishing under the mill." And she waved her small cap of silver fox, calling in a clear, sweet voice the Indian cry of triumph, "Koue!"

VIII
RIDING THE BOUNDS

For the first half-mile our road lay over that same golden, hilly country, and through the same splendid forests which I had traversed on my way to the manor. Then we galloped past cultivated land, where clustered spears of Indian corn sprouted above the reddish golden soil, and sheep fed in stony pastures.

Around the cabins of the tenantry, fields of oats and barley glimmered, thin blades pricking the loam, brilliant as splintered emeralds.

A few dropping blossoms still starred the apple-trees, pears showed in tiny bunches, and once I saw a late peach-tree in full pink bloom and an old man hoeing the earth around it. He looked up as we galloped past, saluted sullenly, and leaned on his hoe, looking after us.

Dorothy said he was a Palatine refugee and a rebel, like the majority of Sir Lupus's tenants; and I gazed curiously at these fields and cabins where gaunt men and gaunter women, laboring among their sprouting vegetables, turned sun-dazzled eyes to watch us as we clattered by; where ragged children, climbing on the stockades, called out to us in little, shrill voices; where feeding cattle lifted sober heads to stare; where lank, yellow dogs rushed out barking and snapping till a cut of the whip sent them scurrying back.

Once a woman came to her gate and hailed us, asking if it was true that the troops had been withdrawn from Johnstown and Kingsborough.

"Which troops?" I asked.

"Ours," began the woman, then checked herself, and shot a suspicious glance at me.

"The Provincials are still at Johnstown and Kingsborough," said Dorothy, gently.

A gleam of relief softened the woman's haggard features. Then her face darkened again and she pointed at two barefooted children shrinking against the fence.

"If my man and I were alone we would not be afraid of the Mohawks; but these--"

She made a desperate gesture, and stood staring at the blue Mayfield hills where, perhaps at that moment, painted Mohawk scouts were watching the Sacandaga.

"If your men remain quiet, Mrs. Schell, you need fear neither rebel, savage, nor Tory," said Dorothy. "The patroon will see that you have ample protection."

Mrs. Schell gave her a helpless glance. "Did you not know that the district scout-call has gone out?" she asked.

"Yes; but if the tenants of Sir Lupus obey it they do so at their peril," replied Dorothy, gravely. "The militia scouts of this district must not act hastily. Your husband would be mad to answer a call and leave you here alone."

"What would you have him do?" muttered the woman.

"Do?" repeated Dorothy. "He can do one thing or the other--join his regiment and take his family to the district fort, or stay at home and care for you and the farm. These alarms are all wrong--your men are either soldiers or farmers; they cannot be both unless they live close enough to the forts. Tell Mr. Schell that Francy McCraw and his riders are in the forest, and that the Brandt-Meester of Balston saw a Mohawk smoke-signal on the mountain behind Mayfield."

The woman folded her bony arms in her apron, cast one tragic glance at her children, then faced us again, hollow-eyed but undaunted.

"My man is with Stoner's scout," she said, with dull pride.

"Then you must go to the block-house," began Dorothy, but the woman pointed to the fields, shaking her head.

"We shall build a block-house here," she said, stubbornly. "We cannot leave our corn. We must eat, Mistress Varick. My man is too poor to be a Provincial soldier, too brave to refuse a militia call--"

She choked, rubbed her eyes, and bent her stern gaze on the hills once more. Presently we rode on, and, turning in my saddle, I saw her standing as we had left her, gaunt, rigid, staring steadily at the dreaded heights in the northwest.

As we galloped, cultivated fields and orchards became rarer; here and there, it is true, some cabin stood on a half-cleared hill-side, and we even passed one or two substantial houses on the flat ridge to the east, but long, solid stretches of forest intervened, and presently we left the highway and wheeled into a cool wood-road bordered on either side by the forest.

"Here we find our first landmark," said Dorothy, drawing bridle.

A white triangle glimmered, cut in the bark of an enormous pine; and my cousin rode up to the tree and patted the bark with her little hand. On the triangle somebody had cut a V and painted it black.

"This is a boundary mark," said Dorothy. "The Mohawks claim the forest to the east; ride around and you will see their sign."

I guided my horse around the huge, straight trunk. An oval blaze scarred it and on the wood was painted a red wolf.

"It's the wolf-clan, Brant's own clan of the Mohawk nation," she called out to me. "Follow me, cousin." And she dashed off down the wood-road, I galloping behind, leaping windfalls, gullies, and the shallow forest brooks that crossed our way. The road narrowed to a trodden trail; the trail faded, marked at first by cut undergrowth, then only by the white scars on the tree-trunks.

These my cousin followed, her horse at a canter, and I followed her, halting now and again to verify the white triangle on the solid flank of some forest giant, passing a sugar-bush with the shack still standing and the black embers of the fire scattered, until we came to a logging-road and turned into it, side by side. A well-defined path crossed this road at right angles, and Dorothy pointed it out. "The Iroquois trail," she said. "See how deeply it is worn--nearly ten inches deep--where the Five Nations have trodden it for centuries. Over it their hunting-parties pass, their scouts, their war-parties. It runs from the Kennyetto to the Sacandaga and north over the hills to the Canadas."

We halted and looked down the empty, trodden trail, stretching away through the forest. Thousands and thousands of light, moccasined feet had worn it deep and patted it hard as a sheep-path. On what mission would the next Mohawk feet be speeding on that trail?

"Those people at Fonda's Bush had best move to Johnstown," said Dorothy. "If the Mohawks strike, they will strike through here at Balston or Saratoga, or at the half-dozen families left at Fonda's Bush, which some of them call Broadalbin."

"Have these poor wretches no one to warn them?" I asked.

"Oh, they have been warned and warned, but they cling to their cabins as cats cling to soft cushions. The Palatines seem paralyzed with fear, the Dutch are too lazy to move in around the forts, the Scotch and English too obstinate. Nobody can do anything for them--you heard what that Schell woman said when I urged her to prudence."

I bent my eyes on the ominous trail; its very emptiness fascinated me, and I dismounted and knelt to examine it where, near a dry, rotten log, some fresh marks showed.

Behind me I heard Dorothy dismount, dropping to the ground lightly as a tree-lynx; the next moment she laid her hand on my shoulder and bent over where I was kneeling.

"Can you read me that sign?" she asked, mischievously.

"Something has rolled and squatted in the dry wood-dust--some bird, I think."

"A good guess," she said; "a cock-partridge has dusted here; see those bits of down? I say a cock-bird because I know that log to be a drumming-log."

She raised herself and guided her horse along the trail, bright eyes restlessly scanning ground and fringing underbrush.

"Deer passed here--one--two--three--the third a buck--a three-year old," she said, sinking her voice by instinct. "Yonder a tree-cat dug for a wood-mouse; your lynx is ever hanging about a drumming-log."

I laid my hand on her arm and pointed to a fresh, green maple leaf lying beside the trail.

"Ay," she murmured, "but it fell naturally, cousin. See; here it parted from the stalk, clean as a poplar twig, leaving the shiny cup unbruised. And nothing has passed here--this spider's web tells that, with a dead moth dangling from it, dead these three days, from its brittle shell."

"I hear water," I said, and presently we came to it, where it hurried darkling across the trail.

There were no human signs there; here a woodcock had peppered the mud with little holes, probing for worms; there a raccoon had picked his way; yonder a lynx had left the great padded mark of its foot, doubtless watching for yonder mink nosing us from the bank of the still pool below.

Silently we mounted and rode out of the still Mohawk country; and I was not sorry to leave, for it seemed to me that there was something unfriendly in the intense stillness--something baleful in the silence; and I was glad presently to see an open road and a great tree marked with Sir Lupus's mark, the sun shining on the white triangle and the painted V.

Entering a slashing where the logging-road passed, we moved on, side by side, talking in low tones. And my cousin taught me how to know these Northern trees by bark and leaf; how to know the shrubs new to me, like that strange plant whose root is like a human body and which the Chinese value at its weight in gold; and the aromatic root used in beer, and the bark of the sweet-birch whose twigs are golden-black.

Now, though the birds and many of the beasts and trees were familiar to me in this Northern forest, yet I was constantly at fault, as I have said. Plumage and leaf and fur puzzled me; our gray rice-bird here wore a velvet livery of black and white and sang divinely, though with us he is mute as a mullet; many squirrels were striped with black and white; no rosy lichen glimmered on the tree-trunks; no pink-stemmed pines softened sombre forest depths; no great tiger-striped butterflies told me that the wild orange was growing near at hand; no whirring, olive-tinted moth signalled the hidden presence of the oleander. But I saw everywhere unfamiliar winged things, I heard unfamiliar bird-notes; new colors perplexed me, new shapes, nay, the very soil smelled foreign, and the water tasted savorless as the mist of pine barrens in February. Still, my Maker had set eyes in my head and given me a nose to sniff with; and I was learning every moment, tasting, smelling, touching, listening, asking questions unashamed; and my cousin Dorothy seemed never to tire in aiding me, nor did her eager delight and sympathy abate one jot.

Dressed in full deer-skin as was I, she rode her horse astride with a grace as perfect as it was unstudied and unconscious, neither affecting the slothful carriage of our Southern saddle-masters nor the dragoons' rigid seat, but sat at ease, hollow-backed, loose-thighed, free-reined and free-stirruped.

Her hair, gathered into a golden club at the nape of the neck, glittered in the sun, her eyes deepened like the violet depths of mid-heaven. Already the sun had lent her a delicate, creamy mask, golden on her temples where the hair grew paler;

and I thought I had never seen such wholesome sweetness and beauty in any living being.

We now rode through a vast flat land of willows, headed due north once more, and I saw a little river which twisted a hundred times upon itself like a stricken snake, winding its shimmering coils out and in through woodland, willow-flat, and reedy marsh.

"The Kennyetto," said Dorothy, "flowing out of the great Vlaie to empty its waters close to its source after a circle of half a hundred miles. Yonder lies the Vlaie--it is that immense flat country of lake and marsh and forest which is wedged in just south of the mountain-gap where the last of the Adirondacks split into the Mayfield hills and the long, low spurs rolling away to the southeast. Sir William Johnson had a lodge there at Summer-house Point. Since his death Sir George Covert has leased it from Sir John. That is our trysting-place."

To hear Sir George's name now vaguely disturbed me, yet I could not think why, for I admired and liked him. But at the bare mention of his name a dull uneasiness came over me and I turned impatiently to my cousin as though the irritation had come from her and she must explain it.

"What is it?" she inquired, faintly smiling.

"I asked no question," I muttered.

"I thought you meant to speak, cousin."

I had meant to say something. I did not know what.

"You seem to know when I am about to speak," I said; "that is twice you have responded to my unasked questions."

"I know it," she said, surprised and a trifle perplexed. "I seem to hear you when you are mute, and I turn to find you looking at me, as though you had asked me something."

We rode on, thoughtful, silent, aware of a new and wordless intimacy.

"It is pleasant to be with you," she said at last. "I have never before found untroubled contentment save when I am alone.... Everything that you see and think of on this ride I seem to see and think of, too, and know that you are observing with the same delight that I feel.... Nor does anything in the world disturb my happiness. Nor do you vex me with silence when I would have you speak; nor with speech when I ride dreaming--as I do, cousin, for hours and hours--not sadly, but in the sweetest peace--"

Her voice died out like a June breeze; our horses, ear to ear moved on slowly in the fragrant silence.

"To ride ... forever ... together," she mused, "looking with perfect content on all the world.... I teaching you, or you me; ... it's all one for the delight it gives to be alive and young.... And no trouble to await us, ... nothing malicious to do a harm to any living thing.... I could renounce Heaven for that.... Could you?"

"Yes.... For less."

"I know I ask too much; grief makes us purer, fitting us for the company of blessed souls. They say that even war may be a holy thing--though we are commanded otherwise.... Cousin, at moments a demon rises in me and I desire some forbidden thing so ardently, so passionately, that it seems as if I could fight a path through paradise itself to gain what I desire.... Do you feel so?"

"Yes."

"Is it not consuming--terrible to be so shaken?... Yet I never gain my desire, for there in my path my own self rises to confront me, blocking my way. And I can never pass--never.... Once, in winter, our agent, Mr. Fonda, came driving a trained caribou to a sledge. A sweet, gentle thing, with dark, mild eyes, and I was mad to drive it--mad, cousin! But Sir Lupus learned that it had trodden and gored a man, and put me on my honor not to drive it. And all day Sir Lupus was away at Kingsborough for his rents and I free to drive the sledge, ... and I was mad to do it--and could not. And the pretty beast stabled with our horses, and every day I might have driven it.... I never did.... It hurts yet, cousin.... How strange is it that to us the single word, 'honor,' blocks the road and makes the King's own highway no thorough-fare forever!"

She gathered bridle nervously, and we launched our horses through a willow fringe and away over a soft, sandy intervale, riding knee to knee till the wind whistled in our ears and the sand rose fountain high at every stride of our bounding horses.

"Ah!" she sighed, drawing bridle. "That clears the heart of silly troubles. Was it not glorious? Like a plunge to the throat in an icy pool!"

Her face, radiant, transfigured, was turned to the north, where, glittering under the westward sun, the sunny waters of the Vlaie sparkled between green reeds and rushes. Beyond, smoky blue mountains tumbled into two uneven walls, spread southeast and southwest, flanking the flat valley of the Vlaie.

Thousands of blackbirds chattered and croaked and trilled and whistled in the reeds, flitting upward, with a flash of scarlet on their wings; hovering, dropping again amid a ceaseless chorus from the half-hidden flock. Over the marshes slow hawks sailed, rose, wheeled, and fell; the gray ducks, whose wings bear purple diamond-squares, quacked in the tussock ponds, guarded by their sentinels, the tall, blue herons. Everywhere the earth was sheeted with marsh-marigolds and violets.

Across the distant grassy flat two deer moved, grazing. We rode to the east, skirting the marshes, following a trail made by cattle, until beyond the flats we saw the green roof of the pleasure-house which Sir William Johnson had built for himself. Our ride together was nearly ended.

As at the same thought we tightened bridle and looked at each other gravely.

"All rides end," I said.

"Ay, like happiness."

"Both may be renewed."

"Until they end again."

"Until they end forever."

She clasped her bare hands on her horse's neck, sitting with bent head as though lost in sombre memories.

"What ends forever might endure forever," I said.

"Not our rides together," she murmured. "You must return to the South one day. I must wed.... Where shall we be this day a year hence?"

"Very far apart, cousin."

"Will you remember this ride?"

"Yes," I said, troubled.

"I will, too.... And I shall wonder what you are doing."

"And I shall think of you," I said, soberly.

"Will you write?"

"Yes. Will you?"

"Yes."

Silence fell between us like a shadow; then:

"Yonder rides Sir George Covert," she said, listlessly.

I saw him dismounting before his door, but said nothing.

"Shall we move forward?" she asked, but did not stir a finger towards the bridle lying on her horse's neck.

Another silence; and, impatiently:

"I cannot bear to have you go," she said; "we are perfectly contented together--and I wish you to know all the thoughts I have touching on the world and on people. I cannot tell them to my father, nor to Ruyven--and Cecile is too young--"

"There is Sir George," I said.

"He! Why, I should never think of telling him of these thoughts that please or trouble or torment me!" she said, in frank surprise. "He neither cares for the things you care for nor thinks about them at all."

"Perhaps he does. Ask him."

"I have. He smiles and says nothing. I am afraid to tax his courtesy with babble of beast and bird and leaf and flower; and why one man is rich and another poor; and whether it is right that men should hold slaves; and why our Lord permits evil, having the power to end it for all time. I should like to know all these things," she said, earnestly.

"But I do not know them, Dorothy."

"Still, you think about them, and so do I. Sir Lupus says you have liberated your Greeks and sent them back. I want to know why. Then, too, though neither you nor I can know our Lord's purpose in enduring the evil that Satan plans, it is pleasant, I think, to ask each other."

"To think together," I said, sadly.

"Yes; that is it. Is it not a pleasure?"

"Yes, Dorothy."

"It does not matter that we fail to learn; it is the happiness in knowing that the other also cares to know, the delight in seaching for reason together. Cousin, I have so longed to say this to somebody; and until you came I never believed it possible.... I wish we were brother and sister! I wish you were Cecile, and I could be with you all day and all night.... At night, half asleep, I think of wonderful things to talk about, but I forget them by morning. Do you?"

"Yes, cousin."

"It is strange we are so alike!" she said, staring at me thoughtfully.

IX
HIDDEN FIRE

After a few moments' silence we moved forward towards the pleasure-house, and we had scarcely started when down the road, from the north, came the patroon riding a powerful black horse, attended by old Cato mounted on a raw-boned hunter, and by one Peter Van Horn, the district Brandt-Meester, or fire-warden. As they halted at Sir George Covert's door, we rode up to join them at a gallop, and the patroon, seeing us far off, waved his hat at us in evident good humor.

"Not a landmark missing!" he shouted, "and my signs all witnessed for record by Peter and Cato! How do the southwest landmarks stand?"

"The tenth pine is blasted by lightning," said Dorothy, walking her beautiful gray to Sir Lupus's side.

"Pooh! We've a dozen years to change trees," said Sir Lupus, in great content. "All's well everywhere, save at the Fish-House near the Sacandaga ford, where some impudent rascal says he saw smoke on the hills. He's doubtless a liar. Where's Sir George?"

Sir George sauntered forth from the doorway where he had been standing, and begged us to dismount, but the patroon declined, saying that we had far to ride ere sundown, and that one of us should go around by Broadalbin. However, Dorothy and I slipped from our saddles to stretch our legs while a servant brought stirrup-cups and Sir George gathered a spray of late lilac which my cousin fastened to her leather belt.

"Tory lilacs," said Sir George, slyly; "these bushes came from cuttings of those Sir William planted at Johnson Hall."

"If Sir William planted them, a rebel may wear them," replied Dorothy, gayly.

"Ay, it's that whelp, Sir John, who has marred what the great baronet left as his monument," growled old Peter Van Horn.

"That's treason!" snapped the patroon. "Stop it. I won't have politics talked in my presence, no! Dammy, Peter, hold your tongue, sir!"

Dorothy, wearing the lilac spray, vaulted lightly into her saddle, and I mounted my mare. Stirrup-cups were filled and passed up to us, and we drained a cooled measure of spiced claret to the master of the pleasure-house, who pledged us gracefully in return, and then stood by Dorothy's horse, chatting and laughing until, at a sign from Sir Lupus, Cato sounded "Afoot!" on his curly hunting-horn, and the patroon wheeled his big horse out into the road, with a whip-salute to our host.

"Dine with us to-night!" he bawled, without turning his fat head or waiting for a reply, and hammered away in a torrent of dust. Sir George glanced wistfully at Dorothy.

"There's a district officer-call gone out," he said. "Some of the Palatine officers desire my presence. I cannot refuse. So ... it is good-bye for a week."

"Are you a militia officer?" I asked, curiously.

"Yes," he said, with a humorous grimace. "May I say that you also are a candidate?"

Dorothy turned squarely in her saddle and looked me in the eyes.

"At the district's service, Sir George," I said, lightly.

"Ha! That is well done, Ormond!" he exclaimed. "Nothing yet to inconvenience you, but our Governor Clinton may send you a billet doux from Albany before May ends and June begins--if this periwigged beau, St. Leger, strolls out to ogle Stanwix--"

Dorothy turned her horse sharply, saluted Sir George, and galloped away towards her father, who had halted at the cross-roads to wait for us.

"Good-bye, Sir George," I said, offering my hand. He took it in a firm, steady clasp.

"A safe journey, Ormond. I trust fortune may see fit to throw us together in this coming campaign."

I bowed, turned bridle, and cantered off, leaving him standing in the road before his gayly painted pleasure-house, an empty wine-cup in his hand.

"Damnation, George!" bawled Sir Lupus, as I rode up, "have we all day to stand nosing one another and trading gossip! Some of us must ride by Fonda's Bush, or Broadalbin, whatever the Scotch loons call it; and I'll say plainly that I have no stomach for it; I want my dinner!"

"It will give me pleasure to go," said I, "but I require a guide."

"Peter shall ride with you," began Sir Lupus; but Dorothy broke in, impatiently:

"He need not. I shall guide Mr. Ormond to Broadalbin."

"Oh no, you won't!" snapped the patroon; "you've done enough of forest-running for one day. Peter, pilot Mr. Ormond to the Bush."

And he galloped on ahead, followed by Cato and Peter; so that, by reason of their dust, which we did not choose to choke in, Dorothy and I slackened our pace and fell behind.

"Do you know why you are to pass by Broadalbin?" she asked, presently.

I said I did not.

"Folk at the Fish-House saw smoke on the Mayfield hills an hour since. That is twice in three days!"

"Well," said I, "what of that?"

"It is best that the Broadalbin settlement should hear of it."

"Do you mean that it may have been an Indian signal?"

"It may have been. I did not see it--the forest cut our view."

The westering sun, shining over the Mayfield hills, turned the dust to golden fog. Through it Cato's red coat glimmered, and the hunting-horn, curving up over his bent back, struck out streams of blinding sparks. Brass buttons on the patroon's broad coat-skirts twinkled like yellow stars, and the spurs flashed on his quarter-gaiters as he pounded along at a solid hand-gallop, hat crammed over his fat ears, pig-tail a-bristle, and the blue coat on his enormous body white with dust.

In the renewed melody of the song-birds there was a hint of approaching evening; shadows lengthened; the sunlight grew redder on the dusty road.

"The Broadalbin trail swings into the forest just ahead," said Dorothy, pointing with her whip-stock. "See, there where they are drawing bridle. But I mean to ride with you, nevertheless.... And I'll do it!"

The patroon was waiting for us when we came to the weather-beaten finger-post:

"FONDA'S BUSH   4 MILES."

And Peter Van Horn had already ridden into the broad, soft wood-road, when Dorothy, swinging her horse past him at a gallop, cried out, "I want to go with them! Please let me!" And was gone like a deer, tearing away down the leafy trail.

"Come back!" roared Sir Lupus, standing straight up in his ponderous stirrups. "Come back, you little vixen! Am I to be obeyed, or am I not? Baggage! Undutiful tree-cat! Dammy, she's off!"

He looked at me and smote his fat thigh with open hand.

"Did you ever see the like of her!" he chuckled, in his pride. "She's a Dutch Varick for obstinacy, but the rest is Ormond--all Ormond. Ride on, George, and tell those rebel fools at Fonda's Bush that they should be hunting cover in the forts if folk at the Fish-House read that smoke aright. Follow the Brandt-Meester if Dorothy slips you, and tell her I'll birch her, big as she is, if she's not home by the new moon rise."

Then he dragged his hat over his mottled ears, grasped the bridle and galloped on, followed by old Cato and his red coat and curly horn.

I had ridden a cautious mile on the dim, leafy trail ere I picked up Van Horn, only to quit him. I had ridden full three before I caught sight of Dorothy, sitting her gray horse, head at gaze in my direction.

"What in the world set you tearing off through the forest like that?" I asked, laughing.

She turned her horse and we walked on, side by side.

"I wished to come," she said, simply. "The pleasures of this day must end only with the night. Besides, I was burning to ask you if it is true that you mean to stay here and serve with our militia?"

"I mean to stay," I said, slowly.

"And serve?"

"If they desire it."

"Why?" she asked, raising her bright eyes.

I thought a moment, then said:

"I have decided to resist our King's soldiers."

"But why here?" she repeated, clear eyes still on mine. "Tell me the truth."

"I think it is because you are here," I said, soberly.

The loveliest smile parted her lips.

"I hoped you would say that.... Do I please you? Listen, cousin: I have a mad impulse to follow you--to be hindered rages me beyond endurance--as when Sir Lupus called me back. For, within the past hour the strangest fancy has possessed me that we have little time left to be together; that I should not let one moment slip to enjoy you."

"Foolish prophetess," I said, striving to laugh.

"A prophetess?" she repeated under her breath. And, as we rode on through the forest dusk, her head drooped thoughtfully, shaded by her loosened hair. At last she looked up dreamily, musing aloud:

"No prophetess, cousin; only a child, nerveless and over-fretted with too much pleasure, tired out with excitement, having played too hard. I do not know quite how I should conduct. I am unaccustomed to comrades like you, cousin; and, in the untasted delights of such companionship, have run wild till my head swims wi' the humming thoughts you stir in me, and I long for a dark, still room and a bed to lie on, and think of this day's pleasures."

After a silence, broken only by our horses treading the moist earth: "I have been starving for this companionship.... I was parched!... Cousin, have you let me drink too deeply? Have you been too kind? Why am I in this new terror lest you--lest you tire of me and my silly speech? Oh, I know my thoughts have been too long pent! I could talk to you forever! I could ride with you till I died! I am like a caged thing loosed, I tell you--for I may tell you, may I not, cousin?"

"Tell me all you think, Dorothy."

"I could tell you all--everything! I never had a thought that I do not desire you to know, ... save one.... And that I do desire to tell you ... but cannot.... Cousin, why did you name your mare Isene?"

"An Indian girl in Florida bore that name; the Seminoles called her Issena."

"And so you named your mare from her?"

"Yes."

"Was she your friend--that you named your mare from her?"

"She lived a century ago--a princess. She wedded with a Huguenot."

"Oh," said Dorothy, "I thought she was perhaps your sweetheart."

"I have none."

"You never had one?"

"No."

"Why?"

I turned in my saddle.

"Why have you never had a gallant?"

"Oh, that is not the same. Men fall in love--or protest as much. And at wine they boast of their good fortunes, swearing each that his mistress is the fairest, and bragging till I yawn to listen.... And yet you say you never had a sweetheart?"

"Neither titled nor untitled, cousin. And, if I had, at home we never speak of it, deeming it a breach of honor."

"Why?"

"For shame, I suppose."

"Is it shameless to speak as I do?" she asked.

"Not to me, Dorothy. I wish you might be spared all that unlicensed gossip that you hear at table--not that it could harm such innocence as yours! For, on my honor, I never knew a woman such as you, nor a maid so nobly fashioned!"

I stopped, meeting her wide eyes.

"Say it," she murmured. "It is happiness to hear you."

"Then hear me," I said, slowly. "Loyalty, devotion, tenderness, all are your due; not alone for the fair body that holds your soul imprisoned, but for the pure tenant that dwells in it so sweetly behind the blue windows of your eyes! Dorothy! Dorothy! Have I said too much? Yet I beg that you remember it, lest you forget me when I have gone from you.... And say to Sir George that I said it.... Tell him after you are wedded, and say that all men envy him, yet wish him well. For the day he weds he weds the noblest woman in all the confines of this earth!"

Dazed, she stared at me through the fading light; and I saw her eyes all wet in the shadow of her tangled hair and the pulse beating in her throat.

"You are so good--so pitiful," she said; "and I cannot even find the words to tell you of those deep thoughts you stir in me--to tell you how sweetly you use me--"

"Tell me no more," I stammered, all a-quiver at her voice. She shrank back as at a blow, and I, head swimming, frighted, penitent, caught her small hand in mine and drew her nearer; nor could I speak for the loud beating of my heart.

"What is it?" she murmured. "Have I pained you that you tremble so? Look at me, cousin. I can scarce see you in the dusk. Have I hurt you? I love you dearly."

Her horse moved nearer, our knees touched. In the forest darkness I found I held her waist imprisoned, and her arms were heavy on my shoulders. Then her lips yielded and her arms tightened around my neck, and that swift embrace in the swimming darkness kindled in me a flame that has never died--that shall live when this poor body crumbles into dust, lighting my soul through its last dark pilgrimage.

As for her, she sat up in her saddle with a strange little laugh, still holding to my hand. "Oh, you are divine in all you lead me to," she whispered. "Never, never have I known delight in a kiss; and I have been kissed, too, willing and against my will. But you leave me breathing my heart out and all a-tremble with a tenderness for you--no, not again, cousin, not yet."

Then slowly the full wretchedness of guilt burned me, bone and soul, and what I had done seemed a black evil to a maid betrothed, and to the man whose wine had quenched my thirst an hour since.

Something of my thoughts she may have read in my bent head and face averted, for she leaned forward in her saddle, and drawing me by the arm, turned me partly towards her.

"What troubles you?" she said, anxiously.

"My treason to Sir George."

"What treason?" she said, amazed.

"That I--caressed you."

She laughed outright.

"Am I not free-until I wed? Do you imagine I should have signed my liberty away to please Sir George? Why, cousin, if I may not caress whom I choose and find a pleasure in the way you use me, I am no better than the winter log he buys to toast his shins at!"

Then she grew angry in her impatience, slapping her bridle down to range her horse up closer to mine.

"Am I not to wed him?" she said. "Is not that enough? And I told him so, flatly, I warrant you, when Captain Campbell kissed me on the porch--which maddened me, for he was not to my fancy--but Sir George saw him and there was like to be a silly scene until I made it plain that I would endure no bonds before I wore a wedding-ring!" She laughed deliciously. "I think he understands now that I am not yoked until I bend my neck. And until I bend it I am free. So if I please you, kiss me, ... but leave me a little breath to draw, cousin, ... and a saddle to cling to.... Now loose me--for the forest ends!"

A faint red light grew in the woodland gloom; a rushing noise like swiftly flowing water filled my ears--or was it the blood that surged singing through my heart?

"Broadalbin Bush," she murmured, clearing her eyes of the clouded hair and feeling for her stirrups with small, moccasined toes. "Hark! Now we hear the Kennyetto roaring below the hill. See, cousin, it is sunset, the west blazes, all heaven is afire! Ah! what sorcery has turned the world to paradise--riding this day with you?"

She turned in her saddle with an exquisite gesture, pressed her outstretched hand against my lips, then, gathering bridle, launched her horse straight through the underbrush, out into a pasture where, across a naked hill, a few log-houses reddened in the sunset.

There hung in the air a smell of sweetbrier as we drew bridle before a cabin under the hill. I leaned over and plucked a handful of the leaves, bruising them in my palm to savor the spicy perfume.

A man came to the door of the cabin and stared at us; a tap-room sluggard, a-sunning on the west fence-rail, chewed his cud solemnly and watched us with watery eyes.

"Andrew Bowman, have you seen aught to fright folk on the mountain?" asked Dorothy, gravely.

The man in the doorway shook his head. From the cabins near by a few men and women trooped out into the road and hastened towards us. One of the houses bore a bush, and I saw two men peering at us through the open window, pewters in hand.

"Good people," said Dorothy, quietly, "the patroon sends you word of a strange smoke seen this day in the hills."

"There's smoke there now," I said, pointing into the sunset.

At that moment Peter Van Horn galloped up, halted, and turned his head, following the direction of my outstretched arm. Others came, blinking into the ruddy evening glow, craning their necks to see, and from the wretched tavern a lank lout stumbled forth, rifle shouldered, pewter a-slop, to learn the news that had brought us hither at that hour.

"It is mist," said a woman; but her voice trembled as she said it.

"It is smoke," growled Van Horn. "Read it, you who can."

Whereat the fellow in the tavern window fell a-laughing and called down to his companion: "Francy McCraw! Francy McCraw! The Brandt-Meester says a Mohawk fire burns in the north!"

"I hear him," cried McCraw, draining his pewter.

Dorothy turned sharply. "Oh, is that you, McCraw? What brings you to the Bush?"

The lank fellow turned his wild, blue eyes on her, then gazed at the smoke. Some of the men scowled at him.

"Is that smoke?" I asked, sharply. "Answer me, McCraw!"

"A canna' deny it," he said, with a mad chuckle.

"Is it Indian smoke?" demanded Van Horn.

"Aweel," he replied, craning his skinny neck and cocking his head impudently--"aweel, a'll admit that, too. It's Indian smoke; a canna deny it, no."

"Is it a Mohawk signal?" I asked, bluntly.

At which he burst out into a crowing laugh.

"What does he say?" called out the man from the tavern. "What does he say, Francy McCraw?"

"He says it maun be Mohawk smoke, Danny Redstock."

"And what if it is?" blustered Redstock, shouldering his way to McCraw, rifle in hand. "Keep your black looks for your neighbors, Andrew Bowman. What have we to do with your Mohawk fires?"

"Herman Salisbury!" cried Bowman to a neighbor, "do you hear what this Tory renegade says?"

"Quiet! Quiet, there," said Redstock, swaggering out into the road. "Francy McCraw, our good neighbors are woful perplexed by that thread o' birch smoke yonder."

"Then tell the feckless fools tae watch it!" screamed McCraw, seizing his rifle and menacing the little throng of men and women who had closed swiftly in on him. "Hands off me, Johnny Putnam--back, for your life, Charley Cady! Ay, stare at the smoke till ye're eyes drop frae th' sockets! But no; there's some foulk 'ill tak' nae warnin'!"

He backed off down the road, followed by Redstock, rifles cocked.

"An' ye'll bear me out," he shouted, "that there's them wha' hear these words now shall meet their weirds ere a hunter's moon is wasted!"

He laughed his insane laugh and, throwing his rifle over his shoulder, halted, facing us.

"Hae ye no heard o' Catrine Montour?" he jeered. "She'll come in the night, Andrew Bowman! Losh, mon, but she's a grewsome carlin', wi' the witch-locks hangin' to her neck an' her twa een blazin'!"

"You drive us out to-night!" shouted Redstock. "We'll remember it when Brant is in the hills!"

"The wolf-yelp! Clan o' the wolf!" screamed McCraw. "Woe! Woe to Broadal-bane! 'Tis the pibroch o' Glencoe shall wake ye to the woods afire! Be warned! Be warned, for ye stand knee-deep in ye're shrouds!"

In the ruddy dusk their dark forms turned to shadows and were gone.

Van Horn stirred in his saddle, then shook his shoulders as though freeing them from a weight.

"Now you have it, you Broadalbin men," he said, grimly. "Go to the forts while there's time."

In the darkness around us children began to whimper; a woman broke down, sobbing.

"Silence!" cried Bowman, sternly. And to Dorothy, who sat quietly on her horse beside him, "Say to the patroon that we know our enemies. And you, Peter Van Horn, on whichever side you stand, we men of the Bush thank you and this young lady for your coming."

And that was all. In silence we wheeled our horses northward, Van Horn rid-ing ahead, and passed out of that dim hamlet which lay already in the shadows of an unknown terror.

Behind us, as we looked back, one or two candles flickered in cabin windows, pitiful, dim lights in the vast, dark ocean of the forest. Above us the stars grew clearer. A vesper-sparrow sang its pensive song. Tranquil, sweet, the serene notes floated into silver echoes never-ending, till it seemed as if the starlight all around us quivered into song.

I touched Dorothy, riding beside me, white as a spirit in the pale radiance, and she turned her sweet, fearless face to mine.

"There is a sound," I whispered, "very far away."

She laid her hand in mine and drew bridle, listening. Van Horn, too, had halted.

Far in the forest the sound stirred the silence; soft, stealthy, nearer, nearer, till it grew into a patter. Suddenly Van Horn's horse reared.

"It's there! it's there!" he cried, hoarsely, as our horses swung round in terror.

"Look!" muttered Dorothy.

Then a thing occurred that stopped my heart's blood. For straight through the forest came running a dark shape, a squattering thing that passed us ere we could draw breath to shriek; animal, human, or spirit, I knew not, but it ran on, thuddy-thud, thuddy-thud! and we struggling with our frantic horses to master them ere they dashed us lifeless among the trees.

"Jesu!" gasped Van Horn, dragging his powerful horse back into the road. "Can you make aught o' yonder fearsome thing, like a wart-toad scrabbling on two legs?"

Dorothy, teeth set, drove her heels into her gray's ribs and forced him to where my mare stood all a-quiver.

"It's a thing from hell," panted Van Horn, fighting knee and wrist with his roan. "My nag shies at neither bear nor wolf! Look at him now!"

"Nor mine at anything save a savage," said I, fearfully peering behind me while my mare trembled under me.

"I think we have seen a savage, that is all," fell Dorothy's calm voice. "I think we have seen Catrine Montour."

At the name, Van Horn swore steadily.

"If that be the witch Montour, she runs like a clansman with the fiery cross," I said, shuddering.

"And that is like to be her business," muttered Van Horn. "The painted forest-men are in the hills, and if Senecas, Cayugas, and Onondagas do not know it this night, it will be no fault of Catrine Montour."

"Ride on, Peter," said Dorothy, and checked her horse till my mare came abreast.

"Are you afraid?" I whispered.

"Afraid? No!" she said, astonished. "What should arouse fear in me?"

"Your common-sense!" I said, impatiently, irritated to rudeness by the shocking and unearthly spectacle which had nigh unnerved me. But she answered very sweetly:

"If I fear nothing, it is because there is nothing that I know of in the world to fright me. I remember," she added, gravely, "'A thousand shall fall at my side and ten thousand at my right hand. And it shall not come nigh me.' How can I fear, believing that?"

She leaned from her saddle and I saw her eyes searching my face in the darkness.

"Silly," she said, tenderly, "I have no fear save that you should prove unkind."

"Then give yourself to me, Dorothy," I said, holding her imprisoned.

"How can I? You have me."

"I mean forever."

"But I have."

"I mean in wedlock!" I whispered, fiercely.

"How can I, silly--I am promised!"

"Can I not stir you to love me?" I said.

"To love you?... Better than I do?... You may try."

"Then wed me!"

"If I were wed to you would I love you better than I do?" she asked.

"Dorothy, Dorothy," I begged, holding her fast, "wed me; I love you."

She swayed back into her saddle, breaking my clasp.

"You know I cannot," she said.... Then, almost tenderly: "Do you truly desire it? It is so dear to hear you say it--and I have heard the words often enough, too, but never as you say them.... Had you asked me in December, ere I was in honor bound.... But I am promised; ... only a word, but it holds me like a chain.... Dear lad, forget it.... Use me kindly.... Teach me to love, ... an unresisting pupil, ... for all life is too short for me to learn in, ... alas!... God guard us both from love's unhappiness and grant us only its sweetness--which you have taught me; to which I am--I am awaking, ... after all these years, ... after all these years without you.

* * * * *

Perhaps it were kinder to let me sleep.... I am but half awake to love.

* * * * *

Is it best to wake me, after all? Is it too late?... Draw bridle in the starlight. Look at me.... It is too late, for I shall never sleep again."

X
TWO LESSONS

For two whole days I did not see my cousin Dorothy, she lying abed with hot and aching head, and the blinds drawn to keep out all light. So I had time to consider what we had said and done, and to what we stood committed.

Yet, with time heavy on my hands and full leisure to think, I could make nothing of those swift, fevered hours together, nor what had happened to us that the last moments should have found us in each other's arms, her tear-stained eyes closed, her lips crushed to mine. For, within that same hour, at table, she told Sir Lupus to my very face that she desired to wed Sir George as soon as might be, and would be content with nothing save that Sir Lupus despatch a messenger to the pleasure house, bidding Sir George dispose of his affairs so that the marriage fall within the first three days of June.

I could not doubt my own ears, yet could scarce credit my shocked senses to hear her; and I had sat there, now hot with anger, now in cold amazement; not touching food save with an effort that cost me all my self-command.

As for Sir Lupus, his astonishment and delight disgusted me, for he fell a-blubbering in his joy, loading his daughter with caresses, breaking out into praises of her, lauding above all her filial gratitude and her constancy to Sir George, whom he also larded and smeared with compliments till his eulogium, buttered all too thick for my weakened stomach, drove me from the table to pace the dark porch and strive to reconcile all these warring memories a-battle in my swimming brain.

What demon possessed her to throw away time, when time was our most precious ally, our only hope! With time--if she truly loved me--what might not be done! And here, too, was another ally swiftly coming to our aid on Time's own wings--the war!--whose far breath already fanned the Mohawk smoke on the northern hills! And still another friendly ally stood to aid us--absence! For, with Sir George away, plunged into new scenes, new hopes, new ambitions, he might well change in his affections. An officer, and a successful one, rising higher every day in the esteem of his countrymen, should find all paths open, all doors unlocked, and a gracious welcome among those great folk of New York city, whose princely mode of living might not only be justified, but even titled under a new regime and a new monarchy.

These were the half-formed, maddened thoughts that went a-racing through my mind as I paced the porch that night; and I think they were, perhaps, the most unworthy thoughts that ever tempted me. For I hated Sir George and wished him a quick flight to immortality unless he changed in his desire for wedlock with my cousin.

Gnawing my lips in growing rage I saw the messenger for the pleasure house mount and gallop out of the stockade, and I wished him evil chance and a fall to dash his senses out ere he rode up with his cursed message to Sir George's door.

Passion blinded and deafened me to all whispers of decency; conscience lay stunned within me, and I think I know now what black obsession drives men's bodies into murder and their souls to punishments eternal.

Quivering from head to heel, now hot, now cold, and strangling with the fierce desire for her whom I was losing more hopelessly every moment, I started aimlessly through the starlight, pacing the stockade like a caged beast, and I thought my swelling heart would choke me if it broke not to ease my breath.

So this was love! A ghastly thing, God wot, to transform an honest man, changing and twisting right and wrong until the threads of decency and duty hung too hopelessly entangled for him to follow or untwine. Only one thing could I see or understand: I desired her whom I loved and was now fast losing forever.

Chance and circumstance had enmeshed me; in vain I struggled in the net of fate, bruised, stunned, confused with grief and this new fire of passion which had flashed up around me until I had inhaled the flames and must forever bear their scars within as long as my seared heart could pulse.

As I stood there under the dim trees, dumb, miserable, straining my ears for the messenger's return, came my cousin Dorothy in the pale, flowered gown she wore at supper, and ere she perceived me I saw her searching for me, treading the new grass without a sound, one hand pressed to her parted lips.

When she saw me she stood still, and her hands fell loosely to her side.

"Cousin," she said, in a faint voice.

And, as I did not answer, she stepped nearer till I could see her blue eyes searching mine.

"What have you done!" I cried, harshly.

"I do not know," she said.

"I know," I retorted, fiercely. "Time was all we had--a few poor hours--a day or two together. And with time there was chance, and with chance, hope. You have killed all three!"

"No; ... there was no chance; there is no longer any time; there never was any hope."

"There was hope!" I said, bitterly.

"No, there was none," she murmured.

"Then why did you tell me that you were free till the yoke locked you to him? Why did you desire to love? Why did you bid me teach you? Why did you consent to my lips, my arms? Why did you awake me?"

"God knows," she said, faintly.

"Is that your defence?" I asked. "Have you no defence?"

"None.... I had never loved.... I found you kind and I had known no man like you.... Every moment with you entranced me till, ... I don't know why, ... that sweet madness came upon ... us ... which can never come again--which must never come.... Forgive me. I did not understand. Love was a word to me."

"Dorothy, Dorothy, what have I done!" I stammered.

"Not you, but I, ... and now it is plain to me why, unwedded, I stand yoked together with my honor, and you stand apart, fettered to yours.... We have shaken our chains in play, the links still hold firm and bright; but if we break them, then, as they snap, our honor dies forever. For what I have done in idle ignorance forgive me, and leave me to my penance, ... which must last for all my life, cousin.... And you will forget.... Hush! dearest lad, and let me speak. Well, then I will say that I pray you may forget! Well, then I will not say that to grieve you.... I wish you to remember--yet not know the pain that I--"

"Dorothy, Dorothy, do you still love me?"

"Oh, I do love you!... No, no! I ask you to spare me even the touch of your hand! I ask it, I beg you to spare me! I implore--Be a shield to me! Aid me, cousin. I ask it for the Ormond honor and for the honor of the roof that shelters us both!... Now do you understand?... Oh, I knew you to be all that I adore and worship!

*   *   *   *   *

Our fault was in our ignorance. How could we know of that hidden fire within us, stirring its chilled embers in all innocence until the flames flashed out and clothed us both in glory, cousin? Heed me, lest it turn to flames of hell!

*   *   *   *   *

And now, dear lad, lest you should deem me mad to cut short the happy time we had to hope for, I must tell you what I have never told before. All that we have in all the world is by charity of Sir George. He stood in the breach when the Cosby heirs made ready to foreclose on father; he held off the Van Rensselaers; he threw the sop to Billy Livingston and to that great villain, Klock. To-day, unsecured, his loans to my father, still unpaid, have nigh beggared him. And the little he has he is about to risk in this war whose tides are creeping on us through this very night.

*   *   *   *   *

And when he honored me by asking me in marriage, I, knowing all this, knowing all his goodness and his generosity--though he was not aware I knew it--I was thankful to say yes--deeming it little enough to please him--and I not knowing what love meant--"

Her soft voice broke; she laid her hands on her eyes, and stood so, speaking blindly. "What can I do, cousin? What can I do? Tell me! I love you. Tell me, use me kindly; teach me to do right and keep my honor bright as you could desire it were

I to be your wife!"

It was that appeal, I think, that brought me back through the distorted shadows of my passion; through the dark pit of envy, past snares of jealousy and malice, and the traps and pitfalls dug by Satan, safe to the trembling rock of honor once again.

Like a blind man healed by miracle, yet still groping in the precious light that mazed him, so I peering with aching eyes for those threads to guide me in my stunned perplexity. But when at last I felt their touch, I found I held one already-- the thread of hope--and whether for good or evil I did not drop it, but gathered all together and wove them to a rope to hold by.

"What is it I must swear," I asked, cold to the knees.

"Never again to kiss me."

"Never again."

"Nor to caress me."

"Nor to caress you."

"Nor speak of love."

"Nor speak of love."

"And ... that is all," she faltered.

"No, not all. I swear to love you always, never to forget you, never to prove unworthy in your eyes, never to wed; living, to honor you; dying, with your name upon my lips."

She had stretched out her arms towards me as though warning me to stop; but, as I spoke slowly, weighing each word and its cost, her hands trembled and sought each other so that she stood looking at me, fingers interlocked and her sweet face as white as death.

And after a long time she came to me, and, raising my hands, kissed them; and I touched her hair with dumb lips; and she stole away through the starlight like a white ghost returning to its tomb.

And long after, long, long after, as I stood there, broke on my wrapt ears the far stroke of horse's hoofs, nearer, nearer, until the black bulk of the rider rose up in the night and Sir Lupus came to the porch.

"Eh! What?" he cried. "Sir George away with the Palatine rebels? Where? Gone to Stanwix? Now Heaven have mercy on him for a madman who mixes in this devil's brew! And he'll drown me with him, too! Dammy, they'll say that I'm in with him.

But I'm not! Curse me if I am. I'm neutral--neither rebel nor Tory--and I'll let 'em know it, too; only desiring quiet and peace and a fair word for all. Damnation!"

*   *   *   *   *

And so had ended that memorable day and night; and now for two whole wretched days I had not seen Dorothy, nor heard of her save through Ruyven, who brought us news that she lay on her bed in the dark with no desire for company.

"There is a doctor at Johnstown," he said; "but Dorothy refuses, saying that she is only tired and requires peace and rest. I don't like it, Cousin George. Never have I seen her ill, nor has any one. Suppose you look at her, will you?"

"If she will permit me," I said, slowly. "Ask her, Ruyven."

But he returned, shaking his head, and I sat down once more upon the porch to think of her and of all I loved in her; and how I must strive to fashion my life so that I do naught that might shame me should she know.

Now that it was believed that factional bickering between the inhabitants of Tryon County might lead, in the immediate future, to something more serious than town brawls and tavern squabbles; and, more-over, as the Iroquois agitation had already resulted in the withdrawal to Fort Niagara of the main body of the Mohawk nation--for what ominous purpose it might be easy to guess--Sir Lupus forbade the children to go a-roaming outside his own boundaries.

Further, he had cautioned his servants and tenants not to rove out of bounds, to avoid public houses like the "Turtle-dove and Olive," and to refrain from busying themselves about matters in which they had no concern.

Yet that very day, spite of the patroon's orders, when General Schuyler's militia-call went out, one-half of his tenantry disappeared overnight, abandoning everything save their live-stock and a rough cart heaped with household furniture; journeying with women and children, goods and chattels, towards the nearest block-house or fort, there to deposit all except powder-horn, flint, and rifle, and join the district regiment now laboring with pick and shovel on the works at Fort Stanwix.

As I sat there on the porch, wretched, restless, debating what course I should take in the presence of this growing disorder which, as I have said, had already invaded our own tenantry, came Sir Lupus a-waddling, pipe in hand, and Cato bearing his huge chair so he might sit in the sun, which was warm on the porch.

"You've heard what my tenant rascals have done?" he grunted, settling in his chair and stretching his fat legs.

"Yes, sir," I said.

"What d' ye think of it? Eh? What d' ye think?"

"I think it is very pitiful and sad to see these poor creatures leaving their little farms to face the British regulars--and starvation."

"Face the devil!" he snorted. "Nobody forces 'em!"

"The greater honor due them," I retorted.

"Honor! Fol-de-rol! Had it been any other patroon but me, he'd turn his manor-house into a court-house, arrest 'em, try 'em, and hang a few for luck! In the old days, I'll warrant you, the Cosbys would have stood no such nonsense--no, nor the Livingstons, nor the Van Cortlandts. A hundred lashes here and there, a debtor's jail, a hanging or two, would have made things more cheerful. But I, curse me if I could ever bring myself to use my simplest prerogatives; I can't whip a man, no! I can't hang a man for anything--even a sheep-thief has his chance with me--like that great villain, Billy Bones, who turned renegade and joined Danny Redstock and the McCraw."

He snorted in self-contempt and puffed savagely at his clay pipe.

"La patroon? Dammy, I'm an old woman! Get me my knitting! I want my knitting and a sunny spot to mumble my gums and wait for noon and a dish o' porridge!... George, my rents are cut in half, and half my farms left to the briers and wolves in one day, because his Majesty, General Schuyler, orders his Highness, Colonel Dayton, to call out half the militia to make a fort for his Eminence, Colonel Gansevoort!"

"At Stanwix?"

"They call it Fort Schuyler now--after his Highness in Albany."

"Sir Lupus," I said, "if it is true that the British mean to invade us here with Brant's Mohawks, there is but one bulwark between Tryon County and the enemy, and that is Fort Stanwix. Why, in Heaven's name, should it not be defended? If this British officer and his renegades, regulars, and Indians take Stanwix and fortify

Johnstown, the whole country will swarm with savages, outlaws, and a brutal soldiery already hardened and made callous by a year of frontier warfare!

"Can you not understand this, sir? Do you think it possible for these blood-
drunk ruffians to roam the Mohawk and Sacandaga valleys and respect you and
yours just because you say you are neutral? Turn loose a pack of famished panthers
in a common pasture and mark your sheep with your device and see how many are
alive at daybreak!"

"Dammy, sir!" cried Sir Lupus, "the enemy are led by British gentlemen."

"Who doubtless will keep their own cuffs clean; it were shame to doubt it! But
if the Mohawks march with them there'll be a bloody page in Tryon County an-
nals."

"The Mohawks will not join!" he said, violently. "Has not Schuyler held a
council-fire and talked with belts to the entire confederacy?"

"The confederacy returned no belts," I said, "and the Mohawks were not present."

"Kirkland saw Brant," he persisted, obstinately.

"Yes, and sent a secret report to Albany. If there had been good news in that
report, you Tryon County men had heard it long since, Sir Lupus."

"With whom have you been talking, sir?" he sneered, removing his pipe from
his yellow teeth.

"With one of your tenants yesterday, a certain Christian Schell, lately returned
with Stoner's scout."

"And what did Stoner's men see in the northwest?" he demanded, contemptuously.

"They saw half a thousand Mohawks with eyes painted in black circles and
white, Sir Lupus."

"For the planting-dance!" he muttered.

"No, Sir Lupus. The castles are empty, the villages deserted. There is not one
Mohawk left on their ancient lands, there is not one seed planted, not one foot of
soil cultivated, not one apple-bough grafted, not one fish-line set!

"And you tell me the Mohawks are painted for the planting-dance, in black and
white? With every hatchet shining like silver, and every knife ground to a razor-
edge, and every rifle polished, and every flint new?"

"Who saw such things?" he asked, hoarsely.

"Christian Schell, of Stoner's scout."

"Now God curse them if they lift an arm to harm a Tryon County man!" he burst out. "I'll not believe it of the British gentlemen who differ with us over taxing tea! No, dammy if I'll credit such a monstrous thing as this alliance!"

"Yet, a few nights since, sir, you heard Walter Butler and Sir John threaten to use the Mohawks."

"And did not heed them!" he said, angrily. "It is all talk, all threats, and empty warning. I tell you they dare not for their names' sakes employ the savages against their own kind--against friends who think not as they think--against old neighbors, ay, their own kin!

"Nor dare we. Look at Schuyler--a gentleman, if ever there was one on this rotten earth--standing, belts in hand, before the sachems of the confederacy, not soliciting Cayuga support, not begging Seneca aid, not proposing a foul alliance with the Onondagas; but demanding right manfully that the confederacy remain neutral; nay, more, he repulsed offers of warriors from the Oneidas to scout for him, knowing what that sweet word 'scout' implied--God bless him I ... I have no love for Schuyler.... He lately called me 'malt-worm,' and, if I'm not at fault, he added, 'skin-flint Dutchman,' or some such tribute to my thrift. But he has conducted like a man of honor in this Iroquois matter, and I care not who hears me say it!"

He settled himself in his chair, mumbling in a rumbling voice, and all I could make out was here and there a curse or two distributed impartially 'twixt Tory and rebel and other asses now untethered in the world.

"Well, sir," I said, "from all I can gather, Burgoyne is marching southward through the lakes, and Clinton is gathering an army in New York to march north and meet Burgoyne, and now comes this Barry St. Leger on the flank, aiming to join the others at Albany after taking Stanwix and Johnstown on the march--three spears to pierce a common centre, three torches to fire three valleys, and you neutral Tryon men in the centre, calm, undismayed, smoking your pipes and singing songs of peace and good-will for all on earth."

"And why not, sir!" he snapped.

"Did you ever hear of Juggernaut?"

"I've heard the name--a Frenchman, was he not? I think he burned

Schenectady."

"No, sir; he is a heathen god."

"And what the devil, sir, has Tryon County to do with heathen gods!" he bawled.

"You shall see--when the wheels pass," I said, gloomily.

He folded his fat hands over his stomach and smoked in obstinate silence. I, too, was silent; again a faint disgust for this man seized me. How noble and unselfish now appeared the conduct of those poor tenants of his who had abandoned their little farms to answer Schuyler's call!--trudging northward with wives and babes, trusting to God for bread to fall like manna in this wilderness to save the frail lives of their loved ones, while they faced the trained troops of Great Britain, and perhaps the Iroquois.

And here he sat, the patroon, sucking his pipe, nursing his stomach; too cautious, too thrifty to stand like a man, even for the honor of his own roof-tree! Lord! how mean, how sordid did he look to me, sulking there, his mottled double-chin crowded out upon his stock, his bow-legs wide to cradle the huge belly, his small eyes obstinately a-squint and partly shut, which lent a gross shrewdness to the expanse of fat, almost baleful, like the eye of a squid in its shapeless, jellied body!

"What are your plans?" he said, abruptly.

I told him that, through Sir George, I had placed my poor services at the State's disposal.

"You mean the rebel State's disposal?"

"Yes, sir."

"Then you are ready to enlist?"

"Quite ready, Sir Lupus."

"Only awaiting summons from Clinton and Schuyler?" he sneered.

"That is all, sir."

"And what about your properties in Florida?"

"I can do nothing there. If they confiscate them in my absence, they might do worse were I to go back and defy them. I believe my life is worth something to our cause, and it would be only to waste it foolishly if I returned to fight for a few indigo-vats and canefields."

"While you can remain here and fight for other people's hen-coops, eh?"

"No, sir; only to take up the common quarrel and stand for that liberty which we inherited from those who now seek to dispossess us."

"Quite an orator!" he observed, grimly. "The Ormonds were formerly more ready with their swords than with their tongues."

"I trust I shall not fail to sustain their traditions," I said, controlling my anger with a desperate effort.

He burst out into a hollow laugh.

"There you go, red as a turkey-cock and madder than a singed tree-cat! George, can't you let me plague you in comfort! Dammy, it's undutiful! For pity's sake! let me sneer--let me gibe and jeer if it eases me."

I glared at him, half inclined to laugh.

"Curse it!" he said, wrathfully, "I'm serious. You don't know how serious I am. It's no laughing matter, George. I must do something to ease me!" He burst out into a roar, swearing in volleys.

"D' ye think I wish to appear contemptible?" he shouted. "D' ye think I like to sit here like an old wife, scolding in one breath and preaching thrift in the next? A weak-kneed, chicken-livered, white-bellied old bullfrog that squeaks and jumps, plunk! into the puddle when a footstep falls in the grass! Am I not a patroon? Am I not Dutch? Granted I'm fat and slow and a glutton, and lazy as a wolverine. I can fight like one, too! Don't make any mistake there, George!"

His broad face flushed crimson, his little, green eyes snapped fire.

"D' ye think I don't love a fight as well as my neighbor? D' ye think I've a stomach for insults and flouts and winks and nudges? Have I a liver to sit doing sums on my thumbs when these impudent British are kicking my people out of their own doors? Am I of a kidney to smile and bow, and swallow and digest the orders of Tory swashbucklers, who lay down a rule of conduct for men who should be framing rules of common decency for them? D' ye think I'm a snail or a potato or an empty pair o' breeches? Damnation!"

Rage convulsed him. He recovered his self-command slowly, smashing his pipe in the interval; and I, astonished beyond measure, waited for the explanation which he appeared to be disposed to give.

"If I'm what I am," he said, hoarsely, "an old jack-ass he-hawing 'Peace! peace! thrift! thrift!' it is because I must and not because the music pleases me.... And I had not meant to tell you why--for none other suspects it--but my personal honor is at stake. I am in debt to a friend, George, and unless I am left in peace here to collect my tithes and till my fields and run my mills and ship my pearl-ashes, I can never hope to pay a debt of honor incurred--and which I mean to pay, if I live, so help me God!

"Lad, if this house, these farms, these acres were my own, do you think I'd hesitate to polish up that old sword yonder that my father carried when Schenectady went up in flames?... Know me better, George!... Know that this condemnation to inaction is the bitterest trial I have ever known. How easy it would be for me to throw my own property into one balance, my sword into the other, and say, 'Defend the one with the other or be robbed!' But I can't throw another man's lands into the balance. I can't raise the war-yelp and go careering about after glory when I owe every shilling I possess and thousands more to an honorable and generous gentleman who refused all security for the loan save my own word of honor.

"And now, simple, brave, high-minded as he is, he offers to return me my word of honor, free me from his debt, and leave me unshackled to conduct in this coming war as I see fit.

"But that is more than he can do, George. My word once pledged can only be redeemed by what it stood for, and he is powerless to give it back.

"That is all, sir.... Pray think more kindly of an old fool in future, when you plume yourself upon your liberty to draw sword in the most just cause this world has ever known."

"It is I who am the fool, Sir Lupus," I said, in a low voice.

XI
LIGHTS AND SHADOWS

I remember it was the last day of May before I saw my cousin Dorothy again. Late that afternoon I had taken a fishing-rod and a book, The Poems of Pansard, and had set out for the grist-mill on the stream below the log-bridge; but did not go by road, as the dust was deep, so instead crossed the meadow and entered the cool thicket, making a shorter route to the stream.

Through the woodland, as I passed, I saw violets in hollows and blue innocence starring moist glades with its heavenly color, and in the drier woods those slender-stemmed blue bell-flowers which some call the Venus's looking-glass.

In my saddened and rebellious heart a more innocent passion stirred and awoke--the tender pleasure I have always found in seeking out those shy people of the forest, the wild blossoms--a harmless pleasure, for it is ever my habit to leave them undisturbed upon their stalks.

Deeper in the forest pink moccasin-flowers bloomed among rocks, and the air was tinctured with a honeyed smell from the spiked orchis cradled in its sheltering leaf under the hemlock shade.

Once, as I crossed a marshy place, about me floated a violet perfume, and I was at a loss to find its source until I espied a single purple blossom of the Arethusa bedded in sturdy thickets of rose-azalea, faintly spicy, and all humming with the wings of plundering bees.

Underfoot my shoes brushed through spikenard, and fell silently on carpets of moss-pinks, and once I saw a matted bed of late Mayflower, and the forest dusk grew sweeter and sweeter, saturating all the woodland, until each breath I drew seemed to intoxicate.

Spring languor was in earth and sky, and in my bones, too; yet, through this

Northern forest ever and anon came faint reminders of receding snows, melting beyond the Canadas--delicate zephyrs, tinctured with the far scent of frost, flavoring the sun's balm at moments with a sharper essence.

Now traversing a ferny space edged in with sweetbrier, a breeze accompanied me, caressing neck and hair, stirring a sudden warmth upon my cheek like a breathless maid close beside me, whispering.

Then through the rustle of leafy depths I heard the stream's laughter, very far away, and I turned to the left across the moss, walking more swiftly till I came to the log-bridge where the road crosses. Below me leaped the stream, deep in its ravine of slate, roaring over the dam above the rocky gorge only to flow out again between the ledge and the stone foundations of the grist-mill opposite. Down into the ravine and under the dam I climbed, using the mossy steps that nature had cut in the slate, and found a rock to sit on where the spray from the dam could not drench me. And here I baited my hook and cast out, so that the swirling water might carry my lure under the mill's foundations, where Ruyven said big, dusky trout most often lurked.

But I am no fisherman, and it gives me no pleasure to drag a finny creature from its element and see its poor mouth gasp and its eyes glaze and the fiery dots on its quivering sides grow dimmer. So when a sly trout snatched off my bait I was in no mood to cover my hook again, but set the rod on the rocks and let the bright current waft my line as it would, harmless now as the dusty alder leaves dimpling yonder ripple. So I opened my book, idly attentive, reading The Poems of Pansard, while dappled shadows of clustered maple leaves moved on the page, and droning bees set old Pansard's lines to music.

> "Like two sweet skylarks springing skyward, singing,
>   Piercing the empyrean of blinding light,
> So shall our souls take flight, serenely winging,
>   Soaring on azure heights to God's delight;
> While from below through sombre deeps come stealing
> The floating notes of earthward church-bells pealing."

My thoughts wandered and the yellow page faded to a glimmer amid pale spots of sunshine waning when some slow cloud drifted across the sun. Again my eyes returned to the printed page, and again thought parted from its moorings, a derelict upon the tide of memory. Far in the forest I heard the white-throat's call with the endless, sad refrain, "Weep-wee-p! Dorothy, Dorothy, Dorothy!" Though some vow that the little bird sings plainly, "Sweet-sw-eet! Canada, Canada, Canada!"

Then for a while I closed my eyes until, slowly, that awakening sense that somebody was looking at me came over me, and I raised my head.

Dorothy stood on the log-bridge above the dam, elbows on the rail, gazing pensively at me.

"Well, of all idle men!" she said, steadying her voice perceptibly. "Shall I come down?"

And without waiting for a reply she walked around to the south end of the bridge and began to descend the ravine.

I offered assistance; she ignored it and picked her own way down the cleft to the stream-side.

"It seems a thousand years since I have seen you," she said. "What have you been doing all this while? What are you doing now? Reading? Oh! fishing! And can you catch nothing, silly?... Give me that rod.... No, I don't want it, after all; let the trout swim in peace.... How pale you have grown, cousin!"

"You also, Dorothy," I said.

"Oh, I know that; there's a glass in my room, thank you.... I thought I'd come down.... There is company at the house--some of Colonel Gansevoort's officers, Third Regiment of the New York line, if you please, and two impudent young ensigns of the Half-moon Regiment, all on their way to Stanwix fort."

She seated herself on the deep moss and balanced her back against a silver-birch tree.

"They're at the house, all these men," she said; "and what do you think? General Schuyler and his lady are to arrive this evening, and I'm to receive them, dressed in my best tucker!... and there may be others with them, though the General comes on a tour of inspection, being anxious lest disorder break out in this district if he is compelled to abandon Ticonderoga.... What do you think of that--George?"

My name fell so sweetly, so confidently, from her lips that I looked up in warm pleasure and found her grave eyes searching mine.

"Make it easier for me," she said, in a low voice. "How can I talk to you if you do not answer me?"

"I--I mean to answer, Dorothy," I stammered; "I am very thankful for your kindness to me."

"Do you think it is hard to be kind to you?" she murmured. "What happiness if I only might be kind!" She hid her face in her hands and bowed her head. "Pay no heed to me," she said; "I--I thought I could see you and control this rebel tongue of mine. And here am I with heart insurgent beating the long roll and every nerve a-quiver with sedition!"

"What are you saying?" I protested, miserably.

She dropped her hands from her face and gazed at me quite calmly.

"Saying? I was saying that these rocks are wet, and that I was silly to come down here in my Pompadour shoes and stockings, and I'm silly to stay here, and I'm going!"

And go she did, up over the moss and rock like a fawn, and I after her to the top of the bank, where she seemed vastly surprised to see me.

"Now I pray you choose which way you mean to stroll," she said, impatiently. "Here lie two paths, and I will take this straight and narrow one."

She turned sharply and I with her, and for a long time we walked swiftly, side by side, exchanging neither word nor glance until at last she stopped short, seated herself on a mossy log, and touched her hot face with a crumpled bit of lace and cambric.

"I tell you what, Mr. Longshanks!" she said. "I shall go no farther with you unless you talk to me. Mercy on the lad with his seven-league boots! He has me breathless and both hat-strings flying and my shoe-points dragging to trip my heels! Sit down, sir, till I knot my ribbons under my ear; and I'll thank you to tie my shoe-points! Not doubled in a sailor's-knot, silly!... And, oh, cousin, I would I had a sun-mask!... Now you are laughing! Oh, I know you think me a country hoyden, careless of sunburn and dust! But I'm not. I love a smooth, white skin as well as any London beau who praises it in verses. And I shall have one for myself, too. You may see, to-night, if the Misses Carmichael come with Lady Schuyler, for we'll have a dance, perhaps, and I mean to paint and patch and powder till you'd swear me a French marquise!... Cousin, this narrow forest pathway leads across the water back to the house. Shall we take it?... You will have to carry me over the stream, for I'll not wet my shins for love of any man, mark that!"

She tied her pink hat-ribbons under her chin and stood up while I made ready; then I lifted her from the ground. Very gravely she dropped her arms around my neck as I stepped into the rushing current and waded out, the water curling almost to my knee-buckles. So we crossed the grist-mill stream in silence, eyes averted from each other's faces; and in silence, too, we resumed the straight and narrow path, now deep with last year's leaves, until we came to a hot, sandy bank covered with wild strawberries, overlooking the stream.

In a moment she was on her knees, filling her handkerchief with strawberries, and I sat down in the yellow sand, eyes following the stream where it sparkled deep under its leafy screen below.

"Cousin," she said, timidly, "are you displeased?"

"Why?"

"At my tyranny to make you bear me across the stream--with all your heavier burdens, and my own--"

"I ask no sweeter burdens," I replied.

She seated herself in the sand and placed a scarlet berry between lips that matched it.

"I have tried very hard to talk to you," she said.

"I don't know what to say, Dorothy," I muttered. "Truly I do desire to amuse you and make you laugh--as once I did. But the heart of everything seems dead. There! I did not mean that! Don't hide your face, Dorothy! Don't look like that! I--I cannot bear it. And listen, cousin; we are to be quite happy. I have thought it all out, and I mean to be gay and amuse you.... Won't you look at me, Dorothy?" "Wh--why?" she asked, unsteadily.

"Just to see how happy I am--just to see that I pull no long faces--idiot that I was!... Dorothy, will you smile just once?"

"Yes," she whispered, lifting her head and raising her wet lashes. Presently her lips parted in one of her adorable smiles. "Now that you have made me weep till my nose is red you may pick me every strawberry in sight," she said, winking away the bright tears. "You have heard of the penance of the Algonquin witch?"

I knew nothing of Northern Indian lore, and I said so.

"What? You never heard of the Stonish Giants? You never heard of the Flying Head? Mercy on the boy! Sit here and we'll eat strawberries and I shall tell you tales of the Long House.... Sit nearer, for I shall speak in a low voice lest old Atotarho awake from his long sleep and the dead pines ring hollow, like witch-drums under the yellow-hammer's double blows.... Are you afraid?"

"All a-shiver," I whispered, gayly.

"Then listen," she breathed, raising one pink-tipped finger. "This is the tale of the Eight Thunders, told in the oldest tongue of the confederacy and to all ensigns of the three clans ere the Erians sued for peace. Therefore it is true.

"Long ago, the Holder of the Heavens made a very poisonous blue otter, and the Mohawks killed it and threw its body into the lake. And the Holder of Heaven came to the eastern door of the Long House and knocked, saying: 'Where is the very poisonous blue otter that I made, O Keepers of the Eastern Door?'

"'Who calls?' asked the Mohawks, peeping out to see.

"Then the Holder of the Heavens named himself, and the Mohawks were afraid and hid in the Long House, listening.

"'Be afraid! O you wise men and sachems! The wisdom of a child alone can save you!' said the Holder of the Heavens. Saying this he wrapped himself in a bright cloud and went like a swift arrow to the sun."

My cousin's voice had fallen into a low, melodious sing-song; her rapt eyes were fixed on me.

"A youth of the Mohawks loved a maid, and they sat by the lake at night, counting the Dancers in the sky--which we call stars of the Pleiades.

"'One has fallen into the lake,' said the youth.

"'It is the eye of the very poisonous blue otter,' replied the maid, beginning to cry.

"'I see the lost Dancer shining down under the water,' said the youth again. Then he bade the maid go back and wait for him; and she went back and built a fire and sat sadly beside it. Then she heard some one coming and turned around. A young man stood there dressed in white, and with white feathers on his head. 'You are sad,' he said to the maid, 'but we will help you.' Then he gave her a belt of purple wampum to show that he spoke the truth.

"'Follow,' he said; and she followed to a place in the forest where smoke rose.

There she saw a fire, and, around it, eight chiefs sitting, with white feathers on their heads.

"'These chiefs are the Eight Thunders,' she thought; 'now they will help me.' And she said: 'A Dancer has fallen out of the sky and a Mohawk youth has plunged for it.'

"'The blue otter has turned into a serpent, and the Mohawk youth beheld her eye under the waters,' they said, one after the other. The maid wept and laid the wampum at her feet. Then she rubbed ashes on her lips and on her breasts and in the palms of her hands.

"'The Mohawk youth has wedded the Lake Serpent,' they said, one after the other. The maid wept; and she rubbed ashes on her thighs and on her feet.

"'Listen,' they said, one after another; 'take strawberries and go to the lake. You will know what to do. When that is done we will come in the form of a cloud on the lake, not in the sky.'

"So she found strawberries in the starlight and went to the lake, calling, 'Friend! Friend! I am going away and wish to see you!'

"Out on the lake the water began to boil, and coming out of it she saw her friend. He had a spot on his forehead and looked like a serpent, and yet like a man. Then she spread the berries on the shore and he came to the land and ate. Then he went back to the shore and placed his lips to the water, drinking. And the maid saw him going down through the water like a snake. So she cried, 'Friends! Friends! I am going away and wish to see you!'

"The lake boiled and her friend came out of it. The lake boiled once more; not in one spot alone, but all over, like a high sea spouting on a reef.

"Out of the water came her friend's wife, beautiful to behold and shining with silver scales. Her long hair fell all around her, and seemed like silver and gold. When she came ashore she stretched out on the sand and took a strawberry between her lips. The young maid watched the lake until she saw something moving on the waters a great way off, which seemed like a cloud.

"In a moment the stars went out and it grew dark, and it thundered till the skies fell down, torn into rain by the terrible lightning. All was still at last, and it grew lighter. The maid opened her eyes to find herself in the arms of her friend. But at their feet lay the dying sparks of a shattered star.

"Then as they went back through the woods the eight chiefs passed them in Indian file, and they saw them rising higher and higher, till they went up to the sky like mists at sunrise."

Dorothy's voice died away; she stretched out one arm.

"This is the end, O you wise men and sachems, told since the beginning to us People of the Morning. Hiro [I have spoken]!"

Then a startling thing occurred; up from the underbrush behind us rose a tall Indian warrior, naked to the waist, painted from belt to brow with terrific, nameless emblems and signs. I sprang to my feet, horror-struck; the savage folded his arms, quietly smiling; and I saw knife and hatchet resting in his belt and a long rifle on the moss at his feet.

"Koue! That was a true tale," he said, in good English. "It is a miracle that one among you sings the truth concerning us poor Mohawks."

"Do you come in peace?" I asked, almost stunned.

He made a gesture. "Had I come otherwise, you had known it!" He looked straight at Dorothy. "You are the patroon's daughter. Does he speak as truthfully of the Mohawks as do you?"

"Who are you?" I asked, slowly.

He smiled again. "My name is Brant," he said.

"Joseph Brant! Thayendanegea!" murmured Dorothy, aloud.

"A cousin of his," said the savage, carelessly. Then he turned sternly on me. "Tell that man who follows me that I could have slain him twice within the hour; once at the ford, once on Stoner's hill. Does he take me for a deer? Does he believe I wear war-paint? There is no war betwixt the Mohawks and the Boston people--yet! Tell that fool to go home!"

"What fool?" I asked, troubled.

"You will meet him--journeying the wrong way," said the Indian, grimly.

With a quick, guarded motion he picked up his rifle, turned short, and passed swiftly northward straight into the forest, leaving us listening there together long after he had disappeared.

"That chief was Joseph Brant, ... but he wore no war-paint," whispered my cousin. "He was painted for the secret rites of the False-Faces."

"He could have slain us as we sat," I said, bitterly humiliated.

She looked up at me thoughtfully; there was not in her face the slightest trace of the deep emotions which had shocked me.

"A tribal fire is lighted somewhere," she mused. "Chiefs like Brant do not travel alone--unless--unless he came to consult that witch Catrine Montour, or to guide her to some national council-fire in the North."

She pondered awhile, and I stood by in silence, my heart still beating heavily from my astonishment at the hideous apparition of a moment since.

"Do you know," she said, "that I believe Brant spoke the truth. There is no war yet, as far as concerns the Mohawks. The smoke we saw was a secret signal; that hag was scuttling around to collect the False-Faces for a council. They may mean war; I'm sure they mean it, though Brant wore no war-paint. But war has not yet been declared; it is no scant ceremony when a nation of the Iroquois decides on war. And if the confederacy declares war the ceremonies may last a fortnight. The False-Faces must be heard from first. And, Heaven help us! I believe their fires are lighted now."

"What ghastly manner of folk are these False-Faces?" I asked.

"A secret clan, common to all Northern and Western Indians, celebrating secret rites among the six nations of the Iroquois. Some say the spectacle is worse than the orgies of the Dream-feast--a frightful sight, truly hellish; and yet others say the False-Faces do no harm, but make merry in secret places. But this I know; if the False-Faces are to decide for war or peace, they will sway the entire confederacy, and perhaps every Indian in North America; for though nobody knows who belongs to the secret sect, two-thirds of the Mohawks are said to be numbered in its ranks; and as go the Mohawks, so goes the confederacy."

"How is it you know all this?" I asked, amazed.

"My playmate was Magdalen Brant," she said. "Her playmates were pure Mohawk."

"Do you mean to tell me that this painted savage is kin to that lovely girl who came with Sir John and the Butlers?" I demanded.

"They are related. And, cousin, this 'painted savage' is no savage if the arts of civilization which he learned at Dr. Wheelock's school count for anything. He was secretary to old Sir William. He is an educated man, spite of his naked body and paint, and the more to be dreaded, it appears to me.... Hark! See those branches moving beside the trail! There is a man yonder. Follow me."

On the sandy bank our shoes made little sound, yet the unseen man heard us and threw up a glittering rifle, calling out: "Halt! or I fire."

Dorothy stopped short, and her hand fell on my arm, pressing it significantly. Out into the middle of the trail stepped a tall fellow clad from throat to ankle in deer-skin. On his curly head rested a little, round cap of silvery mole-skin, light as a feather; his leggings' fringe was dyed green; baldrick, knife-sheath, bullet-pouch, powder-horn, and hatchet-holster were deeply beaded in scarlet, white, and black, and bands of purple porcupine-quills edged shoulder-cape and moccasins, around which were painted orange-colored flowers, each centred with a golden bead.

"A forest-runner," she motioned with her lips, "and, if I'm not blind, he should answer to the name of Mount--and many crimes, they say."

The forest-runner stood alert, rifle resting easily in the hollow of his left arm.

"Who passes?" he called out.

"White folk," replied Dorothy, laughing. Then we stepped out.

"Well, well," said the forest-runner, lifting his mole-skin cap with a grin; "if this is not the pleasantest sight that has soothed my eyes since we hung that Tory whelp last Friday--and no disrespect to Mistress Varick, whose father is more patriot than many another I might name!"

"I bid you good-even, Jack Mount," said Dorothy, smiling.

"To you, Mistress Varick," he said, bowing the deeper; then glanced keenly at me and recognized me at the same moment. "Has my prophecy come true, sir?" he asked, instantly.

"God save our country," I said, significantly.

"Then I was right!" he said, and flushed with pleasure when I offered him my hand.

"If I am not too free," he muttered, taking my hand in his great, hard paw, almost affectionately.

"You may walk with us if you journey our way," said Dorothy; and the great fellow shuffled up beside her, cap in hand, and it amused me to see him strive to shorten his strides to hers, so that he presently fell into a strange gait, half-skip, half-toddle.

"Pray cover yourself," said Dorothy, encouragingly, and Mount did so, dumb as a Matanzas oyster and crimson as a boiled sea-crab. Then, doubtless, deeming that gentility required some polite observation, he spoke in a high-pitched voice of the balmy weather and the sweet profusion of birds and flowers, when there was more like to be a "sweet profusion" of Indians; and I nigh stifled with laughter to see this lumbering, free-voiced forest-runner transformed to a mincing, anxious, backwoods macaroni at the smile of a pretty woman.

"Do you bring no other news save of the birds and blossoms?" asked Dorothy, mischievously. "Tell us what we all are fearful of. Have the Senecas and Cayugas risen to join the British?"

Mount stole a glance at me.

"I wish I knew," he muttered.

"We will know soon, now," I said, soberly.

"Sooner, perhaps, than you expect, sir," he said. "I am summoned to the manor to confer with General Schuyler on this very matter of the Iroquois."

"Is it true that the Mohawks are in their war-paint?" asked Dorothy, maliciously.

"Stoner and Timothy Murphy say so," replied Mount. "Sir John and the Butlers are busy with the Onondagas and Oneidas; Dominic Kirkland is doing his best to keep them peaceable; and our General played his last cards at their national council. We can only wait and see, Mistress Varick."

He hesitated, glancing at me askance.

"The fact is," he said, "I've been sniffing at moccasin tracks for the last hour, up hill, down dale, over the ford, where I lost them, then circled and picked them up again on the moss a mile below the bridge. If I read them right, they were Mohawk tracks and made within the hour, and how that skulking brute got away from me I cannot think."

He looked at us in an injured manner, for we were striving not to smile.

"I'm counted a good tracker," he muttered. "I'm as good as Walter Butler or Tim Murphy, and my friend, the Weasel, now with Morgan's riflemen, is no keener forest-runner than am I. Oh, I do not mean to brag, or say I can match my cunning against such a human bloodhound as Joseph Brant."

He paused, in hurt surprise, for we were laughing. And then I told him of the Indian and what message he had sent by us, and Mount listened, red as a pippin, gnawing his lip.

"I am glad to know it," he said. "This will be evil news to General Schuyler, I have no doubt. Lord! but it makes me mad to think how close to Brant I stood and could not drill his painted hide!"

"He spared you," I said.

"That is his affair," muttered Mount, striding on angrily.

"There speaks the obstinate white man, who can see no good in any savage," whispered Dorothy. "Nothing an Indian does is right or generous; these forest-runners hate them, distrust them, fear them--though they may deny it--and kill all they can. And you may argue all day with an Indian-hater and have your trouble to pay you. Yet I have heard that this man Mount is brave and generous to enemies of his own color."

We had now come to the road in front of the house, and Mount set his cap rakishly on his head, straightened cape and baldrick, and ran his fingers through the gorgeous thrums rippling from sleeve and thigh.

"I'd barter a month's pay for a pot o' beer," he said to me. "I learned to drink serving with Cresap's riflemen at the siege of Boston; a godless company, sir, for an innocent man to fall among. But Morgan's rifles are worse, Mr. Ormond; they drink no water save when it rains in their gin toddy."

"Sir Lupus says you tried to join them," said Dorothy, to plague him.

"So I did, Mistress Varick, so I did," he stammered; "to break 'em o' their habits, ma'am. Trust me, if I had that corps I'd teach 'em to let spirits alone if I had to drink every drop in camp to keep 'em sober!"

"There's beer in the buttery," she said, laughing; "and if you smile at Tulip she'll see you starve not."

"Nobody," said I, "goes thirsty or hungry at Varick Manor."

"Indeed, no," said Dorothy, much amused, as old Cato came down the path, hat in hand. "Here, Cato! do you take Captain Mount and see that he is comfortable and that he lacks nothing."

So, standing together in the stockade gateway, we watched Cato conducting Mount towards the quarters behind the guard-house, then walked on to meet the children, who came dancing down the driveway to greet us.

"Dorothy! Dorothy!" cried Cecile, "we've shaved candles and waxed the library floors. Lady Schuyler is here and the General and the Carmichael girls we knew at school, and their cousin, Maddaleen Dirck, and Christie McDonald and Marguerite Haldimand--cousin to the Tory general in Canada--and--"

"I'm to walk a minuet with Madge Haldimand!" broke in Ruyven; "will you lend me your gold stock-buckle, Cousin Ormond?"

"I mean to dance, too," cried Harry, crowding up to pluck my sleeve. "Please, Cousin Ormond, lend me a lace handkerchief."

"Paltz Clavarack, of the Half-moon Regiment, asked me to walk a minuet," observed Cecile, tossing her head. "I'm sure I don't know what to say. He's so persistent."

Benny's clamor broke out: "Thammy thtole papath betht thnuff-boxth! Thammy thtole papath betht thnuff-boxth!"

"Sammy!" cried Dorothy, "what did you steal your father's best snuff-box for?"

"I only desired to offer snuff to General Schuyler," said Sammy, sullenly, amid a roar of laughter.

"We're to dine at eight! Everybody is dressing; come on, Dorothy!" cried Cecile. "Mr. Clavarack vowed he'd perish if I kept him waiting--"

"You should see the escort!" said Ruyven to me. "Dragoons, cousin, in leather helmets and jack-boots, and all wearing new sabres taken from the Hessian cavalry. They're in the quarters with Tim Murphy, of Morgan's, and, Lord! how thirsty they appear to be!"

"There's the handsomest man I ever saw," murmured Cecile to Dorothy, "Captain O'Neil, of the New York line. He's dying to see you; he said so to Mr. Clavarack, and I heard him."

Dorothy looked up with heightened color.

"Will you walk the minuet with me, Dorothy?" I whispered.

She looked down, faintly smiling:

"Perhaps," she said.

"That is no answer," I retorted, surprised and hurt.

"I know it," she said, demurely.

"Then answer me, Dorothy!"

She looked at me so gravely that I could not be certain whether it was pretence or earnest.

"I am hostess," she said; "I belong to my guests. If my duties prevent my walking the minuet with you, I shall find a suitable partner for you, cousin."

"And no doubt for yourself," I retorted, irritated to rudeness.

Surprise and disdain were in her eyes. Her raised brows and cool smile boded me no good.

"I thought I was free to choose," she said, serenely.

"You are, and so am I," I said. "Will you have me for the minuet?"

We paused in the hallway, facing each other.

She gave me a dangerous glance, biting her lip in silence.

And, the devil possessing me, I said, "For the last time, will you take me?"

"No!" she said, under her breath. "You have your answer now."

"I have my answer," I repeated, setting my teeth.

XII
THE GHOST-RING

I had bathed and dressed me in my best suit of pale-lilac silk, with flapped waist-coat of primrose stiff with gold, and Cato was powdering my hair; when Sir Lupus waddled in, magnificent in scarlet and white, and smelling to heaven of French perfume and pomatum.

"George!" he cried, in his brusque, explosive fashion, "I like Schuyler, and I care not who knows it! Dammy! I was cool enough with him and his lady when they arrived, but he played Valentine to my Orson till I gave up; yes, I did, George, I capitulated. Says he, 'Sir Lupus, if a painful misunderstanding has kept us old neighbors from an exchange of civilities, I trust differences may be forgotten in this graver crisis. In our social stratum there is but one great line of cleavage now, opened by the convulsions of war, sir.'

"'Damn the convulsions of war, sir!' says I.

"'Quite right,' says he, mildly; 'war is always damnable, Sir Lupus.'

"'General Schuyler,' says I, 'there is no nonsense about me. You and Lady Schuyler are under my roof, and you are welcome, whatever opinion you entertain of me and my fashion of living. I understand perfectly that this visit is not a visit of ceremony from a neighbor, but a military necessity.'

"'Sir Lupus,' says Lady Schuyler, 'had it been only a military necessity I should scarcely have accompanied the General and his guests.'

"'Madam,' says I, 'it is commonly reported that I offended the entire aristocracy of Albany when I had Sir John Johnson's sweetheart to dine with them. And for that I have been ostracized. For which ostracism, madam, I care not a brass farthing. And, madam, were I to dine all Albany to-night, I should not ignore my old neigh-bors and friends, the Putnams of Tribes Hill, to suit the hypocrisy of a few strangers from Albany. Right is right, madam, and decency is decency! And I say now that to honest men Claire Putnam is Sir John's wife by every law of honor, decency, and chivalry; and I shall so treat her in the face of a rotten world and to the undying shame of that beast, Sir John!'

"Whereupon--would you believe it, George?--Schuyler took both my hands in his and said my conduct honored me, and more of the same sort o' thing, and Lady Schuyler gave me her hand in that sweet, stately fashion; and, dammy! I saluted her finger-tips. Heaven knows how I found it possible to bend my waist, but I did, George. And there's an end to the whole matter!"

He took snuff, blew his nose violently, snapped his gold snuff-box, and waddled to the window, where, below, in the early dusk, torches and rush-lights burned, illuminating the cavalry horses tethered along their picket-rope, and the trooper on guard, pacing his beat, musket shining in the wavering light.

"That escort will be my undoing," he muttered. "Folk will dub me a partisan now. Dammy! a man under my roof is a guest, be he Tory or rebel. I do but desire to cultivate my land and pay my debts of honor; and I'll stick to it till they leave me in peace or hang me to my barn door!"

And he toddled out, muttering and fumbling with his snuff-box, bidding me hasten and not keep them waiting dinner.

I stood before the mirror with its lighted sconces, gazing grimly at my sober face while Cato tied my queue-ribbon and dusted my silken coat-skirts. Then I fastened the brilliant buckle under my chin, shook out the deep, soft lace at throat and wristband, and took my small-sword from Cato.

"Mars' George," murmured the old man, "yo' look lak yo' is gwine wed wif mah li'l Miss Dorry."

I stared at him angrily. "What put that into your head?" I demanded.

"I dunno, suh; hit dess look dat-a-way to me, suh."

"You're a fool," I said, sharply.

"No, suh, I ain' no fool, Mars' George. I done see de sign! Yaas, suh, I done see de sign."

"What sign?"

The old man chuckled, looked slyly at my left hand, then chuckled again.

"Mars' George, yo' is wearin' yo' weddin'-ring now!"

"A ring! There is no ring on my hand, you rascal!" I said.

"Yaas, suh; dey sho' is, Mars' George," he insisted, still chuckling.

"I tell you I never wear a ring," I said, impatiently.

"'Scuse me, Mars' George, suh," he said, humbly. And, lifting my left hand, laid it in his wrinkled, black palm, peering closely. I also looked, and saw at the base of my third finger a circle like the mark left by a wedding-ring.

"That is strange," I said; "I never wore a ring in all my life!"

"Das de sign, suh," muttered the old man; "das de Ormond sign, suh. Yo' pap wore de ghos'-ring, an' his pap wore it too, suh. All de Ormonds done wore de ghos'-ring fore dey wus wedded. Hit am dess dat-a-way. Mars' George--"

He hesitated, looking up at me with gentle, dim eyes.

"Miss Dorry, suh--"

He stopped short, then dropped his voice to a whisper.

"'Fore Miss Dorry git up outen de baid, suh, I done tote de bre'kfus in de mawnin'. An' de fustest word dat li'l Miss Dorry say, 'Cato,' she say, 'whar Mars' George?' she say. 'He 'roun' de yahd, Miss Dorry,' I say. ''Pears lak he gettin' mo' res'less an' mis'ble, Miss Dorry.'

"'Cato,' she 'low, 'I spec' ma' haid gwine ache if I lie hyah in dishyere baid mo'n two free day. Whar ma' milk an' co'n pone, Cato?'

"So I des sot de salver down side de baid, suh, an' li'l Miss Dorry she done set up in de baid, suh, an' hole out one li'l bare arm--"

He laid a wrinkled finger on his lips; his dark face quivered with mystery and emotion.

"One li'l bare arm," he repeated, "an' I see de sign!"

"What sign?" I stammered.

"De bride-sign on de ring-finger! Yaas, suh. An' I say, 'Whar yo' ring, Miss Dorry?' An' she 'low ain' nebber wore no ring. An' I say, 'Whar dat ring, Miss Dorry?'

"Den Miss Dorry look kinder queer, and rub de ghos'-ring on de bridal-finger.

"'What dat?' she 'low.

"'Dasser ghos'-ring, honey.'

"Den she rub an' rub, but, bless yo' heart, Mars' George! she dess natch'ly gwine wear dat pink ghos'-ring twill yo' slip de bride-ring on.... Mars' George! Honey! What de matter, chile?... Is you a-weepin', Mars' George?"

"Oh, Cato, Cato!" I choked, dropping my head on his shoulder.

"What dey do to mah l'il Mars' George?" he said, soothingly. "'Spec' some one done git saucy! Huh! Who care? Dar de sign! Dar de ghos'-ring! Mars' George, yo' is dess boun' to wed, suh! Miss Dorry, she dess boun' to wed, too--"

"But not with me, Cato, not with me. There's another man coming for Miss Dorry, Cato. She has promised him."

"Who dat?" he cried. "How come dishyere ghost-ring roun' yo' weddin'-finger?"

"I don't know," I said; "the chance pressure of a riding-glove, perhaps. It will fade away, Cato, this ghost-ring, as you call it.... Give me that rag o' lace; ... dust the powder away, Cato.... There, I'm smiling; can't you see, you rascal?... And tell Tulip she is right."

"What dat foolish wench done tole you?" he exclaimed, wrathfully.

But I only shook my head impatiently and walked out. Down the hallway I halted in the light of the sconces and looked at the strange mark on my finger. It was plainly visible. "A tight glove," I muttered, and walked on towards the stairs.

From the floor below came a breezy buzz of voices, laughter, the snap of ivory fans spreading, the whisk and rustle of petticoats. I leaned a moment over the rail which circled the stair-gallery and looked down.

Unaccustomed cleanliness and wax and candle-light made a pretty background for all this powdered and silken company swarming below. The servants and children had gathered ground-pine to festoon the walls; stair-rail, bronze cannon, pictures, trophies, and windows were all bright with the aromatic green foliage; enormous bunches of peonies perfumed the house, and everywhere masses of yellow and white elder-bloom and swamp-marigold brightened the corners.

Sir Lupus, standing in the hallway with a tall gentleman who wore the epaulets and the buff-and-blue uniform of a major-general, beckoned me, and I descended the stairs to make the acquaintance of that noblest and most generous of soldiers, Philip Schuyler. He held my hand a moment, scrutinizing me with kindly eyes, and, turning to Sir Lupus, said, "There are few men to whom my heart surrenders at sight, but your young kinsman is one of the few, Sir Lupus."

"He's a good boy, General, a brave lad," mumbled Sir Lupus, frowning to hide his pride. "A bit quick at conclusions, perhaps--eh, George?"

"Too quick, sir," I said, coloring.

"A fault you have already repaired by confession," said the General, with his kindly smile. "Mr. Ormond, I had the pleasure of receiving Sir George Covert the day he left for Stanwix, and Sir George mentioned your desire for a commission."

"I do desire it, sir," I said, quickly.

"Have you served, Mr. Ormond?" he asked, gravely.

"I have seen some trifling service against the Florida savages, sir."

"As officer, of course."

"As officer of our rangers, General."

"You were never wounded?"

"No, sir; ... not severely."

"Oh!... not severely."

"No, sir."

"There are some gentlemen of my acquaintance," said Schuyler, turning to Sir Lupus, "who might take a lesson in modesty from Mr. Ormond."

"Yes," broke out Sir Lupus--"that pompous ass, Gates."

"General Gates is a loyal soldier," said Schuyler, gravely.

"Who the devil cares?" fumed Sir Lupus. "I call a spade a spade! And I say he is at the head of that infamous cabal which seeks to disgrace you. Don't tell me, sir! I'm an older man than you, sir! I've a right to say it, and I do. Gates is an envious ass, and unfit to hold your stirrup!"

"This is a painful matter," said Schuyler, in a low voice. "Indiscreet friendship may make it worse. I regard General Gates as a patriot and a brother soldier.... Pray let us choose a gayer topic ... friends."

His manner was so noble, his courtesy so charming, that there was no sting in his snub to Sir Lupus. Even I had heard of the amazing jealousies and intrigues which had made Schuyler's life miserable--charges of incompetency, of indifference, of corruption--nay, some wretched creatures who sought to push Gates into Schuyler's command even hinted at cowardice and treason. And none could doubt that Gates knew it and encouraged it, for he had publicly spoken of Schuyler in slighting and contemptuous terms.

Yet the gentleman whose honor had been the target for these slanderers never uttered one word against his traducers: and, when a friend asked him whether he was too proud to defend himself, replied, serenely, "Not too proud, but too sensible to spread discord in my country's army."

"Lady Schuyler desires to know you," said the General, "for I see her fan-signal, which I always obey." And he laid his arm on mine as a father might, and led me across the room to where Dorothy stood with Lady Schuyler on her right, surrounded by a bevy of bright-eyed girls and gay young officers.

Dorothy presented me in a quiet voice, and I bowed very low to Lady Schuyler, who made me an old-time reverence, gave me her fingers to kiss, and spoke most kindly to me, inquiring about my journey, and how I liked this Northern climate.

Then Dorothy made me known to those near her, to the pretty Carmichael twins, whose black eyes brimmed purest mischief; to Miss Haldimand, whose cold beauty had set the Canadas aflame; and to others of whom I have little recollection save their names. Christie McDonald and Lysbet Dirck, two fashionable New York belles, kin to the Schuylers.

As for the men, there was young Paltz Clavarack, ensign in the Half-moon Regiment, very fine in his orange-faced uniform; and there was Major Harrow, of the New York line; and a jolly, handsome dare-devil, Captain Tully O'Neil, of the escort of horse, who hung to Dorothy's skirts and whispered things that made her laugh. There were others, too, aides in new uniforms, a medical officer, who bustled about in the role of everybody's friend; and a parcel of young subalterns, very serious, very red, and very grave, as though the destiny of empires reposed in their blue-and-gold despatch pouches.

"I wonder," murmured Dorothy, leaning towards me and speaking behind her rose-plumed fan--"I wonder why I answered you so."

"Because I deserved it," I muttered,

"Cousin I Cousin!" she said, softly, "you deserve all I can give--all that I dare not give. You break my heart with kindness."

I stepped to her side; all around us rose the hum of voices, laughter, the click of spurs, the soft sounds of silken gowns on a polished floor.

"It is you who are kind to me, Dorothy," I whispered, "I know I can never have you, but you must never doubt my constancy. Say you will not?"

"Hush!" she whispered; "come to the dining-hall; I must look at the table to see that all is well done, and there is nobody there.... We can talk there."

She slipped off through the throng, and I sauntered into the gun-room, from whence I crossed the hallway and entered the dining-hall. Dorothy stood inspecting the silver and linen, and giving orders to Cato in a low voice. Then she dismissed the row of servants and sat down in a leather chair, resting her forehead in her hands.

"Deary me! Deary me!" she murmured, "how my brain whirls!... I would I were abed!... I would I were dead!... What was it you said concerning constancy? Oh, I remember; I am never to doubt your constancy." She raised her fair head from between her hands.

"Promise you will never doubt it," I whispered.

"I--I never will," she said. "Ask me again for the minuet, dear. I--I refused everybody--for you."

"Will you walk it with me, Dorothy?"

"Yes--yes, indeed! I told them all I must wait till you asked me."

"Good heavens!" I said, laughing nervously, "you didn't tell them that, did you?"

She bent her lovely face, and I saw the smile in her eyes glimmering through unshed tears.

"Yes; I told them that. Captain O'Neil protests he means to call you out and run you through. And I said you would probably cut off his queue and tie him up by his spurs if he presumed to any levity. Then he said he'd tell Sir George Covert, and I said I'd tell him myself and everybody else that I loved my cousin Ormond better than anybody in the world and meant to wed him--"

"Dorothy!" I gasped.

"Wed him to the most, beautiful and lovely and desirable maid in America!"

"And who is that, if it be not yourself?" I asked, amazed.

"It's Maddaleen Dirck, the New York heiress, Lysbet's sister; and you are to take her to table."

"Dorothy," I said, angrily, "you told me that you desired me to be faithful to my love for you!"

"I do! Oh, I do!" she said, passionately. "But it is wrong; it is dreadfully wrong. To be safe we must both wed, and then--God knows!--we cannot in honor think of one another."

"It will make no difference," I said, savagely.

"Why, of course, it will!" she insisted, in astonishment. "We shall be married."

"Do you suppose love can be crushed by marriage?" I asked.

"The hope of it can."

"It cannot, Dorothy."

"It must be crushed!" she exclaimed, flushing scarlet. "If we both are tied by honor, how can we hope? Cousin, I think I must be mad to say it, but I never see you that I do not hope. We are not safe, I tell you, spite of all our vows and promises.... You do not need to woo me, you do not need to persuade me! Ere you could speak I should be yours, now, this very moment, for a look, a smile--were it not for that pale spectre of my own self which rises ever before me, stern, inexorable, blocking every path which leads to you, and leaving only that one path free where the sign reads 'honor.' ... And I--I am sometimes frightened lest, in an overwhelming flood of love, that sign be torn away and no spectre of myself rise to confront me, barring those paths that lead to you.... Don't touch me; Cato is looking at us.... He's gone.... Wait, do not leave me.... I have been so wretched and unhappy.... I could scarce find strength and heart to let them dress me, thinking on your face when I answered you so cruelly.... Oh, cousin! where are our vows now? Where are the solemn promises we made never to speak of love?... Lovers make promises like that in story-books-- and keep them, too, and die sanctified, blessing one another and mounting on radiant wings to heaven.... Where I should find no heaven save in you! Ah, God! that is the most terrible. That takes my heart away--to die and wake to find myself still his wife--to live through all eternity without you--and no hope of you--no hope!... For I could be patient through this earthly life, losing my youth and yours forever, ... but not after death! No, no! I cannot.... Better hell with you than endless heaven with him!... Don't speak to me.... Take your hand from my hand.... Can you not see that I mean nothing of what I say--that I do not know what I am saying?... I must go back; I am hostess--a happy one, as you perceive.... Will I never learn to curb my tongue? You must forget every word I uttered--do you hear me?"

She sprang up in her rustling silks and took a dozen steps towards the door, then turned.

"Do you hear me?" she said. "I bid you remember every word I uttered--every word!"

She was gone, leaving me staring at the flowers and silver and the clustered lights. But I saw them not; for before my eyes floated the vision of a slender hand, and on the wedding-finger I saw a faint, rosy circle, as I had seen it there a moment since, when Dorothy dropped her bare arms on the cloth and laid her head between them.

So it was true; whether for good or ill my cousin wore the ghost-ring which for ages, Cato says, we Ormonds have worn before the marriage-ring. There was Ormond blood in Dorothy. Did she wear the sign as prophecy for that ring Sir George should wed her with? I dared not doubt it--and yet, why did I also wear the sign?

Then in a flash the forgotten legend of the Maid-at-Arms came back to me, ringing through my ears in clamorous words:

"Serene, 'mid love's alarms,   For all time shall the Maids-at-Arms,   Wearing the ghost-ring, triumph with their constancy!"

I sprang to the door in my excitement and stared at the picture of the Maid-at-Arms.

Sweetly the violet eyes of the maid looked back at me, her armor glittered, her soft throat seemed to swell with the breath of life.

Then I crept nearer, eyes fixed on her wedding-finger. And I saw there a faint rosy circle as though a golden ring had pressed the snowy flesh.

XIII
THE MAID-AT-ARMS

I remember little of that dinner save that it differed vastly from the quarrelsome carousal at which the Johnsons and Butlers figured in so sinister a role, and at which the Glencoe captains disgraced themselves. But now, if the patroon's wine lent new color to the fair faces round me, there was no feverish laughter, nothing of brutal license. Healths were given and drunk with all the kindly ceremony to which I had been accustomed. At times pattering gusts of hand-clapping followed some popular toast, such as "Our New Flag," to which General Schuyler responded in perfect taste, veiling the deep emotions that the toast stirred in many with graceful allegory tempered by modesty and self-restraint.

At the former dinner I had had for my neighbors Dorothy and Magdalen Brant. Now I sat between Miss Haldimand and Maddaleen Dirck, whom I had for partner, a pretty little thing, who peppered her conversation with fashionable New York phrases and spiced the intervals with French. And I remember she assured me that New York was the only city fit to live in and that she should never survive a prolonged transportation from that earthly paradise of elegance and fashion. Which made me itch to go there.

I think, without meaning any unkindness, that Miss Haldimand, the Canadian beauty, was somewhat surprised that I had not already fallen a victim to her lovely presence; but, upon reflection, set it down to my stupidity; for presently she devoted her conversation exclusively to Ruyven, whose delight and gratitude could not but draw a smile from those who observed him. I saw Cecile playing the maiden's game with young Paltz Clavarack, and Lady Schuyler on Sir Lupus's right, charmingly demure, faintly amused, and evidently determined not to be shocked by the free bluntness of her host.

The mischievous Carmichael twins had turned the batteries of their eyes on two solemn, faultlessly dressed subalterns, and had already reduced them to the verge of capitulation; and busy, bustling Dr. Sleeper cracked witticisms with all who offered him the fee of their attention, and the dinner went very well.

Radiant, beautiful beyond word or thought, Dorothy sat, leaning back in her chair, and the candle-light on the frosty-gold of her hair and on her bare arms and neck made of her a miracle of celestial loveliness. And it was pleasant to see the stately General on her right bend beside her with that grave gallantry which young girls find more grateful than the privileged badinage of old beaus. At moments her sweet eyes stole towards me, and always found mine raised to greet her with that silent understanding which brought the faintest smile to her quiet lips. Once, above the melodious hum of voices, the word "war" sounded distinctly, and General Schuyler said:

"In these days of modern weapons of precision and long range, conflicts are doubly deplorable. In the times of the old match-locks and blunderbusses and unwieldly weapons weighing more than three times what our modern light rifles weigh, there was little chance for slaughter. But now that we have our deadly flint-locks, a battle-field will be a sad spectacle. Bunker Hill has taught the whole world a lesson that might not be in vain if it incites us to rid the earth of this wicked frenzy men call war."

"General," said Sir Lupus, "if weapons were twenty times as quick and deadly--which is, of course, impossible, thank God!--there would always be enough men in the world to get up a war, and enjoy it, too!"

"I do not like to believe that," said Schuyler, smiling.

"Wait and see," muttered the patroon. "I'd like to live a hundred years hence, just to prove I'm right."

"I should rather not live to see it," said the General, with a twinkle in his small, grave eyes.

Then quietly the last healths were given and pledged; Dorothy rose, and we all stood while she and Lady Schuyler passed out, followed by the other ladies; and I had to restrain Ruyven, who had made plans to follow Marguerite Haldimand. Then we men gathered once more over our port and walnuts, conversing freely, while the fiddles and bassoons tuned up from the hallway, and General Schuyler told us pleasantly as much of the military situation as he desired us to know. And it did amuse me to observe the solemn subalterns nodding all like wise young owlets, as though they could, if they only dared, reveal secrets that would astonish the General himself.

Snuff was passed, offered, and accepted with ceremony befitting; spirits replaced the port, but General Schuyler drank sparingly, and his well-trained suite perforce followed his example. So that when it came time to rejoin our ladies there was no evidence of wandering legs, no amiably vacant laughter, no loud voices to strike the postprandial discord at the dance or at the card-tables.

"How did I conduct, cousin?" whispered Ruyven, arm in arm with me as we entered the long drawing-room. And my response pleasing him, he made off straight towards Marguerite Haldimand, who viewed his joyous arrival none too cordially, I thought. Poor Ruyven! Must he so soon close the gate of Eden behind him?--leaving forever his immortal boyhood sleeping amid the never-fading flowers.

It was a fascinating and alarming spectacle to see Sir Lupus walking a minuet with Lady Schuyler, and I marvelled that the gold buttons on his waistcoat did not fly off in volleys when he strove to bend what once, perhaps, had been his waist.

Ceremony dictated what we had both forgotten, and General Schuyler led out Dorothy, who, scarlet in her distress, looked appealingly at me to see that I understood. And I smiled back to see her sweet face brighten with gratitude and confidence and a promise to make up to me what the stern rule of hospitality had deprived us of.

So it was that I had her for the Sir Roger de Coverley, and after that for a Delaware reel, which all danced with a delightful abandon, even Miss Haldimand unbending like a goddess surprised to find a pleasure in our mortal capers. And it was a pretty sight to see the ladies pass, gliding daintily under the arch of glittering swords, led by Lady Schuyler and Dorothy in laughing files, while the fiddle-bows whirred, and the music of bassoon and hautboys blended and ended in a final mellow crash. Then breathless voices rose, and skirts swished and French heels tapped the polished floor and solemn subalterns stalked about seeking ices and lost buckles and mislaid fans; and a faint voice said, "Oh!" when a jewelled garter was found, and a very red subaltern said, "Honi soit!" and everybody laughed.

Presently I missed the General, and, a moment later, Dorothy. As I stood in the hallway, seeking for her, came Cecile, crying out that they were to have pictures and charades, and that General Schuyler, who was to be a judge, awaited me in the gun-room.

The door of the gun-room was closed. I tapped and entered.

The General sat at the mahogany table, leaning back in his arm-chair; opposite sat Dorothy, bare elbows on the table, fingers clasped. Standing by the General, arms folded, Jack Mount loomed a colossal figure in his beaded buckskins.

"Ah, Mr. Ormond!" said the General, as I closed the door quietly behind me; "pray be seated. They are to have pictures and charades, you know; I shall not keep Miss Dorothy and yourself very long."

I seated myself beside Dorothy, exchanging a smile with Mount.

"Now," said the General, dropping his voice to a lower tone, "what was it you saw in the forest to-day?"

So Mount had already reported the apparition of the painted savage!

I told what I had seen, describing the Indian in detail, and repeating word for word his warning message to Mount.

The General looked inquiringly at Dorothy. "I understand," he said, "that you know as much about the Iroquois as the Iroquois do themselves."

"I think I do," she said, simply.

"May I ask how you acquired your knowledge, Miss Dorothy?"

"There have always been Iroquois villages along our boundary until last spring, when the Mohawks left with Guy Johnson," she said. "I have always played with Iroquois children; I went to school with Magdalen Brant. I taught among our Mohawks and Oneidas when I was thirteen. Then I was instructed by sachems and I learned what the witch-drums say, and I need use no signs in the six languages or the clan dialects, save only when I speak with the Lenni-Lenape. Maybe, too, the Hurons and Algonquins have words that I know not, for many Tuscaroras do not understand them save by sign."

"I wish that some of my interpreters had your knowledge, or a fifth of it," said the General, smiling. "Tell me, Miss Dorothy, who was that Indian and what did that paint mean?"

"The Indian was Joseph Brant, called Thayendanegea, which means, 'He who holds many peoples together,' or, in plainer words, 'A bundle of sticks.'"

"You are certain it was Brant?"

"Yes. He has dined at this table with us. He is an educated man." She hesitated, looking down thoughtfully at her own reflection in the polished table. "The paint he wore was not war-paint. The signs on his body were emblems of the secret clan called the 'False-Faces.'"

The General looked up at Jack Mount.

"What did Stoner say?" he asked.

"Stoner reports that all the Iroquois are making ready for some unknown rite, sir. He saw pyramids of flat river-stones set up on hills and he saw smoke answering smoke from the Adirondack peaks to the Mayfield hills."

"What did Timothy Murphy observe?" asked Schuyler, watching Mount intently.

"Murphy brings news of their witch, Catrine Montour, sir. He. chased her till he dropped--like all the rest of us--but she went on and on a running, hop! tap! hop! tap! and patter, patter, patter! It stirs my hair to think on her, and I'm no coward, sir. We call her 'The Toad-woman.'"

"I'll make you chief of scouts if you catch her," said the General, sharply.

"Very good, sir," replied Mount, pulling a wry face, which made us all laugh.

"It has been reported to me," said the General, quietly, "that the Butlers, father and son, are in this county to attend a secret council; and that, with the help of Catrine Montour, they expect to carry the Mohawk nation with them as well as the Cayugas and the Senecas.

"It has further been reported to me by the Palatine scout that the Onondagas are wavering, that the Oneidas are disposed to stand our friends, that the Tuscaroras are anxious to remain neutral.

"Now, within a few days, news has reached me that these three doubtful nations are to be persuaded by an unknown woman who is, they say, the prophetess of the False-Faces."

He paused, looking straight at Dorothy.

"From your knowledge," he said, slowly, "tell me who is this unknown woman."

"Do you not know, sir?" she asked, simply.

"Yes, I think I do, child. It is Magdalen Brant."

"Yes," she said, quietly; "from childhood she stood as prophetess of the False-Faces. She is an educated girl, sweet, lovable, honorable, and sincere. She has been petted by the fine ladies of New York, of Philadelphia, of Albany. Yet she is partly Mohawk."

"Not that charming girl whom I had to dinner?" I cried, astonished.

"Yes, cousin," she said, tranquilly. "You are surprised? Why? You should see, as I have seen, pupils from Dr. Wheelock's school return to their tribes and, in a summer, sink to the level of the painted sachem, every vestige of civilization vanished with the knowledge of the tongue that taught it."

"I have seen that," said Schuyler, frowning.

"And I--by your leave, sir--I have seen it, too!" said Mount, savagely. "There may be some virtue in the rattlesnake; some folk eat 'em! But there is none in an Indian, not even stewed--"

"That will do," said the General, ignoring the grim jest. "Do you speak the Iroquois tongues, or any of them?" he asked, wheeling around to address me.

"I speak Tuscarora, sir," I replied. "The Tuscaroras understand the other five nations, but not the Hurons or Algonquins."

"What tongue is used when the Iroquois meet?" he asked Dorothy.

"Out of compliment to the youngest nation they use the Tuscarora language," she said.

The General rose, bowing to Dorothy with a charming smile.

"I must not keep you from your charades any longer," he said, conducting her to the door and thanking her for the great help and profit he had derived from her knowledge of the Iroquois.

He had not dismissed us, so we awaited his return; and presently he appeared, calm, courteous, and walked up to me, laying a kindly hand on my shoulder.

"I want an officer who understands Tuscarora and who has felt the bite of an Indian bullet," he said, earnestly.

I stood silent and attentive.

"I want that officer to find the False-Faces' council-fire and listen to every word said, and report to me. I want him to use every endeavor to find this woman, Magdalen Brant, and use every art to persuade her to throw all her influence with the Onondagas, Oneidas, and Tuscaroras for their strict neutrality in this coming war. The service I require may be dangerous and may not. I do not know. Are you ready, Captain Ormond?"

"Ready, sir!" I said, steadily.

He drew a parchment from his breast-pocket and laid it in my hands. It was my commission in the armies of the United States of America as captain in the militia battalion of Morgan's regiment of riflemen, and signed by our Governor, George Clinton.

"Do you accept this commission, Mr. Ormond?" he asked, regarding me pleasantly.

"I do, sir."

Sir Lupus's family Bible lay on the window-sill; the General bade Mount fetch it, and he did so. The General placed it before me, and I laid my hand upon it, looking him in the face. Then, in a low voice, he administered the oath, and I replied slowly but clearly, ending, "So help me God," and kissed the Book.

"Sit down, sir," said the General; and when I was seated he told me how the Continental Congress in July of 1775 had established three Indian departments; how that he, as chief commissioner of this Northern department, which included the Six Nations of the Iroquois confederacy, had summoned the national council, first at German Flatts, then at Albany; how he and the Reverend Mr. Kirkland and Mr. Dean had done all that could be done to keep the Iroquois neutral, but that they had not fully prevailed against the counsels of Guy Johnson and Brant, though the venerable chief of the Mohawk upper castle had seemed inclined to neutrality. He told me of General Herkimer's useless conference with Brant at Unadilla, where that chief had declared that "The King of England's belts were still lodged with the Mohawks, and that the Mohawks could not violate their pledges."

"I think we have lost the Mohawks," said the General, thoughtfully. "Perhaps also the Senecas and Cayugas; for this she-devil, Catrine Montour, is a Huron-Seneca, and her nation will follow her. But, if we can hold the three other nations back, it will be a vast gain to our cause--not that I desire or would permit them to do battle for me, though our Congress has decided to enlist such Indians as wish to serve; but because there might be some thousand warriors the less to hang on our flanks and do the dreadful work among the people of this country which these people so justly fear."

He rose, nodding to me, and I followed him to the door.

"Now," he said, "you know what you are to do."

"When shall I set out, sir?" I asked.

He smiled, saying, "I shall give you no instructions, Captain Ormond; I shall only concern myself with results."

"May I take with me whom I please?"

"Certainly, sir."

I looked at Mount, who had been standing motionless by the door, an attentive spectator.

"I will take the rifleman Mount," I said, "unless he is detailed for other service--"

"Take him, Mr. Ormond. When do you wish to start? I ask it because there is a gentleman at Broadalbin who has news for you, and you must pass that way."

"May I ask who that is?" I inquired, respectfully.

"The gentleman is Sir George Covert, captain on my personal staff, and now under your orders."

"I shall set out to-night, sir," I said, abruptly; then stepped back to let him pass me into the hallway beyond.

"Saddle my mare and make every preparation," I said to Mount. "When you are ready lead the horses to the stockade gate.... How long will you take?"

"An hour, sir, for rubbing down, saddling, and packing fodder, ammunition, and provisions."

"Very well," I said, soberly, and walked out to the long drawing-room, where the company had taken chairs and were all whispering and watching a green baize curtain which somebody had hung across the farther end of the room.

"Charades and pictures," whispered Cecile, at my elbow. "I guessed two, and Mr. Clavarack says it was wonderful."

"It certainly was," I said, gravely. "Where is Ruyven? Oh, sitting with Miss Haldimand? Cecile, would you ask Miss Haldimand's indulgence for a few moments? I must speak to Sir Lupus and to you and Ruyven."

I stepped back of the rows of chairs to where Sir Lupus sat in his great arm-chair by the doorway; and in another moment Cecile and Ruyven came up, the latter polite but scarcely pleased to be torn away from his first inamorata.

"Sir Lupus, and you, Cecile and Ruyven," I said, in a low voice, "I am going on a little journey, and shall be absent for a few days, perhaps longer. I wish to take this opportunity to say good-bye, and to thank you all for your great kindness to me."

"Where the devil are you going?" snapped Sir Lupus.

"I am not at liberty to say, sir; perhaps General Schuyler may tell you."

The patroon looked up at me sorrowfully. "George! George!" he said, "has it touched us already?"

"Yes, sir," I muttered.

"What?" whispered Cecile.

"Father means the war. Our cousin Ormond is going to the war," exclaimed Ruyven, softly.

There was a pause; then Cecile flung both arms around my neck and kissed me in choking silence. The patroon's great, fat hand sought mine and held it; Ruyven placed his arm about my shoulder. Never had I imagined that I could love these kinsmen of mine so dearly.

"There's always a bed for you here; remember that, my lad," growled the patroon.

"Take me, too," sniffed Ruyven.

"Eh! What?" cried the patroon. "I'll take you; oh yes--over my knee, you impudent puppy! Let me catch you sneaking off to this war and I'll--"

Ruyven relapsed into silence, staring at me in troubled fascination.

"The house is yours, George," grunted the patroon. "Help yourself to what you need for your journey."

"Thank you, sir; say good-bye to the children, kiss them all for me, Cecile. And don't run away and get married until I come back."

A stifled snivel was my answer.

Then into the room shuffled old Cato, and began to extinguish the candles; and I saw the green curtain twitch, and everybody whispered "Ah-h!"

General Schuyler arose in the dim light when the last candle was blown out. "You are to guess the title of this picture!" he said, in his even, pleasant voice. "It is a famous picture, familiar to all present, I think, and celebrated in the Old World as well as in the New.... Draw the curtain, Cato!"

Suddenly the curtain parted, and there stood the living, breathing figure of the

"Maid-at-Arms." Her thick, gold hair clouded her cheeks, her eyes, blue as wood-violets, looked out sweetly from the shadowy background, her armor glittered.

A stillness fell over the dark room; slowly the green curtains closed; the figure vanished.

There was a roar of excited applause in my ears as I stumbled forward through the darkness, groping my way towards the dim gun-room through which she must pass to regain her chamber by the narrow stairway which led to the attic.

She was not there; I waited a moment, listening in the darkness, and presently I heard, somewhere overhead, a faint ringing sound and the deadened clash of armed steps on the garret floor.

"Dorothy!" I called.

The steps ceased, and I mounted the steep stairway and came out into the garret, and saw her standing there, her armor outlined against the window and the pale starlight streaming over her steel shoulder-pieces.

I shall never forget her as she stood looking at me, her steel-clad figure half buried in the darkness, yet dimly apparent in its youthful symmetry where the starlight fell on the curve of cuisse and greave, glimmering on the inlaid gorget with an unearthly light, and stirring pale sparks like fire-flies tangled in her hair.

"Did I please you?" she whispered. "Did I not surprise you? Cato scoured the armor for me; it is the same armor she wore, they say--the Maid-at-Arms. And it fits me like my leather clothes, limb and body. Hark!... They are applauding yet! But I do not mean to spoil the magic picture by a senseless repetition.... And some are sure to say a ghost appeared.... Why are you so silent?... Did I not please you?"

She flung casque and sword on the floor, cleared her white forehead from its tumbled veil of hair; then bent nearer, scanning my eyes closely.

"Is aught amiss?" she asked, under her breath.

I turned and slowly traversed the upper hallway to her chamber door, she walking beside me in silence, striving to read my face.

"Let your maids disarm you," I whispered; "then dress and tap at my door. I shall be waiting."

"Tell me now, cousin."

"No; dress first."

"It will take too long to do my hair. Oh, tell me! You have frightened me."

"It is nothing to frighten you," I said. "Put off your armor and come to my door. Will you promise?"

"Ye-es," she faltered; and I turned and hastened to my own chamber, to pre-pare for the business which lay before me.

I dressed rapidly, my thoughts in a whirl; but I had scarcely slung powder-horn and pouch, and belted in my hunting-shirt, when there came a rapping at the door, and I opened it and stepped out into the dim hallway.

At sight of me she understood, and turned quite white, standing there in her boudoir-robe of China silk, her heavy, burnished hair in two loose braids to her waist.

In silence I lifted her listless hands and kissed the fingers, then the cold wrists and palms. And I saw the faint circlet of the ghost-ring on her bridal finger, and touched it with my lips.

Then, as I stepped past her, she gave a low cry, hiding her face in her hands, and leaned back against the wall, quivering from head to foot.

"Don't go!" she sobbed. "Don't go--don't go!"

And because I durst not, for her own sake, turn or listen, I reeled on, seeing nothing, her faint cry ringing in my ears, until darkness and a cold wind struck me in the face, and I saw horses waiting, black in the starlight, and the gigantic form of a man at their heads, fringed cape blowing in the wind.

"All ready?" I gasped.

"All is ready and the night fine! We ride by Broadalbin, I think.... Whoa! back up! you long-eared ass! D'ye think to smell a Mohawk?... Or is it your comrades on the picket-rope that bedevil you?... Look at the troop-horses, sir, all a-rolling on their backs in the sand, four hoofs waving in the air. It's easier on yon sentry than when they're all a-squealin' and a-bitin'--This way, sir. We swing by the bush and pick up the Iroquois trail 'twixt the Hollow and Mayfield."

XIV
ON DUTY

As we galloped into Broadalbin Bush a house on our right loomed up black and silent, and I saw shutters and doors swinging wide open, and the stars shining through. There was something sinister in this stark and tenant-less homestead, whose void casements stared, like empty eye-sockets.

"They have gone to the Middle Fort--all of them except the Stoners," said Mount, pushing his horse up beside mine. "Look, sir! See what this red terror has already done to make a wilderness of County Try on--and not a blow struck yet!"

We passed another house, doorless, deserted; and as I rode abreast of it, to my horror I saw two shining eyes staring out at me from the empty window.

"A wolf--already!" muttered Mount, tugging at his bridle as his horse sheered off, snorting; and I saw something run across the front steps and drop into the shadows.

The roar of the Kennyetto sounded nearer. Woods gave place to stump-fields in which the young corn sprouted, silvered by the stars. Across a stony pasture we saw a rushlight burning in a doorway; and, swinging our horses out across a strip of burned stubble, we came presently to Stoner's house and heard the noise of the stream rushing through the woods below.

I saw Sir George Covert immediately; he was sitting on a log under the window, dressed in his uniform, a dark military cloak mantling his shoulders and knees. When he recognized me he rose and came to my side.

"Well, Ormond," he said, quietly, "it's a comfort to see you. Leave your horses with Elerson. Who is that with you--oh, Jack Mount? These are the riflemen, Elerson and Murphy--Morgan's men, you know."

The two riflemen saluted me with easy ceremony and sauntered over to where

Mount was standing at our horses' heads.

"Hello, Catamount Jack," said Elerson, humorously. "Where 'd ye steal the squaw-buckskins? Look at the macaroni, Tim--all yellow and purple fringe!"

Mount surveyed the riflemen in their suits of brown holland and belted rifle-frocks.

"Dave Elerson, you look like a Quakeress in a Dutch jerkin," he observed.

"'Tis the nate turrn to yere leg he grudges ye," said Murphy to Elerson. "Wisha, Dave, ye've the legs av a beau!"

"Bow-legs, Dave," commented Mount. "It's not your fault, lad. I've seen 'em run from the Iroquois as fast as Tim's--"

The bantering reply of the big Irishman was lost to me as Sir George led me out of earshot, one arm linked in mine.

I told him briefly of my mission, of my new rank in the army. He congratulated me warmly, and asked, in his pleasant way, for news of the manor, yet did not name Dorothy, which surprised me to the verge of resentment. Twice I spoke of her, and he replied courteously, yet seemed nothing eager to learn of her beyond what I volunteered.

And at last I said: "Sir George, may I not claim a kinsman's privilege to wish you joy in your great happiness?"

"What happiness?" he asked, blankly; then, in slight confusion, added: "You speak of my betrothal to your cousin Dorothy. I am stupid beyond pardon, Ormond; I thank you for your kind wishes.... I suppose Sir Lupus told you," he added, vaguely.

"My cousin Dorothy told me," I said.

"Ah! Yes--yes, indeed. But it is all in the future yet, Ormond." He moved on, switching the long weeds with a stick he had found. "All in the future," he murmured, absently--"in fact, quite remote, Ormond.... By-the-way, you know why you were to meet me?"

"No, I don't," I replied, coldly.

"Then I'll tell you. The General is trying to head off Walter Butler and arrest him. Murphy and Elerson have just heard that Walter Butler's mother and sister, and a young lady, Magdalen Brant--you met her at Varicks'--are staying quietly at the house of a Tory named Beacraft. We must strive to catch him there; and, failing that, we must watch Magdalen Brant, that she has no communication with the Iroquois." He hesitated, head bent. "You see, the General believes that this young girl can sway the False-Faces to peace or war. She was once their pet--as a child.... It seems hard to believe that this lovely and cultivated young girl could revert to such savage customs.... And yet Murphy and Elerson credit it, and say that she will surely appear at the False-Faces' rites.... It is horrible, Ormond; she is a sweet child--by Heaven, she would turn a European court with her wit and beauty!"

"I concede her beauty," I said, uneasy at his warm praise, "but as to her wit, I confess I scarcely exchanged a dozen words with her that night, and so am no judge."

"Ah!" he said, with an absent-minded stare.

"I naturally devoted myself to my cousin Dorothy," I added, irritated, without knowing why.

"Quite so--quite so," he mused. "As I was saying, it seems cruel to suspect Magdalen Brant, but the General believes she can sway the Oneidas and Tusca-roras.... It is a ghastly idea. And if she does attempt this thing, it will be through the infernal machinations and devilish persuasions of the Butlers--mark that, Or-mond!"

He turned short in his tracks and made a fierce gesture with his stick. It broke short, and he flung the splintered ends into the darkness.

"Why," he said, warmly, "there is not a gentler, sweeter disposition in the world than Magdalen Brant's, if no one comes a-tampering to wake the Iroquois blood in her. These accursed Butlers seem inspired by hell itself--and Guy Johnson!--What kind of a man is that, to take this young girl from Albany, where she had forgotten what a council-fire meant, and bring her here to these savages--sacrifice her!--undo all those years of culture and education!--rouse in her the dormant traditions and passions which she had imbibed with her first milk, and which she forgot when she was weaned! That is the truth, I tell you! I know, sir! It was my uncle who took her from Guy Park and sent her to my aunt Livingston. She had the best of schooling; she was reared in luxury; she had every advantage that could be gained in Albany; my aunt took her to London that she might acquire those graces of deportment which we but roughly imitate.... Is it not sickening to see Guy Johnson and Sir John exercise their power of relationship and persuade her from a good home back to this?... Think of it, Ormond!"

"I do think of it," said I. "It is wrong--it is cruel and shameful!"

"It is worse," said Sir George, bitterly. "Scarce a year has she been at Guy Park, yet to-day she is in full sympathy with Guy and Sir John and her dusky kinsman, Brant. Outwardly she is a charming, modest maid, and I do not for an instant mean you to think she is not chaste! The Irish nation is no more famed for its chastity than the Mohawk, but I know that she listens when the forest calls--listens with savant ears, Ormond, and her dozen drops of dusky blood set her pulses flying to the free call of the Wolf clan!"

"Do you know her well?" I asked.

"I? No. I saw her at my aunt Livingston's. It was the other night that I talked long with her--for the first time in my life."

He stood silent, knee-deep in the dewy weeds, hand worrying his sword-hilt, long cloak flung back.

"You have no idea how much of a woman she is," he said, vaguely.

"In that case," I replied, "you might influence her."

He raised his thoughtful face to the stars, studying the Twin Pointers.

"May I try?" he asked.

"Try? Yes, try, in Heaven's name, Sir George! If she must speak to the Oneidas, persuade her to throw her influence for peace, if you can. At all events, I shall know whether or not she goes to the fire, for I am charged by the General to find the False-Faces and report to him every word said.... Do you speak Tuscarora, Sir George?"

"No; only Mohawk," he said. "How are you going to find the False-Faces' meeting-place?"

"If Magdalen Brant goes, I go," said I. "And while I'm watching her, Jack Mount is to range, and track any savage who passes the Iroquois trail.... What do you mean to do with Murphy and Elerson?"

"Elerson rides back to the manor with our horses; we've no further use for them here. Murphy follows me.... And I think we should be on our way," he added, impatiently.

We walked back to the house, where old man Stoner and his two big boys stood with our riflemen, drinking flip.

"Elerson," I said, "ride my mare and lead the other horses back to Varicks'. Murphy, you will pilot us to Beacraft's. Jack, go forward with Murphy."

Old Stoner wiped his mouth with the back of his hand, bit into a twist of tobacco, spat derisively, and said: "This pup Beacraft swares he'll lift my haar 'fore he gits through with me! Threatened men live long. Kindly tell him me an' my sons is to hum. Sir George."

The big, lank boys laughed, and winked at me as I passed.

"Good trail an' many skelps to ye!" said old Stoner. "If ye see Francy McCraw, jest tell him thar's a rope an' a apple-tree waitin' fur him down to Fundy's Bush!"

"Tell Danny Redstock an' Billy Bones that the Stoner boys is smellin' almighty close on their trail!" called out the elder youth.

Elerson, in his saddle, gathered the bridles that Mount handed him and rode off into the darkness, leading Mount's horse and Sir George's at a trot. We filed off due west, Murphy and Mount striding in the lead, the noise of the river below us on our left. A few rods and we swung south, then west into a wretched stump-road, which Sir George said was the Mayfield road and part of the Sacandaga trail.

The roar of the Kennyetto accompanied us, then for a while was lost in the swaying murmur of the pines. Twice we passed trodden carrying-places before the rushing of the river sounded once more far below us in a gorge; and we descended into a hollow to a ford from which an Indian trail ran back to the north. This was the Balston trail, which joined the Fish-House road; and Sir George said it was the trail I should have followed had it not been necessary for me to meet him at Fonda's Bush to relieve him of his horse.

Now, journeying rapidly west, our faces set towards the Mayfield hills, we passed two or three small, cold brooks, on stepping-stones, where the dark sky, set with stars, danced in the ripples. Once, on a cleared hill, we saw against the sky the dim bulk of a lonely barn; then nothing more fashioned by human hands until, hours later, we found Murphy and Mount standing beside some rough pasture bars in the forest. How they had found them in the darkness of the woods--for we had long since left the stump-road--I do not know; but the bars were there, and a brush fence; and Murphy whispered that, beyond, a cow-path led to Beacraft's house.

Now, wary of ambuscade, we moved on, rifles primed and cocked, traversing a wet path bowered by willow and alder, until we reached a cornfield, fenced with split rails. The path skirted this, continuing under a line of huge trees, then ascended a stony little hill, on which a shadowy house stood.

"Beacraft's," whispered Murphy.

Sir George suggested that we surround the house and watch it till dawn; so Mount circled the little hill and took station in the north, Sir George moved eastward, Murphy crept to the west, and I sat down under the last tree in the lane, cocked rifle on my knees, pan sheltered under my round cap of doeskin.

Sunrise was to be our signal to move forward. The hours dragged; the stars grew no paler; no sign of life appeared in the ghostly house save when the west wind brought to me a faint scent of smoke, invisible as yet above the single chimney.

But after a long while I knew that dawn was on the way towards the western hills, for a bird twittered restlessly in the tree above me, and I began to feel, rather than hear, a multitude of feathered stirrings all about me in the darkness.

Would dawn never come? The stars seemed brighter than ever--no, one on the eastern horizon twinkled paler; the blue-black sky had faded; another star paled; others lost their diamond lustre; a silvery pallor spread throughout the east, while the increasing chorus of the birds grew in my ears.

Then a cock-crow rang out, close by, and the bird o' dawn's clear fanfare roused the feathered world to a rushing outpour of song.

All the east was yellow now; a rose-light quivered behind the forest like the shimmer of a hidden fire; then a blinding shaft of light fell across the world.

Springing to my feet, I shouldered my rifle and started across the pasture, ankle deep in glittering dew; and as I advanced Sir George appeared, breasting the hill from the east; Murphy's big bulk loomed in the west; and, as we met before the door of the house, Jack Mount sauntered around the corner, chewing a grass-stem, his long, brown rifle cradled in his arm.

"Rap on the door, Mount," I said. Mount gave a round double rap, chewed his grass-stem, considered, then rapped again, humming to himself in an under-tone:

> "Is the old fox in?
> Is the old fox out?
> Is the old fox gone to Glo-ry?
> Oh, he's just come in,

But he's just gone out,
And I hope you like my sto-ry!
Tink-a-diddle-diddle-diddle,
Tink-a-diddle-diddle-dum--"

"Rap louder," I said.
Mount obeyed, chewed reflectively, and scratched his ear.

"Is the Tory in?
Is the Tory out?
Is the Tory gone to Glo-ry?
Oh, he's just come in.
But he's just gone out--"

"Knock louder," I repeated.
Murphy said he could drive the door in with his gun-butt; I shook my head.
"Somebody's coming," observed Mount--

"Tink-a-diddle-diddle--"

The door opened and a lean, dark-faced man appeared, dressed in his smalls and shirt. He favored us with a sour look, which deepened to a scowl when he recognized Mount, who saluted him cheerfully.

"Hello, Beacraft, old cock! How's the mad world usin' you these palmy, balmy days?"

"Pretty well," said Beacraft, sullenly.

"That's right, that's right," cried Mount. "My friends and I thought we'd just drop around. Ain't you glad, Beacraft, old buck?"

"Not very," said Beacraft.

"Not very!" echoed Mount, in apparent dismay and sorrow. "Ain't you enj'yin' good health, Beacraft?"

"I'm well, but I'm busy," said the man, slowly.

"So are we, so are we," cried Mount, with a brisk laugh. "Come in, friends; you must know my old acquaintance Beacraft better; a King's man, gentlemen, so we can all feel at home now!"

For a moment Beacraft looked as though he meant to shut the door in our faces, but Mount's huge bulk was in the way, and we all followed his lead, entering a large, unplastered room, part kitchen, part bedroom.

"A King's man," repeated Mount, cordially, rubbing his hands at the smouldering fire and looking around in apparent satisfaction. "A King's man; what the nasty rebels call a 'Tory,' gentlemen. My! Ain't this nice to be all together so friendly and cosey with my old friend Beacraft? Who's visitin' ye, Beacraft? Anybody sleepin' up-stairs, old friend?"

Beacraft looked around at us, and his eyes rested on Sir George.

"Who be you?" he asked.

"This is my friend, Mr. Covert," said Mount, fairly sweating cordiality from every pore--"my dear old friend, Mr. Covert--"

"Oh," said Beacraft, "I thought he was Sir George Covert.... And yonder stands your dear old friend Timothy Murphy, I suppose?"

"Exactly," smiled Mount, rubbing his palms in appreciation.

The man gave me an evil look.

"I don't know you," he said, "but I could guess your business." And to Mount: "What do you want?"

"We want to know," said I, "whether Captain Walter Butler is lodging here?"

"He was," said Beacraft, grimly; "he left yesterday."

"And I hope you like my sto-ry!"

hummed Mount, strolling about the room, peeping into closets and cupboards, poking under the bed with his rifle, and finally coming to a halt at the foot of the stairs with his head on one side, like a jay-bird immersed in thought.

Murphy, who had quietly entered the cellar, returned empty-handed, and, at a signal from me, stepped outside and seated himself on a chopping-block in the yard, from whence he commanded a view of the house and vicinity.

"Now, Mr. Beacraft," I said, "whoever lodges above must come down; and it would be pleasanter for everybody if you carried the invitation."

"Do you propose to violate the privacy of my house?" he asked.

"I certainly do."

"Where is your warrant of authority?" he inquired, fixing his penetrating eyes on mine.

"I have my authority from the General commanding this department. My instructions are verbal--my warrant is military necessity. I fear that this explanation must satisfy you."

"It does not," he said, doggedly.

"That is unfortunate," I observed. "I will give you one more chance to answer my question. What person or persons are on the floor above?"

"Captain Butler was there; he departed yesterday with his mother and sister," replied Beacraft, maliciously.

"Is that all?"

"Miss Brant is there," he muttered.

I glanced at Sir George, who had risen to pace the floor, throwing back his military cloak. At sight of his uniform Beacraft's small eyes seemed to dart fire.

"What were you doing when we knocked?" I inquired.

"Cooking," he replied, tersely.

"Then cook breakfast for us all--and Miss Brant," I said. "Mount, help Mr. Beacraft with the corn-bread and boil those eggs. Sir George, I want Murphy to stay outside, so if you would spread the cloth--"

"Of course," he said, nervously; and I started up the flimsy wooden stairway, which shook as I mounted. Beacraft's malignant eyes followed me for a moment, then he thrust his hands into his pockets and glowered at Mount, who, whistling cheerfully, squatted before the fireplace, blowing the embers with a pair of home-made bellows.

On the floor above, four doors faced the narrow passage-way. I knocked at one. A gentle, sleepy voice answered:

"Very well."

Then, in turn, I entered each of the remaining rooms and searched. In the first room there was nothing but a bed and a bit of mirror framed in pine; in the second, another bed and a clothes-press which contained an empty cider-jug and a tattered almanac; in the third room a mattress lay on the floor, and beside it two ink-horns, several quills, and a sheet of blue paper, such as comes wrapped around a sugar-loaf. The sheet of paper was pinned to the floor with pine splinters, as though a draughtsman had prepared it for drawing some plan, but there were no lines on it, and I was about to leave it when a peculiar odor in the close air of the room brought me back to re-examine it on both sides.

There was no mark on the blue surface. I picked up an ink-horn, sniffed it, and spilled a drop of the fluid on my finger. The fluid left no stain, but the odor I had noticed certainly came from it. I folded the paper and placed it in my beaded pouch, then descended the stairs, to find Mount stirring the corn-bread and Sir George laying a cloth over the kitchen table, while Beacraft sat moodily by the window, watching everybody askance. The fire needed mending and I used the bellows. And, as I knelt there on the hearth, I saw a milky white stain slowly spread over the finger which I had dipped into the ink-horn. I walked to the door and stood in the cool morning air. Slowly the white stain disappeared.

"Mount," I said, sharply, "you and Murphy and Beacraft will eat your breakfast at once--and be quick about it." And I motioned Murphy into the house and sat down on an old plough to wait.

Through the open door I could see the two big riflemen plying spoon and knife, while Beacraft picked furtively at his johnny-cake, eyes travelling restlessly from Mount to Murphy, from Sir George to the wooden stairway.

My riflemen ate like hounds after a chase, tipping their porridge-dishes to scrape them clean, then bolted eggs and smoking corn-bread in a trice, and rose, taking Beacraft with them to the doorway.

"Fill your pipes, lads," I said. "Sit out in the sun yonder. Mr. Beacraft may have some excellent stories to tell you."

"I must do my work," said Beacraft, angrily, but Mount and Murphy each took an arm and led the unwilling man across the strip of potato-hills to a grassy knoll under a big oak, from whence a view of the house and clearing could be obtained. When I entered the house again, Sir George was busy removing soiled plates and ar- ranging covers for three; and I sat down close to the fire, drawing the square of blue paper from my pouch and spreading it to the blaze. When it was piping hot I laid it upon my knees and examined the design. What I had before me was a well-drawn map of the Kingsland district, made in white outline, showing trails and distances between farms. And, out of fifty farms marked, forty-three bore the word "Rebel," and were ornamented by little red hatchets.

Also, to every house was affixed the number, sex, and age of its inhabitants, even down to the three-months babe in the cradle, the number of cattle, the amount of grain in the barns.

Further, the Kingsland district of the county was divided into three sections, the first marked "McCraw's Operations," the second "Butler and Indians," the third "St. Leger's Indians and Royal Greens." The paper was signed by Uriah Beacraft.

After a few moments I folded this carefully prepared plan for deliberate and wholesale murder and placed it in my wallet.

Sir George looked up at me with a question in his eyes. I nodded, saying: "We have enough to arrest Beacraft. If you cannot persuade Magdalen Brant, we must arrest her, too. You had best use all your art, Sir George."

"I will do what I can," he said, gravely.

A moment later a light step sounded on the stairs; we both sprang to our feet and removed our hats. Magdalen Brant appeared, fresh and sweet as a rose-peony on a dewy morning.

"Sir George!" she exclaimed, in flushed dismay--"and you, too, Mr. Ormond!"

Sir George bowed, laughingly, saying that our journey had brought us so near her that we could not neglect to pay our respects.

"Where is Mr. Beacraft?" she said, bewildered, and at the same moment caught sight of him through the open doorway, seated under the oak-tree, apparently in delightful confab with Murphy and Mount.

"I do not quite understand," she said, gazing steadily at Sir George. "We are King's people here. And you--"

She looked at his blue-and-buff uniform, shaking her head, then glanced at me in my fringed buckskins.

"I trust this war cannot erase the pleasant memories of other days, Miss Brant," said Sir George, easily. "May we not have one more hour together before the storm breaks?"

"What storm, Sir George?" she asked, coloring up.

"The British invasion," I said. "We have chosen our colors; your kinsmen have chosen theirs. It is a political, not a personal difference, Miss Brant, and we may honorably clasp hands until our hands are needed for our hilts."

Sir George, graceful and debonair, conducted her to her place at the rough table; I served the hasty-pudding, making a jest of the situation. And presently we were eating there in the sunshine of the open doorway, chatting over the dinner at Varicks', each outvying the others to make the best of an unhappy and delicate situation.

Sir George spoke of the days in Albany spent with his aunt, and she responded in sensitive reserve, which presently softened under his gentle courtesy, leaving her beautiful, dark eyes a trifle dim and her scarlet mouth quivering,

"It is like another life," she said. "It was too lovely to last. Ah, those dear people in Albany, and their great kindness to me! And now I shall never see them again."

"Why not?" asked Sir George. "My aunt Livingston would welcome you."

"I cannot abandon my own kin, Sir George," she said, raising her distressed eyes to his.

"There are moments when it is best to sever such ties," I observed.

"Perhaps," she said, quickly; "but this is not the moment, Mr. Ormond. My kinsmen are exiled fugitives, deprived of their own lands by those who have risen in rebellion against our King. How can I, whom they loved in their prosperity, leave them in their adversity?"

"You speak of Guy Johnson and Sir John?" I asked.

"Yes; and of those brave people whose blood flows in my veins," she said, quietly. "Where is the Mohawk nation now, Sir George? This is their country, secured to them by solemn oath and covenant, inviolate for all time. Their belts lie with the King of England; his belts lie still with my people, the Mohawks. Where are they?"

"Fled to Oswego with Sir John," I said.

"And homeless!" she added, in a low, tense voice--"homeless, without clothing, without food, save what Guy Johnson gives them; their women and children utterly helpless, the graves of their fathers abandoned, their fireplace at Onondaga cold, and the brands scattered for the first time in a thousand years I This have you Boston people done--done already, without striking a blow."

She turned her head proudly and looked straight at Sir George.

"Is it not the truth?" she asked.

"Only in part," he said, gently. Then, with infinite pains and delicacy, he told her of our government's desire that the Iroquois should not engage in the struggle;

that if they had consented to neutrality they might have remained in possession of their lands and all their ancient rights, guaranteed by our Congress.

He pointed out the fatal consequences of Guy Johnson's councils, the effect of Butler's lying promises, the dreadful results of such a struggle between Indians, maddened by the loss of their own homes, and settlers desperately clinging to theirs.

"It is not the Mohawks I blame," he said, "it is those to whom opportunity has given wider education and knowledge--the Tories, who are attempting to use the Six Nations for their own selfish and terrible ends!... If in your veins run a few drops of Mohawk blood, my child, English blood runs there, too. Be true to your bright Mohawk blood; be true to the generous English blood. It were cowardly to deny either--shameful to betray the one for the other."

She gazed at him, fascinated; his voice swayed her, his handsome, grave face held her. Whether it was reason or emotion, mind or heart, I know not, but her whole sensitive being seemed to respond to his voice; and as he played upon this lovely human instrument, varying his deep theme, she responded in every nerve, every breath. Reason, hope, sorrow, tenderness, passion--all these I read in her deep, velvet eyes, and in the mute language of her lips, and in the timing pulse-beat under the lace on her breast.

I rose and walked to the door. She did not heed my going, nor did Sir George.

Under the oak-tree I found Murphy and Mount, smoking their pipes and watching Beacraft, who lay with his rough head pillowed on his arms, feigning slumber.

"Why did you mark so many houses with the red hatchet?" I asked, pleasantly.

He did not move a muscle, but over his face a deep color spread to the neck and hair.

"Murphy," I said, "take that prisoner to General Schuyler!"

Beacraft sprang up, glaring at me out of bloodshot eyes.

"Shoot him if he breaks away," I added.

From his convulsed and distorted lips a torrent of profanity burst as Murphy laid a heavy hand on his shoulder and faced him eastward. I drew the blue paper from my wallet, whispered to Murphy, and handed it to him. He shoved it inside the breast of his hunting-shirt, cocked his rifle, and tapped Beacraft on the arm.

So they marched away across the sunlit pasture, where blackbirds walked among the cattle, and the dew sparkled in tinted drops of fire.

In all my horror of the man I pitied him, for I knew he was going to his death, there through the fresh, sweet morning, under the blue heavens. Once I saw him look up, as though to take a last long look at a free sky, and my heart ached heavily. Yet he had plotted death in its most dreadful shapes for others who loved life as well as he--death to neighbors, death to strangers--whole families, whom he had perhaps never even seen--to mothers, to fathers, old, young, babes in the cradle, babes at the breast; and he had set down the total of one hundred and twenty-nine scalps at twenty dollars each, over his own signature.

Schuyler had said to me that it was not the black-eyed Indians the people of Tryon County dreaded, but the blue-eyed savages. And I had scarcely understood at that time how the ferocity of demons could lie dormant in white breasts.

Standing there with Mount under the oak, I saw Sir George and Magdalen Brant leave the house and stroll down the path towards the stream. Sir George was still speaking in his quiet, earnest manner; her eyes were fixed on him so that she scarce heeded her steps, and twice long sprays of sweetbrier caught her gown, and Sir George freed her. But her eyes never wandered from him; and I myself thought he never looked so handsome and courtly as he did now, in his officer's uniform and black cockade.

Where their pathway entered the alders, below the lane, they vanished from our sight; and, leaving Mount to watch I went back to the house, to search it thoroughly from cellar to the dark garret beneath the eaves.

At two o'clock in the afternoon Sir George and Magdalen Brant had not returned. I called Mount into the house, and we cooked some eggs and johnny-cake to stay our stomachs. An hour later I sent Mount out to make a circle of a mile, strike the Iroquois trail and hang to it till dark, following any traveller, white or red, who might be likely to lead him towards the secret trysting-place of the False-Faces.

Left alone at the house, I continued to rummage, finding nothing of importance, however; and towards dusk I came out to see if I might discover Sir George and Magdalen Brant. They were not in sight. I waited for a while, strolling about the deserted garden, where a few poppies turned their crimson disks towards the setting sun, and a peony lay dead and smelling rank, with the ants crawling all over it. In the mellow light the stillness was absolute, save when a distant white-throat's silvery call, long drawn out, floated from the forest's darkening edge.

The melancholy of the deserted home oppressed me, as though I had wronged it; the sad little house seemed to be watching me out of its humble windows, like a patient dog awaiting another blow. Beacraft's worn coat and threadbare vest, limp and musty as the garments of a dead man, hung on a peg behind the door. I searched the pockets with repugnance and found a few papers, which smelled like the covers of ancient books, memoranda of miserable little transactions--threepence paid for soling shoes, twopence here, a penny there; nothing more. I threw the papers on the grass, dipped up a bucket of well-water, and rinsed my fingers. And always the tenantless house watched me furtively from its humble windows.

The sun's brassy edge glittered above the blue chain of hills as I walked across the pasture towards the path that led winding among the alders to the brook below. I followed it in the deepening evening light and sat down on a log, watching the water swirling through the flat stepping-stones where trout were swarming, leaping for the tiny winged creatures that drifted across the dusky water. And as I sat there I became aware of sounds like voices; and at first, seeing no one, I thought the noises came from the low bubbling monotone of the stream. Then I heard a voice murmuring: "I will do what you ask me--I will do everything you desire."

Fearful of eavesdropping, I rose, peering ahead to make myself known, but saw nothing in the deepening dusk. On the point of calling, the words died on my lips as the same voice sounded again, close to me:

"I pray you let me have my way. I will obey you. How can you doubt it? But I must obey in my own way."

And Sir George's deep, pleasant voice answered: "There is danger to you in this. I could not endure that, Magdalen."

They were on a path parallel to the trail in which I stood, separated from me by a deep fringe of willow. I could not see them, though now they were slowly passing abreast of me.

"What do you care for a maid you so easily persuade?" she asked, with a little laugh that rang pitifully false in the dusk.

"It is her own merciful heart that persuades her," he said, under his breath.

"I think my heart is merciful," she said--"more merciful than even I knew. The restless blood in me set me afire when I saw the wrong done to these patient people of the Long House.... And when they appealed to me I came here to justify them, and bid them stand for their own hearths.... And now you come, teaching me the truth concerning right and wrong, and how God views justice and injustice; and how this tempest, once loosened, can never be chained until innocent and guilty are alike ingulfed.... I am very young to know all these things without counsel.... I needed aid--and wisdom to teach me--your wisdom. Now, in my turn, I shall teach; but you must let me teach in my way. There is only one way that the Long House can be taught.... You do not believe it, but in this I am wiser than you--I know."

"Will you not tell me what you mean to do, Magdalen?"

"No, Sir George."

"When will you tell me?"

"Never. But you will know what I have done. You will see that I hold three nations back. What else can you ask? I shall obey you. What more is there?"

Her voice lingered in the air like an echo of flowing water, then died away as they moved on, until nothing sounded in the forest stillness save the low ripple of the stream. An hour later I picked my way back to the house and saw Sir George standing in the starlight, and Mount beside him, pointing towards the east.

"I've found the False-Faces' trysting-place," said Mount, eagerly, as I came up. "I circled and struck the main Iroquois trail half a mile yonder in the bottom land--a smooth, hard trail, worn a foot deep, sir. And first comes an Onondaga war-party, stripped and painted something sickening, and I dogged 'em till they turned off into the bush to shoot a doe full of arrows--though all had guns!--and left 'em eating. Then comes three painted devils, all hung about with witch-drums and rattles, and I tied to them. And, would you believe it, sir, they kept me on a fox-trot straight east, then south along a deer-path, till they struck the Kennyetto at that sulphur spring under the big cliff--you know, Sir George, where Klock's old line cuts into the Mohawk country?"

"I know," said Sir George.

Mount took off his cap and scratched his ear.

"The forest is full of little heaps of flat stones. I could see my painted friends with the drums and rattles stop as they ran by, and each pull a flat stone from the river and add it to the nearest heap. Then they disappeared in the ravine--and I guess that settles it, Captain Ormond."

Sir George looked at me, nodding.

"That settles it, Ormond," he said.

I bade Mount cook us something to eat. Sir George looked after him as he entered the house, then began a restless pacing to and fro, arms loosely clasped behind him.

"About Magdalen Brant," he said, abruptly. "She will not speak to the three nations for Butler's party. The child had no idea of this wretched conspiracy to turn the savages loose in the valley. She thought our people meant to drive the Iroquois from their own lands--a black disgrace to us if we ever do!... They implored her to speak to them in council. Did you know they believe her to be inspired? Well, they do. When she was a child they got that notion, and Guy Johnson and Walter Butler have been lying to her and telling her what to say to the Oneidas and Onondagas."

He turned impatiently, pacing the yard, scowling, and gnawing his lip.

"Where is she?" I asked.

"She has gone to bed. She would eat nothing. We must take her back with us to Albany and summon the sachems of the three nations, with belts."

"Yes," I said, slowly. "But before we leave I must see the False-Faces."

"Did Schuyler make that a point?"

"Yes, Sir George."

"They say the False-Faces' rites are terrific," he muttered. "Thank God, that child will not be lured into those hideous orgies by Walter Butler!"

We walked towards the house where Mount had prepared our food. I sat down on the door-step to eat my porridge and think of what lay before me and how best to accomplish it. And at first I was minded to send Sir George back with Magdalen Brant and take only Mount with me. But whether it was a craven dread of despatching to Dorothy the man she was pledged to wed, or whether a desire for his knowledge and experience prompted me to invite his attendance at the False-Faces' rites, I do not know clearly, even now. He came out of the house presently, and I asked him if he would go with me.

"One of us should stay here with Magdalen Brant," he said, gravely.

"Is she not safe here?" I asked.

"You cannot leave a child like that absolutely alone," he answered.

"Then take her to Varicks'," I said, sullenly. "If she remains here some of Butler's men will be after her to attend the council."

"You wish me to go up-stairs and rouse her for a journey--now?"

"Yes; it is best to get her into a safe place," I muttered. "She may change her ideas, too, betwixt now and dawn."

He re-entered the house. I heard his spurs jingling on the stairway, then his voice, and a rapping at the door above.

Jack Mount appeared, rifle in hand, wiping his mouth with his fingers; and together we paced the yard, waiting for Sir George and Magdalen Brant to set out before we struck the Iroquois trail.

Suddenly Sir George's heavy tread sounded on the stairs; he came to the door, looking about him, east and west. His features were pallid and set and seamed with stern lines; he laid an unsteady hand on my arm and drew me a pace aside.

"Magdalen Brant is gone," he said.

"Gone!" I repeated. "Where?"

"I don't know!" he said, hoarsely.

I stared at him in astonishment. Gone? Where? Into the tremendous blackness of this wilderness that menaced us on all sides like a sea? And they had thought to tame her like a land-blown gull among the poultry!

"Those drops of Mohawk blood are not in her veins for nothing," I said, bitterly. "Here is our first lesson."

He hung his head. She had lied to him with innocent, smooth face, as all such fifth-castes lie. No jewelled snake could shed her skin as deftly as this young maid had slipped from her shoulders the frail garment of civilization.

The man beside me stood as though stunned. I was obliged to speak to him thrice ere he roused to follow Jack Mount, who, at a sign from me, had started across the dark hill-side to guide us to the trysting-place of the False-Faces' clan.

"Mount," I whispered, as he lingered waiting for us at the stepping-stones in the dark, "some one has passed this trail since I stood here an hour ago." And, bending down, I pointed to a high, flat stepping-stone, which glimmered wet in the pale light of the stars.

Sir George drew his tinder-box, struck steel to flint, and lighted a short wax dip.

"Here!" whispered Mount.

On the edge of the sand the dip-light illuminated the small imprint of a woman's shoe, pointing southeast.

Magdalen Brant had heard the voices in the Long House.

"The mischief is done," said Sir George, steadily. "I take the blame and disgrace of this."

"No; I take it," said I, sternly. "Step back, Sir George. Blow out that dip! Mount, can you find your way to that sulphur spring where the flat stones are piled in little heaps?"

The big fellow laughed. As he strode forward into the depthless sea of darkness a whippoorwill called.

"That's Elerson, sir," he said, and repeated the call twice.

The rifleman appeared from the darkness, touching his cap to me. "The horses are safe, sir," he said. "The General desires you to send your report through Sir George Covert and push forward with Mount to Stanwix."

He drew a sealed paper from his pouch and handed it to me, saying that I was to read it.

Sir George lighted his dip once more. I broke the seal and read my orders under the feeble, flickering light:

"TEMPORARY HEADQUARTERS,
VARICK MANOR, June 1, 1777.

To Captain Ormond, on scout:

Sir,--The General commanding this department desires you to employ all art and persuasion to induce the Oneidas, Tuscaroras, and Onondagas to remain quiet. Failing this, you are again reminded that the capture of Magdalen Brant is of the utmost importance. If possible, make Walter Butler also prisoner, and send him to Albany under charge of Timothy Murphy; but, above all, secure the person of Magdalen Brant

and send her to Varick Manor under escort of Sir George
Covert. If, for any reason, you find these orders impossible
of execution, send your report of the False-Faces' council
through Sir George Covert, and push forward with the riflemen
Mount, Murphy, and Elerson until you are in touch with
Gansevoort's outposts at Stanwix. Warn Colonel Gansevoort
that Colonel Barry St. Leger has moved from Oswego, and order
out a strong scout towards Fort Niagara. Although Congress
authorizes the employment of friendly Oneidas as scouts,
General Schuyler trusts that you will not avail yourself of
this liberty. Noblesse oblige! The General directs you to
return only when you have carried out these orders to the
best of your ability. You will burn this paper before you set
out for Stanwix. I am, sir,

"Your most humble and obedient servant,

"JOHN HARROW, Major and A. D. C. to the Major-General
Commanding. (Signed) PHILIP SCHUYLER, Major-General
Commanding the Department of the North."

Hot with mortification at the wretched muddle I had already made of my mission, I thrust the paper into my pouch and turned to Elerson.

"You know Magdalen Brant?" I asked, impatiently.

"Yes, sir."

"There is a chance," I said, "that she may return to that house on the hill behind us. If she comes back you will see that she does not leave the house until we return."

Sir George extinguished the dip once more. Mount turned and set off at a swinging pace along the invisible path; after him strode Sir George; I followed, brooding bitterly on my stupidity, and hopeless now of securing the prisoner in whose fragile hands the fate of the Northland lay.

XV
THE FALSE-FACES

For a long time we had scented green birch smoke, and now, on hands and knees, we were crawling along the edge of a cliff, the roar of the river in our ears, when Mount suddenly flattened out and I heard him breathing heavily as I lay down close beside him.

"Look!" he whispered, "the ravine is full of fire!"

A dull-red glare grew from the depths of the ravine; crimson shadows shook across the wall of earth and rock. Above the roaring of the stream I heard an immense confused murmur and the smothered thumping rhythm of distant drumming.

"Go on," I whispered.

Mount crawled forward, Sir George and I after him. The light below burned redder and redder on the cliff; sounds of voices grew more distinct; the dark stream sprang into view, crimson under the increasing furnace glow. Then, as we rounded a heavy jutting crag, a great light flared up almost in our faces, not out of the kindling ravine, but breaking forth among the huge pines on the cliffs.

"Their council-fire!" panted Mount. "See them sitting there!"

"Flatten out," I whispered. "Follow me!" And I crawled straight towards the fire, where, ink-black against the ruddy conflagration, an enormous pine lay uprooted, smashed by lightning or tempest, I know not which.

Into the dense shadows of the debris I crawled, Mount and Sir George following, and lay there in the dark, staring at the forbidden circle where the secret mysteries of the False-Faces had already begun.

Three great fires roared, set at regular intervals in a cleared space, walled in by the huge black pines. At the foot of a tree sat a white man, his elbows on his knees, his chin in his hands. The man was Walter Butler.

On his right sat Brant, wrapped in a crimson blanket, his face painted black and scarlet. On his left knelt a ghastly figure wearing a scowling wooden mask painted yellow and black.

Six separate groups of Indians surrounded the fires. They were sachems of the Six Nations, each sachem bearing in his hands the symbol of his nation and of his clan. All were wrapped in black-and-white blankets, and their faces were painted white above the upper lip as though they wore skin-tight masks.

Three young girls, naked save for the beaded clout, and painted scarlet from brow to ankle, beat the witch-drums tump-a-tump! tump-a-tump! while a fourth stood, erect as a vermilion statue, holding a chain belt woven in black-and-white wampum.

Behind these central figures the firelight fell on a solid semicircle of savages, crowns shaved, feathers aslant on the braided lock, and all oiled and painted for war.

A chief, wrapped in a blue blanket, stepped out into the circle swinging the carcass of a white dog by the hind-legs. He tied it to a black-birch sapling and left it dangling and turning round and round.

"This for the Keepers of the Fires," he said, in Tuscarora, and flung the dog's entrails into the middle fire.

Three young men sprang into the ring; each threw a log onto one of the fires.

"The name of the Holder of the Heavens may now be spoken and heard without offence," said an old sachem, rising. "Hark! brothers. Harken, O you wise men and sachems! The False-Faces are laughing in the ravine where the water is being painted with firelight. I acquaint you that the False-Faces are coming up out of the ravine!"

The witch-drums boomed and rattled in the silence that followed his words. Far off I heard the sound of many voices laughing and talking all together; nearer, nearer, until, torch in hand, a hideously masked figure bounded into the circle, shaking out his bristling cloak of green reeds. Another followed, another, then three, then six, then a dozen, whirling their blazing torches; all horribly masked and smothered in coarse bunches of long, black hair, or cloaked with rustling river reeds.

"Ha! Ah-weh-hot-kwah!   Ha! Ah-weh-hah!   Ha! The crimson flower!

Ha! The flower!"

they chanted, thronging around the central fire; then falling back in a half-circle, torches lifted, while the masked figures banked solidly behind, chanted monotonously:

"Red fire burns on the maple!   Red fire burns in the pines.   The red flower to the maple!   The red death to the pines!"

At this two young girls, wearing white feathers and white weasel pelts dangling from shoulders to knees, entered the ring from opposite ends. Their arms were full of those spectral blossoms called "Ghost-corn," and they strewed the flowers around the ring in silence. Then three maidens, glistening in cloaks of green pine-needles, slipped into the fire circle, throwing showers of violets and yellow moccasin flowers over the earth, calling out, amid laughter, "Moccasins for whippoorwills! Violets for the two heads entangled!" And, their arms empty of blossoms, they danced away, laughing while the False-Faces clattered their wooden masks and swung their torches till the flames whistled.

Then six sachems rose, casting off their black-and-white blankets, and each in turn planted branches of yellow willow, green willow, red osier, samphire, witch-hazel, spice-bush, and silver birch along the edge of the silent throng of savages.

"Until the night-sun comes be these your barriers, O Iroquois!" they chanted. And all answered:

"The Cherry-maid shall lock the gates to the People of the Morning! A-e! ja-e! Wild cherry and cherry that is red!"

Then came the Cherry-maid, a slender creature, hung from head to foot with thick bunches of wild cherries which danced and swung when she walked; and the False-Faces plucked the fruit from her as she passed around, laughing and tossing her black hair, until she had been despoiled and only the garment of sewed leaves hung from shoulder to ankle.

A green blanket was spread for her and she sat down under the branch of witch-hazel.

"The barrier is closed!" she said. "Kindle your coals from Onondaga, O you Keepers of the Central Fire!"

An aged sachem arose, and, lifting his withered arm, swept it eastward.

"The hearth is cleansed," he said, feebly. "Brothers, attend! She-who-runs is coming. Listen!"

A dead silence fell over the throng, broken only by the rustle of the flames. After a moment, very far away in the forest, something sounded like the muffled gallop of an animal, paddy-pad! paddy-pad, coming nearer and ever nearer.

"It's the Toad-woman!" gasped Mount in my ear. "It's the Huron witch! Ah! My God! look there!"

Hopping, squattering, half scrambling, half bounding into the firelight came running a dumpy creature all fluttering with scarlet rags. A coarse mat of gray hair masked her visage; she pushed it aside and raised a dreadful face in the red fire-glow--a face so marred, so horrible, that I felt Mount shivering in the darkness beside me.

Through the hollow boom-boom of the witch-drums I heard a murmur swelling from the motionless crowd, like a rising wind in the pines. The hag heard it too; her mouth widened, splitting her ghastly visage. A single yellow fang caught the firelight.

"O you People of the Mountain! O you Onondagas!" she cried. "I am come to ask my Cayugas and my Senecas why they assemble here on the Kennyetto when their council-fire and yours should burn at Onondaga! O you Oneidas, People of the Standing Stone! I am come to ask my Senecas, my Mountain-snakes, why the Keepers of the Iroquois Fire have let it go out? O you of the three clans, let your ensigns rise and listen. I speak to the Wolf, the Turtle, and the Bear! And I call on the seven kindred clans of the Wolf, and the two kindred clans of the Turtle, and the four kindred clans of the Bear throughout the Six Nations of the Iroquois confederacy, throughout the clans of the Lenni-Lenape, throughout the Huron-Algonquins and their clans!

"And I call on the False-Faces of the Spirit-water and the Water of Light!"

She shook her scarlet rags and, raising her arm, hurled a hatchet into a painted post which stood behind the central fire.

"O you Cayugas, People of the Carrying-place! Strike that war-post with your hatchets or face the ghosts of your fathers in every trail!"

There was a deathly silence. Catrine Montour closed her horrible little eyes, threw back her head, and, marking time with her flat foot, began to chant.

She chanted the glory of the Long House; of the nations that drove the Eries, the Hurons, the Algonquins; of the nation that purged the earth of the Stonish Giants; of the nation that fought the dreadful battle of the Flying Heads. She sang the triumph of the confederacy, the bonds that linked the Elder Brothers and Elder Sons with the Esaurora, whose tongue was the sign of council unity.

And the circle of savages began to sway in rhythm to her chanting, answering back, calling their challenge from clan to clan; until, suddenly, the Senecas sprang to their feet and drove their hatchets into the war-post, challenging the Lenape with their own battle-cry:

"Yoagh! Yoagh! Ha-ha! Hagh! Yoagh!"

Then the Mohawks raised their war-yelp and struck the post; and the Cayugas answered with a terrible cry, striking the post, and calling out for the Next Youngest Son--meaning the Tuscaroras--to draw their hatchets.

"Have the Seminoles made women of you?" screamed Catrine Montour, menacing the sachems of the Tuscaroras with clinched fists.

"Let the Lenape tell you of women!" retorted a Tuscarora sachem, calmly.

At this opening of an old wound the Oneidas called on the Lenape to answer; but the Lenape sat sullen and silent, with flashing eyes fixed on the Mohawks.

Then Catrine Montour, lashing herself into a fury, screamed for vengeance on the people who had broken the chain-belt with the Long House. Raving and frothing, she burst into a torrent of prophecy, which silenced every tongue and held every Indian fascinated.

"Look!" whispered Mount. "The Oneidas are drawing their hatchets! The Tuscaroras will follow! The Iroquois will declare for war!"

Suddenly the False-Faces raised a ringing shout:

"Kree! Ha-ha! Kre-e!"

And a hideous creature in yellow advanced, rattling his yellow mask.

Catrine Montour, slavering and gasping, leaned against the painted war-post. Into the fire-ring came dancing a dozen girls, all strung with brilliant wampum, their bodies and limbs painted vermilion, sleeveless robes of wild iris hanging to their knees. With a shout they chanted:

"O False-Faces, prepare to do honor to the truth! She who Dreams has come from her three sisters--the Woman of the Thunder-cloud, the Woman of the Sounding Footsteps, the Woman of the Murmuring Skies!"

And, joining hands, they cried, sweetly: "Come, O Little Rosebud Woman!--Ke-neance-e-qua! O-gin-e-o-qua!--Woman of the Rose!"

And all together the False-Faces cried: "Welcome to Ta-lu-la, the leaping waters! Here is I-e-nia, the wanderer's rest! Welcome, O Woman of the Rose!"

Then the grotesque throng of the False-Faces parted right and left; a lynx, its green eyes glowing, paced out into the firelight; and behind the tawny tree-cat came slowly a single figure--a young girl, bare of breast and arm; belted at the hips with silver, from which hung a straight breadth of doeskin to the instep of her bare feet. Her dark hair, parted, fell in two heavy braids to her knees; her lips were tinted with scarlet; her small ear-lobes and finger-tips were stained a faint rose-color.

In the breathless silence she raised her head. Sir George's crushing grip clutched my arm, and he fell a-shuddering like a man with ague.

The figure before us was Magdalen Brant.

The lynx lay down at her feet and looked her steadily in the face.

Slowly she raised her rounded arm, opened her empty palm; then from space she seemed to pluck a rose, and I saw it there between her forefinger and her thumb.

A startled murmur broke from the throng. "Magic! She plucks blossoms from the empty air!"

"O you Oneidas," came the sweet, serene voice, "at the tryst of the False-Faces I have kept my tryst.

"You wise men of the Six Nations, listen now attentively; and you, ensigns and attestants, attend, honoring the truth which from my twin lips shall flow, sweetly as new honey and as sap from April maples."

She stooped and picked from the ground a withered leaf, holding it out in her small, pink palm.

"Like this withered leaf is your understanding. It is for a maid to quicken you to life, ... as I restore this last year's leaf to life," she said, deliberately.

In her open palm the dry, gray leaf quivered, moved, straightened, slowly turned moist and fresh and green. Through the intense silence the heavy, gasping breath of hundreds of savages told of the tension they struggled under.

She dropped the leaf to her feet; gradually it lost its green and curled up again, a brittle, ashy flake.

"O you Oneidas!" she cried, in that clear voice which seemed to leave a floating melody in the air, "I have talked with my Sisters of the Murmuring Skies, and none but the lynx at my feet heard us."

She bent her lovely head and looked into the creature's blazing orbs; after a moment the cat rose, took three stealthy steps, and lay down at her feet, closing its emerald eyes.

The girl raised her head: "Ask me concerning the truth, you sachems of the Oneida, and speak for the five war-chiefs who stand in their paint behind you!"

An old sachem rose, peering out at her from dim, aged eyes.

"Is it war, O Woman of the Rose?" he quavered.

"Neah!" she said, sweetly.

An intense silence followed, shattered by a scream from the hag, Catrine.

"A lie! It is war! You have struck the post, Cayugas! Senecas! Mohawks! It is a lie! Let this young sorceress speak to the Oneidas; they are hers; the Tuscaroras are hers, and the Onondagas and the Lenape! Let them heed her and her dreams and her witchcraft! It concerns not you, O Mountain-snakes! It concerns only these and False-Faces! She is their prophetess; let her dream for them. I have dreamed for you, O Elder Brothers! And I have dreamed of war!!"

"And I of peace!" came the clear, floating voice, soothing the harsh echoes of the hag's shrieking appeal. "Take heed, you Mohawks, and you Cayuga war-chiefs and sachems, that you do no violence to this council-fire!"

"The Oneidas are women!" yelled the hag.

Magdalen Brant made a curiously graceful gesture, as though throwing something to the ground from her empty hand. And, as all looked, something did strike the ground--something that coiled and hissed and rattled--a snake, crouched in the form of a letter S; and the lynx turned its head, snarling, every hair erect.

"Mohawks and Cayugas!" she cried; "are you to judge the Oneidas?--you who dare not take this rattlesnake in your hands?"

There was no reply. She smiled and lifted the snake. It coiled up in her palm, rattling and lifting its terrible head to the level of her eyes. The lynx growled.

"Quiet!" she said, soothingly. "The snake has gone, O Tahagoos, my friend. Behold, my hand is empty; Sa-kwe-en-ta, the Fanged One has gone."

It was true. There was nothing where, an instant before, I myself had seen the dread thing, crest swaying on a level with her eyes.

"Will you be swept away by this young witch's magic?" shrieked Catrine Montour.

"Oneidas!" cried Magdalen Brant, "the way is cleared! Hiro [I have spoken]!"

Then the sachems of the Oneida stood up, wrapping themselves in their blankets, and moved silently away, filing into the forest, followed by the war-chiefs and those who had accompanied the Oneida delegation as attestants.

"Tuscaroras!" said Magdalen Brant, quietly.

The Tuscarora sachems rose and passed out into the darkness, followed by their suite of war-chiefs and attestants.

"Onondagas!"

All but two of the Onondaga delegation left the council-fire. Amid a profound silence the Lenape followed, and in their wake stalked three tall Mohicans.

Walter Butler sprang up from the base of the tree where he had been sitting and pointed a shaking finger at Magdalen Brant:

"Damn you!" he shouted; "if you call on my Mohawks, I'll cut your throat, you witch!"

Brant bounded to his feet and caught Butler's rigid, outstretched arm.

"Are you mad, to violate a council-fire?" he said, furiously. Magdalen Brant looked calmly at Butler, then deliberately faced the sachems.

"Mohawks!" she called, steadily.

There was a silence; Butler's black eyes were almost starting from his bloodless visage; the hag, Montour, clawed the air in helpless fury.

"Mohawks!" repeated the girl, quietly.

Slowly a single war-chief rose, and, casting aside his blanket, drew his hatchet and struck the war-post. The girl eyed him contemptuously, then turned again and called:

"Senecas!"

A Seneca chief, painted like death, strode to the post and struck it with his hatchet.

"Cayuga!" called the girl, steadily.

A Cayuga chief sprang at the post and struck it twice.

Roars of applause shook the silence; then a masked figure leaped towards the central fire, shouting: "The False-Faces' feast! Ho! Hoh! Ho-ooh!"

In a moment the circle was a scene of terrific excesses. Masked figures pelted each other with live coals from the fires; dancing, shrieking, yelping demons leaped about whirling their blazing torches; witch-drums boomed; chant after chant was raised as new dancers plunged into the delirious throng, whirling the carcasses of white dogs, painted with blue and yellow stripes. The nauseating stench of burned roast meat filled the air, as the False-Faces brought quarters of venison and baskets of fish into the circle and dumped them on the coals.

Faster and more furious grew the dance of the False-Faces. The flying coals flew in every direction, streaming like shooting-stars across the fringing darkness. A grotesque masker, wearing the head-dress of a bull, hurled his torch into the air; the flaming brand lodged in the feathery top of a pine, the foliage caught fire, and with a crackling rush a vast whirlwind of flame and smoke streamed skyward from the forest giant.

"To-wen-yon-go [It touches the sky]!" howled the crazed dancers, leaping about, while faster and faster came the volleys of live coals, until a young girl's hair caught fire.

"Kah-none-ye-tah-we!" they cried, falling back and forming a chain-around her as she wrung the sparks from her long hair, laughing and leaping about between the flying coals.

Then the nine sachems of the Mohawks rose, all covering their breasts with their blankets, save the chief sachem, who is called "The Two Voices." The serried circle fell back, Senecas, Cayugas, and Mohawks shouting their battle-cries; scores of hatchets glittered, knives flashed.

All alone in the circle stood Magdalen Brant, slim, straight, motionless as a tinted statue, her hands on her hips. Reflections of the fires played over her, in amber and pearl and rose; violet lights lay under her eyes and where the hair shadowed her brow. Then, through the silence, a loud voice cried: "Little Rosebud Woman, the False-Faces thank you! Koon-wah-yah-tun-was [They are burning the white dog]!"

She raised her head and laid a hand on each cheek.

"Neah-wen-ha [I thank you]," she said, softly.

At the word the lynx rose and looked up into her face, then turned and paced slowly across the circle, green eyes glowing.

The young girl loosened the braids of her hair; a thick, dark cloud fell over her bare shoulders and breasts.

"She veils her face!" chanted the False-Faces. "Respect the veil! Adieu, O Woman of the Rose!"

Her hands fell, and, with bent head, moving slowly, pensively, she passed out of the infernal circle, the splendid lynx stalking at her heels.

No sooner was she gone than hell itself broke loose among the False-Faces; the dance grew madder and madder, the terrible rite of sacrifice was enacted with frightful symbols. Through the awful din the three war-cries pealed, the drums advanced, thundering; the iris-maids lighted the six little fires of black-birch, spice-wood, and sassafras, and crouched to inhale the aromatic smoke until, stupefied and quivering in every limb with the inspiration of delirium, they stood erect, writhing, twisting, tossing their hair, chanting the splendors of the future!

Then into the crazed orgie leaped the Toad-woman like a gigantic scarlet spider, screaming prophecy and performing the inconceivable and nameless rites of Ak-e, Ne-ke, and Ge-zis, until, in her frenzy, she went stark mad, and the devil worship began with the awful sacrifice of Leshee in Biskoonah.

Horror-stricken, nauseated, I caught Mount's arm, whispering: "Enough, in God's name! Come away!"

My ears rang with the distracted yelping of the Toad-woman, who was strangling a dog. Faint, almost reeling, I saw an iris-girl fall in convulsions; the stupefying smoke blew into my face, choking me. I staggered back into the darkness, feeling my way among the unseen trees, gasping for fresh air. Behind me, Mount and Sir George came creeping, groping like blind men along the cliffs.

"This way," whispered Mount.

XVI
ON SCOUT

L ike a pursued man hunted through a dream, I labored on, leaden-limbed, trembling; and it seemed hours and hours ere the blue starlight broke overhead and Beacraft's dark house loomed stark and empty on the stony hill. Suddenly the ghostly call of a whippoorwill broke out from the willows. Mount answered; Elerson appeared in the path, making a sign for silence.

"Magdalen Brant entered the house an hour since," he whispered. "She sits yonder on the door-step. I think she has fallen asleep."

We stole forward through the dusk towards the silent figure on the door-step. She sat there, her head fallen back against the closed door, her small hands lying half open in her lap. Under her closed eyes the dark circles of fatigue lay; a faint trace of rose paint still clung to her lips; and from the ragged skirt of her thorn-rent gown one small foot was thrust, showing a silken shoe and ankle stained with mud.

There she lay, sleeping, this maid who, with her frail strength, had split forever the most powerful and ancient confederacy the world had ever known.

Her superb sacrifice of self, her proud indifference to delicacy and shame, her splendid acceptance of the degradation, her instant and fearless execution of the only plan which could save the land from war with a united confederacy, had left us stunned with admiration and helpless gratitude.

Had she gone to them as a white woman, using the arts of civilized persuasion, she could have roused them to war, but she could not have soothed them to peace. She knew it--even I knew that among the Iroquois the Ruler of the Heavens can never speak to an Indian through the mouth of a white woman.

As an Oneida, and a seeress of the False-Faces, she had answered their appeal. Using every symbol, every ceremony, every art taught her as a child, she had swayed them, vanquishing with mystery, conquering, triumphing, as an Oneida, where a single false step, a single slip, a moment's faltering in her sweet and serene authority might have brought out the appalling cry of accusation:

"Her heart is white!"

And not one hand would have been raised to prevent the sacrificial test which must follow and end inevitably in a dreadful death.

*   *   *   *   *

Mount and Elerson, moved by a rare delicacy, turned and walked noiselessly away towards the hill-top.

"Wake her," I said to Sir George.

He knelt beside her, looking long into her face; then touched her lightly on the hand. She opened her eyes, looked up at him gravely, then rose to her feet, steadying herself on his bent arm.

"Where have you been?" she asked, glancing anxiously from him to me. There was the faintest ring of alarm in her voice, a tint of color on cheek and temple. And Sir George, lying like a gentleman, answered: "We have searched the trails in vain for you. Where have you lain hidden, child?"

Her lips parted in an imperceptible sigh of relief; the pallor of weariness returned.

"I have been upon your business, Sir George," she said, looking down at her mud-stained garments. Her arms fell to her side; she made a little gesture with one limp hand. "You see," she said, "I promised you." Then she turned, mounting the steps, pensively; and, in the doorway, paused an instant, looking back at him over her shoulder.

*   *   *   *   *

And all that night, lying close to the verge of slumber, I heard Sir George pacing the stony yard under the great stars; while the riflemen, stretched beside the hearth, snored heavily, and the death-watch ticked in the wall.

At dawn we three were afield, nosing the Sacandaga trail to count the tracks leading to the north--the dread footprints of light, swift feet which must return one day bringing to the Mohawk Valley an awful reckoning.

At noon we returned. I wrote out my report and gave it to Sir George. We spoke little together. I did not see Magdalen Brant again until they bade me adieu.

And now it was two o'clock in the afternoon; Sir George had already set out with Magdalen Brant to Varicks' by way of Stoner's; Elerson and Mount stood by the door, waiting to pilot me towards Gansevoort's distant outposts; the noon sunshine filled the deserted house and fell across the table where I sat, reading over my instructions from Schuyler ere I committed the paper to the flames.

So far, no thanks to myself, I had carried out my orders in all save the apprehension of Walter Butler. And now I was uncertain whether to remain and hang around the council-fire waiting for an opportunity to seize Butler, or whether to push on at once, warn Gansevoort at Stanwix that St. Leger's motley army had set out from Oswego, and then return to trap Butler at my leisure.

I crumpled the despatch into a ball and tossed it onto the live coals in the fireplace; the paper smoked, caught fire, and in a moment more the black flakes sank into the ashes.

"Shall we burn the house, sir?" asked Mount, as I came to the doorway and looked out.

I shook my head, picked up rifle, pouch, and sack, and descended the steps. At the same instant a man appeared at the foot of the hill, and Elerson waved his hand, saying: "Here's that mad Irishman, Tim Murphy, back already."

Murphy came jauntily up the hill, saluted me with easy respect, and drew from his pouch a small packet of papers which he handed me, nodding carelessly at Elerson and staring hard at Mount as though he did not recognize him.

"Phwat's this?" he inquired of Elerson--"a Frinch cooroor, or maybe a Sac shquaw in a buck's shirrt?"

"Don't introduce him to me," said Mount to Elerson; "he'll try to kiss my hand, and I hate ceremony."

"Quit foolin'," said Elerson, as the two big, over-grown boys seized each other and began a rough-and-tumble frolic. "You're just cuttin' capers, Tim, becuz you've heard that we're takin' the war-path--quit pullin' me, you big Irish elephant! Is it true we're takin' the war-path?"

"How do I know?" cried Murphy; but the twinkle in his blue eyes betrayed him; "bedad, 'tis home to the purty lasses we go this blessed day, f'r the crool war is over, an' the King's got the pip, an--"

"Murphy!" I said.

"Sorr," he replied, letting go of Mount and standing at a respectful slouch.

"Did you get Beacraft there in safety?"

"I did, sorr."

"Any trouble?"

"None, sorr--f'r me."

I opened the first despatch, looking at him keenly.

"Do we take the war-path?" I asked.

"We do, sorr," he said, blandly. "McDonald's in the hills wid the McCraw an'ten score renegades. Wan o' their scouts struck old man Schell's farm an' he put buckshot into sivinteen o' them, or I'm a liar where I shtand!"

"I knew it," muttered Elerson to Mount. "Where you see smoke, there's fire; where you see Murphy, there's trouble. Look at the grin on him--and his hatchet shined up like a Cayuga's war-axe!"

I opened the despatch; it was from Schuyler, countermanding his instructions for me to go to Stanwix, and directing me to warn every settlement in the Kingsland district that McDonald and some three hundred Indians and renegades were loose on the Schoharie, and that their outlying scouts had struck Broadalbin.

I broke the wax of the second despatch; it was from Harrow, briefly thanking me for the capture of Beacraft, adding that the man had been sent to Albany to await court-martial.

That meant that Beacraft must hang; a most disagreeable feeling came over me, and I tore open the third and last paper, a bulky document, and read it:

"VARICK MANOR,
"June the 2d.
"An hour to dawn.

"In my bedroom I am writing to you the adieu I should have
said the night you left. Murphy, a rifleman, goes to you with
despatches in an hour: he will take this to you, ...
wherever you are.

"I saw the man you sent in. Father says he must surely hang.
He was so pale and silent, he looked so dreadfully tired--and
I have been crying a little--I don't know why, because all
say he is a great villain.

"I wonder whether you are well and whether you remember me."
("me" was crossed out and "us" written very carefully.) "The
house is so strange without you. I go into your room
sometimes. Cato has pressed all your fine clothes. I go into
your room to read. The light is very good there. I am reading
the Poems of Pansard. You left a fern between the pages to
mark the poem called 'Our Deaths'; did you know it? Do you
admire that verse? It seems sad to me. And it is not true,
either. Lovers seldom die together." (This was crossed out,
and the letter went on.) "Two people who love--" ("love" was
crossed out heavily and the line continued)--"two friends
seldom die at the same instant. Otherwise there would be no
terror in death.

"I forgot to say that Isene, your mare, is very well. Papa
and the children are well, and Ruyven a-pestering General
Schuyler to make him a cornet in the legion of horse, and
Cecile, all airs, goes about with six officers to carry her
shawl and fan.

"For me--I sit with Lady Schuyler when I have the opportunity. I love her; she is so quiet and gentle and lets me sit by her for hours, perfectly silent. Yesterday she came into your room, where I was sitting, and she looked at me for a long time--so strangely--and I asked her why, and she shook her head. And after she had gone I arranged your linen and sprinkled lavender among it.

"You see there is so little to tell you, except that in the afternoon some Senecas and Tories shot at one of our distant tenants, a poor man, one Christian Schell; and he beat them off and killed eleven, which was very brave, and one of the soldiers made a rude song about it, and they have been singing it all night in their quarters. I heard them from your room--where I sometimes sleep--the air being good there; and this is what they sang:

"'A story, a story
  Unto you I will tell,
Concerning a brave hero,
  One Christian Schell.

"'Who was attacked by the savages.
  And Tories, it is said;
But for this attack
  Most freely they bled.

"'He fled unto his house
  For to save his life.
Where he had left his arms
  In care of his wife.

"'They advanced upon him
  And began to fire,
But Christian with his blunderbuss
  Soon made them retire.

"'He wounded Donald McDonald
  And drew him in the door,
Who gave an account
  Their strength was sixty-four.

"'Six there was wounded
  And eleven there was killed
Of this said party,
  Before they quit the field.'

"And I think there are a hundred other verses, which I will spare you; not that I forget them, for the soldiers sang them over and over, and I had nothing better to do than to lie awake and listen.

"So that is all. I hear my messenger moving about below; I am to drop this letter down to him, as all are asleep, and to open the big door might wake them.

"Good-bye.

*   *   *   *   *

"It was not my rifleman, only the sentry. They keep double watch since the news came about Schell. "Good-bye. I am thinking of you.

"DOROTHY.

"Postscript.--Please make my compliments and adieux to Sir George Covert.

"Postscript.--The rifleman is here; he is whistling like a whippoorwill. I must say good-bye. I am mad to go with him. Do not forget me!

"My memories are so keen, so pitilessly real, I can scarce endure them, yet cling to them the more desperately.

"I did not mean to write this--truly I did not! But here, in the dusk, I can see your face just as it looked when you said good-bye!--so close that I could take it in my arms despite my vows and yours!

"Help me to reason; for even God cannot, or will not, help me; knowing, perhaps, the dreadful after-life He has doomed me to for all eternity. If it is true that marriages are made in heaven, where was mine made? Can you answer? I cannot. (The whimper of the whippoorwill again!) Dearest, good-bye. Where my body lies matters nothing so that you hold my soul a little while. Yet, even of that they must rob you one day. Oh, if even in dying there is no happiness, where, where does it abide? Three places only have I heard of: the world, heaven, and hell. God forgive me, but I think the last could cover all.

"Say that you love me! Say it to the forest, to the wind. Perhaps my soul, which follows you, may hear if you only say it. (Once more the ghost-call of the whippoorwill!) Dear lad, good-bye!"

XVII
THE FLAG

Day after day our little scout of four traversed the roads and forests of the Kingsland district, warning the people at the outlying settlements and farms that the county militia-call was out, and that safety lay only in conveying their families to the forts and responding to the summons of authority without delay.

Many obeyed; some rash or stubborn settlers prepared to defend their homes. A few made no response, doubtless sympathizing with their Tory friends who had fled to join McDonald or Sir John Johnson in the North.

Rumors were flying thick, every settlement had its full covey; every cross-road tavern buzzed with gossip. As we travelled from settlement to settlement, we, too, heard something of what had happened in distant districts: how the Schoharie militia had been called out; how one Huetson had been captured as he was gathering a band of Tories to join the Butlers; how a certain Captain Ball had raised a company of sixty-three royalists at Beaverdam and was fled to join Sir John; how Captain George Mann, of the militia, refused service, declaring himself a royalist, and disbanding his company; how Adam Crysler had thrown his important influence in favor of the King, and that the inhabitants of Tryon County were gloomy and depressed, seeing so many respectable gentlemen siding with the Tories.

We learned that the Schoharie and Schenectady militia had refused to march unless some provision was made to protect their families in their absence; that Congress had therefore established a corps of invalids, consisting of eight companies, each to have one captain, two lieutenants, two ensigns, five sergeants, six corporals, two drums, two fifes, and one hundred men; one company to be stationed in Schoharie, and to be called the "Associate Exempts"; that three forts for the protection of the Schoharie Valley were nearly finished, called the Upper, Lower, and Middle forts.

More sinister still were the rumors from the British armies: Burgoyne was marching on Albany from the north with the finest train of artillery ever seen in America; St. Leger was moving from the west; McDonald had started already, flinging out his Indian scouts as far as Perth and Broadalbin, and Sir Henry Clinton had gathered a great army at New York and was preparing to sweep the Hudson Valley from Fishkill to Albany. And the focus of these three armies and of Butler's, Johnson's, and McDonald's renegades and Indians was this unhappy county of Tryon, torn already with internal dissensions; unarmed, unprovisioned, unorganized, almost ungarrisoned.

I remember, one rainy day towards sunset, coming into a small hamlet where, in front of the church, some score of farmers and yokels were gathered, marshalled into a single line. Some were armed with rifles, some with blunderbusses, some with spears and hay-forks. None wore uniform. As we halted to watch the pathetic array, their fifer and drummer wheeled out and marched down the line, playing Yankee Doodle. Then the minister laid down his blunderbuss and, facing the company, raised his arms in prayer, invoking the "God of Armies" as though he addressed his supplication before a vast armed host.

Murphy strove to laugh, but failed; Mount muttered vaguely under his breath; Elerson gnawed his lips and bent his bared head while the old man finished his prayer to "The God of Armies!" then picked up his blunderbuss and limped to his place in the scanty file.

And again I remember one fresh, sweet morning late in June, standing with my riflemen at a toll-gate to see some four hundred Tryon County militia marching past on their way to Unadilla on the Susquehanna, where Brant, with half a thousand savages, had consented to a last parley. Stout, wholesome lads they were, these Tryon County men; wearing brown and yellow uniforms cut smartly, and their officers in the Continental buff and blue, riding like regulars; curved swords shining and their epaulets striking fire in the sunshine.

"Palatines!" said Mount, standing to salute as an officer rode by. "That's General Herkimer--old Honikol Herkimer--with his hard, weather-tanned jaws and the devil lurking under his eyebrows; and that young fellow in his smart uniform is

Colonel Cox, old George Klock's son-in-law; and yonder rides Colonel Harper! Oh, I know 'em, sir; I was not in these parts for nothing in '74 and '75!"

The drums and fifes were playing "Unadilla" as the regiment marched past; and my riflemen, lounging along the roadside, exchanged pleasantries with the hardy Palatines, or greeted acquaintances in their impudent, bantering manner:

"Hello! What's this Low Dutch regiment? Say, Han Yost, the pigs has eat off your queue-band! Bedad, they marrch like Albany ducks in fly-time! Musha, thin, luk at the fat dhrummer laad! Has he apples in thim two cheeks, Jack? I dunnoa! Hey, there goes Wagner! Hello, Wagner! Wisha, laad, ye're cross-eyed an' shquint-lipped a-playin' yere fife hind-end furrst!"

And the replies from the dusty, brown ranks, steadily passing:

"Py Gott! dere's Jack Mount! Look alretty, Jacob! Hello, Elerson! Ish dot true you patch your breeches mit second-hand scalps you puy in Montreal? Vat you vas doing down here, Tim Murphy? Oh, joost look at dem devils of Morgan! Sure, Emelius, dey joost come so soon as ve go. Ya! Dey come to kiss our girls, py cricky! Uf I catch you round my girl alretty, Dave Elerson--"

"Silence! Silence in the ranks!" sang out an officer, riding up. The brown column passed on, the golden dust hanging along its flanks. Far ahead we could still hear the drums and fifes playing "Unadilla."

"They ought to have a flag; a flag's a good thing to fight for," said Mount, looking after them. "I fought for the damned British rag when I was fifteen. Lord! it makes me boil to think that they've forgot what we did for 'em!"

"We Virginians carried a flag at the siege o' Boston," observed Elerson. "It was a rattlesnake on a white ground, with the motto, 'Don't tread on me!'"

I told them of the new flag that our Congress had chosen, describing it in detail. They listened attentively, but made no comment.

It was on these expeditions that I learned something of these rough riflemen which I had not suspected--their passionate devotion to the forest. What the sea is to mariners, the endless, uncharted wilderness was to these forest runners; they loved and hated it, they suspected and trusted it. A forest voyage finished, they steered for the nearest port with all the eager impatience of sea-cloyed sailors. Yet, scarcely were they anchored in some frontier haven than they fell to dreaming of the wilderness, of the far silences in the trackless sea of trees, of the winds ruffling the forest's crests till ten thousand trees toss their leaves, silver side up, as white-caps flash, rolling in long patches on a heaving waste of waters.

Yet, in all those weeks I never heard one word or hint of that devotion expressed or implied, not one trace of appreciation, not one shadow of sentiment. If I ventured to speak of the vast beauty of the woods, there was no response from my shy companions; one appeared to vie with another in concealing all feeling under a careless mask and a bantering manner.

Once only can I recall a voluntary expression of pleasure in beauty; it came from Jack Mount, one blue night in July, when the heavens flashed under summer stars till the vaulted skies seemed plated solidly with crusted gems.

"Them stars look kind of nice," he said, then colored with embarrassment and spat a quid of spruce-gum into the camp-fire.

Yet humanity demands some outlet for accumulated sentiment, and these men found it in the dirge-like songs and laments and rude ballads of the wilderness, which I think bear a close resemblance to the sailor-men's songs, in words as well as in the dolorous melodies, fit only for the scraping whine of a two-string fiddle in a sugar-camp.

The magic of June faded from the forests, smothered under the magnificent and deeper glory of July's golden green; the early summer ripened into August, finding us still afoot in the Kingsland district gathering in the loyal, warning the rash, comforting the down-cast, threatening the suspected. Twice, by expresses bound for Saratoga, I sent full reports to Schuyler, but received no further orders. I wondered whether he was displeased at my failure to arrest Walter Butler; and we redoubled our efforts to gain news of him. Three times we heard of his presence in or near the Kingsland district: once at Tribes Hill, once at Fort Plain, and once it was said he was living quietly in a farm-house near Johnstown, which he had the effrontery to enter in broad daylight. But we failed to come up with him, and to this day I do not know whether any of this information we received was indeed correct. It was the first day of August when we heard of Butler's presence near Johnstown; we had been lying at a tavern called "The Brick House," a two-story inn standing where the Albany and Schenectady roads fork near Fox Creek, and there had been great fear of McDonald's renegades that week, and I had advised the despatch of an express to Albany asking for troops to protect the valley when I chanced to overhear a woman say that firing had been heard in the direction of Stanwix.

The woman, a slattern, who was known by the unpleasant name of Rya's Pup, declared that Walter Butler had gone to Johnstown to join St. Leger before Stanwix, and that the Tories would give the rebels such a drubbing that we would all be crawling on our bellies yelling for quarter this day week. As the wench was drunk, I made little of her babble; but the next day Murphy and Elerson, having been in touch with Gansevoort's outposts, returned to me with a note from Colonel Willett:

"FORT SCHUYLER (STANWIX),
"August 2d,

"DEAR SIR,--I transmit to you the contents of a letter from Colonel Gansevoort, dated July 28th:

"'Yesterday, at three o'clock in the afternoon, our garrison was alarmed with the firing of four guns. A party of men was instantly despatched to the place where the guns were fired, which was in the edge of the woods, about five hundred yards from the fort; but they were too late. The villains were fled, after having shot three young girls who were out picking raspberries, two of whom were lying scalped and tomahawked; one dead and the other expiring, who died in about half an hour after she was brought home. The third had a bullet through her face, and crawled away, lying hid until we arrived. It was pitiful. The child may live, but has lost her mind.

"'This was accomplished by a scout of sixteen Tories of Colonel John Butler's command and two savages, Mohawks, all under direction of Captain Walter Butler.'

"This, sir, is a revised copy of Colonel Gansevoort's letter

to Colonel Van Schaick. Permit me to add, with the full
approval of Colonel Gansevoort, that the scout under your
command warns the militia at Whitestown of the instant
approach of Colonel Barry St. Leger's regular troops,
reinforced by Sir John Johnson's regiment of Royal Greens,
Colonel Butler's Rangers, McCraw's outlaws, and seven hundred
Mohawk, Seneca, and Cayuga warriors under Brant and Walter
Butler. I will add, sir, that we shall hold this fort to the
end. Respectfully,

"MARINUS WILLETT,
Lieutenant-Colonel."

Standing knee-deep in the thick undergrowth, I read this letter aloud to my
riflemen, amid a shocked silence; then folded it for transmission to General Schuyler when opportunity might offer, and signed Murphy to lead forward.

So Rya's Pup was right. Walter Butler had made his first mark on the red Oswego trail!

We marched in absolute silence, Murphy leading, every nerve on edge, straining eye and ear for a sign of the enemy's scouts, now doubtless swarming forward
and to cover the British advance.

But the wilderness is vast, and two armies might pass each other scarcely out
of hail and never know.

Towards sundown I caught my first glimpse of a hostile Iroquois war-party.
We had halted behind some rocks on a heavily timbered slope, and Mount was
scrutinizing the trail below, where a little brook crossed it, flowing between mossy
stones; when, without warning, a naked Mohawk stalked into the trail, sprang from
rock to rock, traversing the bed of the brook like a panther, then leaped lightly
into the trail again and moved on. After him, in file, followed some thirty warriors,
naked save for the clout, all oiled and painted, and armed with rifles. One or two
glanced up along our slope while passing, but a gesture from the leader hastened
their steps, and more quickly than I can write it they had disappeared among the
darkening shadows of the towering timber.

"Bad luck!" breathed Murphy; "'tis a rocky road to Dublin, but a shorter wan to hell! Did you want f'r to shoot, Jack? Look at Dave Elerson an' th' thrigger finger av him twitchin' all a-thremble! Wisha, lad! lave the red omadhouns go. Arre you tired o' the hair ye wear, Jack Mount? Come on out o' this, ye crazy divil!"

Circling the crossing-place, we swung east, then south, coming presently to a fringe of trees through which the red sunset glittered, illuminating a great stretch of swamp, river, and cleared land beyond. "Yonder's the foort," whispered Murphy--"ould Stanwix--or Schuyler, as they call it now. Step this way, sorr; ye can see it plain across the Mohawk shwamps."

The red sunshine struck the three-cornered bastions of the rectangular fort; a distant bayonet caught the light and twinkled above the stockaded ditch like a slender point of flame. Outside the works squads of troops moved, relieving the nearer posts; working details, marching to and from the sawmill, were evidently busy with the unfinished abattis; a long, low earth-work, surmounted by a stockade and a block-house, which. Murphy said, guarded the covered way to the creek, swarmed with workmen plying pick and shovel and crowbar, while the sentries walked their beats above, watching the new road which crossed the creek and ran through the swamp to the sawmill.

"It is strange," said Mount, "that they have not yet finished the fort."

"It is stranger yet," said Elerson, "that they should work so close to the forest yonder. Look at that fatigue-party drawing logs within pistol-shot of the woods--"

Before the rifleman could finish, a sentinel on the northwest parapet fired his musket; the entire scene changed in a twinkling; the fatigue-party scattered, dropping chains and logs; the workmen sprang out of ditch and pit, running for the stockade; a man, driving a team of horses along the new road, jumped up in his wagon and lashed his horses to a gallop across the rough meadow; and I saw the wagon swaying and bumping up the slope, followed by a squad of troops on the double. Behind these ran a dozen men driving some frightened cattle; soldiers swarmed out on the bastions, soldiers flung open the water gates, soldiers hung over parapets, gesticulating and pointing westward.

Suddenly from the bastion on the west angle of the fort a shaft of flame leaped; a majestic cloud buried the parapet, and the deep cannon-thunder shook the evening air. Above the writhing smoke, now stained pink in the sunset light, a flag crept jerkily up the halyards of a tall flag-staff, higher, higher, until it caught the evening wind aloft and floated lazily out.

"It's the new flag," whispered Elerson, in an awed voice.

We stared at it, fascinated. Never before had the world seen that flag displayed. Blood-red and silver-white the stripes rippled; the stars on the blue field glimmered peacefully. There it floated, serene above the drifting cannon--smoke, the first American flag ever hoisted on earth. A freshening wind caught it, blowing strong out of the flaming west; the cannon-smoke eddied, settled, and curled, floating across its folds. Far away we heard a faint sound from the bastions. They were cheering.

Cap in hand I stood, eyes never leaving the flag; Mount uncovered, Elerson and Murphy drew their deer-skin caps from their heads in silence.

After a little while we caught the glimmer of steel along the forest's edge; a patch of scarlet glowed in the fading rays of sunset. Then, out into the open walked a red-coated officer bearing a white flag and attended by a drummer in green and scarlet.

Far across the clearing we heard drums beating the parley; and we knew the British were at the gates of Stanwix, and that St. Leger had summoned the garrison to surrender.

We waited; the white flag entered the stockade gate, only to reappear again, quickly, as though the fort's answer to the summons had been brief and final. Scarcely had the ensign reached the forest than bang! bang! bang! bang! echoed the muskets, and the rifles spat flame into the deepening dusk and the dark woods rang with the war-yell of half a thousand Indians stripped for the last battles that the Long House should ever fight.

About ten o'clock that night we met a regiment of militia on the Johnstown road, marching noisily north towards Whitestown, and learned that General Herkimer's brigade was concentrating at an Oneida hamlet called Oriska, only eight miles by the river highway from Stanwix, and a little to the east of Oriskany creek. An officer named Van Slyck also informed me that an Oneida interpreter had just come in, reporting St. Leger's arrival before Stanwix, and warning Herkimer that an ambuscade had been prepared for him should he advance to raise the siege of the beleaguered fort.

Learning that we also had seen the enemy at Stanwix, this officer begged us to accompany him to Oriska, where our information might prove valuable to General Herkimer. So I and my three riflemen fell in as the troops tramped past; and I, for one, was astonished to hear their drums beating so loudly in the enemy's country, and to observe the careless indiscipline in the ranks, where men talked loudly and their reckless laughter often sounded above the steady rolling of the drums.

"Are there no officers here to cuff their ears!" muttered Mount, in disgust.

"Bah!" sneered Elerson; "officers can't teach militia--only a thrashing does 'em any good. After all, our people are like the British, full o' contempt for untried enemies. Do you recall how the red-coats went swaggering about that matter o' Bunker Hill? They make no more frontal attacks now, but lay ambuscades, and thank their stars for the opportunity."

A soldier, driving an ox-team behind us, began to sing that melancholy ballad called "St. Clair's Defeat." The entire company joined in the chorus, bewailing the late disaster at Ticonderoga, till Jack Mount, nigh frantic with disgust, leaped up into the cart and bawled out:

"If you must sing, damn you, I'll give something that rings!"

And he lifted his deep, full-throated voice, sounding the marching song of "Morgan's Men."

"The Lord He is our rampart and our buckler and our shield!
We must aid Him cleanse His temple; we must follow Him afield.
To His wrath we leave the guilty, for their punishment is sure;
To His justice the downtrodden, for His mercy shall endure!"

And out of the darkness the ringing chorus rose, sweeping the column from end to end, and the echoing drums crashed amen!

Yet there is a time for all things--even for praising God.

XVIII
ORISKANY

It is due, no doubt, to my limited knowledge of military matters and to my lack of practical experience that I did not see the battle of Oriskany as our historians have recorded it; nor did I, before or during the affair, notice any intelligent effort towards assuming the offensive as described by those whose reports portray an engagement in which, after the first onset, some semblance of military order reigned.

So, as I do not feel at liberty to picture Oriskany from the pens of abler men, I must be content to describe only what I myself witnessed of that sad and unnecessary tragedy.

For three days we had been camped near the clearing called Oriska, which is on the south bank of the Mohawk. Here the volunteers and militia of Tryon County were concentrating from Fort Dayton in the utmost disorder, their camps so foolishly pitched, so slovenly in those matters pertaining to cleanliness and health, so inadequately guarded, that I saw no reason why our twin enemies, St. Leger and disease, should not make an end of us ere we sighted the ramparts of Stanwix.

All night long the volunteer soldiery had been in-subordinate and riotous in the hamlet of Oriska, thronging the roads, shouting, singing, disputing, clamoring to be led against the enemy. Popular officers were cheered, unpopular officers jeered at, angry voices raised outside headquarters, demanding to know why old Honikol Herkimer delayed the advance. Even officers shouted, "Forward! forward! Wake up Honikol!" And spoke of the old General derisively, even injuriously, to their own lasting disgrace.

Towards dawn, when I lay down on the floor of a barn to sleep, the uproar had died out in a measure; but lights still flickered in the camp where soldiers were smoking their pipes and playing cards by the flare of splinter-wood torches. As for the pickets, they paid not the slightest attention to their duties, continually leaving their posts to hobnob with neighbors; and the indiscipline alarmed me, for what could one expect to find in men who roamed about where it pleased them, howling their dissatisfaction with their commander, and addressing their officers by their first names?

At eight o'clock on that oppressive August morning, while writing a letter to my cousin Dorothy, which an Oneida had promised to deliver, he being about to start with a message to Governor Clinton, I was interrupted by Jack Mount, who came into the barn, saying that a company of officers were quarrelling in front of the sugar-shack occupied as headquarters.

I folded my letter, sealed it with a bit of blue balsam gum, and bade Mount deliver it to the Oneida runner, while I stepped up the road.

Of all unseemly sights that I have ever had the misfortune to witness, what I now saw was the most shameful. I pushed and shouldered my way through a riotous mob of soldiers and teamsters which choked the highway; loud, angry voices raised in reproach or dispute assailed my ears. A group of militia officers were shouting, shoving, and gesticulating in front of the tent where, rigid in his arm-chair, the General sat, grim, narrow-eyed, silent, smoking a short clay pipe. Bolt upright, behind him, stood his chief scout and interpreter, a superb Oneida, in all the splendor of full war-paint, blazing with scarlet.

Colonel Cox, a swaggering, intrusive, loud-voiced, and smartly uniformed officer, made a sign for silence and began haranguing the old man, evidently as spokesman for the party of impudent malcontents grouped about him. I heard him demand that his men be led against the British without further delay. I heard him condemn delay as unreasonable and unwarrantable, and the terms of speech he used were unbecoming to an officer.

"We call on you, sir, in the name of Tryon County, to order us forward!" he said, loudly. "We are ready. For God's sake give the order, sir! There is no time to waste, I tell you!"

The old General removed the pipe from his teeth and leaned a little forward in his chair.

"Colonel Cox," he said, "I haff Adam Helmer to Stanvix sent, mit der opject of inviting Colonel Gansevoort to addack py de rear ven ve addack py dot left flank.

"So soon as Helmer comes dot fort py, Gansevoort he fire cannon; und so soon I hear cannon, I march! Not pefore, sir; not pefore!"

"How do we know that Helmer and his men will ever reach Stanwix?" shouted Colonel Paris, impatiently.

"Ve vait, und py un' py ve know," replied Herkimer, undisturbed.

"He may be dead and scalped by now," sneered Colonel Visscher.

"Look you, Visscher," said the old General; "it iss I who am here to answer for your safety. Now comes Spencer, my Oneida, mit a pelt, who svears to me dot Brant und Butler an ambuscade haff made for me. Vat I do? Eh? I vait for dot sortie? Gewiss!"

He waved his short pipe.

"For vy am I an ass to march me py dot ambuscade? Such a foolishness iss dot talk! I stay me py Oriskany till I dem cannon hear."

A storm of insolent protest from the mob of soldiers greeted his decision; the officers gesticulated and shouted insultingly, shoving forward to the edge of the porch. Fists were shaken at him, cries of impatience and contempt rose everywhere. Colonel Paris flung his sword on the ground. Colonel Cox, crimson with anger, roared: "If you delay another moment the blood of Gansevoort's men be on your head!"

Then, in the tumult, a voice called out: "He's a Tory! We are betrayed!" And Colonel Cox shouted: "He dares not march! He is a coward!"

White to the lips, the old man sprang from his chair, narrow eyes ablaze, hands trembling. Colonel Bellinger and Major Frey caught him by the arm, begging him to remain firm in his decision.

"Py Gott, no!" he thundered, drawing his sword. "If you vill haff it so, your blood be on your heads! Vorwaerts!"

It is not for me to blame him in his wrath, when, beside himself with righteous fury, he gave the bellowing yokels their heads and swept on with them to destruction. The mutinous fools who had called him coward and traitor fell back as their outraged commander strode silently through the disordered ranks, noticing neither the proffered apologies of Colonel Paris nor the stammered excuses of Colonel Cox. Behind him stalked the tall Oneida, silent, stern, small eyes flashing. And now began the immense uproar of departure; confused officers ran about cursing and shouting; the smashing roll of the drums broke out, beating the assembly; teamsters rushed to harness horses; dismayed soldiers pushed and struggled through the mass, searching for their regiments and companies.

Mounted on a gaunt, gray horse, the General rode through the disorder, quietly directing the incompetent militia officers in their tasks of collecting their men; and behind him, splendidly horsed and caparisoned, cantered the tall Oneida, known as Thomas Spencer the Interpreter, calm, composed, inscrutable eyes fixed on his beloved leader and friend.

The drums of the Canajoharie regiment were beating as the drummers swung past me, sleeves rolled up to the elbows, sweat pouring down their sunburned faces; then came Herkimer, all alone, sitting his saddle like a rock, the flush of anger still staining his weather-ravaged visage, his small, wrathful eyes fixed on the north.

Behind him rode Colonels Cox and Paris, long, heavy swords drawn, heading the Canajoharie regiment, which pressed forward excitedly. The remaining regiments of Tryon County militia followed, led by Colonel Seeber, Colonel Bellenger, Majors Frey, Eisenlord, and Van Slyck. Then came the baggage-wagons, some drawn by oxen, some by four horses; and in the rear of these rode Colonel Visscher, leading the Caughnawaga regiment, closing the dusty column.

"Damn them!" growled Elerson to Murphy, "they're advancing without flanking-parties or scouts. I wish Dan'l Morgan was here."

"'Tis th' Gineral's jooty to luk out f'r his throops, not Danny Morgan's or mine," replied the big rifleman in disgust.

The column halted. I signalled my men to follow me and hastened along the flanks under a fire of chaff: "Look at young buckskins! There go Morgan's macaronis! God help the red-coats this day! How's the scalp trade, son?"

Herkimer was sitting his horse in the middle of the road as I came up; and he scowled down at me when I gave him the officer's salute and stood at attention beside his stirrup.

"Veil, you can shpeak," he said, bluntly; "efery-body shpeaks but me!"

I said that I and my riflemen were at his disposal if he desired leaders for flanking-parties or scouts; and his face softened as he listened, looking down at me in silence.

"Sir," he said, "it iss to my shame I say dot my sodgers command me, not I my sodgers."

Then, looking back at Colonel Cox, he added, bitterly:

"I haff ordered flanking-parties and scouts, but my officers, who know much more than I, haff protested against dot useless vaste of time. I thank you, sir; I can your offer not accept."

The drums began again; the impatient Palatine regiment moved forward, yelling their approval, and we fell back to the roadside, while the boisterous troops tramped past, cheering, singing, laughing in their excitement. Mechanically we fell in behind the Caughnawagas, who formed the rear-guard, and followed on through the dust; meaning to go with them only a mile or so before we started back across country with the news which I was now at liberty to take in person to General Schuyler.

For I considered my mission at an end. In one thing only had I failed: Walter Butler was still free; but now that he commanded a company of outlaws and savages in St. Leger's army, I, of course, had no further hope of arresting him or of dealing with him in any manner save on the battle-field.

So at last I felt forced to return to Varick Manor; but the fear of the dread future was in me, and all the hopeless misery of a hopeless passion made of me a coward, so that I shrank from the pain I must surely inflict and endure. Kinder for her, kinder for me, that we should never meet again.

Not that I desired to die. I was too young in life and love to wish for death as a balm. Besides, I knew it could not bring us peace. Still, it was one solution of a problem otherwise so utterly hopeless that I, heartsick, had long since wearied of the solving and carried my hurt buried deep, fearful lest my prying senses should stir me to disinter the dead hope lying there.

Absence renders passion endurable. But at sight of her I loved I knew I could not endure it; and, uncertain of myself, having twice nigh failed under the overwhelming provocations of a love returned, I shrank from the coming duel 'twixt love and duty which must once more be fought within my breast.

Nor could my duty, fighting blindly, expect encouragement from her I loved, save at the last gasp and under the heel of love. Then, only, at the very last would she save me; for there was that within her which revolted at a final wrong, and I knew that not even our twin passion could prevail to stamp out the last spark of conscience and slay our souls forever.

Brooding, as I trudged forward through the dust, I became aware that the drums had ceased their beating, and that the men were marching quietly with little laughter or noise of song.

The heat was intense, although a black cloud had pushed up above the west, veiling the sun. Flies swarmed about the column; sweat poured from men and horses; the soldiers rolled back their sleeves and plodded on, muskets a-trail and coats hanging over their shoulders. Once, very far away, the looming horizon was veined with lightning; and, after a long time, thunder sounded.

We had marched northward on a rutty road some two miles or more from our camp at Oriska, and I was asking Mount how near we were to the old Algonquin-Iroquois trail which runs from the lakes across the wilderness to the healing springs at Saratoga, when the column halted and I heard an increasing confusion of voices from the van.

"There's a ravine ahead," said Elerson. "I'm thinking they'll have trouble with these wagons, for there's a swamp at the bottom and only a log-road across."

"Tis the proper shpot f'r to ambuscade us," observed Murphy, craning his neck and standing on tiptoe to see ahead.

We walked forward and sat down on the bank close to the brow of the hill. Directly ahead a ravine, shaped like a half-moon, cut the road, and the noisy Canajoharie regiment was marching into it. The bottom of the ravine appeared to be a swamp, thinly timbered with tamarack and blue-beech saplings, where the reeds and cattails grew thick, and little, dark pools of water spread, all starred with water-lilies, shining intensely white in the gloom of the coming storm.

"There do be wild ducks in thim rushes," said Murphy, musingly. "Sure I count it sthrange, Jack Mount, that thim burrds sit quiet-like an' a screechin' rigiment marchin' acrost that log-road."

"You mean that somebody has been down there before and scared the ducks away?" I asked.

"Maybe, sorr," he replied, grimly.

Instinctively we leaned forward to scan the rising ground on the opposite side of the ravine. Nothing moved in the dense thickets. After a moment Mount said quietly: "I'm a liar or there's a barked twig showing raw wood alongside of that ledge."

He glanced at the pan of his rifle, then again fixed his keen, blue eyes on the tiny glimmer of white which even I could distinguish now, though Heaven only knows how his eyes had found it in all that tangle.

"That's raw wood," he repeated.

"A deer might bark a twig," said I.

"Maybe, sorr," muttered Murphy; "but there's divil a deer w'ud nibble sheep-laurel."

The men of the Canajoharie regiment were climbing the hill on the other side of the ravine now. Colonel Cox came galloping back, shouting: "Bring up those wagons! The road is clear! Move your men forward there!"

Whips cracked; the vehicles rattled off down hill, drivers yelling, soldiers pushing the heavy wheels forward over the log-road below which spurted water as the bumping wagons struck the causeway.

I remember that Colonel Cox had just drawn bridle, half-way up the opposite incline, and was leaning forward in his saddle to watch the progress of an ox-team, when a rifle-shot rang out and he tumbled clean out of his saddle, striking the shallow water with a splash.

Then hell itself broke loose in that black ravine; volley on volley poured into the Canajoharie regiment; officers fell from their horses; drivers reeled and pitched forward under the heels of their plunging teams; wagons collided and broke down, choking the log-road. Louder and louder the terrific yells of the outlaws and savages rang out on our flanks; I saw our soldiers in the ravine running frantically in all directions, falling on the log-road, floundering waist-deep in the water and mud, slipping, stumbling, staggering; while faster and faster cracked the hidden rifles, and the pitiless bullets pelted them from the heights above.

"Stand! Stand! you fools!" bawled Elerson. "Take to the timber! Every man to a tree! For God's sake remember Braddock!"

"Look out!" shouted Mount, dragging me with him to a rock. "Close up, Elerson! Close up, Murphy!"

Straight into the stupefied ranks of the Caughnawaga company came leaping the savages, shooting, stabbing, clubbing the dazed men, dragging them from the ranks with shrieks of triumph. I saw one half-naked creature, awful in his paint, run up and strike a soldier full in the face with his fist, then dash out his brains with a death-maul and tear his scalp off.

Murphy and Mount were loading and firing steadily; Elerson and I kept our rifles ready for a rush. I was perfectly stunned; the spectacle did not seem real to me.

The Caughnawaga men, apparently roused from their momentary stupor, fell back into small squads, shooting in every direction; and the savages, unable to withstand a direct fire, sheered off and came bounding past us to cover, yelping like timber-wolves. Three darted directly at us; a young warrior, painted in bars of bright yellow, raised his hatchet to hurl it; but Murphy's bullet spun him round like a top till he crashed against a tree and fell in a heap, quivering all over.

The two others had leaped on Mount. Swearing, threatening, roaring with rage, the desperate giant shook them off into our midst, and cut the throat of one as he lay sprawling--a sickening spectacle, for the poor wretch floundered and thrashed about among the leaves and sticks, squirting thick blood all over us.

The remaining savage, a chief, by his lock and eagle-quill, had fastened to Elerson's legs with the fury of a tree-cat, clawing and squalling, while Murphy dealt him blow on blow with clubbed stock, and finally was forced to shoot him so close that the rifle-flame set his greased scalp-lock afire.

"Take to the timber, you Tryon County men! Remember Braddock!" shouted Colonel Paris, plunging about on his wounded horse; while from every tree and bush rang out the reports of the rifles; and the steady stream of bullets poured into the Caughnawaga regiment, knocking the men down the hill-side into the struggling mass below. Some dropped dead where they had been shot; some rolled to the log-road; some fell into the marsh, splashing and limping about like crippled wild fowl.

"Advance der Palatine regiment!" thundered Herkimer. "Clear avay dot oxen-team!"

A drummer-boy of the Palatines beat the charge. I can see him yet, a curly-haired youngster, knee-deep in the mud, his white, frightened face fixed on his commander. They shot his drum to pieces; he beat steadily on the flapping parchment.

Across the swamp the Palatines were doggedly climbing the slope in the face of a terrible discharge. Herkimer led them. As they reached the crest of the plateau, and struggled up and over, a rush of men in green uniforms seemed to swallow the entire Palatine regiment. I saw them bayonet Major Eisenlord and finish him with their rifle-stocks; they stabbed Major Van Slyck, and hurled themselves at the mounted Oneida. Hatchet flashing, the interpreter swung his horse straight into the yelling onset and went down, smothered under a mass of enemies.

"Vorwaerts!" thundered Herkimer, standing straight up in his stirrups; but they shot him out of his saddle and closed with the Palatines, hilt to hilt.

Major Frey and Colonel Bellenger fell under their horses, Colonel Seeber dropped dead into the ravine, Captain Graves was dragged from the ranks and butchered by bayonets; but those stubborn Palatines calmly divided into squads, and their steady fusillade stopped the rush of the Royal Greens and sent the flanking savages howling to cover.

Mount, Murphy, Elerson, and I lay behind a fallen hemlock, awaiting the flank attack which we now understood must surely come. For our regiments were at last completely surrounded, facing outward in an irregular circle, the front held by the Palatines, the rear by the Caughnawagas, the west by part of the Canajoharie regiment, and the east by a fraction of unbrigaded militia, teamsters, batt-men, bateaux-men, and half a dozen volunteer rangers reinforced by my three riflemen.

The scene was real enough to me now. Jack Mount, kneeling beside me, was attempting to clean the blood from himself and Elerson with handfuls of dried leaves. Murphy lay on his belly, watching the forest in front of us, and his blue eyes seemed suffused with a light of their own in the deepening gloom of the gathering thunderstorm. My nerves were all a-quiver; the awful screaming from the ravine had never ceased for an instant, and in that darkening, slimy pit I could still see a swaying mass of men on the causeway, locked in a death-struggle. To and fro they reeled; hatchet and knife and gun-stock glittered, rising and falling in the twilight of the storm-cloud; the flames from the rifles flashed crimson.

"Kape ye're eyes to the front, sorr; they do be comin'!" cried Murphy, springing briskly to his feet.

I looked ahead into the darkening woods; the Caughnawaga men were falling back, taking station behind trees; Mount stepped to the shelter of a big oak; Elerson leaped to cover under a pine; a Caughnawaga bateaux-man darted past me, stationing himself on my right behind the trunk of a dapple beech. Suddenly an Indian showed himself close in front; the Caughnawaga man fired and missed; and, quicker than I can write it, the savage was on him before he could reload and had brained him with a single castete-stroke. I fired, but the Mohawk was too quick for me, and a moment later he bounded back into the brush while the forest rang with his triumphant scalp-yell.

"That's what they're doing in front!" shouted Elerson. "When a soldier fires they're on him before he can reload!"

"Two men to a tree!" roared Jack Mount. "Double up there, you Caughnawaga men!"

Elerson glided cautiously to the oak which sheltered Mount; Murphy crept forward to my tree.

"Bedad!" he muttered, "let the ondacent divils dhraw ye're fire an' welcome. I've a pill to purge 'em now. Luk at that, sorr! Shteady! Shteady an' cool does it!"

A savage, with his face painted half white and half red, stepped out from the thicket and dropped just as I fired. The next instant he came leaping straight for our tree, castete poised.

Murphy fired. The effect of the shot was amazing; the savage stopped short in mid-career as though he had come into collision with a stone wall; then Elerson fired, knocking him flat, head doubled under his naked shoulders, feet trailing across a rotting log.

"Save ye're powther, Dave!" sang out Murphy. "Sure he was clean kilt as he shtood there. Lave a dead man take his own time to fall!"

I had reloaded, and Murphy was coolly priming, when on our right the rifles began speaking faster and faster, and I heard the sound of men running hard over the dry leaves, and the thudding gallop of horses.

"A charge!" said Murphy. "There do be horses comin', too. Have they dhragoons?--I dunnoa. Ha! There they go! 'Tis McCraw's outlaws or I'm a Dootchman!"

A shrill cock-crow rang out in the forest.

"'Tis the chanticleer scalp-yell of that damned loon, Francy McCraw!" he cried, fiercely. "Give it to 'em, b'ys! Shoot hell into the dommed Tories!"

The Caughnawaga rifles rang out from every tree; a white man came running through the wood, and I instinctively held my fire.

"Shoot the dhirrty son of a shlut!" yelled Murphy; and Elerson shot him and knocked him down, but the man staggered to his feet again, clutching at his wounded throat, and reeled towards us. He fell again, got on his knees, crawled across the dead leaves until he was scarce fifteen yards away, then fell over and lay there, coughing.

"A dead wan,'" said Murphy, calmly; "lave him."

McCraw's onset passed along our extreme left; the volleys grew furious; the ghastly cock-crow rang out shrill and piercing, and we fired at long range where the horses were passing through the rifle-smoke.

Then, in the roar of the fusillade, a bright flash lighted up the forest; a thundering crash followed, and the storm burst, deluging the woods with rain. Trees rocked and groaned, dashing their tops together; the wind rose to a hurricane; the rain poured down, beating the leaves from the trees, driving friend and foe to shelter. The reports of the rifles ceased; the war-yelp died away. Peal on peal of thunder shook the earth; the roar of the tempest rose to a steady shriek through which the terrific smashing of falling trees echoed above the clash of branches.

Soaked, stunned, blinded by the awful glare of the lightning, I crouched under the great oak, which rocked and groaned, convulsed to its bedded roots, so that the ground heaved under me as I lay.

I could not see ten feet ahead of me, so thick was the gloom with rain and flying leaves and twigs. The thunder culminated in a series of fearful crashes; bolt after bolt fell, illuminating the flying chaos of the tempest; then came a stunning silence, slowly filled with the steady roar of the rain.

A gray pallor grew in the woods. I looked down into the ravine and saw a muddy lake there full of dead men and horses.

The wounded Tory near us was still choking and coughing, dying hard out there in the rain. Mount and Elerson crept over to where we lay, and, after a moment's conference, Murphy led us in a long circle, swinging gradually northward until we stumbled into the drenched Palatine regiment, which was still holding its ground. There was no firing on either side; the guns were too wet.

On a wooded knoll to the left a group of dripping men had gathered. Somebody said that the old General lay there, smoking and directing the defence, his left leg shattered by a ball. I saw the blue smoke of his pipe curling up under the tree, but I did not see him.

The wind had died out; the thunder rolled off to the northward, muttering among the hills; rain fell less heavily; and I saw wounded men tearing strips from their soaking shirts to bind their hurts. Details from the Canajoharie regiment passed us searching the underbrush for their dead.

I also noticed with a shudder that Elerson and Murphy carried two fresh scalps apiece, tied to the belts of their hunting-shirts; but I said nothing, having been warned by Jack Mount that they considered it their prerogative to take the scalps of those who had failed to take theirs.

How they could do it I cannot understand, for I had once seen the body of a scalped man, with the skin, released from the muscles of the forehead, hanging all loose and wrinkled over the face.

With the ceasing of the rain came the renewed crack of the rifles and the whiz of bullets. We took post on the extreme left, firing deliberately at McCraw's renegades; and I do not know whether I hit any or not, but five men did I see fall under the murderous aim of Murphy; and I know that Elerson shot two savages, for he went down into the ravine after them and returned with the wet, red trophies.

The sun was now shining again with a heat so fierce and intense that the earth smoked vapor all around us. It was at this time that I, personally, experienced the only close fighting of the day, which brought a sudden end to this most amazing and bloody skirmish.

I had been lying full length behind a bush in the lines of the Palatine regiment, eating a crust of bread; for that strange battle-hunger had been gnawing at my vitals for an hour. Some of the men were eating, some firing; the steaming heat almost suffocated me as I lay there, yet I munched on, ravenous as a December wolf.

I heard somebody shout: "Here they come!" and, filling my mouth with bread, I rose to my knees to see.

A body of troops in green uniforms came marching steadily towards us, led by a red-coated officer on horseback; and all around me the Palatines were springing to their feet, uttering cries of rage, cursing the oncoming troops, and calling out to them by name.

For the detachment of Royal Greens which now advanced to the assault was, it appeared, composed of old acquaintances and neighbors of the Palatines, who had fled to join the Tories and Indians and now returned to devastate their own county.

Lashed to ungovernable fury by the sight of these hated renegades, the entire regiment leaped forward with a roar and rushed on the advancing detachment, stabbing, shooting, clubbing, throttling. Mutual hatred made the contest terrible beyond words; no quarter was given on either side. I saw men strangle each other with naked hands; kick each other to death, fighting like dogs, tooth and nail, rolling over the wet ground.

The tide had not yet struck us; we fired at their mounted officer, whom Elerson declared he recognized as Major Watts, brother-in-law to Sir John Johnson; and presently, as usual, Murphy hit him, so that the young fellow dropped forward on his saddle and his horse ran away, flinging him against a tree with a crash, doubtless breaking every bone in his body.

Then, above the tumult, out of the north came booming three cannon-shots, the signal from the fort that Herkimer had desired to wait for.

A detachment from the Canajoharie regiment surged out of the woods with a ringing cheer, pointing northward, where, across a clearing, a body of troops were rapidly advancing from the direction of the fort.

"The sortie! The sortie!" shouted the soldiers, frantic with joy. Murphy and I ran towards them; Elerson yelled: "Be careful! Look at their uniforms! Don't go too close to them!"

"They're coming from the north!" bawled Mount. "They're our own people, Dave! Come on!"

Captain Jacob Gardinier, with a dozen Caughnawaga men, had already reached the advancing troops, when Murphy seized my arm and halted me, crying out, "Those men are wearing their coats turned inside out! They're Johnson's Greens!"

At the same instant I recognized Colonel John Butler as the officer leading them; and he knew me and, without a word, fired his pistol at me. We were so near them now that a Tory caught hold of Murphy and tried to stab him, but the big Irishman kicked him headlong and rushed into the mob, swinging his long hatchet, followed by Gardinier and his Caughnawaga men, whom the treachery had transformed into demons.

In an instant all around me men were swaying, striking, shooting, panting, locked in a deadly embrace. A sweating, red-faced soldier closed with me; chin to chin, breast to breast we wrestled; and I shall never forget the stifling struggle-- every detail remains, his sunburned face, wet with sweat and powder-smeared; his irregular teeth showing when I got him by the throat, and the awful change that came over his visage when Jack Mount shoved the muzzle of his rifle against the struggling fellow and shot him through the stomach.

Freed from his death-grip, I stood breathing convulsively, hands clinched, one foot on my fallen rifle. An Indian ran past me, chased by Elerson and Murphy, but the savage dodged into the underbrush, shrieking, "Oonah! Oonah! Oonah!" and Elerson came back, waving his deer-hide cap.

Everywhere Tories, Royal Greens, and Indians were running into the woods; the wailing cry, "Oonah! Oonah!" rose on all sides now. Gardinier's Caughnawa-ga men were shooting rapidly; the Palatines, master of their reeking brush-field, poured a heavy fire into the detachment of retreating Greens, who finally broke and ran, dropping sack and rifle in their flight, and leaving thirty of their dead under the feet of the Palatines.

The soldiers of the Canajoharie regiment came up, swarming over a wooded knoll on the right, only to halt and stand, silently leaning on their rifles.

For the battle of Oriskany was over.

There was no cheering from the men of Tryon County. Their victory had been too dearly bought; their losses too terrible; their triumph sterile, for they could not now advance the crippled fragments of their regiments and raise the siege in the face of St. Leger's regulars and Walter Butler's Rangers.

Their combat with Johnson's Greens and Brant's Mohawks had been fought; and, though masters of the field, they could do no more than hold their ground. Perhaps the bitter knowledge that they must leave Stanwix to its fate, and that, too, through their own disobedience, made the better soldiers of them in time. But it was a hard and dreadful lesson; and I saw men crying, faces hidden in their powder-blackened hands, as the dying General was borne through the ranks, lying gray and motionless on his hemlock litter.

And this is all that I myself witnessed of that shameful ambuscade and murder-ous combat, fought some two miles north of the dirty camp, and now known as the

Battle of Oriskany.

That night we buried our dead; one hundred on the field where they had fallen, two hundred and fifty in the burial trenches at Oriskany--thirty-five wagon-loads in all. Scarcely an officer of rank remained to lead the funeral march when the muffled drums of the Palatines rolled at midnight, and the smoky torches moved, and the dead-wagons rumbled on through the suffocating darkness of a starless night. We had few wounded; we took no prisoners; Oriskany meant death. We counted only thirty men disabled and some score missing.

"God grant the missing be safely dead," prayed our camp chaplain at the burial trench. We knew what that meant; worse than dead were the wretched men who had fallen alive into the hands of old John Butler and his son, Walter, and that vicious drunkard, Barry St. Leger, who had offered, over his own signature, two hundred and forty dollars a dozen for prime Tryon County scalps.

I slept little that night, partly from the excitement of my first serious combat, partly because of the terrible heat. Our outposts, now painfully overzealous and alert, fired off their muskets at every fancied sound or movement, and these continual alarms kept me awake, though Mount and Murphy slept peacefully, and Elerson yawned on guard.

Towards sunrise rain fell heavily, but brought no relief from the heat; the sun, a cherry-red ball, hung a hand's-breadth over the forests when the curtain of rain faded away. The riflemen, curled up in the hay on the barn floor, snored on, unconscious; the batt-horses crunched and munched in the manger; flies whirled and swarmed over a wheelbarrow piled full of dead soldier's shoes, which must to-day be distributed among the living.

All the loathsome and filthy side of war seemed concentrated around the barnyard, where sleepy, unshaven, half-dressed soldiers were burning the under-clothes of a man who had died of the black measles; while a great, brawny fellow, naked to the waist and smeared from hair to ankles with blood, butchered sheep, so that the army might eat that day.

The thick stench of the burning clothing, the odor of blood, the piteous bleating of the doomed creatures sickened me; and I made my way out of the barn and down to the river, where I stripped and waded out to wash me and my clothes.

A Caughnawaga soldier gave me a bit of soap; and I spent the morning there.

By noon the fierce heat of the sun had dried my clothes; by two o'clock our small scout of four left the Stanwix and Johnstown road and struck out through the unbroken wilderness for German Flatts.

XIX
THE HOME TRAIL

For eleven days we lay at German Flatts, Colonel Visscher begging us to aid in the defence of that threatened village until the women and children could be conveyed to Johnstown. But Sir John Johnson remained before Stanwix, and McCraw's riders gave the village wide berth, and on the 18th of August we set out for Varicks'.

Warned by our extreme outposts, we bore to the south, forced miles out of our course to avoid the Oneida country, where a terrific little war was raging. For the Senecas, Cayugas, a few Mohawks, and McCraw's renegade Tories, furious at the neutral and pacific attitude of the Oneidas towards our people, had suddenly fallen upon them, tooth and nail, vowing that the Oneida nation should perish from the earth for their treason to the Long House.

We skirted the doomed region cautiously, touching here and there the fringe of massacre and fire, often scenting smoke, sometimes hearing a distant shot. Once we encountered an Oneida runner, painted blue and white, and naked save for the loin-cloth, who told us of the civil war that was already rending the Long House; and I then understood more fully what Magdalen Brant had done for our cause, and how far-reaching had been the effects of her appearance at the False-Faces' council-fire.

The Oneida appeared to be disheartened. He sullenly admitted to us that the Cayugas had scattered his people and laid their village in ashes; he cursed McCraw fiercely and promised a dreadful retaliation on any renegade captured. He also described the fate of the Oriskany prisoners and some bateaux-men taken by Walter Butler's Rangers near Wood Creek; and I could scarcely endure to listen, so horrid were the details of our soldiers' common fate, where Mohawk and Tory, stripped and painted alike, conspired to invent atrocities undreamed of for their wretched victims.

It was then that I heard for the second time the term "Blue-eyed Indian," meaning white men stained, painted, and disguised as savages. More terrifying than the savages themselves, it appeared, were the blue-eyed Indians to the miserable settlers of Tryon. For hellish ingenuity and devilish cruelty these mock savages, the Oneida assured us, had nothing to learn from their red comrades; and I shall never be able to efface from my mind the memory of what we saw, that very day, in a lonely farm-house on the flats of the Mohawk; nor was it necessary that McCraw should have left his mark on the shattered door--a cock crowing, drawn in outline by a man's forefinger steeped in blood--to enlighten those who might not recognize the ghastly work as his.

We stayed there for three hours to bury the dead, an old man and woman, a young mother, and five children, the youngest an infant not a year old. All had been scalped; even the watch-dog lay dead near the bloody cradle. We dug the shallow graves with difficulty, having nothing to work with save our hunting-knives and some broken dishes which we found in the house; and it was close to noon before we left the lonely flat and pushed forward through miles of stunted willow growth towards the river road which led to Johnstown.

I shall never forget Mount's set face nor Murphy's terrible, vacant stare as we plodded on in absolute silence. Elerson led us on a steady trot hour after hour, till, late in the afternoon, we crossed the river road and wheeled into it exhausted.

The west was all aglow; cleared land and fences lay along the roadside; here and there houses loomed up in the red, evening light, but their inhabitants were gone, and not a sign of life remained about them save for the circling swallows whirling in and out of the blackened chimneys.

So still, so sad this solitude that the sudden chirping of a robin in the evening shadows startled us.

The sun sank behind the forest, turning the river to a bloody red; a fox yapped and yapped from a dark hill-side; the moon's yellow light flashed out through the trees; and, with the coming of the moon, far in the wilderness the owls began and the cries of the night-hawks died away in the sky.

The first human being that we encountered was a miller riding an ancient horse towards a lane which bordered a noisy brook.

When he discovered us he whipped out a pistol and bade us stand where we were; and it took all my persuasion to convince him that we were not renegades from McCraw's band.

We asked for news, but he had none, save that a heavy force of our soldiers was lying by the roadside some two miles below on their way to relieve Fort Stanwix. The General, he believed, was named Arnold, and the troops were Massachusetts men; that was all he knew.

He seemed stupid or perhaps stunned, having lost three sons in a battle somewhere near Bennington, and had that morning received word of his loss. How the battle had gone he did not know; he was on his way up the creek to lock his mill before joining the militia at Johnstown. He was not too old to carry the musket he had carried at Braddock's battle. Besides, his boys were dead, and there was no one in his family except himself to help our Congress fight the red-coats.

We watched him ride off into the darkness, gray head erect, pistol shining in his hand; then moved on, searching the distance for the outpost we knew must presently hail us. And, sure enough, from the shadow of a clump of trees came the smart challenge: "Halt! Who goes there?"

"Officer from Herkimer and scout of three with news for General Schuyler!" I answered.

"Halt, officer with scout! Sergeant of the guard! Post number three!"

Dark figures swarmed in the road ahead; a squad of men came up on the double.

"Advance officer!" rang out the summons; a torch blazed, throwing a red glare around us; a red-faced old officer in brown and scarlet walked up and took the packet of papers which I extended.

"Are you Captain Ormond?" he asked, curiously, glancing at the endorsement on my papers.

I replied that I was, and named Murphy, Elerson, and Mount as my scout.

When the soldiers standing about heard the notorious names of men already famed in ballad and story, they craned their necks to see, as my tired riflemen filed into the lines; and the staff-officer made himself exceedingly agreeable and civil, conducting us to a shelter made of balsam branches, before which a smudge was burning.

"General Arnold has despatches for you, Captain Ormond," he said; "I am Drummond, Brigade Major; we expected you at Varick Manor on the ninth--you wrote to your cousin, Miss Varick, from Oriskany, you know."

A soldier came up with two headquarters lanterns which he hung on the cross-bar of the open-faced hut; another soldier brought bread and cheese, a great apple-pie, a jug of spring water, and a bottle of brandy, with the compliments of Brigadier-General Arnold, and apologies that neither cloth, glasses, nor cutlery were included in the camp baggage.

"We're light infantry with a vengeance, Captain Ormond," said Major Drummond, laughing; "we left at twenty-four hours' notice! Gad, sir! the day before we started the General hadn't a squad under his orders; but when Schuyler called for volunteers, and his brigadiers began to raise hell at the idea of weakening the army to help Stanwix, Arnold came out of his fit of sulks on the jump! 'Who'll follow me to Stanwix?' he bawls; and, by gad, sir, the Massachusetts men fell over each other trying to sign the rolls."

He laughed again, waving my papers in the air and slapping them down on a knapsack.

"You will doubtless wish to hand these to the General yourself," he said, pleasantly. "Pray, sir, do not think of standing on ceremony; I have dined, Captain."

Mount, who had been furtively licking his lips and casting oblique glances at the bread and cheese, fell to at a nod from me. Murphy and Elerson joined him, bolting huge mouthfuls. I ate sparingly, having little appetite left after the sights I had seen in that lonely house on the Mohawk flats.

The gnats swarmed, but the smoke of the green-moss smudge kept them from us in a measure. I asked Major Drummond how soon it might be convenient for General Arnold to receive me, and he sent a young ensign to headquarters, who presently returned saying that General Arnold was making the rounds and would waive ceremony and stop at our post on his return.

"There's a soldier, sir!" said Major Drummond, emphasizing his words with a smart blow of his riding-cane on his polished quarter-boots. "He's had us on a dog-trot since we started; up hill, down dale, across the cursed Sacandaga swamps, through fords chin-high! By gad, sir! allow me to tell you that nothing stopped us!

We went through windfalls like partridges; we crossed the hills like a herd o' deer in flight! We ran as though the devil were snapping at our shanks! I'm half dead, thank you--and my shins!--you should see where that razor-boned nag of mine shaved bark enough off the trees with me to start every tannery between the Fish-House and Half-moon!"

The ruddy-faced Major roared at the recital of his own misfortunes. Mount and Murphy looked up with sympathetic grins; Elerson had fallen asleep against the side of the shack, a bit of pie, half gnawed, clutched in his brier-torn fist.

I had a pipe, but no tobacco; the Major filled my pipe, purring contentedly; a soldier, at a sign from him, took Mount and Murphy to the nearest fire, where there was a gill of grog and plenty of tobacco. I roused Elerson, who gaped, bolted his pie with a single mighty effort, and stumbled off after his comrades. Major Drummond squatted down cross-legged before the smudge, lighting his corn-cob pipe from a bit of glowing moss, and leaned back contentedly, crossing his arms behind his head.

"I'm tired, too," he said; "we march again at midnight. If it's no secret, I should like to know what's going on ahead there."

"It's no secret," I said, soberly; "the Senecas and Cayugas are harrying the Onei-das; the renegades are riding the forest, murdering women and infants. St. Leger is firing bombs at Stanwix, and Visscher is holding German Flatts with some Caugh-nawaga militia."

"And Herkimer?" asked Drummond, gravely.

"Dead," I replied, in a low voice.

"Good gad, sir! I had not heard that!" he exclaimed.

"It is true, Major. The old man died while I was at German Flatts. They say the amputation of his leg was a wretched piece of work.... He died bolt upright in his bed, smoking his pipe, and reading aloud the thirty-eighth Psalm.... His men are wild with grief, they say.... They called him a coward the morning of Oriskany."

After a silence the Major's emotion dimmed his twinkling eyes; he dragged a red bandanna handkerchief from his coat-tails and blew his nose violently.

"All flesh is grass--eh, Captain? And some of it devilish poor grass at that, eh? Well, well; we can't make an army in a day. But, by gad, sir, we've done uncommonly well. You've heard of--but no, you haven't, either. Here's news for you, friend, since you've been in the woods. On the sixth, while you fellows were shooting down some three hundred and fifty of the Mohawks, Royal Greens, and renegades, that sly old wolverine, Marinus Willett, slipped out of the fort, fell on Sir John's camp, and took twenty-one wagon-loads of provisions, blankets, ammunition, and tools; also five British standards and every bit of personal baggage belonging to Sir John Johnson, including his private papers, maps, memoranda, and all orders and instructions for the completed plans of campaign.... Wait, if you please, sir. That is not all.

"On the sixteenth, old John Stark fell upon Baum's and Breyman's Hessians at Bennington, killed and wounded over two hundred, captured seven hundred; took a thousand stand of arms, a thousand fine dragoon sabres, and four excellent field-cannon with limbers, harness, and caissons.... And lost fourteen killed!"

Speechless at the good news, I could only lean across the smudge and shake hands with him while he chuckled and slapped his knee, growing ruddier in the face every moment.

"Where are the red-coats now?" he cried. "Look at 'em! Burgoyne, scared witless, badgered, dogged from pillar to post, his army on the defensive from Still water down to Half-moon; St. Leger, destitute of his camp baggage, caught in his own wolf-pit, flinging a dozen harmless bombs at Stanwix, and frightened half to death at every rumor from Albany; McDonald chased out of the county; Mann captured, and Sir Henry Clinton dawdling in New York and bothering his head over Washington while Burgoyne, in a devil of a plight, sits yonder yelling for help!

"Where's the great invasion, Ormond? Where's the grand advance on the centre? Where's the gigantic triple blow at the heart of this scurvy rebellion? I don't know; do you?"

I shook my head, smilingly; he beamed upon me; we had a swallow of brandy together, and I lay back, deathly tired, to wait for Arnold and my despatches.

"That's right," commented the genial Major, "go to sleep while you can; the General won't take it amiss--eh? What? Oh, don't mind me, my son. Old codgers like me can get along without such luxuries as sleep. It's the young lads who require sleep. Eh? Yes, sir; I'm serious. Wait till you see sixty year! Then you'll understand.... So I'll just sit here, ... and smoke, ... and talk away in a buzz-song, ... and that will fix--"

        *   *   *   *   *

I looked up with a start; the Major had disappeared. In my eyes a lantern was shining steadily. Then a shadow moved, and I turned and stumbled to my feet, as a cloaked figure stepped into the shelter and stood before me, peering into my eyes.

"I'm Arnold; how d'ye do," came a quick, nervous voice from the depths of the military cloak. "I've a moment to stay here; we march in ten minutes. Is Herkimer dead?"

I described his death in a few words.

"Bad, bad as hell!" he muttered, fingering his sword-hilt and staring off into the darkness. "What's the situation above us? Gansevoort's holding out, isn't he? I sent him a note to-night. Of course he's holding out; isn't he?"

I made a short report of the situation as I knew it; the General looked straight into my eyes as though he were not listening.

"Yes, yes," he said, impatiently. "I know how to deal with St. Leger and Sir John--I wrote Gansevoort that I understood how to deal with them. He has only to sit tight; I'll manage the rest."

His dark, lean, eager visage caught the lantern light as he turned to scan the moonlit sky. "Ten minutes," he muttered; "we should strike German Flatts by sun-down to-morrow if our supplies come up." And, aloud, with an abrupt and vigorous gesture, "McCraw's band are scalping the settlers, they say?"

I told him what I had seen. He nodded, then his virile face changed and he gave me a sulky look.

"Captain Ormond," he said, "folk say that I brood over the wrongs done me by Congress. It's a lie; I don't care a damn about Congress--but let it pass. What I wish to say is this: On the second of August the best general in these United States except George Washington was deprived of his command and superseded by a--a--thing named Gates.... I speak of General Philip Schuyler, my friend, and now my fellow-victim."

Shocked and angry at the news of such injustice to the man whose splendid energy had already paralyzed the British invasion of New York, I stiffened up, rigid and speechless.

"Ho!" cried Arnold, with a disagreeable laugh. "It mads you, does it? Well, sir, think of me who have lived to see five men promoted over my head--and I left in the anterooms of Congress to eat my heart out! But let that pass, too. By the eternal

God, I'll show them what stuff is in me! Let it pass, Ormond, let it pass."

He began to pace the ground, gnawing his thick lower lip, and if ever the infernal fire darted from human eyes, I saw its baleful flicker then.

With a heave of his chest and a scowl, he controlled his voice, stopping in his nervous walk to face me again.

"Ormond, you've gone up higher--the commission is here." He pulled a packet of papers from his breast-pocket and thrust them at me. "Schuyler did it. He thinks well of you, sir. On the first of August he learned that he was to be superseded. He told Clinton that you deserved a commission for what you did at that Iroquois council-fire. Here it is; you're to raise a regiment of rangers for local defence of the Mohawk district.... I congratulate you, Colonel Ormond."

He offered his bony, nervous hand; I clasped it, dazed and speechless.

"Remember me," he said, eagerly. "Let me count on your voice at the next council of war. You will not regret it, Colonel. Even if you go higher--even if you rise over my luckless head, you will not regret the friendship of Benedict Arnold. For, by Heaven, sir, I have it in me to lead men; and they shall not keep me down, and they shall not fetter me--no, not even this beribboned lap-dog Gates!... Stand my friend, Ormond. I need every friend I have. And I promise you the world shall hear of me one day!"

I shall never forget his worn and shadowy face, the long nose, the strong, selfish chin, the devouring flame burning his soul out through his eyes.

"Luck be with you!" he said, abruptly, extending his hand. Once more that bony, fervid clasp, and he was gone.

A moment later the ground vibrated; a dark, massed column of troops appeared in the moonlight, marching swiftly without drum-tap or spoken command; the dim forms of mounted officers rode past like shadows against the stars; vague shapes of wagons creaked after, rolling on muffled wheels; more troops followed quickly; then the shadowy pageant ended; and there was nothing before me but the moon in the sky above a world of ghostly wilderness.

One camp lantern had been left for my use; by its nickering light I untied the documents left me by Arnold; and, sorting the papers, chose first my orders, reading the formal notice of my transfer from Morgan's Rifles to the militia; then the order detailing me to the Mohawk district, with headquarters at Varick Manor; and, finally, my commission on parchment, signed by Governor Clinton and by Philip Schuyler, Major-General Commanding the Department of the North.

It was, perhaps, the last official act as chief of department of this generous man.

The next letter was in his own handwriting. I broke the heavy seal and read:

"ALBANY,

"August 10, 1777.
"Colonel George Ormond"

"MY DEAR YOUNG FRIEND,--As you have perhaps heard rumors that General Gates has superseded me in command of the army now operating against General Burgoyne, I desire to confirm these rumors for your benefit.

"My orders I now take from General Gates, without the slightest rancor, I assure you, or the least unworthy sentiment of envy or chagrin. Congress, in its wisdom, has ordered it; and I count him unspeakably base who shall serve his country the less ardently because of a petty and personal disappointment in ambitions unfulfilled.

"I remain loyal in heart and deed to my country and to General Gates, who may command my poor talents in any manner he sees fitting.

"I say this to you because I am an older man, and I know something of younger men, and I have liked you from the first. I say it particularly because, now that you also owe duty and instant obedience to General Gates, I do not wish your obedience retarded, or your sense of duty confused by any mistaken ideas of friendship to me or loyalty to my person.

"In these times the individual is nothing, the cause
everything. Cliques, cabals, political conspiracies are
foolish, dangerous--nay, wickedly criminal. For, sir, as long
as the world endures, a house divided against itself
must fall.

"Which leads me with greatest pleasure to mention your wise
and successful diplomacy in the matter of the Long House.
That house you have most cleverly divided against itself; and
it must fall--it is tottering now, shaken to its foundations
of centuries. Also, I have the pleasure to refer to your
capture of the man Beacraft and his papers, disclosing a
diabolical plan of murder. The man has been condemned by a
court on the evidence as it stood, and he is now awaiting
execution.

"I have before me Colonel Visscher's partial report of the
battle of Oriskany. Your name is not mentioned in this
report, but, knowing you as I believe I do, I am satisfied
that you did your full duty in that terrible affair;
although, in your report to me by Oneida runner, you record
the action as though you yourself were a mere spectator.

"I note with pleasure your mention of the gallantry of your
riflemen, Mount, Murphy, and Elerson, and have reported it to
their company captain, Mr. Long, who will, in turn, bring it
to the attention of Colonel Morgan.

"I also note that you have not availed yourself of the
war-services of the Oneidas, for which I beg to thank you
personally.

"I recall with genuine pleasure my visit to your uncle, Sir Lupus Varick, where I had the fortune to make your acquaintance and, I trust, your friendship.

"Mrs. Schuyler joins me in kindest remembrance to you, and to Sir Lupus, whose courtesy and hospitality I have to-day had the honor to acknowledge by letter. Through your good office we take advantage of this opportunity to send our love to Miss Dorothy, who has won our hearts.

"I am, sir, your most obedient,
PHILIP SCHUYLER,
Major-General.

"P.S.--I had almost forgotten to congratulate you on your merited advancement in military rank, for which you may thank our wise and good Governor Clinton.

"I shall not pretend to offer you unasked advice upon this happy occasion, though it is an old man's temptation to do so, perhaps even his prerogative. However, there are younger colonels than you, sir, in our service--ay, and brigadiers, too. So be humble, and lay not this honor with too much unction to your heart. Your friend,

"PH. SCHUYLER."

I sat for a while staring at this good man's letter, then opened the next missive.

"HEADQUARTERS, DEPARTMENT OF THE NORTH, STILLWATER, August

12, 1777.

"Colonel George Ormond, on Scout:

"SIR,--By order of Major-General Gates, commanding this department, you will, upon reception of this order, instantly repair to Varick Manor and report your arrival by express or a native runner to be trusted, preferably an Oneida. At nine o'clock, the day following your arrival at Varicks', you will leave on your journey to Stillwater, where you will report to General Gates for further orders.

"Your small experience in military matters of organization renders it most necessary that you should be aided in the formation of your regiment of rangers by a detail from Colonel Morgan's Rifles, as well as by the advice of General Gates.

"You will, therefore, retain the riflemen composing your scout, but attempt nothing towards enlisting your companies until you receive your instructions personally and in full from headquarters.

"I am, sir,

"Your very obedient servant,

"WILKINSON,
Adjutant-General.
"For Major-General Gates, commanding."

"Why, in Heaven's name, should I lose time by journeying to headquarters?" I said, aloud, looking up from my letter. Ah! There was the difference between Schuyler, who picked his man, told him what he desired, and left him to fulfil it, and Gates, who chose a man, flung his inexperience into his face, and bade him twirl his thumbs and sit idle until headquarters could teach him how to do what he had been chosen to do, presumably upon his ability to do it!

A helpless sensation of paralysis came over me--a restless, confused impression of my possible untrustworthiness, and of unfriendliness to me in high quarters, even of a thinly veiled hostility to me.

What a letter! That was not the way to get work out of a subordinate--this patronizing of possible energy and enthusiasm, this cold dampening of ardor, as though ardor in itself were a reproach and zeal required reproof.

Wondering why they had chosen me if they thought me a blundering and, perhaps, mischievous zealot, I picked up a parcel, undirected, and broke the string.

Out of it fell two letters. The writing was my cousin Dorothy's; and, trembling all over in spite of myself, I broke the seal of the first. It was undated:

"DEAREST,--Your letter from Oriskany is before me. I am here
in your room, the door locked, alone with your letter,
overwhelmed with love and tenderness and fear for you.

"They tell me that you have been made colonel of a regiment,
and the honor thrills yet saddens me--all those colonels
killed at Oriskany! Is it a post of special danger, dear?

"Oh, my brave, splendid lover! with your quiet, steady eyes
and your bright hair--you angel on earth who found me a child
and left me an adoring woman--can it be that in this world
there is such a thing as death for you? And could the world
last without you?

*   *   *   *   *

"Ah me! dreary me! the love that is in me! Who could believe it? Who could doubt that it is divine and not inspired by hell as I once feared; it is so beautiful, so hopelessly beautiful, like that faint thrill of splendor that passes shadowing a dream where, for an instant, we think to see a tiny corner of heaven sparkling out through a million fathoms of terrific night.... Did you ever dream that?

*   *   *   *   *

"We have been gay here. Young Mr. Van Rensselaer came from Albany to heal the breach with father. We danced and had games. He is a good young man, this patroon and patriot. Listen, dear: he permitted all his tenants to join the army of Gates, cancelled their rent-rolls during their service, and promised to provide for their families. It will take a fortune, but his deeds are better than his words.

"Only one thing, dear, that troubled me. I tell it to you, as I tell you everything, knowing you to be kind and pitiful. It is this: he asked father's permission to address me, not knowing I was affianced. How sad is hopeless love!

"There was a battle at Bennington, where General Stark's men whipped the Brunswick troops and took equipments for a thousand cavalry, so that now you should see our Legion of Horse, so gay in their buff-and-blue and their new helmets and great, spurred jack-boots and bright sabres!

"Ruyven was stark mad to join them; and what do you think?
Sir Lupus consented, and General Schuyler lent his kind
offices, and to-day, if you please, my brother is strutting
about the yard in the uniform of a Cornet of Legion cavalry!

"To-night the squadron leaves to chase some of McDonald's
renegades out of Broadalbin. You remember Captain McDonald,
the Glencoe brawler?--it's the same one, and he's done
murder, they say, on the folk of Tribes Hill. I am thankful
that Ruyven is in Sir George Covert's squadron.

"And, dear, what do you think? Walter Butler was taken, three
days since, by some of Sir George Covert's riders, while
visiting his mother and sister at a farm-house near
Johnstown. He was taken within our lines, it seems, and in
civilian's clothes; and the next day he was tried by a
drum-court at Albany and condemned to death as a spy. Is it
not awful? He has not yet been sentenced. It touches us, too,
that an Ormond-Butler should die on the gallows. What horrors
men commit! What horrors! God pity his mother!

*   *   *   *   *

"I am writing at a breathless pace, quill flying, sand
scattered by the handful--for my feverish gossip seems to
help me to endure.

"Time, space, distance vanish while I write; and I am with
you ... until my letter ends.

"Then, quick! my budget of gossip! I said that we had been
gay, and that is true, for what with the Legion camping in
our quarters and General Arnold's men here for two days, and

Schuyler's and Gates's officers coming and going and always remaining to dine, at least, we have danced and picnicked and played music and been frightened when McDonald's men came too near. And oh, the terrible pall that fell on our company when news came of poor Janet McCrea's murder by Indians--you did not know her, but I did, and loved her dearly in school--the dear little thing! But Burgoyne's Indians murdered her, and a fiend called The Wyandot Panther scalped her, they say--all that beautiful, silky, long hair! But Burgoyne did not hang him, Heaven only knows why, for they said Burgoyne was a gentleman and an honorable soldier!

"Then our company forgot the tragedy, and we danced--think of it, dear! How quickly things are forgotten! Then came the terrible news from Oriskany! I was nearly dead with fright until your letter arrived.... So, God help us I we danced and laughed and chattered once more when Arnold's troops came.

"I did not quite share the admiration of the women for General Arnold. He is not finely fibred; not a man who appeals to me; though I am very sorry for the slight that the Congress has put upon him; and it is easy to see that he is a brave and dashing officer, even if a trifle coarse in the grain and inclined to be a little showy. What I liked best about him was his deep admiration and friendship for our dear General Schuyler, which does him honor, and doubly so because General Schuyler has few friends in politics, and Arnold was perfectly fearless in showing his respect and friendship for a man who could do him no favors.

*   *   *   *   *

"Dear, a strange and amusing thing has happened. A few score of friendly Oneidas and lukewarm Onondagas came here to pay their respects to Magdalen Brant, who, they heard, was living at our house.

"Magdalen received them; she is a sweet girl and very good to her wild kin; and so father permitted them to camp in the empty house in the sugar-bush, and sent them food and tobacco and enough rum to please them without starting them war-dancing.

"Now listen. You have heard me tell of the Stonish Giants--those legendary men of stone whom the Iroquois, Hurons, Algonquins, and Lenape stood in such dread of two hundred years ago, and whom our historians believe to have been some lost company of Spaniards in armor, strayed northward from Cortez's army.

"Well, then, this is what occurred:

"They were all at me to put on that armor which hangs in the hall--the same suit which belonged to the first Maid-at-Arms, and which she is painted in, and which I wore that last memorable night--you remember.

"So, to please them, I dressed in it--helmet and all--and came down. Sir George Covert's horse stood at the stockade gate, and somebody--I think it was General Arnold--dared me to ride it in my armor.

"Well, ... I did. Then a mad desire for a gallop seized
me--had not mounted a horse since that last ride with
you--and I set spurs to the poor beast, who was already
dancing under the unaccustomed burden, and away we tore.

"My conscience! what a ride that was! and the clang of my
armor set the poor horse frantic till I could scarce
govern him.

"Then the absurd happened. I wheeled the horse into the
pasture, meaning to let him tire himself, for he was really
running away with me; when, all at once, I saw a hundred
terror-stricken savages rush out of the sugar-house, stand
staring a second, then take to their legs with most doleful
cries and hoots and piteous howls.

"'Oonah! The Stonish Giants have returned! Oonah! Oonah! The
Giants of Stone!'

"My vizor was down and locked. I called out to them in
Delaware, but at the sound of my voice they ran the
faster--five score frantic barbarians! And, dear, if they
have stopped running yet I do not know it, for they never
came back.

"But the most absurd part of it all is that the Onondagas,
who are none too friendly with us, though they pretend to be,
have told the Cayugas that the Stonish Giants have returned
to earth from Biskoona, which is hell. And I doubt not that
the dreadful news will spread all through the Six Nations,
with, perhaps, some astonishing results to us. For scouts
have already come in, reporting trouble between General
Burgoyne and his Wyandots, who declare they have had enough

of the war and did not enlist to fight the Stonish
Giants--which excuse is doubtless meaningless to him.

"And other scouts from the northwest say that St. Leger can
scarce hold the Senecas to the siege of Stanwix because of
their great loss at Oriskany, which they are inclined to
attribute to spells cast by their enemies, who enjoy the
protection of the Stonish Giants.

"Is it not all mad enough for a child's dream?

"Ay, life and love are dreams, dear, and a mad world spins
them out of nothing.... Forgive me ... I have been sewing on
my wedding-gown again. And it is nigh finished.

"Good-night. I love you. D."

Blindly I groped for the remaining letter and tore the seal.

"Sir George has just had news of you from an Oneida who says
you may be here at any moment! And I, O God I terrified at my
own mad happiness, fearing myself in that meeting, begged him
to wed me on the morrow. I was insane, I think, crazed with
fear, knowing that, were I not forever beyond you, I must
give myself to you and abide in hell for all eternity!

"And he was astonished, I think, but kind, as he always is;
and now the dreadful knowledge has come to me that for me
there is no refuge, no safety in marriage which I, poor fool,
fled to for sanctuary lest I do murder on my own soul!

"What shall I do? What can I do? I have given my word to wed
him on the morrow. If it be mortal sin to show ingratitude to

a father and deceive a lover, what would it be to deceive a husband and disgrace a father?

"And I, silly innocent, never dreamed but that temptation ceased within the holy bonds of wedlock--though sadness might endure forever.

"And now I know! In the imminent and instant presence of my marriage I know that I shall love you none the less, shall tempt and be tempted none the less. And, in this resistless, eternal love, I may fall, dragging you down with me to our endless punishment.

"It was not the fear of punishment that kept me true to my vows before; it was something within me, I don't know what.

"But, if I were wedded with him, it would be fear of punishment alone that could save me--not terror of flames; I could endure them with you, but the new knowledge that has come to me that my punishment would be the one thing I could not endure--eternity without you!

"Neither in heaven nor in hell may I have you. Is there no way, my beloved? Is there no place for us?

*   *   *   *   *

"I have been to the porch to tell Sir George that I must postpone the wedding. I did not tell him. He was standing with Magdalen Brant, and she was crying. I did not know she had received bad news. She said the news was bad. Perhaps Sir George can help her.

"I will tell him later that the wedding must be postponed....
I don't know why, either. I cannot think. I can scarcely see
to write. Oh, help me once more, my darling! Do not come to
Varicks'! That is all I desire on earth! For we must never,
never, see each other again!"

*   *   *   *   *

Stunned, I reeled to my feet and stumbled out into the moonlight, staring across the misty wilderness into the east, where, beyond the forests, somewhere, she lay, perhaps a bride.

A deathly chill struck through and through me. To a free man, with one shred of pity, honor, unselfish love, that appeal must be answered. And he were the basest man in all the world who should ignore it and show his face at Varick Manor--were he free to choose.

But I was not free; I was a military servant, pledged under solemn oath and before God to obedience--instant, unquestioning, unfaltering obedience.

And in my trembling hand I held my written orders to report at Varick Manor.

XX
COCK-CROW

At dawn we left the road and struck the Oneida trail north of the river, following it swiftly, bearing a little north of east until, towards noon, we came into the wagon-road which runs over the Mayfield hills and down through the outlying bush farms of Mayfield and Kingsborough.

Many of the houses were deserted, but not all; here and there smoke curled from the chimney of some lonely farm; and across the stump pasture we could see a woman laboring in the sun-scorched fields and a man, rifle in hand, standing guard on a vantage-point which overlooked his land.

Fences and gates became more frequent, crossing the rough road every mile or two, so that we were constantly letting down and replacing cattle-bars, unpinning rude gates, or climbing over snake fences of split rails.

Once we came to a cross-roads where the fence had been demolished and a warning painted on a rough pine board above a wayside watering-trough.

"WARNING!

All farmers and townsfolk are hereby requested and ordered to remove gates, stiles, cow-bars, and fences, which includes all obstructions to the public highway, in order that the cavalry may pass without difficulty. Any person found felling trees across this road, or otherwise impeding the operations of cavalry by building brush, stump, rail, or stone fences across this road, will be arrested and tried before a court on charge of aiding and giving comfort to the enemy.

G. COVERT,

"Captain Commanding Legion."

Either this order did not apply to the cross-road which we now filed into, or the owners of adjacent lands paid no heed to it; for presently, a few rods ahead of us, we saw a snake fence barring the road and a man with a pack on his back in the act of climbing over it.

He was going in the same direction that we were, and seemed to be a fur-trader laden with packets of peltry.

I said this to Murphy, who laughed and looked at Mount.

"Who carries pelts to Quebec in August?" asked Elerson, grinning.

"There's the skin of a wolverine dangling from his pack," I said, in a low voice.

Murphy touched Mount's arm, and they halted until the man ahead had rounded a turn in the road; then they sprang forward, creeping swiftly to the shelter of the undergrowth at the bend of the road, while Elerson and I followed at an easy pace.

"What is it?" I asked, as we rejoined them where they were kneeling, looking after the figure ahead.

"Nothing, sir; we only want to see them pelts, Tim and me."

"Do you know the man?" I demanded.

Murphy gazed musingly at Mount through narrowed eyes. Mount, in a brown study, stared back.

"Phwere th' divil have I seen him, I dunnoa!" muttered Murphy. "Jack, 'tis wan mush-rat looks like th' next, an' all thrappers has the same cut to them! Yonder's no thrapper!"

"Nor peddler," added Mount; "the strap of the Delaware baskets never bowed his legs."

"Thrue, avick! Wisha, lad, 'tis horses he knows better than snow-shoes, bed-plates, an' thrip-sticks! An' I've seen him, I think!"

"Where?" I asked.

He shook his head, vacantly staring. Moved by the same impulse, we all started forward; the man was not far ahead, but our moccasins made no noise in the dust and we closed up swiftly on him and were at his elbow before he heard us.

Under the heavy sunburn the color faded in his cheeks when he saw us. I noted it, but that was nothing strange considering the perilous conditions of the country and the sudden shock of our appearance.

"Good-day, friend," cried Mount, cheerily.

"Good-day, friends," he replied, stammering as though for lack of breath.

"God save our country, friend," added Elerson, gravely.

"God save our country, friends," repeated the man.

So far, so good. The man, a thick, stocky, heavy-eyed fellow, moistened his broad lips with his tongue, peered furtively at me, and instantly dropped his eyes. At the same instant memory stirred within me; a vague recollection of those heavy, black eyes, of that broad, bow-legged figure set me pondering.

"Me fri'nd," purred Murphy, persuasively, "is th' Frinch thrappers balin' August peltry f'r to sell in Canady?"

"I've a few late pelts from the lakes," muttered the man, without looking up.

"Domned late," cried Murphy, gayly. "Sure they do say, if ye dhraw a summer mink an' turrn th' pelt inside out like a glove, the winther fur will sprout inside-- wid fashtin' an' prayer."

The man bent his eyes obstinately on the ground; instead of smiling he had paled.

"Have you the skin of a wampum bird in that bale?" asked Mount, pleasantly.

Elerson struck the pack with the flat of his hand; the mangy wolverine pelt crackled.

"Green hides! Green hides!" laughed Mount, sarcastically. "Come, my friend, we're your customers. Down with your bales and I'll buy."

Murphy had laid a heavy hand on the man's shoulder, halting him short in his tracks; Elerson, rifle cradled in the hollow of his left arm, poked his forefinger into the bales, then sniffed at the aperture.

"There are green hides there!" he exclaimed, stepping back. "Jack, slip that pack off!"

The man started forward, crying out that he had no time to waste, but Murphy jerked him back by the collar and Elerson seized his right arm.

"Wait!" I said, sharply. "You cannot stop a man like this on the highway!"

"You don't know us, sir," replied Mount, impudently.

"Come, Colonel Ormond," added Elerson, almost savagely. "You're our captain no longer. Give way, sir. Answer for your own men, and we'll answer to Danny Morgan!"

Mount, struggling to unfasten the pack, looked over his huge shoulders at me.

"Not that we're not fond of you, sir; but we know this old fox now--"

"You lie!" shrieked the man, hurling his full weight at Murphy and tearing his right arm free from Elerson's grip.

There came a flash, an explosion; through a cloud of smoke I saw the fellow's right arm stretched straight up in the air, his hand clutching a smoking pistol, and Elerson holding the arm rigid in a grip of steel.

Instantly Mount tripped the man flat on his face in the dust, and Murphy jerked his arms behind his back, tying them fast at the wrists with a cord which Elerson cut from the pack and flung to him.

"Rip up thim bales, Jack!" said Murphy. "Yell find them full o' powther an' ball an' cutlery, sorr, or I'm a liar!" he added to me. "This limb o' Lucifer is wan o' Francy McCraw's renegados!--Danny Redstock, sorr, th' tirror av the Sacandaga!"

Redstock! I had seen him at Broadalbin that evening in May, threatening the angry settlers with his rifle, when Dorothy and the Brandt-Meester and I had ridden over with news of smoke in the hills.

Murphy tied the prostrate man's legs, pulled him across the dusty road to the bushes, and laid him on his back under a great maple-tree.

Mount, knife in hand, ripped up the bales of crackling peltry, and Elerson delved in among the skins, flinging them right and left in his impatient search.

"There's no powder here," he exclaimed, rising to his knees on the road and staring at Mount; "nothing but badly cured beaver and mangy musk-rat."

"Well, he baled 'em to conceal something!" insisted Mount. "No man packs in this moth-eaten stuff for love of labor. What's that parcel in the bottom?"

"Not powder," replied Elerson, tossing it out, where it rebounded, crackling.

"Squirrel pelts," nodded Mount, as I picked up the packet and looked at the sealed cords. The parcel was addressed: "General Barry St. Leger, in camp before Stanwix." I sat down on the grass and began to open it, when a groan from the prostrate prisoner startled me. He had struggled to a sitting posture, and was facing me, eyes bulging from their sockets. Every vestige of color had left his visage.

"For God's sake don't open that!" he gasped--"there is naught there, sir--"

"Silence!" roared Mount, glaring at him, while Murphy and Elerson, dropping their armfuls of pelts, came across the road to the bank where I sat.

"I will not be silent!" screamed the man, rocking to and fro on the ground. "I did not do that!--I know nothing of what that packet holds! A Mohawk runner gave it to me--I mean that I found it on the trail--"

The riflemen stared at him in contempt while I cut the strings of the parcel and unrolled the bolt of heavy miller's cloth.

At first I did not comprehend what all that mass of fluffy hair could be. A deep gasp from Mount enlightened me, and I dropped the packet in a revulsion of horror indescribable. For the parcel was fairly bursting with tightly packed scalps.

In the deathly silence I heard Redstock's hoarse breathing. Mount knelt down and gently lifted a heavy mass of dark, silky hair.

At last Elerson broke the silence, speaking in a strangely gentle and monotonous voice.

"I think this hair was Janet McCrea's. I saw her many times at Half-moon. No maid in Tryon County had hair like hers."

Shuddering, Mount lifted a long braid of dark-brown hair fastened to a hoop painted blue. And Elerson, in that strange monotone, continued speaking:

"The hair on this scalp is braided to show that the woman was a mother; the skin stretched on a blue hoop confirms it.

"The murderer has painted the skin yellow with red dots to represent tears shed for the dead by her family. There is a death-maul painted below in black; it shows how she was killed."

He laid the scalp back very carefully. Under the mass of hair a bit of paper stuck out, and I drew it from the dreadful packet. It was a sealed letter directed to General St. Leger, and I opened and read the contents aloud in the midst of a terrible silence.

"SACANDAGA VLAIE,
August 17, 1777

"General Barry St. Leger

"SIR,--I send you under care of Daniel Redstock the first
packet of scalps, cured, dried, hooped, and painted; four
dozen in all, at twenty dollars a dozen, which will be eighty
dollars. This you will please pay to Daniel Redstock, as I
need money for tobacco and rum for the men and the Senecas
who are with me.

"Return invoice with payment acquitted by the bearer, who
will know where to find me. Below I have prepared a true
invoice. Your very humble servant,

"F. MCCRAW.

"Invoice.

(6) Six scalps of farmers, green hoops to show they were killed
in their fields; a large white circle for the sun, showing
it was day; black bullet mark on three; hatchet on two.

(2) Two of settlers, surprised and killed in their houses or barns;
hoops red; white circle for the sun; a little red foot to show
they died fighting. Both marked with bullet symbol.

(4) Four of settlers. Two marked by little yellow flames to show
how they died. (My Senecas have had no prisoners for
burning since August third.) One a rebel clergyman, his
band tied to the scalp-hoop, and a little red foot under a red
cross painted on the skin. (He killed two of my men before

we got him.) One, a poor scalp, the hair gray and
thin; the hoop painted brown. (An old man whom we
found in bed in a rebel house.)

(12) Twelve of militia soldiers; stretched on black hoops four inches
     in diameter, inside skin painted red; a black circle showing
     they were outposts surprised at night; hatchet as usual.

(12) Twelve of women; one unbraided--a very fine scalp (bought
     of a Wyandot from Burgoyne's army), which I paid full
     price for; nine braided, hoops blue, red tear-marks; two
     very gray; black hoops, plain brown color inside; death-maul
     marked in red.

(6) Six of boys' scalps; small green hoops; red tears; symbols
    in black of castete, knife, and bullet.

(5) Five of girls' scalps; small yellow hoops. Marked with the
    Seneca symbol to whom they were delivered before scalping.

(l) One box of birch-bark containing an infant's scalp; very little
    hair, but well dried and cured. (I must ask full price
    for this.)

48 scalps assorted, @ 20 dollars a dozen..............80 dollars.

"Received payment, F. McCRAW."

The ghastly face of the prisoner turned livid, and he shrieked as Mount caught
him by the collar and dragged him to his feet.

"Jack," I said, hoarsely, "the law sends that man before a court."

"Court be damned!" growled Mount, as Elerson uncoiled the pack-rope, flung
one end over a maple limb above, and tied a running noose on the other end.

Murphy crowded past me to seize the prisoner, but I caught him by the arm and pushed him aside.

"Men!" I said, angrily; "I don't care whose command you are under. I'm an officer, and you'll listen to me and obey me with respect. Murphy!"

The Irishman gave me a savage stare.

"By God!" I cried, cocking my rifle, "if one of you dares disobey, I'll shoot him where he stands! Murphy! Stand aside! Mount, bring that prisoner here!"

There was a pause; then Murphy touched his cap and stepped back quietly, nodding to Mount, who shuffled forward, pushing the prisoner and darting a venomous glance at me.

"Redstock," I said, "where is McCraw?"

A torrent of filthy abuse poured out of the prisoner's writhing mouth. He cursed us, threatening us with a terrible revenge from McCraw if we harmed a hair of his head.

Astonished, I saw that he had mistaken my attitude for one of fear. I strove to question him, but he insolently refused all information. My men ground their teeth with impatience, and I saw that I could control them no longer.

So I gave what color I could to the lawless act of justice, partly to save my waning authority, partly to save them the consequences of executing a prisoner who might give valuable information to the authorities in Albany.

I ordered Elerson to hold the prisoner and adjust the noose; Murphy and Mount to the rope's end. Then I said: "Prisoner, this field-court finds you guilty of murder and orders your execution. Have you anything to say before sentence is carried out?"

The wretch did not believe we were in earnest. I nodded to Elerson, who drew the noose tight; the prisoner's knees gave way, and he screamed; but Mount and Murphy jerked him up, and the rope strangled the screech in his throat.

Sickened, I bent my head, striving to count the seconds as he hung twisting and quivering under the maple limb.

Would he never die? Would those spasms never end?

"Shtep back, sorr, if ye plaze, sorr," said Murphy, gently. "Sure, sorr, ye're as white as a sheet. Walk away quiet-like; ye're not used to such things, sorr."

I was not, indeed; I had never seen a man done to death in cold blood. Yet I fought off the sickening faintness that clutched at my heart; and at last the dangling thing hung limp and relaxed, turning slowly round and round in mid-air.

Mount nodded to Murphy and fell to digging with a sharpened stick. Elerson quietly lighted his pipe and aided him, while Murphy shaved off a white square of bark on the maple-tree under the slow-turning body, and I wrote with the juice of an elderberry:

"Daniel Redstock, a child murderer, executed by American Riflemen for his crimes, under order of George Ormond, Colonel of Rangers, August 19, 1777. Renegades and Outlaws take warning!"

When Mount and Elerson had finished the shallow grave, they laid the scalps of the murdered in the hole, stamped down the earth, and covered it with sticks and branches lest a prowling outlaw or Seneca disinter the remains and reap a ghastly reward for their redemption from General the Hon. Barry St. Leger, Commander of the British, Hessians, Loyal Colonials, and Indians, in camp before Fort Stanwix.

As we left that dreadful spot, and before I could interfere to prevent them, the three riflemen emptied their pieces into the swinging corpse--a useless, foolish, and savage performance, and I said so sharply.

They were very docile and contrite and obedient now, explaining that it was a customary safeguard, as hanged men had been revived more than once--a flimsy excuse, indeed!

"Very well," I said; "your shots may draw McCraw's whole force down on us. But doubtless you know much more than your officers--like the militia at Oriskany."

The reproof struck home; Mount muttered his apology; Murphy offered to carry my rifle if I was fatigued.

"It was thoughtless, I admit that," said Elerson, looking backward, uneasily. "But we're close to the patroon's boundary."

"We're within bounds now," said Mount. "Fonda's Bush lies over there to the southeast, and the Vlaie is yonder below the mountain-notch. This wagon-track runs into the Fish-House road."

"How far are we from the manor?" I asked.

"About two miles and a half, sir," replied Mount. "Doubtless some of Sir George Covert's horsemen heard our shots, and we'll meet 'em cantering out to investigate."

I had not imagined we were as near as that. A painful thrill passed through me; my heart leaped, beating feverishly in my breast.

Minute after minute dragged as we filed swiftly onward, mechanically treading in each other's tracks. I strove to consider, to think, to picture the sad, strange home-coming--to see her as she would stand, stunned, astounded that I had ignored her appeal to help her by my absence.

I could not think; my thoughts were chaos; my brain throbbed heavily; I fixed my hot eyes on the road and strode onward, numbed, seeing, hearing nothing.

And, of a sudden, a shout rang out ahead; horsemen in line across the road, rifles on thigh, moved forward towards us; an officer reversed his sword, drove it whizzing into the scabbard, and spurred forward, followed by a trooper, helmet flashing in the sun.

"Ormond!" cried the officer, flinging himself from his horse and holding out both white-gloved hands.

"Sir George, ... I am glad to see you.... I am very--happy," I stammered, taking his hands.

"Cousin Ormond!" came a timid voice behind me.

I turned; Ruyven, in full uniform of a cornet, flung himself into my arms.

I could scarce see him for the mist in my eyes; I pressed the boy close to my breast and kissed him on both cheeks.

Utterly unable to speak, I sat down on a log, holding Sir George's gloved hand, my arm on Ruyven's laced shoulder. An immense fatigue came over me; I had not before realized the pace we had kept up for these two months nor the strain I had been under.

"Singleton!" called out Sir George, "take the men to the barracks; take my horse, too--I'll walk back. And, Singleton, just have your men take these fine fellows up behind"--with a gesture towards the riflemen. "And see that they lack for nothing in quarters!"

Grinning sheepishly, the riflemen climbed up behind the troopers assigned them; the troop cantered off, and Sir George pointed to Ruyven's horse, indicating that it was for me when I was rested.

"We heard shots," he said; "I mistrusted it might be a salute from you, but came ready for anything, you see--Lord! How thin you've grown, Ormond!"

"I'm cornet, cousin!" burst out Ruyven, hugging me again in his excitement. "I charged with the squadron when we scattered McDonald's outlaws! A man let drive at me--"

"Oh, come, come," laughed Sir George, "Colonel Ormond has had more bullets driven at him than our Legion pouches in their bullet-bags!"

"A man let drive at me!" breathed Ruyven, in rapture. "I was not hit, cousin! A man let drive at me, and I heard the bullet!"

"Nonsense!" said Sir George, mischievously; "you heard a bumble-bee!"

"He always says that," retorted Ruyven, looking at me. "I know it was a bullet, for it went zo-o-zip-tsing-g! right past my ear; and Sergeant West shouted, 'Cut him down, sir!' ... But another trooper did that. However, I rode like the devil!"

"Which way?" inquired Sir George, in pretended anxiety. And we all laughed.

"It's good to see you back all safe and sound," said Sir George, warmly. "Sir Lupus will be delighted and the children half crazed. You should hear them talk of their hero!"

"Dorothy will be glad, too," said Ruyven. "You'll be in time for the wedding."

I strove to smile, facing Sir George with an effort. His face, in the full sunlight, seemed haggard and careworn, and the light had died out in his eyes.

"For the wedding," he repeated. "We are to be wedded to-morrow. You did not know that, did you?"

"Yes; I did know it. Dorothy wrote me," I said. A numbed feeling crept over me; I scarce heard the words I uttered when I wished him happiness. He held my proffered hand a second, then dropped it listlessly, thanking me for my good wishes in a low voice.

There was a vague, troubled expression in his eyes, a strange lack of feeling. The thought came to me like a stab that perhaps he had learned that the woman he was to wed did not love him.

"Did Dorothy expect me?" I asked, miserably.

"I think not," said Sir George.

"She believed you meant to follow Arnold to Stanwix," broke in Ruyven. "I should have done it! I regard General Arnold as the most magnificent soldier of the age!" he added.

"I was ordered to Varick Manor," I said, looking at Sir George. "Otherwise I might have followed Arnold. As it is I cannot stay for the wedding; I must report at Stillwater, leaving by nine o'clock in the morning."

"Lord, Ormond, what a fire-eater you have become!" he said, smiling from his abstraction. "Are you ready to mount Ruyven's nag and come home to a good bed and a glass of something neat?"

"Let Ruyven ride," I said; "I need the walk, Sir George."

"Need the walk!" he exclaimed. "Have you not had walks enough?--and your moccasins and buckskins in rags!"

But I could not endure to ride; a nerve-racking restlessness was on me, a desire for movement, for utter exhaustion, so that I could no longer have even strength to think.

Ruyven, protesting, climbed into his dragoon-saddle; Sir George walked beside him and I with Sir George.

Long, soft August lights lay across the leafy road; the blackberries were in heavy fruit; scarlet thimble-berries, over-ripe, dropped from their pithy cones as we brushed the sprays with our sleeves.

Sir George was saying: "No, we have nothing more to fear from McDonald's gang, but a scout came in, three days since, bringing word of McCraw's outlaws who have appeared in the west--"

He stopped abruptly, listening to a sound that I also heard; the sudden drumming of unshod hoofs on the road behind us.

"What the devil--" he began, then cocked his rifle; I threw up mine; a shrill cock-crow rang out above the noise of tramping horses; a galloping mass of horsemen burst into view behind us, coming like an avalanche.

"McCraw!" shouted Sir George. Ruyven fired from his saddle; Sir George's rifle and mine exploded together; a horse and rider went down with a crash, but the others came straight on, and the cock-crow rang out triumphantly above the roar of the rushing horses.

"Ruyven!" I shouted, "ride for your life!"

"I won't!" he cried, furiously; but I seized his bridle, swung his frightened horse, and struck the animal across the buttocks with clubbed rifle. Away tore the maddened beast, almost unseating his rider, who lost both stirrups at the first frantic bound and clung helplessly to his saddle-pommel while the horse carried him away like the wind.

Then I sprang into the ozier thicket, Sir George at my side, and ran a little way; but they caught us, even before we reached the timber, and threw us to the ground, tying us up like basted capons with straps from their saddles. Maltreated, struck, kicked, mauled, and dragged out to the road, I looked for instant death; but a lank creature flung me across his saddle, face downward, and, in a second, the whole band had mounted, wheeled about, and were galloping westward, ventre a terre.

Almost dead from the saddle-pommel which knocked the breath from my body, suffocated and strangled with dust, I hung dangling there in a storm of flying sticks and pebbles. Twice consciousness fled, only to return with the blood pounding in my ears. A third time my senses left me, and when they returned I lay in a cleared space in the woods beside Sir George, the sun shining full in my face, flung on the ground near a fire, over which a kettle was boiling. And on every side of us moved McCraw's riders, feeding their horses, smoking, laughing, playing at cards, or coming up to sniff the camp-kettle and poke the boiling meat with pointed sticks.

Behind them, squatted in rows, sat two dozen Indians, watching us in ferocious silence.

XXI
THE CRISIS

For a while I lay there stupefied, limp-limbed, lifeless, closing my aching eyes under the glittering red rays of the westering sun.

My parched throat throbbed and throbbed; I could scarcely stir, even to close my swollen hands where they had tied my wrists, although somebody had cut the cords that bound me.

"Sir George," I said, in a low voice.

"Yes, I am here," he replied, instantly.

"Are you hurt?"

"No, Ormond. Are you?"

"No; very tired; that is all."

I rolled over; my head reeled and I held it in my benumbed hands, looking at Sir George, who lay on his side, cheek pillowed on his arms.

"This is a miserable end of it all," he said, with calm bitterness. "But that it involves you, I should not dare blame fortune for the fool I acted. I have my deserts; but it's cruel for you."

The sickening whirling in my head became unendurable. I lay down, facing him, eyes closed.

"It was not your fault," I said, dully.

"There is no profit in discussing that," he muttered. "They took us alive instead of scalping us; while there's life there's hope, ... a little hope.... But I'd sooner they'd finish me here than rot in their stinking prison-ships.... Ormond, are you awake?"

"Yes, Sir George."

"If they--if the Indians get us, and--and begin their--you know--"

"Yes; I know."

"If they begin ... that ... insult them, taunt them, sneer at them, laugh at them!--yes, laugh at them! Do anything to enrage them, so they'll--they'll finish quickly.... Do you understand?"

"Yes," I muttered; and my voice sounded miles away.

He lay brooding for a while; when I opened my eyes he broke out fretfully: "How was I to dream that McCraw could be so near!--that he dared raid us within a mile of the house! Oh, I could die of shame, Ormond! die of shame!... But I won't die that way; oh no," he added, with a frightful smile that left his face distorted and white.

He raised himself on one elbow.

"Ormond," he said, staring at vacancy, "what trivial matters a man thinks of in the shadow of death. I can't consider it; I can't be reconciled to it; I can't even pray. One absurd idea possesses me--that Singleton will have the Legion now; and he's a slack drill-master--he is, indeed!... I've a million things to think of--an idle life to consider, a misspent career to repent, but the time is too short, Ormond.... Perhaps all that will come at the instant of--of--"

"Death," I said, wearily.

"Yes, yes; that's it, death. I'm no coward; I'm calm enough--but I'm stunned. I can't think for the suddenness of it!... And you just home; and Ruyven there, snuggled close to you as a house-cat--and then that sound of galloping, like a fly-stung herd of cattle in a pasture!"

"I think Ruyven is safe," I said, closing my eyes.

"Yes, he's safe. Nobody chased him; they'll know at the manor by this time; they knew long ago.... My men will be out.... Where are we, Ormond?"

"I don't know," I murmured, drowsily. The months of fatigue, the unbroken strain, the feverish weeks spent in endless trails, the constant craving for movement to occupy my thoughts, the sleepless nights which were the more unendurable because physical exhaustion could not give me peace or rest, now told on me. I drowsed in the very presence of death; and the stupor settled heavily, bringing, for the first time since I left Varick Manor, rest and immunity from despair or even desire.

I cared for nothing: hope of her was dead; hope of life might die and I was acquiescent, contented, glad of the end. I had endured too much.

My sleep--or unconsciousness--could not have lasted long; the sun was not yet level with my eyes when I roused to find Sir George tugging at my sleeve and a man in a soiled and tarnished scarlet uniform standing over me.

But that brief respite from the strain had revived me; a bucket of cold water stood near the fire, and I thrust my burning face into it, drinking my fill, while the renegade in scarlet bawled at me and fumed and cursed, demanding my attention to what he was saying.

"You damned impudent rebel!" he yelled; "am I to stand around here awaiting your pleasure while you swill your skin full?"

I wiped my lips with my torn hands, and got to my feet painfully, a trifle dizzy for a moment, but perfectly able to stand and to comprehend.

"I'm asking you," he snarled, "why we can't send a flag to your people without their firing on it?"

"I don't know what you mean," I said.

"I do," said Sir George, blandly.

"Oh, you do, eh?" growled the renegade, turning on him with a scowl. "Then tell me why our flag of truce is not respected, if you can."

"Nobody respects a flag from outlaws," said Sir George, coolly.

The fellow's face hardened and his eyes blazed. He started to speak, then shut his mouth with a snap, turned on his heel, and strode across the treeless glade to where his noisy riders were saddling up, tightening girths, buckling straps, and examining the unshod feet of their horses or smoothing out the burrs from mane and tail. The red sun glittered on their spurs, rifles, and the flat buckles of their cross-belts. Their uniform was scarlet and green, but some wore beaded shirts of scarlet holland, belted in with Mohawk wampum, and some were partly clothed like Cayuga Indians and painted with Seneca war-symbols--a grewsome sight.

There were savages moving about the fire--or I took them for savages, until one half-naked lout, lounging near, taunted me with a Scotch burr in his throat, and I saw, in his horribly painted face, a pair of flashing eyes fixed on me. And the eyes were blue.

There was something in that ghastly masquerade so horrible, so unspeakably revolting, that a shiver of pure fear touched me in every nerve. Except for the voice and the eyes, he looked the counterpart of the Senecas moving about near us; his skin, bare to the waist, was stained a reddish copper hue; his black hair was shaved except for the knot; war-paint smeared visage and chest, and two crimson quills rose from behind his left ear, tied to the scalp-lock.

"Let him alone; don't answer him; he's worse than the Indians," whispered Sir George.

Among the savages I saw two others with light eyes, and a third I never should have suspected had not Sir George pointed out his feet, which were planted on the ground like the feet of a white man when he walked, and not parallel or toed-in.

But now the loud-voiced riders were climbing into their saddles; the officer in scarlet, who had cursed and questioned us, came towards us leading a horse.

"You treacherous whelps!" he said, fiercely; "if a flag can't go to you safely, we must send one of you with it. By Heaven! you're both fit for roasting, and it sickens me to send you! But one of you goes and the other stays. Now fight it out--and be quick!"

An amazed silence followed; then Sir George asked why one of us was to be liberated and the other kept prisoner.

"Because your sneaking rebel friends fire on the white flag, I tell you!" cried the fellow, furiously; "and we've got to get a message to them. You are Captain Sir George Covert, are you not? Very good. Your rebel friends have taken Captain Walter Butler and mean to hang him. Now you tell your people that we've got Colonel Ormond and we'll exchange you both, a colonel and a captain, for Walter Butler. Do you understand? That's what we value you at; a rebel colonel and a rebel captain for a single loyal captain."

Sir George turned to me. "There is not the faintest chance of an exchange," he said, in French.

"Stop that!" threatened the man in scarlet, laying his hand on his hanger. "Speak English or Delaware, do you hear?"

"Sir George," I said, "you will go, of course. I shall remain and take the chance of exchange."

"Pardon," he said, coolly; "I remain here and pay the piper for the tune I danced to. You will relieve me of my obligations by going," he added, stiffly.

"No," I said; "I tell you I don't care. Can't you understand that a man may not care?"

"I understand," he replied, staring at me; "and I am that man, Ormond. Come, get into your saddle. Good-bye. It is all right; it is perfectly just, and--it doesn't matter."

A shrill voice broke out across the cleared circle. "Billy Bones! Billy Bones! Hae ye no flints f'r the lads that ride? Losh, mon, we'll no be ganging north the day, an' ye bide droolin' there wi' the blitherin' Jacobites!"

"The flints are in McBarron's wagon! Wait, wait, Francy McCraw!" And he hurried away, bawling for the teamster McBarron.

"Sir George," I said, "take the chance, in Heaven's name, for I shall not go. Don't dispute; don't stand there! Man, man, don't delay, I tell you, or they'll change their plan!"

"I won't go," he said, sharply. "Ormond, am I a contemptible poltroon that I should leave you here to endure the consequences of my own negligence? Do you think I could accept life at that price?"

"I tell you to go!" I said, harshly. A horrid hope, a terrible and unworthy temptation, had seized me like a thing from hell. I trembled; sweat broke out on me, and I set my teeth, striving to think as the woman I had lost would have had me think. "Quick!" I muttered, "don't wait, don't delay; don't talk to me, I tell you! Go! Go! Get out of my sight--"

And all the time, pounding in my brain, the pulse beat out a shameful thought; and mad temptations swarmed, whispering close to my ringing ears that his death was my only chance, my only possible salvation--and hers!

"Go!" I stammered, pushing him towards the horse; "get into your saddle! Quick, I tell you--I--I can't endure this! I am not made to endure everything, I tell you! Can't you have a little mercy on me and leave me?"

"I refuse," he said, sullenly.

"You refuse!" I stammered, beside myself with the torture I could no longer bear. "Then stand aside! I'll go--I'll go if it costs me--No! No! I can't; I can't, I tell you; it costs too much!... Damn you, you may have the woman I love, but you shall leave me her respect!"

"Ormond! Ormond!" he cried, in sorrowful amazement; but I was clean out of my head now, and I closed with him, dragging him towards the horse.

He shook himself free, glaring at me.

"I am ... your superior ... officer!" I panted, advancing on him; "I order you to go!"

He looked me narrowly in the eyes. "And I refuse obedience," he said, hoarsely. "You are out of your mind!"

"Then, by God!" I shrieked, "I'll force you!"

Billy Bones, Francy McCraw, and a Seneca came hastening up. I leaped on Mc-Craw and dealt him a blow full in his bony face, splitting the lean cheek open.

They overpowered me before I could repeat the blow; they flung me down, kicking and pounding me as I lay there, but the death-stroke I awaited was with-held; the castete of the Seneca was jerked from his fist.

Then they seized Sir George and forced him into his saddle, calling on four troopers to pilot him within sight of the manor and shoot him if he attempted to return.

"You tell them that if they refuse to exchange Walter Butler for Ormond, we've torments for Colonel Ormond that won't kill him under a week!" roared Billy Bones.

McCraw, stupefied with amazement and rage, stood mopping the blood from his blotched face, staring at me out of his crazy blue eyes. For a moment his hand fiddled with his hatchet, then Bones shoved him away, and he strode off towards his horsemen, who were forming in column of fours.

"You tell 'em," shouted Bones, "that before we finish him they'll hear his screams in Albany! If they want Colonel Ormond," he added, his voice rising to a yell, "tell 'em to send a single man into the sugar-bush. But if they hang Walter Butler, or if you try to catch us with your cavalry, we'll take Ormond where we'll have leisure to see what our Senecas can do with him! Now ride! you damned--"

He struck Sir George's horse with the flat of his hanger; the horse bounded off, followed by four of McCraw's riders, pistols cocked and hatchets loosened.

Bruised, dazed, exhausted, I lay there, listening to the receding thudding of their horses' feet on the moss.

The crisis was over, and I had won--not as I might have chosen to win, but by a compromise with death for deliverance from temptation.

If it was the compromise of a crazed creature, insane from mental and physical exhaustion, it was not the compromise of a weak man; I did not desire death as long as she lived. I dreaded to leave her alone in the world. But, though she loved him not--and did love me--I could not accept the future through his sacrifice and live to remember that he had laid down his life for a friend who desired from him more than he had renounced.

I was perfectly sane now; a strange calmness came over me; my mind was clear and composed; my meditations serene. Free at last from hope, from sorrowful passion, from troubled desire, I lay there thinking, watching the long, red sun-rays slanting through the woods.

Gratitude to God for a life ended ere I fell from His grace, ere temptation entangled me beyond deliverance; humble pride in the honorable traditions that I had received and followed untainted; deep, reverent thankfulness for the strength vouchsafed me in this supreme crisis of my life--the strength of a madman, perhaps, but still strength to be true, the power to renounce--these were the meditations that brought me rest and a quietude I had never known when death seemed a long way off and life on earth eternal.

The setting sun crimsoned the pines; the riders were gathered along the hillside, bending far out in their saddles to scan the valley below. McCraw, his white face bound with a bloody rag, drew his straight claymore and wound the tattered tartan around his wrist, motioning Billy Bones to ride on.

"March!" he cried, in his shrill voice, laying his claymore level; and the long files moved off, spurs and scabbards clanking, horses crowding and trampling in, faster and faster, till a far command set them trotting, then galloping away into the west, where the kindling sky reddened the world.

The world!--it would be the same to-morrow without me: that maple-tree would not have changed a leaf; that tiny, hovering, gauze-winged creature, drifting through the calm air, would be alive when I was dead.

It was difficult to understand. I repeated it to myself again and again, but the phrases had no meaning to me.

The sun set; cool, violet lights lay over the earth; a thrush, awakened by the sweetness of the twilight from his long summer moping, whistled timidly, tentatively; then the silvery, evanescent notes floated away, away, in endless, heavenly serenity.

A soft, leather-shod foot nudged me; I sat up, then rose, holding out my wrists.

They tied me loosely; a tall warrior stepped beside me; others fell in behind with a patter of moccasined feet.

Then came an officer, pistol cocked and held muzzle up. He was the only white man left.

"Forward," he said, nervously; and we started off through the purple dusk.

Physical weariness and pain had left me; I moved as in a dream. Nothing of apprehension or dismay disturbed the strange calm of my soul; even desire for meditation left me; and a vague content wrapped me, mind and body.

Distance, time, were meaningless to me now; I could go on forever; I could lie down forever; nothing mattered; nothing could touch me now.

The moon came up, flooding the woods with a creamy light; then a little stream, sparkling like molten silver, crossed our misty path; then a bare hill-side stretched away, pale in the moonlight, vanishing into a luminous veil of vapor, floating over a hollow where unseen water lay.

We entered a grove of still trees standing wide apart--maple-trees, with the sap-pegs still in the bark. I sat down on a log; the Indians seated themselves in a wide circle around me; the renegade officer walked to the fringe of trees and stood there motionless.

Time passed serenely; I had fallen drowsing, soothed by the silvered silence; when through a dream I heard a cock-crow.

Around me the Indians rose, all listening. Far away a sound grew in the night--the dull blows of horses' hoofs on sod; a shot rang faintly, a distant cry was echoed by a long-drawn yell and a volley.

The renegade officer came running back, calling out, "McCraw has struck the Legion at the grist-mill!" In the intense silence around me the noise of the conflict grew, increasing, then became fainter and fainter until it died out to the westward and all was still.

The Indians came crowding back from the edge of the grove, shoving through the circle of those who guarded me, pushing, pressing, surging around me.

"Give him to us!" they muttered, under their breath. "The flag has not come; they will hang your Walter Butler! Give him to us! The Legion cavalry is driving your riders into the west! Give him to us! We wish to see how the Oriskany man can die!"

Dragged, pulled from one to another, I scarcely felt their clutch; I scarcely felt the furtive blows that fell on me. The officer clung to me, fighting the savages back with fist and elbow.

"Wait for McCraw!" he panted. "The flag may come yet, you fools! Would you murder him and lose Walter Butler forever? Wait till McCraw comes, I tell you!"

"McCraw is riding for his life!" said a chief, fiercely.

"It's a lie!" said the officer; "he is drawing them to ambush!"

"Give the prisoner to us!" cried the savages, closing in. "After all, what do we care for your Walter Butler!" And again they rushed forward with a shout.

Twice the officer drove them back with kicks and blows, cursing their treachery in McCraw's absence; then, as they drew their knives, clamoring, threatening, gathering for a last rush, into their midst bounded an unearthly shape--a squat and hideous figure, fluttering with scarlet rags. Arms akimbo, the thing planted itself before me, mouthing and slavering in fury.

"The Toad-woman! Catrine Montour! The Toad-witch!" groaned the Senecas, shrinking back, huddling together as the hag whirled about and pointed at them.

"I want him! I want him! Give him to me!" yelped the Toad-woman. "Fools! Do you know where you are? Do you know this grove of maple-trees?"

The Indians, amazed and cowed, slunk farther back. The hag fixed her blazing eyes on them and raised her arms.

"Fools! Fools!" she mouthed, "what madness brought you here to this grove?-- to this place where the Stonish Giants have returned, riding out of Biskoona!"

A groan burst from the Indians; a chief raised his arms, making the False-Faces' sign.

"Mother," he stammered, "we did not know! We heard that the Stonish Giants had returned; the Onondagas sent us word, but we did not know this grove was where they gathered from Biskoona! McCraw sent us here to await the flag."

"Liar!" hissed the hag.

"It is the truth," muttered the chief, shuddering. "Witness if I speak the truth, O ensigns of the three clans!"

And a hollow groan burst from the cowering savages. "We witness, mother. It is the truth!"

"Witch!" cried the officer, in a shaking voice, "what would you do with my prisoner? You shall not have him, by the living God!"

"Senecas, take him!" howled the hag, pointing at the officer. The fellow strove to draw his claymore, but staggered and sank to the ground, covered under a mass of savages. Then, dragged to his feet, they pulled him back, watching the Toad-woman for a sign.

"To purge this grove! To purge the earth of the Stonish Giants!" she howled. "For this I ask this prisoner. Give him to me!--to me, priestess of the six fires! Tiya-noga calls from behind the moon! What Seneca dares disobey? Give him to me for a sacrifice to Biskoona, that the Stonish ghosts be laid and the doors of fire be closed forever!"

"Take him! Spare us the dreadful rites, O mother!" answered the chief, in a quivering voice. "Slay him before us now and let us see the color of his blood, so that we may depart in peace ere the Stonish Giants ride forth from Biskoona and leave not one among us!"

"Neah!" cried the hag, furiously. "He dies in secret!"

There was a silence of astonishment. Spite of their superstitious terror, the Senecas knew that a sacrificial death, to close Biskoona, could not occur in secret. Suddenly the chief leaped forward and dealt me a blow with his castete. I fell, but staggered to my feet again.

"Mother!" began the chief, "let him die quickly--"

"Silence!" screamed the hag, supporting me. "I hear, far off, the gates of Bisk-oona opening! Hark! Ta-ho-ne-ho-ga-wen! The doors open--the doors of flame! The Stonish Giants ride forth! O chief, for your sacrilege you die!"

A horrified silence followed; the chief reeled back, dropping the death-maul.

Suddenly a horse's iron-shod foot rang out on a stone, close at hand. Straight through the moonlight, advancing steadily, came a snorting horse; and, towering in the saddle, a magic shape clad in complete steel, glittering in the moonlight.

"Oonah!" shrieked the hag, seizing me in both arms.

With an unearthly howl the Senecas fled; the Toad-woman dropped me and bounded on the dazed renegade; he turned, crying out in horror, stumbled, and fell headlong down the bushy slope.

Then, as the hag halted, she seemed to grow, straightening up, tall, broad, su-perb; towering into a supple shape from which the scarlet rags fell fluttering around her like painted maple-leaves.

"Magdalen Brant!" I gasped, swaying where I stood, the blood almost blinding me.

From behind two steel-clad arms seized me and dragged me backward; I stumbled against the horse; the armored figure bent swiftly, caught me up, swung me clear into the saddle in front, while the armor creaked and strained and clashed with the effort.

Then my head was drawn gently back, falling on a steel shoulder; two arms were thrust under mine, seizing the bridle. The horse wheeled towards the north, stepping quietly through the moonlight, steadily, slowly northward, through misty woodlands and ferny glades and deep fields swimming under the moon, across a stony stream, up through wet meadows, into a silvery road, and across a bridge which echoed mellow thunder under the trample of the iron-shod horse.

The stockade gate was shut; an old slave opened it--a trembling black man, who shot the bolts and tottered beside us, crying and pressing my hand to his eyes.

Men came from the stables, men ran from the quarters, lanterns glimmered, windows in the house opened, and I heard a vague clamor growing around me, fainter now, yet dinning in my ears until a soft, dense darkness fell, weighing on my lids till they closed.

XXII
THE END OF THE BEGINNING

ay broke with a thundering roll of drums. Instinctively I stumbled out of bed, dragged on my clothes, and, half awake and half dressed, crept to the open window. The level morning sun blazed on acres of slanting rifles passing; a solid column of Continental infantry, drums and fifes leading, came swinging along the stockade; knapsacks, cross-belts, gaiters, gray with dust; officers riding ahead with naked swords drawn, color-bearers carrying the beautiful new standard, stars shining, red and white stripes stirring lazily in brilliant, silken billows.

The morning air rang with the gusty music of the fifes, the drums beat steadily in solid cadence to the long, rippling trample of feet.

Within the stockade an incessant clamor filled the air; the grounds around the house were packed with soldiers, some leading out mules, some loading batt-horses, some drawing and carrying water, some forming ranks, shouting their numbers for column of fours.

Sir George Covert's riders of the Legion had halted under my window, rifles slung, helmets strapped; a trumpeter in embroidered jacket sat his horse in front, corded trumpet reversed flat on his thigh.

Clearing my eyes with unsteady hand, I peered dizzily at the spectacle below; my ears rang with the tumult of arrival and departure; and, through the increasing uproar and the thundering rhythm of the drums, memories of the past night flashed up, livid as flames in darkness.

The endless columns of Continentals were still pouring by the stockade, when, above the dinning drums, I heard my door shaking and a voice calling me by name.

"Ormond! Ormond! Open the door, man!"

With stiff limbs dragging, I made my way to the door and pulled back the bolt. Sir George Covert, in full uniform, sprang in and caught my hands in his.

"Ormond! Ormond!" he cried, in deep reproach. "Why did you not tell me long since that you loved her? You knew she loved you! What blind violence have you and Dorothy done yourselves and each other--and me, Ormond!--and yet another very dear to me--with your mad obstinacy and mistaken chivalry!"

I saw the grave, kind eyes searching mine, I heard his unsteady voice, but I could not respond. An immense fatigue chained mind and tongue; intelligence was there, but the tension had relaxed, and I stood dull, nerveless, my hands limp in his.

"Ormond," he said, gently, "we ride south in a few moments; you will be leaving for Stillwater in an hour. Gates's left wing is marching on Balston, and news is in by an Oneida runner that Arnold has swept all before him; Stanwix is safe; St. Leger routed. Do you understand? Every man in Tryon County is marching on Burgoyne! You, too, will be on the way towards headquarters within the hour!"

Trembling from weakness and excitement, I could only look at him in silence.

"So all is well," he said, gravely, holding my hands tighter. "Do you understand? All is well, Ormond.... We struck McCraw at Schell's last night and tore him to atoms. We punished the Senecas dreadfully. We have cleared the land of the Johnsons, the Butlers, the McDonalds, and the Mohawks, and now we're concentrating on Burgoyne. Ormond, he is a doomed man! He can never leave this land save as a prisoner!"

His grip tightened; a smile lighted his careworn face as though a ray of pure sunshine had struck his eyes.

"Ormond," he said, "I have bred much mischief among us all, yet with the kindest motives in the world. If honor and modesty forbids an explanation, at least let me repair what I can. I have given your cousin Dorothy her freedom; and now, before I go, I ask your friendship. Nay, give me more--give me joy, Ormond! Man, man, must I speak more plainly still? Must I name the bravest maid in county Tryon? Must I say that the woman I love loves me--Magdalen Brant?"

He laughed like a boy in his excitement. "We wed in Albany on Thursday! Think of it, man! I showed her no mercy, I warrant you, soon as I was free!"

He colored vividly. "Nay, that's ungallant to our Maid-at-Arms," he stammered. "I'm flustered--you will pardon that. She rides with us to Albany--I mean Magdalen--we wed at my aunt's house--"

The trumpet of the Legion was sounding persistently; the clatter of spurred boots filled the hallway; Ruyven burst in, sabre banging, and flung himself into my arms.

"Good-bye! Good-bye!" he cried. "We are marching with the left wing to Balston. I'll write you, cousin, when we take Burgoyne--I'll write you all about it and exactly how I conducted!"

I felt the parting clasp of their hands, but scarcely saw them through the tears of sheer weakness that filled my eyes. The capacity for deep emotion was deadened in me; the strain had been too great; the reaction had left me scarcely capable of realizing the instant portent of events.

The mellow trampling of horses came from below. I hobbled to the window and looked down where the troopers were riding in fours, falling in behind a train of artillery which passed jolting and bumping along the stockade.

A young girl, superbly mounted, came galloping by, and behind her spurred Sir George Covert and Ruyven. At full speed she turned her head and looked up at my window, and I think I never saw such radiant happiness in any woman's face as in Magdalen Brant's when she swept past with a gesture of adieu and swung her horse out into the road. A general's escort and staff checked their horses to make way for her. The officers lifted their black cockaded hats; a slim, boyish officer, in a white-and-gold uniform, rode forward to receive her, with a low salute that only a Frenchman could imitate.

So, escorted by prancing, clattering cavalry, and surrounded by a brilliant staff, Magdalen Brant rode away from Varicks'; and beside her, alert, upright, transfigured, rode Sir George Covert, whose life she had accepted only after she had paid her debt to Dorothy by offering her own life to rescue mine.

Dim-eyed, I stared at the passing troops, the blurred colors of their uniforms ever changing as the regiments succeeded each other, now brown and red, now green and red, now gray and yellow, as Massachusetts infantry, New York line, and Morgan's Rifles poured steadily by in unbroken columns.

Wrapped in my chamber-robe, head supported on my hand, I sat by the window, dully content, striving to think, to realize all that had befallen me. The glitter of the passing rifles, the constantly changing hues and colors, the movement, the noise, set my head swimming. Yet I must prepare to leave within the hour, for the stable bells were ringing for eight o'clock.

Cato scratched at the door and entered, bringing me hot water, and hovering around me with napkin, salve, and basin, till my battered body had been bathed, my face shaved, and my bruised head washed where the Seneca castete had glanced, tearing the skin. Clothed in fresh linen and a new uniform, sent by Schuyler, I bade him call Sir Lupus; who came presently, his mouth full of toast, a mug of cooled ale in one hand, clay pipe in the other.

He laid his pipe on the mantel, set his mug on a chair, and embraced me, shaking his head in solemn silence; and we sat for a space, considering one another, while Cato filled my bowl with chocolate and removed the cover from my smoking porridge-dish.

"They beat all," said Sir Lupus, at length; "don't they, George?"

"Do you mean our troops, sir?" I asked.

"No, sir, I don't. I mean our women."

He struck his fat leg with his palm, drew a long breath, and regarded me, arms akimbo.

"Mad, sir; all stark, raving mad! Look at those two chits of girls! The Legion had gone tearing off after you to Schell's with an Oneida scout; Sir George pops in with his tale of your horrid plight, then pelts off to find his troopers and do what he could to save you. Gad, George! it looked bad for you. I--I was half out o' my senses, thinking of you; and what with the children a-squalling and the household rushing up stairs and down, and the militia marching to the grist-mill bridge, I did nothing. What the devil was I to do? Eh?"

"You did quite right, sir," I said, gravely.

He lay back, staring at me, shoving his fat hands into his breeches pockets.

"If I'd known what that baggage o' mine was bent on, I'd ha' locked her in the cellar!... George, you won't hold that against me, will you? She's my own daughter. But the hussy was gone with Magdalen Brant before I dreamed of it--gone on the maddest moonlight quest that mortal ever dared conceive!--one in rags cut from a red blanket, t'other in that rotten old armor that your aunt thought fit to ship from

England when her father stripped the house to cross an ocean and build in the forests of a new world. George, she's all Ormond, that girl o' mine. A Varick would never have thought to cut such a caper, I tell you. It isn't in our line; it isn't in Dutch blood to imagine such things, or do 'em either!"

He seized pipe and mug, swearing under his breath.

"It was the bravest thing I ever knew," I said, huskily.

He dipped his nose into his mug, pulled at his long pipe, and eyed me askance.

"What the devil's this between you and Dorothy?" he growled.

"Nothing, I trust now, sir," I answered, in a low voice.

"Oh! 'nothing, you trust now, sir!'" he mimicked, striving to turn a sour face. "Dammy, d' ye know that I meant her for Sir George Covert?" His broad face softened; he attempted to scowl, and failed utterly. "Thank God, the land's clear of these bandits of St. Leger, anyhow!" he snorted. "I'll work my mills and I'll scrape enough to pay my debts. I suppose I'll have you on my hands when you've finished with Burgoyne."

"No," I said, smiling, "the blow that Arnold struck at Stanwix will be felt from Maine to the Florida Keys. The blow to be delivered twenty miles north of us will settle any questions of land confiscation. No, Sir Lupus, I shall not be on your hands, but ... you may be on mine if you turn Tory!"

"You impudent rogue!" he cried, struggling to his feet; then, still clutching pipe and pewter, he embraced me, and choked and chuckled, laying his fat head on my shoulder. "Be a son to me, George," he whimpered, sentimentally; "if you won't, you're a damned ungrateful pup!"

And he took himself off, sniffing, and sucking at his long clay, which had gone out.

I turned to the window, drawing in deep breaths of sweet, pure morning air. Troops were still passing in solid column, grim, dirty soldiers in heavy cowhide knapsacks, leather gaiters, and blue great-coats buttoned back at the skirts; and I heard the militia at the quarters calling across the stable-yard that these grimy battalions were some of Washington's veterans, hurried north from West Point by his Excellency to stiffen the backbone of Lincoln's militia, who prowled, growling and snarling, around Burgoyne's right flank.

They were a gaunt, hard-eyed, firm-jawed lot, marching with a peculiar cadence and swing which set all their muskets and buckles glittering at one moment, as though a thousand tiny mirrors had been turned to the light, then turned away. And, pat! pat! patter! patter! pat! went their single company drums, and their drummers seemed to beat mechanically, without waste of energy, yet with a dry, rattling precision that I had never heard save in the old days when the British troops at New Smyrna or St. Augustine marched out.

"Good--mornin', sorr," came a hearty and somewhat loud voice from below; and I saw Murphy, Elerson, and Mount, arm in arm, swaggering past with that saunter that none but a born forest runner may hope to imitate. They were not sober.

I spoke to them kindly, however, asking them if their wants were fully supplied; and they acknowledged with enthusiasm that they could desire nothing better than Sir Lupus's buttery ale.

"Wisha, then, sorr," said Murphy, jerking his thumb towards the sombre column passing, "thim laads is the laads f'r to twisht th' Dootch pigtails on thim Hissians at Half-moon. They do be pigtails on th' Dootch a fut long in the eel-skin. Faith, I saw McCraw's scalp--'twas wan o' Harrod's men tuk it, not I, sorr!--an' 'twas red an' ratty, wid nary a lock to lift it, more shame to McCraw!"

Mount stood, balancing now on his heels, now on his toes, inhaling and expelling his breath like a man who has had more than a morning draught of cider.

He laid his head on one side, like an enormous bird, and regarded me with a simper, as though lost in admiration.

"Three cheers for the Colonel," he observed, thickly, and took off his cap.

"'Ray!" echoed Elerson, regarding the unsteadiness of Mount's legs with an expression of wonder and pity.

I bade Mount saddle my mare and prepare to accompany me to headquarters. He saluted amiably; presently they started across the yard for their quarters, distributing morsels of wisdom and advice among the militiamen, who stared at them with awe and pointed at their beaded shot--pouches, which were, alas! adorned with fringes of coarse hair, dyed scarlet.

But Morgan must worry over that. I had other matters to stir me and set my pulses beating heavily as I walked to the door, opened it, and looked out into the hallway.

Children's voices came from the library below; I rested my hand on the banisters, aiding my stiffened limbs in the descent, and limped down the stairs.

Cecile spied me first. She was sitting on the porch with a very, very young ensign of Half-moon militia, watching the passing troops; and she sprang to her feet and threw her arms about my neck, kissing me again and again, a proceeding viewed with concern by the very young ensign of Half-moon militia.

"You darling!" she whispered. "Dorothy's in the library with father and the children. Lean on me, you poor boy! How you have suffered! And to think that you loved her all the time! Ah!" she whispered, sentimentally, pressing my arm, "how rare is constancy! How adorable it must be to be adored!"

There was a rush of children as we entered, and Cecile cried, "You little beasts, have you no manners?" But they were clinging to me, limb and body, and I stood there, caressing them, eyes fixed on my cousin Dorothy, who had risen from her chair.

She was very pale and quiet, and the hand she left in mine seemed lifeless as I bent to kiss it. But, upon the bridal finger, I saw the ghost-ring, a thin, rosy band, and I thrilled from head to foot with happiness unspeakable.

"Get him a chair, Harry!" said Sir Lupus. "Sit down, George; and what shall it be, my boy, cold mulled or spiced to cheer you on your journey? Or, as the Glencoe brawlers have it, 'Wha's f'r poonch?'"

I sank into my chair, saying I desired nothing; and my eyes never left Dorothy, who sat with golden head bent, folding and refolding the ruffled corner of her apron, raising her lovely eyes at moments to look across at me.

The morning had turned raw and chilly; a log-fire crackled on the hearth, where Benny had set a row of early harvest apples to sizzle and steam and perfume the air, the while Dorothy heard Harry, Sammy, and Benny read their morning lessons, so that they might hurry away to watch the passing army of their pet hero, Gates.

"Come," cried the patroon, "read your lessons and get out, you young dunces! Now, Sammy!"

Dorothy looked at me and took up her book.

"If Amos gives Joseph sixteen apples, and Joseph gives Amanda two times one half of one half of the apples, how many will Amanda have?" demanded Samuel, with labored breath. "And the true answer to that is six."

Dorothy nodded and stole a glance at me.

"That doesn't sound quite right to me," said Sir Lupus, wrinkling his brows and counting on his fingers. "Is that the answer, Dorothy?"

"I don't know," she murmured, eyes fixed on me.

Sir Lupus glared at Dorothy, then at me. Then he stuffed his pipe full of tobacco and sat in grim silence while Benny repeated:

"Theven timeth theven ith theventy-theven; theven timeth eight ith thixty-thix." While Dorothy nodded absently and plaited the edges of her lace apron, and looked at me under lowered lashes. And Benny lisped on: "Theven timeth nine ith theventy-thix; theven--"

"Stop that nonsense!" burst out Sir Lupus. "Take 'em away, Cecile! Take 'em out o' my sight!"

The children, only too delighted to escape, rushed forth with whoops and hoots, demanding to be shown their hero, General Gates. Sir Lupus looked after them sardonically.

"We're a race o' glory--mongers these days," he said. "Gad, I never thought to see offspring o' mine chasing the drums! Look at 'em now! Ruyven hunting about Tryon County for a Hessian to knock him in the head; Cecile sitting in rapture with every cornet or ensign who'll notice her; the children yelling for Lafayette and Washington; Dorothy, here, playing at Donna Quixota, and you starting for Stillwater to teach that fool, Gates, how to catch Burgoyne. Set an ass to catch an ass--eh, George?--"

He stopped, his small eyes twinkling with a softer light.

"I suppose you want me to go," he said.

We did not reply.

"Oh, I'm going," he added, fretfully; "I'm no company for a pair o' heroes, a colonel, and--"

"Touching the colonelcy," I said, "I want to make it plain that I shall refuse the promotion. I did nothing; the confederacy was split by Magdalen Brant, not by me; I did nothing at Oriskany; I cannot understand how General Schuyler should think me deserving of such promotion. And I am ashamed to take it when such men as Arnold are passed over, and such men as Schuyler are slighted--"

"Folderol! What the devil's this?" bawled Sir Lupus. "Do you think you know more than your superior officers--hey? You're a colonel, George. Let well enough alone, for if you make a donkey of yourself, they'll make you a major-general!"

With a spasmodic effort he got on his feet, seized glass and pipe, and waddled out of the room, slamming the door behind him.

In the ringing silence a charred log broke and fell in a shower of sparks, tincturing the air with the perfume of sweet birch smoke.

I rose from my chair. Dorothy rose, too, trembling. A strange shyness seemed to hold us apart. She stood there, the forced smile stamped on her lips, watching me with the fascination of fear; and I steadied myself on the arm of my chair, looking deep into her eyes, seeking to recognize in her the child I had known.

The child had gone, and in her place stood this lovely, silent stranger, with all the mystery of woman-hood in her eyes--that sweet light, exquisitely prophetic, divinely sad.

"Dorothy," I said, under my breath. "All that is brave and adorable in you, I love and worship. You have risen so far above me--and I am so weak and--and broken, and unworthy--"

"I love you," she faltered, her lips scarcely moving. Then the color surged over brow and throat; she laid her hands on her hot cheeks; I took her in my arms, holding her imprisoned. At my touch the color faded from her face, leaving it white as a flower.

"I fear you--maid spiritual, maid militant--Maid-at-Arms!" I stammered.

"And I fear you," she murmured, looking at me. "What lover does the whole world hold like you? What hero can compare with you? And who am I that I should take you away from the whole world? Sweetheart, I am afraid."

"Then fear no more," I whispered, and bent my head. She raised her pale face; her arms crept up around my neck and tightened, clinging closer as her closing lips met mine.

There came a tapping at the door, a shuffle of felt-shod feet--

"Mars' Gawge, suh, yo' hoss done saddle', suh."

The Codes Of Hammurabi And Moses
W. W. Davies

QTY

The discovery of the Hammurabi Code is one of the greatest achievements of archaeology, and is of paramount interest, not only to the student of the Bible, but also to all those interested in ancient history...

Religion **ISBN: *1-59462-338-4*** Pages:132
MSRP $12.95

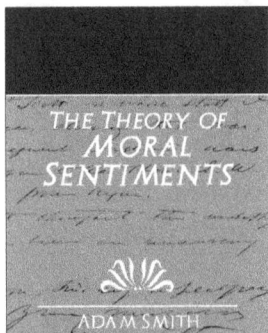

The Theory of Moral Sentiments
Adam Smith

QTY

This work from 1749. contains original theories of conscience amd moral judgment and it is the foundation for systemof morals.

Philosophy ISBN: *1-59462-777-0* Pages:536
MSRP $19.95

Jessica's First Prayer
Hesba Stretton

QTY

In a screened and secluded corner of one of the many railway-bridges which span the streets of London there could be seen a few years ago, from five o'clock every morning until half past eight, a tidily set-out coffee-stall, consisting of a trestle and board, upon which stood two large tin cans, with a small fire of charcoal burning under each so as to keep the coffee boiling during the early hours of the morning when the work-people were thronging into the city on their way to their daily toil...

Pages:84

Childrens **ISBN: *1-59462-373-2*** *MSRP $9.95*

My Life and Work
Henry Ford

QTY

Henry Ford revolutionized the world with his implementation of mass production for the Model T automobile. Gain valuable business insight into his life and work with his own auto-biography... "We have only started on our development of our country we have not as yet, with all our talk of wonderful progress, done more than scratch the surface. The progress has been wonderful enough but..."

Pages:300

Biographies/ **ISBN: *1-59462-198-5*** *MSRP $21.95*

The Art of Cross-Examination
Francis Wellman

QTY

I presume it is the experience of every author, after his first book is published upon an important subject, to be almost overwhelmed with a wealth of ideas and illustrations which could readily have been included in his book, and which to his own mind, at least, seem to make a second edition inevitable. Such certainly was the case with me; and when the first edition had reached its sixth impression in five months, I rejoiced to learn that it seemed to my publishers that the book had met with a sufficiently favorable reception to justify a second and considerably enlarged edition. ..

Pages:412

Reference   **ISBN:** *1-59462-647-2*   *MSRP $19.95*

On the Duty of Civil Disobedience
Henry David Thoreau

QTY

Thoreau wrote his famous essay, On the Duty of Civil Disobedience, as a protest against an unjust but popular war and the immoral but popular institution of slave-owning. He did more than write—he declined to pay his taxes, and was hauled off to gaol in consequence. Who can say how much this refusal of his hastened the end of the war and of slavery ?

Law   **ISBN:** *1-59462-747-9*   **Pages:48**

MSRP $7.45

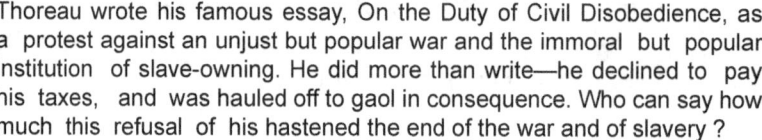

Dream Psychology Psychoanalysis for Beginners
Sigmund Freud

QTY

Sigmund Freud, born Sigismund Schlomo Freud (May 6, 1856 - September 23, 1939), was a Jewish-Austrian neurologist and psychiatrist who co-founded the psychoanalytic school of psychology. Freud is best known for his theories of the unconscious mind, especially involving the mechanism of repression; his redefinition of sexual desire as mobile and directed towards a wide variety of objects; and his therapeutic techniques, especially his understanding of transference in the therapeutic relationship and the presumed value of dreams as sources of insight into unconscious desires.

Pages:196

Psychology   **ISBN:** *1-59462-905-6*   *MSRP $15.45*

The Miracle of Right Thought
Orison Swett Marden

QTY

Believe with all of your heart that you will do what you were made to do. When the mind has once formed the habit of holding cheerful, happy, prosperous pictures, it will not be easy to form the opposite habit. It does not matter how improbable or how far away this realization may see, or how dark the prospects may be, if we visualize them as best we can, as vividly as possible, hold tenaciously to them and vigorously struggle to attain them, they will gradually become actualized, realized in the life. But a desire, a longing without endeavor, a yearning abandoned or held indifferently will vanish without realization.

Pages:360

Self Help   **ISBN:** *1-59462-644-8*   *MSRP $25.45*

☐ **The Rosicrucian Cosmo-Conception Mystic Christianity** *by Max Heindel* ISBN: *1-59462-188-8* **$38.95**
The Rosicrucian Cosmo-conception is not dogmatic, neither does it appeal to any other authority than the reason of the student. It is: not controversial, but is: sent forth in the, hope that it may help to clear... New Age/Religion Pages 646

☐ **Abandonment To Divine Providence** *by Jean-Pierre de Caussade* ISBN: *1-59462-228-0* **$25.95**
"The Rev. Jean Pierre de Caussade was one of the most remarkable spiritual writers of the Society of Jesus in France in the 18th Century. His death took place at Toulouse in 1751. His works have gone through many editions and have been republished... Inspirational/Religion Pages 400

☐ **Mental Chemistry** *by Charles Haanel* ISBN: *1-59462-192-6* **$23.95**
Mental Chemistry allows the change of material conditions by combining and appropriately utilizing the power of the mind. Much like applied chemistry creates something new and unique out of careful combinations of chemicals the mastery of mental chemistry... New Age Pages 354

☐ **The Letters of Robert Browning and Elizabeth Barret Barrett 1845-1846 vol II** ISBN: *1-59462-193-4* **$35.95**
by Robert Browning and Elizabeth Barrett Biographies Pages 596

☐ **Gleanings In Genesis (volume I)** *by Arthur W. Pink* ISBN: *1-59462-130-6* **$27.45**
Appropriately has Genesis been termed "the seed plot of the Bible" for in it we have, in germ form, almost all of the great doctrines which are afterwards fully developed in the books of Scripture which follow... Religion/Inspirational Pages 420

☐ **The Master Key** *by L. W. de Laurence* ISBN: *1-59462-001-6* **$30.95**
In no branch of human knowledge has there been a more lively increase of the spirit of research during the past few years than in the study of Psychology, Concentration and Mental Discipline. The requests for authentic lessons in Thought Control, Mental Discipline and... New Age/Business Pages 422

☐ **The Lesser Key Of Solomon Goetia** *by L. W. de Laurence* ISBN: *1-59462-092-X* **$9.95**
This translation of the first book of the "Lernegton" which is now for the first time made accessible to students of Talismanic Magic was done, after careful collation and edition, from numerous Ancient Manuscripts in Hebrew, Latin, and French... New Age/Occult Pages 92

☐ **Rubaiyat Of Omar Khayyam** *by Edward Fitzgerald* ISBN:*1-59462-332-5* **$13.95**
Edward Fitzgerald, whom the world has already learned, in spite of his own efforts to remain within the shadow of anonymity, to look upon as one of the rarest poets of the century, was born at Bredfield, in Suffolk, on the 31st of March, 1809. He was the third son of John Purcell... Music Pages 172

☐ **Ancient Law** *by Henry Maine* ISBN: *1-59462-128-4* **$29.95**
The chief object of the following pages is to indicate some of the earliest ideas of mankind, as they are reflected in Ancient Law, and to point out the relation of those ideas to modern thought. Religion/History Pages 452

☐ **Far-Away Stories** *by William J. Locke* ISBN: *1-59462-129-2* **$19.45**
"Good wine needs no bush, but a collection of mixed vintages does. And this book is just such a collection. Some of the stories I do not want to remain buried for ever in the museum files of dead magazine-numbers an author's not unpardonable vanity..." Fiction Pages 272

☐ **Life of David Crockett** *by David Crockett* ISBN: *1-59462-250-7* **$27.45**
"Colonel David Crockett was one of the most remarkable men of the times in which he lived. Born in humble life, but gifted with a strong will, an indomitable courage, and unremitting perseverance... Biographies/New Age Pages 424

☐ **Lip-Reading** *by Edward Nitchie* ISBN: *1-59462-206-X* **$25.95**
Edward B. Nitchie, founder of the New York School for the Hard of Hearing, now the Nitchie School of Lip-Reading, Inc, wrote "LIP-READING Principles and Practice". The development and perfecting of this meritorious work on lip-reading was an undertaking... How-to Pages 400

☐ **A Handbook of Suggestive Therapeutics, Applied Hypnotism, Psychic Science** ISBN: *1-59462-214-0* **$24.95**
by Henry Munro Health/New Age/Health/Self-help Pages 376

☐ **A Doll's House: and Two Other Plays** *by Henrik Ibsen* ISBN: *1-59462-112-8* **$19.95**
Henrik Ibsen created this classic when in revolutionary 1848 Rome. Introducing some striking concepts in playwriting for the realist genre, this play has been studied the world over. Fiction/Classics/Plays 308

☐ **The Light of Asia** *by sir Edwin Arnold* ISBN: *1-59462-204-3* **$13.95**
In this poetic masterpiece, Edwin Arnold describes the life and teachings of Buddha. The man who was to become known as Buddha to the world was born as Prince Gautama of India but he rejected the worldly riches and abandoned the reigns of power when... Religion/History/Biographies Pages 170

☐ **The Complete Works of Guy de Maupassant** *by Guy de Maupassant* ISBN: *1-59462-157-8* **$16.95**
"For days and days, nights and nights, I had dreamed of that first kiss which was to consecrate our engagement, and I knew not on what spot I should put my lips..." Fiction/Classics Pages 240

☐ **The Art of Cross-Examination** *by Francis L. Wellman* ISBN: *1-59462-309-0* **$26.95**
Written by a renowned trial lawyer, Wellman imparts his experience and uses case studies to explain how to use psychology to extract desired information through questioning. How-to/Science/Reference Pages 408

☐ **Answered or Unanswered?** *by Louisa Vaughan* ISBN: *1-59462-248-5* **$10.95**
Miracles of Faith in China Religion Pages 112

☐ **The Edinburgh Lectures on Mental Science (1909)** *by Thomas* ISBN: *1-59462-008-3* **$11.95**
This book contains the substance of a course of lectures recently given by the writer in the Queen Street Hail, Edinburgh. Its purpose is to indicate the Natural Principles governing the relation between Mental Action and Material Conditions... New Age/Psychology Pages 148

☐ **Ayesha** *by H. Rider Haggard* ISBN: *1-59462-301-5* **$24.95**
Verily and indeed it is the unexpected that happens! Probably if there was one person upon the earth from whom the Editor of this, and of a certain previous history, did not expect to hear again... Classics Pages 380

☐ **Ayala's Angel** *by Anthony Trollope* ISBN: *1-59462-352-X* **$29.95**
The two girls were both pretty, but Lucy who was twenty-one who supposed to be simple and comparatively unattractive, whereas Ayala was credited, as her Bombwhat romantic name might show, with poetic charm and a taste for romance. Ayala when her father died was nineteen... Fiction Pages 484

☐ **The American Commonwealth** *by James Bryce* ISBN: *1-59462-286-8* **$34.45**
An interpretation of American democratic political theory. It examines political mechanics and society from the perspective of Scotsman James Bryce Politics Pages 572

☐ **Stories of the Pilgrims** *by Margaret P. Pumphrey* ISBN: *1-59462-116-0* **$17.95**
This book explores pilgrims religious oppression in England as well as their escape to Holland and eventual crossing to America on the Mayflower, and their early days in New England... History Pages 268

QTY

The Fasting Cure *by Sinclair Upton*   ISBN: *1-59462-222-1*   **$13.95**
In the Cosmopolitan Magazine for May, 1910, and in the Contemporary Review (London) for April, 1910, I published an article dealing with my experiences in fasting. I have written a great many magazine articles, but never one which attracted so much attention... New Age/Self Help/Health Pages 164

Hebrew Astrology *by Sepharial*   ISBN: *1-59462-308-2*   **$13.45**
In these days of advanced thinking it is a matter of common observation that we have left many of the old landmarks behind and that we are now pressing forward to greater heights and to a wider horizon than that which represented the mind-content of our progenitors... Astrology Pages 144

Thought Vibration or The Law of Attraction in the Thought World   ISBN: *1-59462-127-6*   **$12.95**
by William Walker Atkinson   Psychology/Religion Pages 144

Optimism *by Helen Keller*   ISBN: *1-59462-108-X*   **$15.95**
Helen Keller was blind, deaf, and mute since 19 months old, yet famously learned how to overcome these handicaps, communicate with the world, and spread her lectures promoting optimism. An inspiring read for everyone... Biographies/Inspirational Pages 84

Sara Crewe *by Frances Burnett*   ISBN: *1-59462-360-0*   **$9.45**
In the first place, Miss Minchin lived in London. Her home was a large, dull, tall one, in a large, dull square, where all the houses were alike, and all the sparrows were alike, and where all the door-knockers made the same heavy sound... Childrens/Classic Pages 88

The Autobiography of Benjamin Franklin *by Benjamin Franklin*   ISBN: *1-59462-135-7*   **$24.95**
The Autobiography of Benjamin Franklin has probably been more extensively read than any other American historical work, and no other book of its kind has had such ups and downs of fortune. Franklin lived for many years in England, where he was agent... Biographies/History Pages 332

Name	
Email	
Telephone	
Address	
City, State ZIP	

☐ **Credit Card**   ☐ **Check / Money Order**

Credit Card Number	
Expiration Date	
Signature	

Please Mail to: Book Jungle
PO Box 2226
Champaign, IL 61825
or Fax to: 630-214-0564

ORDERING INFORMATION

web: *www.bookjungle.com*
email: *sales@bookjungle.com*
fax: *630-214-0564*
mail: *Book Jungle PO Box 2226 Champaign, IL 61825*
or PayPal *to sales@bookjungle.com*

Please contact us for bulk discounts

DIRECT-ORDER TERMS

**20% Discount if You Order
Two or More Books**
Free Domestic Shipping!
Accepted: Master Card, Visa,
Discover, American Express

www.ingramcontent.com/pod-product-compliance
Lightning Source LLC
Chambersburg PA
CBHW080953020726
47505CB00009B/2188